The Reluctant Countess

By

Annie Parnell

The Paper Pollinator

Boulder, CO

Published by **The Paper Pollinator**, Boulder, CO
"Because a good story should fertilize your mind"

The Griffin and the Rat-Catcher is available exclusively at Amazon.com

Edited by: Lorelei Logsdon

Cover Art by: Dar of Wicked Smart Designs

"My ambition was never to rule the world.
It was to change the world."

Lady Gaga
Glamour
December 2013

Dedication

To the women in my life who know and live the true meaning of Sisterhood. Bless you all.

Chapter One

Kent, April 1766.

Eight-year-old Eleanor Augusta T. Barrett was *not* by nature a patient child, as everyone continuously reminded her. And yet tonight she overcame her natural tendency and created what she thought to be the perfect imitation of a slumbering child. While her eyes were closed, she conjugated her Latin verbs while she waited for the remainder of the residents of Barrett Hall to drift into deep— and therefore inattentive—sleep. *Ego veho*—I ride. *Ego diligo ut veho meus equus*—I love to ride my horse.

The clock in the foyer chimed 2:00 a.m. and she cracked open one eye. *Everyone must be asleep by now.*

Eleanor crept down the servants' staircase, wearing the jacket from her oldest riding habit over her night-rail. A green dress sash hung around her neck, and she carried her riding boots in one hand and her new pony's bridle that she'd hidden in her wardrobe in the other.

She made a quick stop in the pantry before heading down to the stables to visit her best birthday present ever—Sir Gawain, her new Welsh pony.

With a smallish apple stuffed into her jacket pocket for him, and a butter biscuit for herself between her teeth, Eleanor pulled the French door shut at the back of the house. When she heard that final soft click of the latch, she heaved a sigh of relief.

A soft, victorious giggle bubbled up and the biscuit slipped from between her lips. It hit the stones of the terrace and broke in two.

The late spring moon smiled down on Eleanor as she crouched down to inspect the damage. She picked up the two flakey, sweet pieces. "Botheration. Well, Mama shall never know I ate these off the ground, will she?" She brushed the pieces against her night-rail and popped the smallest bit into her mouth and chewed. *Mmm.* She plunked down on the stony steps leading down to the gardens and devoured the second biscuit piece while shoving her bare feet into her boots.

No one understood her desire to spend the night with her new pony. An image of her father's face when he was angry popped into her head. She hesitated as fear of causing that sort of reaction nibbled away at her resolve and she gazed up at her bedroom window.

"Stuff and nonsense. Sir Gawain is worth any punishment Papa might dole out. Besides, when he roars his displeasure, I'll make me lower lip quiver and apologize in that tiny voice me older sisters declare quite vomitus."

With boots tied, Eleanor jumped up. She pulled the dress sash from
around her neck and tied it about her waist. She yanked handfuls of her night-rail's voluminous fabric over the top of her makeshift belt, freeing her legs. The excess cloth pouffed out like a great doughy belly. "Gaahh." *Whoever designed these garments was a fool.* With her hem riding just below her knees, Eleanor scampered down the path to the stable.

The fragrance of leather, horse, and straw filled her nostrils as she slipped through the stable's partially open door and began to wander down the main alley.

Heaven.

One lamp with its wick turned quite low hung from crossbeams halfway down. She found Sir Gawain in his box. Eleanor softly crooned as she undid the latch. "It's me—Eleanor." She stepped inside his stall, then turned her back on him to close the door. His cold nose nuzzled her neck and his steady horsey breathing filled her ears. "Ahh, boy, I just knew you'd be happy to see me." Eleanor threw her arms around his neck and kissed his nose.

He lipped his apple off her palm and then she began brushing his coat. Eleanor worked her way from his shoulder, across his back to his hip, when a sound outside the stall caught her attention. Her heart jumped.

She stopped brushing.

Cocked her head and listened.

Nothing. Eleanor let out the breath she was holding. "Whew. Guess it was only my imagination." She went back to brushing Sir Gawain's coat.

A young man's voice uttered from somewhere else in the stable, "You've got lovely skin."

Eleanor's brush stroke halted. "Blast. Someone *is* here. Lovely skin? That's a funny thing to say to a horse."

Whimpers.

Sir Gawain rumbled his discontent.

"Shhh." Eleanor listened harder. "Is that someone crying?" she asked her horse.

The pony's ears went back and he snuffled.

"Be quiet, boy. Or someone will come and check on you and I'll be found."

A panicked young female voice: "Let go. Stop that."

A loud slap.

A startled cry.

The scuffle of feet.

A body hitting the floor of the stable.

That same young man's voice, but angry now, spat, "You ignorant cow."

Mean. Eleanor rubbed her cheek as if she'd been struck.

A girl's whimpered crying.

Gasps and grunts.

The air hummed with fear and a strange tension.

Eleanor dropped into a crouch and wrapped her arms about her legs. Her pony nudged her with his head, almost toppling her over. "I'm scared, S-Sir Gawain. I think something bad is happening."

The sounds outside Sir Gawain's stall grew frantic, thrashing, and finally a muffled scream of pain.

Eleanor started to rise. Then she lost her nerve and dropped back down into a squat. *Fortes fortuna iuvat—Fortune favors the brave.* Eleanor braced her hand against Sir Gawain's leg and stood.

She wished she had a pitchfork or a shovel to brandish, but Mac, the head groom, always put his tools away. To arm herself, Eleanor grabbed Sir Gawain's new bridle, then she crept from his stall.

The lantern's dim light lay ahead. Eleanor peered into the semi-darkness. She slid her feet tentatively across the floor. Moving toward the sounds, the light grew stronger. Deep shadows fading into blackness closed in on either side. Monsters were hiding in every dark shape. Waiting to grab her. With sweaty palms, she flexed her fingers around the bridle. Clenching and unclenching.

Someone was lying on the floor. Face down. Eleanor ran forward. It
was her friend, Betty Longley, the gardener's thirteen-year-old granddaughter. Her skirt was pushed way up, exposing her bare bottom.

What had happened?

A booted foot landed on Betty's back. "I told you to *shut up.*" A faceless male form stood over her. He was fastening his breeches, his back to Eleanor.

Eleanor's legs trembled, so she locked her knees, fighting her impulse to run the other away.

Betty made a choking sob.

The man drew his foot back in preparation to strike. "I told you—"

"Don't you dare kick me friend," Eleanor said.

The young man's head shot up. He was still only a black form outlined in light as he jeered, "Who's going to stop me?"

"Me!" Eleanor raced forward, lashing the bridle back and forth like a whip.

"What?" He made a mad grab for the reins. He snagged them on his second attempt.

Eleanor tugged hard to break free. She dug in her heels. Her shoulder muscles burned but he was bigger and stronger. He wound the reins around his fist. Eleanor was pulled relentlessly forward like a fish on a line.

When she got close, he grabbed Eleanor's braid, pulling up, making her
stand on tiptoe. He towered over her and his sour breath stank from ale. "Interfering little bitch!"

"Should not speak words like that." Eleanor let go of the bridle and flailed about like a stringed puppet, trying to land a blow.

He moved his arm about, making her head snap back and forth. "You're pathetic. Shouldn't stick your nose where it doesn't belong."

"Let go. I'll tell me father."

He pulled her braid up higher. The pain rushing across her scalp made her eyes tear.

"You say *anything* and I'll come back and kill your new pony." Scared and mad, Eleanor's bladder began to give way. *Oh no.* Betty whimpered again.

He raised his booted foot and kicked Eleanor in the stomach.

Her legs crumpled. He released his hold. Eleanor tumbled forward, falling face down beside her friend. She hit the floor and curled up tight on her side, unable to draw breath. Then she felt the warm rush of fluid escaping her bladder. She closed her eyes in shame.

When Eleanor felt a hand gently touch hers, she cracked her eyes open.

Betty was less than a foot away, her lip split and silent tears trickling down her cheeks. She interlaced her fingers with Eleanor's.

Eleanor gazed unblinkingly at her friend. As she tried to draw air into her lungs, she heard the sound of their attacker's feet moving away.

Whoever you are, one day you'll be sorry. I'm going to make you pay. I swear it.

Chapter Two

Covent Garden, London, ten years later, spring 1777.

Eleanor peered over her best friend's slender shoulder, then nudged Elizabeth—Libby—Archer in the back. "Does *he* look like a building to *you*?"

"Not on his best day." Libby held her hands out in front of herself, pretending she had a gigantic imaginary belly. "Especially not with that paunch."

Eleanor smiled.

Libby waved her hand over her head. "And with that hat and coat he's wearing… Have you ever seen such a fellow? I can't turn away."

"That's the point, dearest. While all eyes are glued on him, his companions pluck the unwary spectators like chickens heading for the stew pot."

Libby's eyes grew round with wonder. "Really? How clever."

Eleanor snorted. "Buildings *only*. This was your idea, remember? Make accurate drawings so we can plan accordingly. We need doorways, alleys, things of that nature. Not the populace."

"Spoilsport?"

Eleanor chuckled.

On a small grassy patch, a short distance from the dairy vendors, Eleanor and Libby sat back to back, each facing her easel. Eleanor removed her right glove. Free of its confines, she flexed her fingers and manipulated her charcoal with greater speed and accuracy.

The world around them, on this early morning market day, rang with the clank of cart wheels over cobblestones mixed with the chatter of buyers and sellers—each one haggling over the best price for a chicken, a leg o' mutton, a bushel of turnips, a dozen eggs, or a lump of cheese. The air was redolent with the savory—as well as the unsavory—smells that accompanied this sort of commerce.

All the inhabitants of the market, including the pickpockets *and* honest merchants, kept a respectful distance from Eleanor and Libby. This was due to the presence of the four armed and liveried Barrett outriders who had formed a perimeter about them. Each outrider was tall, built like a brick bake-house, and carried a loaded flintlock. No one with a lick of sense dared come near.

The sky was overcast, and if not refreshingly cool, at least she and Libby weren't plagued by the oppressive heat, which wouldn't settle in until later in the day. Hazy daylight glazed the rooftops, casting the alleys between the buildings that faced the square into fathomless gray crevasses.

Eleanor peered over Libby's shoulder again. "You missed a door."

"Did not," Libby said.

Eleanor pointed to the building in question. "Did." She flicked her wrist. "Right there."

Libby looked in the direction Eleanor pointed. "I don't see it.'"

"To the right of that cheese man you were drawing."

Libby considered the building again.

Eleanor waved her hand in an exasperated fashion. "That fellow in that ridiculous fool's cap—the one you thought so compelling."

Libby nodded. "I know who you mean."

"Now look at his belt buckle, then move your eyes to the right."

"I know where you want me to look. There's nothing there."

Eleanor poked Libby lightly with her elbow. "Obdurate chit."

"Hah. Look who's talking."

"Up. Stand up, Lib."

Libby made an aggrieved huff and stood. Then she sat back down like a dainty queen, arranged her skirts, picked up her charcoal and drew in the door.

"Well?"

Libby crossed her arms over her chest and stuck her nose in the air. "It's not nice to be so enthusiastic when pointing out someone's mistakes. Didn't your mother ever tell you that?"

"Indeed, as you well know. Repeatedly," Eleanor said.

Libby's lips twitched with suppressed laughter.

Eleanor turned back to her work.

A Barrett footman approached carrying a tray with two cups. "Miss Barrett, would you or Miss Archer care for some refreshment?"

Eleanor and Libby each accepted a cup of lemonade. As Eleanor put her cup back on the tray, she made eye contact with a girl in the crowd. She was scrawny and her face and legs were smeared with grime. Her dress was too big and hung from her narrow shoulders like a scarecrow in a farmer's field. And Eleanor couldn't look away.

Libby's hand came to rest on her arm. "Ellie? You can't help everyone."

Eleanor broke eye contact with the child. "Not everyone. If I give her coin, someone will steal it,

but…Eleanor motioned to her footman.

"What now?" Libby asked.

"Making sure *she* eats what I'm sending over. The outrider will stand with her until she finishes."

The footman and the outrider nearest the child approached her presenting her with a small linen-wrapped bundle.

"For me?" The girl's eyes grew round as she pointed to herself. She hesitated but then raised her hand and accepted the food-filled napkin.

"Miss Barrett says you're to stay right here until you eat every last crumb," the footman said.

The girl peeked around the footman at Eleanor, who gave the child a nod of encouragement.

Libby gazed about at the crowd watching them and shuddered with unease, then lowered her voice. "I'm glad we brought the outriders. These people. So much need. I'm frightened."

Eleanor squeezed Libby's hand. "You worry too much."

Libby shook her head. "And you worry *too* little." Libby bowed her head and pulled her hand free. She leafed through the sketches they'd completed. "When we started talking about looking for those missing girls, I never thought we'd end up here. "Libby's brow furrowed.

Eleanor felt a pang of guilt. "It seemed like the logical next step. Perhaps I should've come alone."

"You did a good job with the north side, despite those spirit merchants' wagons being in your way."

Eleanor stared at the top of Libby's bent head. Libby hated to admit she was afraid, so now they were going to pretend Libby had said nothing. "Uhh, thank you."

"Are you almost done with St. Paul's?" Libby asked.

"Yes."

"Good. I'm quite ready to leave." Libby scrunched her nose. "Besides, the smell is quite … overpowering."

"I'm sorry, but if we'd situated ourselves by the flower sellers or the vintners, we wouldn't have this excellent vantage."

"I did try holding me breath, but it just made me lightheaded," Libby added.

Eleanor smiled. "I'm almost done. Me Aunt Bea is expecting us to pick her up tonight."

A commanding male voice cut through the crowd noise. "Who's in charge?"

Libby jumped.

"You there." A tall, well-dressed blond man, accompanied by a large, splendid-looking male collie, marched toward them.

Eleanor bristled.

The man with the collie pointed his cane at her father's coachman. "What do you mean bringing these young ladies into this part of town? Viscount Barrett would not be pleased."

Who the hell did he think he was, interfering with her business?

One of her outriders stepped into the intruder's path, blocking his advance.

Eleanor rose from her stool to confront the handsome interloper. He was still a few feet away, but she would guess he was above six feet. But tall or short, it made little difference to her. She would brook *no* interference—not with those missing girls' lives at stake.

Eleanor walked up beside her guard and laid a hand on his arm. "I'll handle this." Then she stepped between the two men. An air of familiarity swept over her as she looked up into the blond-headed man's face. "It's a perfectly reputable part of town during daylight. Now be off with you before I ask me men to help you on your way."

"I'll not be dismissed by an impetuous female." He looked over her head and addressed the outrider at her back. The stranger didn't appear intimidated in the least by the size or weaponry of her guards. "Is Lord Emory or Lord Harleigh in the vicinity?"

His arrogant meddling and his attempt to ignore her lit a fuse to Eleanor's temper. "Sirrah, cease your nebby inquisition. You sound like a Billingsgate fishwife!"

Her outrider choked back a laugh. "Miss? Perhaps ..." His voice sounded conciliatory.

The intruder narrowed his eyes and his lips pressed into a flat line.

Libby poked Eleanor in the back and whispered, "Stop goading him."

"He called me impetuous."

"I heard. Rise above. Remember, we serve a greater purpose here."

Eleanor looked away, clenching her jaw, biting back her rejoinder. She took a breath, then looked back. The marshal gleam in the obnoxious fellow's deep blue eyes irritated her beyond bearing. She was about to launch her next verbal salvo when he stepped closer and every nerve in her body jumped to attention.

He looked down his nose at her and his voice took on an odious pomposity. "What *is* your name?"

"*Who* is enquiring?" Eleanor raised her chin another notch and leaned forward, for all the world looking like she was begging him to plant her a facer.

His dog jumped up, barking a reprimand and planted his front paws on her skirt, just below her waist. The shove caused her to teeter backward, and the dog's master grabbed Eleanor's elbow to keep her from falling over.

"Sit, Rodrigo." The gentleman made a slight hand gesture, and his dog dropped his posterior to the ground.

Once righted, Eleanor yanked her arm free from his most disconcerting grasp. His touch, although abrupt, had been pleasant. She brushed that thought aside as she brushed off her skirts, dismissing her attraction to him

as annoying. Then she bent down and scratched the dog under his chin. "Protecting your master, me good fellow? I'm sure he's in constant need of your assistance." She gave him one last scratch and stood up.

The man's eyes made a thorough survey of her person and she felt warm in all the wrong places. The wiser voice in her head beseeched her to withdraw from this contest of wills. Instead, Eleanor drew herself up and squared her shoulders. *You arrogant nodcock, you'll rue the day our paths crossed.*

Libby whispered from behind her, "This isn't necessary. You know we're nearly done."

"That's not the point," Eleanor murmured back.

Libby sighed. "Pigheaded."

"What?" Eleanor glared at Libby.

Libby rolled her eyes.

Eleanor turned back to deal with *him*.

He stepped even closer.

Criminy. Eleanor caught a whiff of clean skin, spices and shirt starch. His demeanor, the cut of his coat, the fine linen of his jabot and the brocade of his waistcoat proclaimed his breeding and class. Up close she could see he was about the age of her eldest brother, Harleigh. And hadn't he mentioned her father and brother by their Christian names? *Bags and buttons.* They must be acquainted.

Eleanor tilted her chin up so she would look him in the eye. Tall for a woman but, even in her heeled shoes, she still only came to his shoulder.

Libby huffed, then she nudged Eleanor aside.

The dog cocked its head and studied Libby.

Libby cringed. "Nice doggy."

Large, unpredictable animals still frightened Libby. She cleared her throat and soldiered on, lifting her gloved hand . "I am Miss Elizabeth Archer. And you are?" She smiled up at *him* with great warmth, letting her voice end on a light up-note of enquiry.

Their trespasser gently took her offered hand, stepped back, and made quite a respectable courtly bow, which only confirmed Eleanor's suspicion he was a man of consequence.

"My name is Giles—Lord West—at your service, Miss Archer."

West? Good grief. What rotten luck.

Libby's voice wobbled. "Oh."

Well, that's certainly a finger in the eye. Giles West, my brother's best friend. Well, well, well ... It's been an age since last we laid eyes on one another.

Eleanor shook her head in disbelief. *Hah! Feels like I've fallen into a Goldsmith comedy.* Eleanor snorted at the absurd turn of her thoughts. *No conquering required—just good riddance, if you please.*

Eleanor shrugged, trying to look like she didn't care a fig who he was, totally belying her racing heart and dry mouth.

While Libby made social chitchat with Lord West, Eleanor surveyed the physical changes—the improvements, as it were—that had overtaken the gangly lad who'd spent many a school holiday at her parents' home. If he was cognizant of her perusal, he made no sign of it.

His broad shoulders filled out his coat nicely and his breeches and stockings revealed well-defined, muscular thighs and calves. *You've turned into a well set-up but still provoking Philistine.*

Libby swallowed hard and dipped a curtsy. "Lord West, may I present my dearest friend in all the world."

"*Enchanté*, Miss Archer." Giles West smiled warmly. In the blink of an eye his bellicose attitude had transformed into convivial gentility. His voice softened and the way he looked at Libby, he truly did seem enchanted.

As Eleanor watched them interact, her mother's words wafted through her mind. *Sometimes you bring out the worst in people, dear.*

"Miss, a-ah …" Libby paused and cleared her throat.

He started to bow.

Libby lowered her voice. "Eleanor Barrett."

West stopped bowing abruptly. Still bent over, mid-bow, his head shot up.

Eleanor adopted her haughtiest demeanor.

Lord West righted himself and put his hands on his hips.

Eleanor could hear the cogs whirring in that devilish brain of his. They'd been children the last time they'd laid eyes on one another— well, she had. Being of an age with Harleigh, Giles had been fifteen or sixteen.

Giles appeared thoughtful.

Wondering how long it will take you to locate Harleigh, so you can tattle?

Moments ticked by. Neither Eleanor nor Giles West gave quarter.

Think! Think of some way to mitigate this disaster.

Libby cleared her throat. "Eleanor?"

Eleanor didn't look away from Giles West. "Yes?"

"Shall I have the men pack our things?"

Giles didn't break eye contact with Eleanor. "I think that would be for the best, don't you agree, Miss Archer?"

Eleanor watched a sly grin lift the corners of his well-shaped lips, which caused his dimples to appear and a rascally sort of twinkle came into his eyes.

"You've changed." Giles West nodded. "Improved, even."

Eleanor tipped her head in regal condescension. "*Most kind.*"

He shook his head. "Well, it seems you've grown—a-a-taller, but no wiser."

"Why don't you hie yourself off?"

"Harleigh would wish me to act in your best interest."

"You've no idea what's in *my* best interest."

Giles shook his head. "As willful as ever."

She heard the dismantling and packing of their belongings. She and Giles West hadn't moved one jot.

Libby's small hand came to rest on her arm. "Eleanor, I'll wait for you in the coach." She heard Libby's distinctive limping footsteps moving away.

Giles West pulled his hat from his head. He had such lovely thick blond hair. She wondered what it would feel like to run her fingers through it. Eleanor shook herself.

He handed off his hat and walking stick to the nearest footman, then he wrapped his large hands around her waist and lifted Eleanor straight off the ground.

She felt her feet dangling. It was quite disconcerting. She beat at Giles' arms. "Unhand me, you presumptuous lummox."

"As you wish." Giles loosened his grasp.

He's going to drop me! She began to fall.

He tightened his hold again. Her head fell back and an unexpected laugh burst from her lips. Their eyes met and her breath caught. The way he looked at her made her feel—peculiar. She gave Giles West her most evil look.

He was unfazed by her scowl. In fact, it had the opposite effect, his smile grew larger and warmer. It was quite disorienting to be smiled at like that.

"Put me down," Eleanor said.

"I suggest you remove that fetching chapeau of yours before I help you through the door of your carriage, Miss Barrett."

Eleanor pressed her lips together. Mad as a wet cat. She pulled one long hat pin from the front of her hat's crown. Gazing at its shining sharp tip flashing in the sunlight, she mulled over the prudence of plunging it into Giles West's upper arm, impaling him like an insect specimen.

"Not a sagacious move on your part," Giles said as he gazed at her hatpin. "Just might actually drop you."

Eleanor wanted to scream. Being female at this moment was tantamount to being that stool she'd been sitting on—picked up and moved about at someone else's discretion. She yanked off her hat. This maneuver caused several of her curls to come loose. The breeze carried them across her face where they tangled with her eyelashes.

Giles emitted a soft chuckle. "Most becoming." He pulled Eleanor closer and whispered in her ear, "Harleigh has no idea where you are, does he?"

His warm breath tickled as it swept across her cheek. He held her in mid-air and he wasn't even winded. She, on the other hand, was breathing as if she'd run for miles.

Giles West pulled her against his chest, and her head went under his chin as he bent forward to pass under the lintel. She could see dog hair on his coat. He placed her back onto the seat—firmly—beside Libby.

His hands still around her waist, he remained improperly close, his mouth hovering above hers. Eleanor couldn't tear her gaze from his lips. She had an overwhelming desire to touch them.

Kiss.

When that word streaked across her brain, her eyes darted to his. His unfashionably bronzed skin only made the deep blue of his eyes all the more startling. She scowled, and his eyes crinkled with merriment.

His husky voice made her skin prickle. "Miss Barrett," he said and then paused, "you tempt me."

Eleanor felt the burn of her blush.

"To throw you over me knee and paddle your derrière till it burned and turned as pink as your cheeks are at this moment."

Eleanor slammed her fists into the seat cushion on either side of her hips. "Get out!"

He withdrew from the carriage, shut the door with what Eleanor perceived as a self-satisfied snap, and waved the coachman off.

The Barrett coach lurched into motion.

Eleanor drummed her foot on the carriage floor. "I'm not going to let him get away with this."

"Oh dear. What are you thinking?" Libby slid closer to Eleanor on the bench. When Eleanor didn't answer, Libby squeezed her hand. "Ellie, are you blushing?"

Eleanor turned her head away and looked out the window. "Of course not. Shhh, I need to think."

Libby shifted forward on the bench, then sang out, "You are too-oo."

Eleanor didn't respond.

"Do you think he'll tell?" Libby asked.

Eleanor forced her breathing to slow, just like her teacher, Master Sakegawa, had taught her years before. It helped to restore her calm. She propped her elbow on the window ledge and cradled her chin. "Of course he'll tell."

"Lord West is ver-r-ry handsome," Libby said.

"What does that have to do with the price of butter? Honestly, Lib."

Libby's brow furrowed. "Strange he didn't recognize you."

Eleanor flicked her hand in the air. "It's been years. He and Harleigh went up to University, I went traveling with Aunt Beatrice, and then those two went on their grand tour." She shrugged. "He's changed. And not all of it in the best ways."

Libby started worrying her bottom lip.

Eleanor reached out and took Libby's hand. "Don't worry. I can handle me father *and* brother."

"But can you *handle* Lord West? Hmmm?" Libby said.

Eleanor glowered at her. "Pshaw."

Libby tried unsuccessfully to suppress her giggles. "You should've seen your face when he lifted you off the ground." She gasped for breath.

Eleanor frowned.

"And Lord preserve me, I thought he was going to kiss you right here in front of me when he deposited you on this bench."

Eleanor huffed. "When we get back to me parents, I must send me aunt a note."

"About tonight?" Libby said.

Eleanor gave her a sly grin. "You might say that."

Libby's giggles ceased. "Uh-oh."

‹♦›

As the wheels of the Barrett's coach clattered across the cobblestones and disappeared from view, Giles West placed his hat back on his head.

Woof.

He looked down at his collie, Rodrigo, who dutifully sat beside him, waiting for directions. "So you think she's a handful too, do you?"

Woof.

"By gad, she smelled"—Giles paused— "delightful, but none of that cloying attar of roses nonsense."

He scowled, troubled by his reaction to his best friend's little sister. "And her eyes, the color of a moss-covered rock by a trout stream." A bark of mocking laughter erupted from him. "Christ, what fanciful drivel I'm spouting. Moss-covered rocks, indeed."

Rodrigo exhaled loudly, laid his head on his paws and rolled his eyes upward to look at his master. Giles would've sworn it sounded like a dog's version of exasperation.

"She's all grown up, you see. Quite caught me off guard. And Harleigh said nothing about her being back or the improvement in her looks. She used to be lumpy, then she elongated and got skinny and freckled and she had no—no…" Giles held his cupped hands in front of his chest and motioned right and left.

Woof.

"Botheration." Giles rubbed his forehead. "Almost made an ass out of myself. Damn, but those lips of hers almost made me forget I'm a gentleman."

Chapter Three

Giles heard the last long dramatic note of the violins above the buzz of conversation and the shush-shush of moving feet across the Cunninghams' polished ballroom floor. The cessation of the music signaled the terminus of this socially acceptable brand of torture. His current tribulation was a buxom, golden-haired sylph of marriageable age. She was an ideal piece of fruit, nurtured by his class, now ripe, waiting to be plucked. A pretty doll of a woman in a virginal white dress, with a highly-refined demeanor, and the total absence of intelligent conversation.

He had endured an entire set of dances while listening to her sweet voice recount every bit of ruinous gossip that crossed her mind. Only good manners had kept Giles from yawning in her face. His reputation as a principled man of high standards, who neither listened to, nor passed along gossip, hadn't deterred her from subjecting him to this form of what his peers considered entertainment.

He knew his potential wifely tastes weren't the norm for a man of his class. Except for Harleigh, the rest of his unmarried friends didn't seem to want more in a life partner than a pretty face, a decent pedigree, and a reasonable dowry. Without another moment of hesitation, or a flicker of regret, Giles crossed this young woman's name off his list of potential mates.

As his mental pen slashed through her name, it moved on to scrawl a new one … Eleanor. His palms itched, remembering the feel of his hands wrapped around her voluptuous figure. Lord, what a talent she had for provoking him. She'd possessed that ability since she was a child. Any male who stood in her way got the same treatment. If she couldn't run over you, she would beat you into submission with logic or sheer stubbornness. Now she had added all those luscious curves to her arsenal. But he doubted they were perceived as much of an asset on the marriage mart, not with her temperament and penchant for saying exactly what was on her mind.

Giles recalled the time, as a little girl, she had demanded to be let into the schoolroom with her brothers. He could hear her jabbering voice as she peppered her father with her arguments.

Eleanor believed her gender was irrelevant. Her mind was just as capable of learning as her brothers and she should have the same opportunities to cultivate her abilities.

Her poor father had gotten wrapped about her chubby little fingers like a ribbon around the maypole. Later on, so had Harleigh. He'd even taught her to handle a sword. Giles would never lower himself to be trapped or manipulated by his feelings for a woman. None of his sisters had dared ask him to teach them to fence.

"Is something wrong, my lord?" his empty-headed dance partner enquired.

Giles jolted out of his reverie and cleared his throat. "What makes you ask?"

"You have a look on your face as if you just swallowed something sour," she said.

"Ah." *Damn it.* "Sorry, must be something I ate." Giles tapped one of the buttons on his waistcoat to indicate an upset stomach.

"Oh…um, I just hate that. Mama always says it's best to adhere to a regimen of bland foods, especially before an event." She looked up at him with such earnestness in her eyes.

Good Lord, she had bought his drivel, hook, line and sinker. Unlike the woman currently at his side, he doubted Eleanor would ever allow an answer like that to pass. He huffed as a sardonic thought whispered in his ear. *Neither would she bore you to death, you clod.* Bah. His errant thoughts had once again taken a bad turn.

Giles walked the girl back to her mama. "Thank you, Miss Croft." He bowed over her gloved hand and took a step back, ready to make his escape, when Lady Croft stopped him in his tracks.

"Ah, my lord, you are everything that is kindness itself."

Save me.

"The heat in this ballroom is excessive, is it not?" Lady Croft fanned herself. "I would dearly love a glass of our host's most excellent lemonade."

He wanted to snarl but, alas, his mother had trained him too well. "I'll attend to it immediately. Ladies." Giles gave a quick nod and withdrew. He found the nearest footman and ordered him to take the ladies Croft their sour libation.

His long legs ate up the distance as he strolled to the edge of the ballroom. He was about to make his escape, when some fickle whim made him gaze right. There sat Jemma Peabody, one of his sister Dolly's friends. She sat alone, staring at her dance card.

Her empty dance card, no doubt.

Sweet Miss Peabody. Giles closed his eyes and groaned inwardly. As he approached, she pulled her spectacles from her reticule; they tangled in the draw-cords of her bag. She loudly huffed as she tugged to free her glasses. It was not a dainty sound.

Once firmly in hand, Jemma Peabody hooked her specs about her ears. This maneuver caused her curls, which had formerly dangled in a becoming fashion from her temples, to bunch-up in a loopy manner like mangled insect antennae. Miss Peabody looked like a discomposed grasshopper. She sighed—loudly—and allowed her shoulders to sag.

"Miss Peabody." Giles stood in front of her.

She squinted up at him through the round and slightly foggy lenses. Her hand trembled as she shoved her glasses up onto the bridge of her nose. "I'm sorry, sir, have we been introduced?"

Giles coughed to cover his laugh. "Indeed. I'm Dolly's eldest brother."

She squeaked and then propelled herself off her seat to dip an awkward curtsy. "Oh dear, oh dear, oh dear." She couldn't look him in the eye.

"I'm pleased to see you again. Are you enjoying the dance?" Giles asked.

"Lord West, how foolish of me not to recognize you. What a simpleton you must think me."

"You, a simpleton? Hardly. Do I recall correctly, Miss Peabody, that you've a great interest in philosophical matters?"

Her eyes opened wide in surprise, but she nodded rapidly.

"That hardly qualifies you for the status of simpleton." He waved his arm in the direction of the dancers. "May I have this dance?" She became even more flustered so Giles put her trembling gloved hand on his arm and led her onto the dance floor.

They joined a line that had formed for the next set. The music began and his toes quickly became aware that Jemma Peabody was as awkward on the dance floor as she was off it.

When their first dance concluded, Giles took mercy on his toes and led Miss Peabody to a quiet corner. They found a padded bench.

"Oh, yes, indeed." Jemma Peabody gazed up at him.

"What?"

"I *am* vastly interested in scientific matters, my lord."

Giles felt a moment of confusion. "You're responding to me other question." He hailed a footman, who brought them two glasses of punch. "Which science captures your interest?"

"Ahem, botanical matters. Flowers, to be precise."

"Do you attend many philosophical society meetings?" She pursed her lips and attempted to look stern, but her eyes gave her away. There was a mischievous twinkle hiding in their depths.

"You know perfectly well that men do not allow mere women to attend their meetings. Though I do read extensively. My dear father indulges me shamelessly. His library contains many texts on the subject of botany, which he has purchased for me. My current favorite text is Systema Naturæ by the Swedish botanist and physician, Carolus von Linné. He has eased the task of plant cataloging, you see. He adopted a sexual system of classification using stamens and pistils as important characters."

She stopped abruptly and emitted a soft choking sound. "Oh dear, I shouldn't have said that." She turned quite red and couldn't meet his eye, again.

"Actually, I found your discourse most informative."

"Really?"

"Truly. Carolus von Linné, you said?"

Jemma Peabody nodded.

"Now I know whom to come to when I have a botanical question."

"Oh."

She was such a sweet, intelligent creature, it was too bad he felt no attraction to her; she was the closest thing to his ideal mate that he had spoken to in an age—well, except for Eleanor, but that hadn't been a conversation, more like a skirmish. And where Miss Peabody chose to hide her unconventional interests, Eleanor waved them around like a red flag, daring any male to challenge her. No, Eleanor was *not* suitable at all.

Before he left the ballroom, Giles made sure to leave Jemma Peabody in the company of several kind young matrons he knew would watch over her.

This time he left the ballroom with dispatch and secured directions to their host's study. As the footman opened the portal to this *sancto sanctorum*, Giles' senses were assaulted by the heady aroma of excellently blended cigars and raucous male laughter. The room was already chock-full of refugee males of all ages. He inhaled deeply and his spirits rose.

After procuring a cigar for one hand and a glass of excellent French brandy for the other, he wandered around the room, conversing with several of his father's cronies, elder statesmen, sporting large powdered wigs and faces molded by the triumphs and travails of a life well-lived.

Several enquired how his hunt was going, referring, of course, to his benighted decision to find himself a suitable wife during *this* Season. He took their verbal jabs with aplomb, but a couple of times he did wince and that sent them all off into gales of laughter. He hated being the butt of this kind of laughter, as if his heart's desire was fodder for a comedy.

All he wanted was a modestly pretty, docile female with a companionable personality. Once he became leg-shackled, he intended to be monogamous, so he had to find someone he could tolerate for the next fifty or so years. The Wests were notoriously long-lived.

Making the decision to find a suitable wife and beget brats used to have a certain symmetry to it. Now, he felt like Sisyphus—compelled to roll an immense boulder up a hill, only to watch it roll back down or until he said, 'I do'.

Instead of enjoying the Season of wife-hunting, he found his world overflowing with women of Lady Croft's ilk, replete with their un-married female progeny. He felt his shoulders and neck growing painfully tight. *Sore toes and now a pain in me neck. What next?*

Having made the rounds, he excused himself and escaped out to the terrace to enjoy his cigar under the night sky. His gaze fell on the profile of his oldest and dearest friend, Lord Harleigh Barrett, Eleanor's eldest brother. Seeing Harleigh instantly erased his sour mood.

"What ho, Harleigh."

Harleigh turned at the sound of his name. "Giles, this is splendid to find you here."

Giles shoved his cigar into the corner of his mouth as he crossed to his friend. When he arrived at Harleigh's side, he slapped him on the back and then leaned forward and lowered his voice. "I've had enough of this for one night. Can you steal away with me?"

Harleigh chuckled. "What? Nothing meets your exacting standards in the ballroom this night?"

"I feel rather like a rat that has been cornered by a pack of cats."

Harleigh snorted. "Cats do not run in packs."

"Go ahead and laugh, you jackal," Giles said.

"Now, jackals do run in packs," Harleigh said. "It's your own damned fault for being such a handsome, well-heeled specimen. Me sisters tell me you are considered quite the best catch of the Season." Harleigh sipped his drink.

"Really?" Giles felt quite pleased by that appellation. He very much
doubted one of those sisters had been Eleanor. He doubted she would have anything of a complimentary nature to say about him. Then he took another look at his friend and knew he was being bammed. Giles huffed with indignation.

Harleigh, damn his eyes, was bent over and gasping for breath, he was laughing so hard.

"I shall get even with you for that one."

"P-p-r-robabl-ee-hee," Harleigh gasped.

Giles crossed his arms over his chest. "So, why are you not being hounded, then?"

"Do not give'm the chance, that is me motto." Harleigh's smile grew devilish.

"Well then, it appears we are agreed. Let's make a quick retreat."

Harleigh snagged Giles by the elbow. "Sorry, old friend, I cannot do it. We just arrived."

"We?" Giles said.

"M' parents. They would love to see you."

"And I them."

"Maybe you should take a second look in the ballroom." Harleigh waved his hand that held his glass in the direction of the house. "Time's running out, ye know, the Season's nearly over."

"Bah. Don't need you reminding me, too. I've looked and danced with every eligible chit from here to Timbuktu."

"Look for no sympathy from this quarter," Harleigh said.

Giles leaned against the balustrade. "Hmph. So I've noticed."

"What are your requirements anyway?"

"Pretty, steady, competent."

"That doesn't sound uncommon or impossible," Harleigh said.

"Well, I didn't think so."

"There must be something else. What do you mean by competent?"

"She must manage the household. I've the estates to manage and eventually I'll have Parliamentary concerns as well. She'll have to deal with a great many things on her own and often in a timely way," Giles said.

"You aren't speaking about competence, you want spirit and intelligence. Someone who's not afraid of taking on large tasks and who'll act independently of you."

Giles rubbed his chin. "Are we not saying the same thing?"

"Hardly. Competency implies sufficient skill to perform a particular task, like playing the piano. It speaks to being adequate, not exceptional. You've always been a fellow of exacting standards. Probably why you took that first in mathematics."

Giles opened his mouth to challenge Harleigh's supposition.

"Anyway, what you are describing is an extraordinary woman. No wonder you are failing to find her, since I'm not sure she exists."

Giles took a sip of his drink. An image of the indomitable Eleanor wanting to plunge her hat pin into his arm leapt into his mind. He blinked and then rubbed his forehead, as if he could wipe her out of his thoughts.

Harleigh laid his hand over his heart. "I, myself, am quite happy as I am. In a year, or two, or three, I'll be ready to settle down."

Giles scowled down into his glass.

"You, me friend, are chasing a wild goose," Harleigh said.

"You're turning into a bit of a nag; did you know that?"

Harleigh's eyes lit with merriment. "Only where you're concerned. What's an old friend good for but to remind you of your shortcomings, eh?"

"Friendship aside, I'm having an overpowering urge to plant you a facer."

Harleigh shrugged. "If it'll make you feel better, go ahead and try."

"Cousin Harleigh."

Both Giles and Harleigh turned to watch Francis—Lord Edgerton—sauntering toward them. Although he was really Harleigh's father's cousin, at twenty-six he was just a year older than Harleigh and Giles, so their age proximity had made it easier to refer to each other as cousins.

"Christ, what's he doing here?" Harleigh muttered but didn't extend his hand, and then said with thinly veiled civility, "Evening, Edgerton."

Giles watched Harleigh turn from affable to barely courteous in a blink. He'd never known Harleigh to be anything but kind, friendly and scrupulously polite—well, except where Edgerton was concerned. Giles chose to ignore Harleigh's social lead and follow his own conscience.

Giles was genuinely pleased to see Francis Edgerton and smiled warmly as he turned to face him. As school boys, Giles had been one of the few students who'd liked and befriended Edgerton after his father's accident that had brought the Edgerton family close to financial ruin. Giles had gone so far as to ask his father to make Edgerton a loan for his last year at University.

But Edgerton would have none of it. Too proud to accept help, somehow, he'd squeaked through, and look at him now, he looked hale and hearty, and plump in the pockets to boot. It was a pleasure to see him so.

Edgerton stopped in front of Harleigh. "How are you, cousin? Giles?"

"Passable," Harleigh said. "And you?"

"Are you here escorting Eleanor?" Edgerton asked.

"Eleanor?" Harleigh said.

"Heard she's back," Edgerton said. "After all, 'tis the Season, is it not? And she is the only one left in the nest as I recall."

Harleigh's brow furrowed. "She and Aunt Beatrice returned a few weeks ago."

"Lord, forgot Eleanor was gadding about with our madcap Cousin Beatrice," Edgerton said.

Harleigh's posture stiffened.

Edgerton tipped his head back toward the house. "And shall I find them both in the ballroom this evening?"

"They're attending a salon."

Edgerton shuddered in a mocking way. "Intellectual talks. What does a woman need with those? That's what your father gets for allowing Eleanor into the schoolroom with you fellows."

Harleigh, his lips a flat line, his nostrils flared, took an aggressive step toward Edgerton.

Giles got between them. Christ, he was feeling mildly irked himself at Edgerton's shabby remarks about Eleanor developing her mind.

Harleigh crossed his arms over his chest. "If me father had wanted your opinion—"

"Yes, I know." Edgerton waved his hand dismissively, smiling all the while. He turned to Giles. "Have not seen you in an age, West."

And now, Giles felt irritated at Edgerton's unsolicited criticism of Harleigh's father, but he extended his hand nonetheless. "Just thinking the
same."

Edgerton shook hands with Giles. "We should catch up. Have coffee with me tomorrow, at Travelers."

"Did not think this was your kind of affair, cousin?" Harleigh's voice had an edge.

Edgerton shrugged. "You're correct. It's not. I detest women in white. Makes me feel trapped. I like me women with less clothing on."

Harleigh dipped his head and muttered, "And much younger, from what I've heard."

What?

"What?" Edgerton looked like an inquisitive, well-dressed owl.

Harleigh nudged his chin in the direction of the ballroom. "I said I can see your predicament. But that still does not explain your presence."

"True," Edgerton said.

Harleigh pressed. "Then?"

Edgerton nodded in Giles' direction. "Meeting up with some friends, don't ye know. Would ten o'clock in the morning suit you, West?"

Distracted by the waves of tension flowing between Harleigh and Edgerton, Giles lost the thread of his own conversation with the man. "What?"

"Coffee at Travelers. Tomorrow morning. At ten? If you are up and

about at that hour, that is."

"Oh, I'm up. Got used to being an early riser during me wanderings," Giles said.

"Excellent. Need to get back inside and do the pretty for at least a dance or two before I escape into the night and more libidinous pleasures." Edgerton waggled his brows, saluted them with his glass, then sauntered back inside.

When Edgerton crossed the threshold, Giles turned to Harleigh. "What the hell's going on?"

Harleigh stared after Edgerton's retreating form. "Hmmm?"

"*I said ...*"

"You'd do well to stay a long way away from him," Harleigh said. "And why's he asking after me little sister, anyway? They've *never* gotten on."

"Whatever has ruffled your feathers won't keep me from meeting him tomorrow. Gave me word, and I mean to keep it."

"Suit yourself," Harleigh said. His brow furrowed and he suddenly looked like a man who'd walked under a dark cloud. "Just don't get drawn into anything."

"What does that mean?" Giles said.

"Never mind. Should've kept me mouth shut. I mean I don't any have proof."

"All right. Then let me change the subject. What's this about Eleanor?"

"Like I told Edgerton. Elizabeth Archer, you remember her, Ellie's best friend?"

Giles held his hand in the air, palm downward as if indicating someone's height. "Dainty thing. Reddish-gold hair, a bit of a limp?"

"Yes. She came up with us for the Season. She and Ellie are off at Lady Montagu's with Aunt Beatrice tonight."

Bet little miss high-jinx thinks I'll tattle on her to you and your father. Giles shook his head. *Oh, Eleanor, I'm so tempted.*

Chapter Four

Eleanor Barrett slipped her hand through the break in the brocade drapes and nudged the fabric aside. There wasn't much to see. Below, the flambeau beside the front door of her family's London home cast a small circle of light that barely illuminated the front steps, leaving everything beyond the reach of the undulating light in darkness.

The tension and impatience thrumming through her caused her foot to ceaselessly tap. She was on the lookout for the unmarked coach her aunt was sending to pick her up. But first, she had to sneak out of the house, without anyone knowing, and that included her best friend, who at this moment was seated across the room from her.

Libby held a book in her hands. "What are you looking at?"

"Nothing."

"Are you sure you wouldn't rather go to Lady Montagu's?" Libby said. "We'll be late but I can be ready in a tick."

Eleanor let the curtain fall and gazed over at Libby "If you want to go I can arrange for a carriage."

"Not without you." Libby turned a page.

Guilt pecked at Eleanor's conscience. She didn't like sneaking off, but
Libby needed to stay here. Where it was safe. The only witnesses Eleanor wanted to this night's risky activity were Bart—her Aunt Bea's faithful driver and bodyguard, and the sentinel moon.

Eleanor had promised her aunt there would be no 'funny business.' She just wanted to complete her drawing on the south side of Saint Paul's. Nothing formal, just a few quick sketches should do the trick. That should give them what they needed to move their investigation forward.

To calm her fidgets, she walked the perimeter of the room, ending back where she started. Damn Giles West. If he hadn't interfered, she and Libby would be sitting in Lady Montagu's parlor right now. There would be no cause to go sneaking around Covent Garden after dark.

A distant tower clock struck nine. Following the last stroke, she heard the faint sound of iron-shod hooves against cobbles. With one finger, Eleanor made a peephole in the drapes and watched Bart climb down from the box. She let the curtain drop and marched to the hallway door. "I need to get something from me room."

Libby put her book aside. "I'll go with you."

Eleanor opened the door. "No need, dearest."

Libby slipped through the doorway before Eleanor could stop her. They stared at each other for a long moment. Eleanor's mind, usually so quick, seemed stuck.

Libby pointed down the hall, away from the stairs. "Um, your room is that way."

Time got stuck like Eleanor's mind and they continued staring at one another. Eleanor threw her hands in the air. "All right, all right, all right. I'm going out."

Libby thrust her index finger at Eleanor. "I knew you were up to something."

Eleanor huffed. "Go back in there," she said, pointing to the room they'd just vacated. "I'll return soon." She moved to the stairs.

A maid approached who carried an armful of linens, she eyed them with great curiosity.

"Yes?" Eleanor glared at the servant. The maid ducked her head and scurried away.

Libby clutched Eleanor's sleeve. "Oh, no. I cannot let you out of me sight. You'll do something foolish if I'm not around. And get into trouble."

Eleanor moved her arm forward, hoping Libby would let go.

Libby didn't let go, instead stepping closer. "If you'll not listen to reason, then I'll have to go with you."

Eleanor wanted to tie Libby up and gag her. "Go back in there or go to bed."

"Take me with you or I'll make such a row you'll never leave this house tonight."

଼

Inside her Aunt Beatrice's carriage, the lamp's wick was turned low and the curtains had been drawn. Eleanor tapped on the small door in the roof and Bart's face appeared. "Take it slow. I need time to change."

He grunted and closed the hatch. The coach lurched into motion.

Libby peered beneath a corner of a curtain. "Where are we bound?"

Eleanor didn't answer as she dug into a large lumpy bag. She extracted a pair of worn men's boots and tossed them onto the floor. Onto the bench beside her, she piled a small corked jar, a man's unadorned shirt dyed a deep mulberry, a dark woolen cap, black breeches, and a heavy black cape.

Libby interlaced her gloved fingers and set them primly in her lap. "Ellie, I know you are put out with me, but please answer me question?"

Eleanor felt the pull of Libby's entreaty; it was always hard to stay angry with her.

Libby remained silent.

Eleanor sighed, kicking off her shoes and tossing them into the now empty sack. "Covent Garden." Eleanor wedged her arms behind her back, trying to position her fingers to undo the knot holding her dress laces tied.

"All right." Libby sat back. "But, wait, then why these mannish clothes? I mean, we're in a carriage…Oh no. You mean to walk about?"

Libby's voice rose in pitch. "No-no-no. That'll never do."

"Shhhh." Eleanor continued to fiddle with the knot at her back, then frustrated, dropped down to one knee and exposed her back to Libby. "Would you mind?" She cocked her arm over her shoulder and pointed downward with her thumb, indicating the laces that needed undoing.

Libby sat on her hands. "I'm not going to help you do something so ill-advised."

Eleanor picked up one of her mannish boots from the floor of the carriage. She ran her fingers around the inside rim on the boot top. When she found the hidden sheath, she pulled the small knife out and held it up. "You either do it or I'll cut the strings."

Libby's mouth gaped open. "Put that nasty thing away."

Eleanor felt Libby's fingers working at the strings.

"For goodness' sake, you keep this up and I just might come around to your mother's point of view."

Eleanor looked over her shoulder. "What do you mean?"

"That your interest in manly things is … is …"

"Unnatural?" Eleanor said.

Libby waved her hands in the air. "No, not that. Not ever. It's just that you're so brave and courageous and you care so deeply about the wrongs of this world that sometimes your passions override your good sense."

"We need this information. You know that as surely as I do. This is the fastest and surest way to get it. I don't trust Giles West. He'll tell Harleigh or me father where he found us and we'll never be let back into Covent Garden on our own. We need to find out what's happening to those missing girls and the clues have led us here. These girls' families have no consequence, or the money to pay for anyone to look for them. We're their only hope. Do you want me to sit in someone's parlor and make chitchat when we might be able to bring those girls home?"

"Certainly not." Libby twirled one finger in the air, indicating Eleanor should turn around. Libby loosened the laces the rest of the way. "But this situation is much more dangerous than us cavorting in the country like boys after dark."

"Aaahhh." With her laces now undone, Eleanor returned to sit on the bench opposite and pulled her bodice down, withdrew her arms from the sleeves, then pulled it off over her head and tossed it on the floor. "I *never* cavort."

Libby snorted and then grabbed Eleanor's discarded bodice and folded it and put it in the sack. "Besides, practicing our fighting skills against one another isn't the same thing at all as coming up against a big ugly man."

Eleanor took off her skirts and petticoats, leaving her in a chemise, short stays, and stockings. "I *have* practiced against a man…Master Sakegawa."

"That was years ago, when you were a girl," Libby said.

"The body's memory is long. And yes, it's been years since he left, but he trained me well. Do not doubt me. I'll bring us home safe."

Libby nibbled her lip and her brows drew together.

Eleanor reached over and squeezed her hand. "Have faith in me."

"You were the only one who believed I'd walk again. Of course I've faith in you."

Eleanor sat back, undid her garters, and got rid of her stockings. She got the breeches up to her knees, but then had to stand, albeit bent over, to pull them on completely. With the coach in motion, she staggered. Eleanor's hand came to rest above Libby's head to brace herself and keep from falling over. The pouch she wore on a ribbon around her neck nearly hit Libby in the forehead.

"What is that? Around your neck?" Libby pointed at the pouch.

Eleanor sat back down opposite her friend and partially buttoned the falls of her breeches. She pulled a voluminous man's shirt over her head, hiding the pouch from view.

Libby gave her a questioning glance but let the subject drop. Instead, she pointed at the yards of fabric of Eleanor's chemise, which hung down to her shins. "What're you going to do about that?"

"At least I had the presence of mind to wear a sleeveless chemise." Eleanor extracted the boot knife again. "There's nothing for it." She plunged the tip of her knife into the fabric of the chemise right at her hips and began cutting away the thin material.

Libby gasped.

"Well, I cannot go stuffing all of this fabric into me breeches, now can I? Here, cut the back part off, will you?"

Libby took the knife. "Not while we're moving."

The carriage made a sharp turn.

Libby braced herself with her arms.

Eleanor tumbled to the floor. She brushed her hair off her face and grinned. "Point well taken."

"Hardy har," Libby said.

By the time they reached Covent Garden, Eleanor was completely transformed. The small corked jar contained soot and ashes, which she had smeared over her face, down her neck and over the back of her hands.

"Yilch, why'd you do that?" Libby pointed to Eleanor's face.

"The moon's full. Want nothing to reflect light, me face included, and a mask would impair me vision."

"Reflect light?" Libby said.

"I'll be nothing more than a shadow."

The coach stopped. As Bart, who wasn't a small man, came down off the driver's box, he set the coach rocking.

Bart's formidable size made him an excellent guardian for Libby, but the swaying of the coach caused Eleanor's stomach to heave. She gulped in some air and swallowed hard.

The door opened. Bart caught sight of Eleanor and grunted. "Now what?"

Eleanor motioned with her hand for him to move aside. She jumped out. "You two stay here. I'll be back soon."

Bart grabbed Eleanor by the back of her cape, jerking her unceremoniously to a halt. "Nothin' doin', miss. Yer aunt said I wasn't to let you outta me sight."

Eleanor looked up at Bart, with his square granite jaw and pugilist's broken nose, and knew he'd follow her aunt's orders.

Drat!

"You can let go of me now, Bart." Once he released her, Eleanor turned to face him, crossing her arms over her chest. "I see."

Libby leaned out of the carriage door and sniffed the air. "What's that dreadful odor?"

Eleanor pointed to Libby. "Well, we can't leave her here alone, can we?"

Grinning, whip in hand, Bart rocked back on his heels. "Well, then I guess that means nobody goes nowheres."

Eleanor wanted to hit someone. "First Giles West's high-handed interfering, now you and me aunt. I don't think so. Step down, Lib."

"What?" Libby said.

"If he"—Eleanor thrust her finger at Bart—"must stay with me, then you must come with us."

Bart's grin disappeared. "Miss Eleanor, you be the stubbornest female I done ever met."

"No more talk. The quickest way to complete the logistical diagrams of this locale is to get on with it."

Bart helped Libby from the coach. He moved to the box and whispered. "Here, boy." When Bart turned back to them, he held a small scrappy dog in his hands. He placed the mongrel on the ground. "Guard, Leo."

Eleanor headed off with a quick light step. A few beats later she heard Bart and Libby's footsteps following her down the alley. She leaned against the building at the mouth of the alley and pulled her woolen cap down firmly upon her head.

A chilly breeze whistled under her cape and up her sleeves, sending shivers across her shoulders and down her spine.

Bart and Libby were a few yards back and it was dark, so Eleanor pulled the ribbon that hung around her neck out from under her shirt. She loosened the mouth of the small velvet pouch and slipped her fingers inside. They came to rest against a child's toy. A small lump of baked clay. It had once been a round marble, but now it was rather misshapen. As her fingertips rested on the hard lump, her resolve grew firm. In her mind, she ticked off the steps they needed to take to ensure a safe and victorious outcome for this night's work.

She withdrew her fingers from the tiny sack, tugged it closed, and slipped it back under her shirt. How odd life was. Giles West had given her that marble and if it weren't for his interference they wouldn't be here right now.

She remembered him sitting quietly on her bed. He'd held her hand. Everyone else—her parents, Harleigh, the doctor, her governess—were badgering her to tell them what had happed in the barn. But Eleanor couldn't explain. Not with Betty's attacker's words playing like an endless litany in her aching head.

Giles had placed that marble in the palm of her hand, telling her it was his good-luck token and she looked like she could use a bit of luck. She'd carried it as her talisman ever since.

Thinking of Giles was a mistake. Her restless imagination pictured him
dancing around the Cunninghams' ballroom tonight, holding some marriageable young woman in his arms—his future countess, no doubt. Eleanor pinched herself. She needed all her attention focused in the here and now, not distracted by some childhood memory. She crouched and peered around the corner just as Libby and Bart came up behind her.

Libby sank her fingers into Eleanor's shoulder and leaned forward and whispered, "If you ask me, that doesn't look good."

Eleanor whispered back, "You have, as always, a gift for understatement."

"What's amiss?" Towering over both, Bart took his turn to have a peek.

"Two lumps with an unwilling woman between them," Eleanor said.

Libby poked Eleanor in the shoulder. "She needs help."

"Me thought exactly." Eleanor sprang up.

Libby fell back. "No, no, no," she shook her head. "I didn't mean we should do the helping."

Eleanor placed her finger over her lips. "Shhhh. Well … to whom would you suggest that young woman apply for assistance?"

Libby gazed about frantically. "There must be someone else about."

"I'm afraid Miss Eleanor is correct. There be only us," Bart said.

Eleanor gazed up at him. "Do you have a gun?"

Bart raised his hand with the whip. "Don't need no gun."

Eleanor believed him. She flipped the edge of her cape over her right shoulder and reached around her back and pulled out the twig flintlock she had tucked into the waistband of her breeches. She released the safety and handed it to Libby. "Here."

Libby took the gun.

Eleanor gave Libby's shoulder a squeeze. "I know you don't want to shoot anyone. But if it comes to it, you know what to do."

Libby nodded.

Eleanor wrapped her fingers into the front of Bart's overcoat and tugged so he lowered his face to hers. "I taught her to shoot, but whether she'll pull the trigger is another matter."

Bart grunted.

"I can take care of myself. I'm counting on *you* to take care of *her*."

Bart darted an assessing glance at Libby, who was nibbling her lip. He cleared his throat and rubbed his chin. "I sees what ye mean. Cannot picture her pullin' that trigger meself."

"Good." Eleanor let go of Bart's coat, then she whispered into Libby's ear, "Stay close to him. He'll keep you safe."

Eleanor slipped around the corner. A sign that was hanging on a rusty bit of iron above her head creaked as it swung in the breeze. The louts across the street were coming closer.

She dropped her hands to her sides. Rolled her shoulders. Took a deep, calming breath, and flexed her fingers. Harleigh and their father had given her training in guns, archery, swords, and horses. But it had been her secret childhood teacher, Sakegawa Sensei, who had taught Eleanor to subdue her enemies without drawing blood.

Following the incident in the barn, Eleanor's father had brought her to see a London doctor. She'd been waiting in his carriage when three oafs had tried to waylay a small, wiry man with marzipan-colored skin.

She'd watched in silent awe as he magically dispatched his adversaries. She'd begged the strange little man to teach her so she'd never be vulnerable again. He'd finally acquiesced but made her promise to use her skills for defense only.

So far, she'd trained Libby and Betty, turning them both into a formidable sisterhood of warriors.

The two men, with their hapless victim sandwiched between, were now right across the street from her. The larger man wore a ratty frockcoat and a misshapen wig. His arm was about the woman's neck and his hand clamped over her mouth.

His accomplice wore no wig. Moonlight revealed an enormous bulbous nose and a jiggly potbelly.

The men dragged their captive into a narrow passageway. Eleanor
followed her quarry into the alley. Sliding into the shadows. She crept along the west wall. A thick wedge of blue-white moonlight illuminated the east side of the passage, revealing the positions of her adversaries.

Eleanor unhooked her cape and laid it soundlessly on the ground as Ratty-Frockcoat shoved the woman against the wall.

"L-leave me alone," the young woman said, desperation and fear making her voice shake.

"Why would we leaves ye alone, dearie?" Bulbous-Nose said.

"Yeah, alls we wants is a little tail tickle, thas all," Ratty-Frockcoat said.

The sound of fabric ripping.

"Leave off, I ain't no whore. Da ya hear me?" She shoved their hands away and then covered her exposed chest with her trembling fingers.

"None of that now." Bulbous-Nose belched as he knocked the young woman's hands aside. "We likes to see yer wares, in the flesh, so to speak."

Eleanor came up close behind Frockcoat. She planted one foot on the paving stones, raised her other, then snapped the heel of her boot into the backside of Frockcoat's knee.

He stumbled forward. When he caught his balance, he turned his head and stared into the darkness where Eleanor stood, holding her breath.

Moving on the balls of her feet, she stepped to his left as he came toward her. Eleanor slapped him hard and fast across the head.

He fell to the ground.

She stepped silently to her opponent's right.

The woman made a run for it. Bulbous-Nose caught her and hauled her back against his chest and gazed down at his friend. "Wha' happened?"

"Nuffin' happened." Frockcoat adjusted his wig and squinted into the shadows.

Eleanor took another small step back.

"If nuffin' happened, what ye doin' on the ground?" Bulbous-Nose said.

"Shut yer trap," Frockcoat said.

"Too much drink, I reckon. Think ye can still gets it up?" Bulbous-Nose taunted.

The woman pulled, trying to break away from Bulbous-Nose.

Bulbous-Nose shook her. "Quit that."

"Let go," the woman said.

Frockcoat stood up and his arm shot out.

Eleanor ducked.

Swish-swish. Frockcoat swung his arm back and forth, failing to connect with anything.

He spit and turned back to face their captive. He grabbed his crotch. "I'll show you who's got it up all right. Come on, girlie, ye been bobbling them tiddies under our noses all night."

"I done no such thing," she said as she shook her head.

You've got pluck.

Frockcoat laid a large paw over one very ample breast. She struggled and opened her mouth to cry out. He slapped her. "I says ye did, back there at the Cock 'n' Bull. And me words are the only ones that counts. Right?"

Bulbous-Nose chortled. "Damn straight."

"Holds her tight." Frockcoat bent his head and began undoing the laces of his breeches.

Eleanor was beside Bulbous-Nose. She raised her leg and delivered a hard, fast snap-kick. She drove her heel into the side of his soft protuberant belly.

As he fell sideways, toward the wall, he let go of his captive, freeing his hands to stop his fall.

Their captive landed on her bottom.

Bulbous-Nose's head bounced off the wall and he landed face-down.

Frockcoat threw his head back and guffawed. "Jaysus, we must ha' drunk a helluva lot more than I thought. Neither of us seems to be able to stay off 'n the ground."

From the ground, Bulbous-Nose swung his head up. "Sumpin' hit me."

"Sure, sure," Frockcoat said, his voice dripping disbelief.

Breathing hard, Libby limped quickly into the alley, waving the gun. "I'm here, Ellie."

Damn, where the hell is Bart?

Frockcoat grabbed his untied, sagging breeches with one hand and back-handed Libby with his other. She crumpled to the ground.

Their captive, on hands and knees, was crawling away.

Holding up his untied breeches with one hand, Frockcoat leaned down and grabbed their captive's hair and yanked. "Nows we gots two of 'em, one for you *and* one for me."

Before Bulbous-Nose could rise, Eleanor charged out of the darkness.

"Is that yer name? Ellie?" Frockcoat said.

Eleanor dropped to one knee beside Bulbous-Nose and drove her elbow into his back, right into his kidney.

Bulbous-Nose roared. "Christ Almi-hee."

Frockcoat caught sight of Eleanor. He let go of the tavern wench and grabbed Libby by the front of her dress and shook. "Where's that damn gun of yers?"

Crack! Frockcoat's ratty wig went flying.

Frockcoat yelped and grabbed his now bald head. "Bloody hell."

Libby and the captive were standing up against the wall, holding on to one another.

Crack!

"Yow!" Frockcoat rubbed his backside with one hand and held his pants up with the other.

Eleanor moved in, getting ready to deal with the repugnant Frockcoat.

"I got this one, Miss Ellie." Bart swung his whip again.

Crack!

Bart struck Frockcoat's hand that was rubbing his backside.

Frockcoat turned toward Bart and away from Libby. "Wha' the hell do ye think yer doin'?"

Crack!

Bart struck the back of Frockcoat's hand that clutched his breeches. "Damn yer eyes." Frockcoat's pants fell around his ankles.

"Leave 'em be, ye rat bastard," Bart said.

Frockcoat was puffing like a bellows.

"Here's how it's gonna be." Bart's voice was malevolent. "Ye and yer friend are getting off easy. Git outta here before I flay ye open and leave ye for the rats to feast on."

Frockcoat yanked up his pants, growling as he did it, then grabbed Bulbous-Nose under the arm, pulling him to standing. They departed quickly.

"Oh, Ellie." Libby was crying.

Eleanor grabbed her cape and tossed it at the nameless woman, who wrapped herself in it. Eleanor pulled Libby into her arms. "Why didn't you stay with Bart?"

Libby gave her a wan smile. "He tangled with a drunk and I slipped away. I couldn't let you have all the fun, could I?"

Eleanor shook her head, then turned to the other woman. "What's your name, miss?"

"Mi-Mildred. But they calls me Millie."

Bart ran up and lifted Libby into his arms. "Bunch a wild women is what ye are. Time I got ye to Miss Perdy's place. Yer aunt's waitin' for ye."

He moved off, back to the coach, carrying Libby while Eleanor and Millie followed.

"I'm ever so sorry 'bout yer friend getting' hurt on a counta me," Millie said.

Eleanor shook her head. "My fault, not yours."

Bart placed Libby in the coach and then lifted Leo back onto the box. "We needs to go, miss," Bart said to Eleanor as he climbed up.

Eleanor yanked her cap off. Her braid swung down her back. She wiped her sleeve across her face, wiping away some of the soot she'd
used as camouflage.

"Why, ye're just a girl. How did you do all that stuff back there?" Millie said.

Eleanor laughed. "That's right, a girl shouldn't be able to defend herself, should she?"

"I meant no harm," Millie said.

With her foot on the step and her hands on the doorframe, Eleanor gazed over her shoulder at Millie. "I understand. We must be on our way. I'm glad you're all right, Mildred."

"Wait, miss, can I comes wit you?" Millie said.

 Cz

Eleanor sat beside Libby on the bench, her arm wrapped around Libby's shoulders. She couldn't relax or make herself let go of her best friend. As the coach headed south out of London, the scene in the alley played over and over in her mind. Her stomach burned and her head pounded out the words: *You're arrogant and impatient and Libby could've died.*

Mildred sat opposite, watching.

After a while Libby fell asleep, her head rested on Eleanor's shoulder.

"Ye looks troubled, miss," Mildred said.

"I am." Eleanor studied Libby's sleeping face. She looked so small and vulnerable.

"She'll be right as rain in a day or two." Mildred nudged her chin at the slumbering Libby. "Course her bruises will takes a bit longer."

"I agree. The bruises will fade, but not the memory. She shouldn't have been there."

"Well, I know nuffin' about tha'. But if ye and her and the big fella up top hadn't come ..." Mildred shuddered. "The way I sees it the nicest thing that would ha' happened to me is an unwanted child, and the worst is a slow death by the pox."

Mildred was right, they'd saved her, but at what cost? Eleanor felt the burn of tears and turned her face away to hide her distress. She never let anyone see her cry.

Silence.

Eleanor cleared her throat. "Try and get some sleep. We'll not arrive at our destination for some time."

Wrapped in Eleanor's cloak, Mildred settled into the corner and closed her eyes.

They were headed for their rendezvous, a cottage north of Chatham that belonged to Eleanor's old governess, Amelia Perdy, and her husband, Mac, her father's former head groom.

Eventually, their speed slowed. The coach turned into a narrow, tree-covered lane. When they came to a stop, Eleanor's Aunt Beatrice and dear tough-as-old-boots Perdy came out onto the doorstep bundled in their shawls. Mac stood beside his wife, holding a lantern aloft.

The women were helped from the coach and ushered into the house while Mac and Bart took the coach back to the stable to tend the horses. Aunt Bea took Mildred off to get her something decent to wear and Perdy, Libby, and Eleanor went into the kitchen.

"Miss Eleanor, put the kettle on," Perdy said as she helped Libby to a chair at the kitchen table and got busy examining her injuries.

Eleanor checked that the kettle was full and then swung it over the fire. Then she paced around the kitchen, like a caged animal.

When Perdy was done, Libby smelled of ointment and the large scrape on her right cheek was clean and purpling.

When Aunt Beatrice and Mildred returned, Mildred was wearing a dark dress with a modest neckline that fit at the bust but bagged everywhere else. She took the seat next to Libby and gazed at her with adoration.

"How are ye feelin', miss?" Mildred said.

Libby looked up and smiled. "Better, miss … ah."

"Mildred, but I prefers to be called Millie."

"Better, Millie." Libby's eyes returned to her hands, which were folded and resting on the tabletop.

Aunt Beatric carried a large brown glazed teapot with steam rising from its spout over to the head of the table and seated herself behind it.

Perdy brought mugs from the sideboard and set them beside the teapot.

Aunt Beatrice filled mugs for Perdy, Libby, and Millie and handed them off. "Niece?"

Eleanor stopped her pacing and gazed at her aunt.

"Tea?" Aunt Beatrice said.

Eleanor shook her head and resumed her pacing. The room was full of tense silence.

Aunt Beatrice pounded her mug onto the tabletop like a magistrate with a gavel calling his court into session. "Eleanor, what happened to Libby?"

Eleanor jerked to a halt and turned to face her aunt.

Aunt Beatrice was in high dudgeon. "You led me to believe it would be only *you* out there tonight."

Libby cleared her throat. "Lady Whitely, it's not Eleanor's fault. I-I forced her. To take me along."

Aunt Beatrice flicked her hand, dismissing Libby's assertion. "Bah, no one forces that child to do anything."

Libby huffed and fisted her hands in front of her.

Aunt Beatrice raised her voice. "Ellie, she should *never* have left your parents' house."

Eleanor opened her mouth to respond.

"You mean because I must always be cosseted! Because of my leg." Libby said.

Aunt Beatrice's eyes went wide at Libby's statement.

Libby stood up quickly. Her chair toppled over behind her. "You all treat me like I'm made of glass. Everyone but Ellie, that is. And I'll not have you blaming her for *my* stupidity. She told me explicitly to stay with Bart. But when he had to deal with a drunken lout... well ... I took the opportunity and slipped away. I-I wanted to ..."

Millie touched Libby's arm. "Go on, miss,"

"...Help." They were all looking at her now. "I had Ellie's gun. And I *do* know how to use it because she taught me. Which is more than I can say for me own family."

Beatrice's brows rose up her forehead. "You can shoot?"

Eleanor righted Libby's fallen chair. "Yes, she's quite good with a pistol. Now, a bow and arrow is another matter altogether." Eleanor smiled when she rested her hand on Libby's shoulder.

Libby elbowed Eleanor. "No jokes. You were right. I should've stayed with Bart ... but I'm not sorry one bit about blackmailing you into to taking me along."

"Family?" Lady Beatrice pressed her hand to her cheek. "However, are we going to explain your face to Eleanor's parents?"

"Well, they can stay here for a few days. Miss Eleanor often comes for visits," Perdy said.

"That bruising and scrape won't heal that fast, Perdy," Eleanor said. "I think we should go home and tell them Libby fell."

"Fell?" Perdy said.

Eleanor shrugged. "On the bright side, my mother won't make us go to any more balls until Libby is once again presentable."

Libby smiled, then winced and touched her scraped cheek.

"Niece, of all the parts of London to go prowling in after dark, why ever did you choose Covent Garden?"

"Because we were following an important clue," Libby said. "And if that handsome dunderhead, Lord West, had minded his own business we would've been done earlier in the day and not had to go back tonight."

"Giles West?" Aunt Beatrice asked. "What do you mean a clue?"

Libby nodded at Ellie's aunt. "Yes, Giles West." Then she turned to Eleanor. "I think it's time to tell them."

Eleanor hesitated, listening to her inner compass—the one that told her

more than her eyes ever could. That compass said, *trust Millie*. "All right. Over a year ago, I started noticing these handbills."

"Concerning what, pray tell?" Aunt Beatrice said.

"Missing girls," Eleanor said.

"That isn't the sort of thing a proper young lady should be readin'," Perdy said as she shook her index finger at Eleanor.

Eleanor and Libby looked at Perdy, then looked back at each other and started to laugh.

Perdy huffed. "Well, it's not, and you two know I'm right."

"Go on." Aunt Beatrice motioned with her mug.

"Over time, I saw the same kind of notices in several different towns and villages."

"You never mentioned any of this to me." Aunt Beatrice put her elbows on the table and leaned forward.

"Sorry, Aunt, but it took us time to catch the pattern of it. The notices were always about girls, of a certain age, and the descriptions said they were pretty. And they all seemed to be daughters of farmers, shop owners, and such."

"We began cataloging the notices," Libby said. "Noting where the girls were from, their ages, the occupation of the fathers. Next, we wondered why these girls? Then we asked ourselves: did they run away, or
were they taken away?"

"Good Lord," Perdy muttered.

"Yes, it is quite horrible to think about, isn't it?" Libby said. "Now, if these girls were taken for ransom that, too, made no sense. These parents could no more afford to pay money to get them back than to hire men to go look for them. So, that meant the girls themselves had to have some value to whoever took them. And, most frustrating of all, we found no one who thought all these missing girls were connected."

"But you do?" Aunt Beatrice asked.

Libby nodded.

Eleanor continued circling the table. "We wondered … was there one person doing the taking … or a group of people? How many girls had been taken and how widespread? Libby suggested we write to some of our friends who live in other counties, asking if they had seen similar notices."

"I made a map," Libby said, "and when one of our friends told us they had seen a notice, I placed a mark on the place. And another common thing about these girls … they don't come from large towns."

"Well now, I can't imagine there are many marks on Miss Libby's map," Perdy said.

"Oh, but there are," Libby said.

"But what has this all have to do with Covent Garden?" Aunt Bea.asked again.

Millie listened intently and her eyes were glued to the face of the person speaking.

Eleanor cleared her throat. "I overheard my brothers talking about"—she wondered what word to use— "women."

"I take it, Niece, your brothers were *not* talking about respectable females." Aunt Beatrice pursed her lips and raised her brows.

Perdy crossed her arms over her midsection and gave Eleanor her most disapproving look. "Eavesdropping. Tsk, tsk. I thought we'd cured you of that bad habit, young lady."

"Oh, Perdy, sometimes it truly proves to be quite useful. What brother is going to discuss with his sister that he had heard rumors that there was a new"—Eleanor paused again—"place in Covent Garden that catered to men who liked girls?"

"Did you hear anything else useful?" Aunt Bea asked.

"Nothing, I'm sorry to say. Father came in and my brothers changed the subject. So, you see, based on what I heard about Covent Garden, we thought it would be a good place to look."

"And earlier today Ellie and I went there under the ruse of drawing pictures," Libby said.

Perdy shook her head. "Pictures? Now I've heard it all. You never liked drawing, or embroidery, or playing an instrument."

"Well, it was the best idea we could come up with. We brought outriders and everything, but we got interrupted," Eleanor said.

Libby laughed. "That's one way of putting it."

"What happened?" Aunt Beatrice asked.

"Lord West picked up Eleanor,"—Libby mimicked Giles lifting Eleanor off the ground—"and put her into the carriage and told our driver to take us home."

Aunt Beatrice chuckled. "Would've liked to have seen that."

"Hah. Well, I wasn't going to let him tell me where I could and couldn't go, so when we got home I wrote you that note. I only intended to take a quick look around. Finish my drawing."

"You're extremely lucky that your misadventure didn't end up with one of you killed. Your face will heal, Libby, and now we must figure out what to do with Millie here." Aunt Beatrice nodded at Millie.

"And them girls, missis. Wha' about them missin' girls?" Millie said.

Chapter Five

Eleanor sat down beside Perdy. "That's an excellent question, Millie."

"Well, Millie," Lady Beatrice said as she tugged her shawl around her shoulders tighter, "have *you* heard anything about pretty, healthy young girls who look like they don't belong?"

"My aunt means girls who don't look or sound like they're city-bred?" Eleanor sipped her tea.

"Yes, you know, especially girls—not women,"—Libby coughed— "in houses that men like to visit."

Millie's brows furrowed in confusion, then shot up her forehead. "Oh, yer talkin' 'bout a brothel, ain't ye?"

"Yes, that's right," Eleanor said.

"Which one does ye want to know about?" Millie said.

"Which one?" Libby squeaked. "How many are there?"

"Two that I dun heard of," Millie said. "I mean ones like ye be talkin' 'bout with young girls. There be one in London. And anuder in Baff."

"Bath?" Perdy stirred her tea.

"Do you know the whereabouts of the one in London?" Eleanor asked.

"I could show ye. It ain't far from where you found me tonight Millie said as she bobbed her head. "I ne'er been to *Bath*, meself."

Millie was trying to ape Perdy's pronunciation of Bath, but she lingered too long on the 'th', which gave the word a sibilant sound. That was a good sign—Millie was trainable.

Perdy wagged her finger at Eleanor. "Now you listen here, you're *not* going near ta any brothel. It's time to take this information to your father. He's a magistrate, after all."

Aunt Beatrice snorted. "Really, Perdy, when we were girls you had so much spunk, now look at you. Sometimes you're positively antiquated in your thinking."

Perdy's eyes went wide at Aunt Beatrice's rebuke and small flags of color appeared high on her cheeks. "Is that so, Miss Bee-in-her-bonnet? With an aunt like yourself, no wonder Miss Ellie has so many strange ideas running around in that head of hers."

Eleanor choked on her tea.

Now Aunt Beatrice had flags of color on her cheeks and her lips were pursed.

Libby slapped her hand down on the table. "Stop it, you two."

Aunt Beatrice and Perdy fell silent.

"These girls' lives are more important than our personal differences. We must put principles first. We may be the only ones who can save them." Libby made eye contact with each woman and held it until she nodded in agreement.

Millie touched Libby's arm. "I agrees with ye, miss."

"Call me Libby."

"All right." Millie smiled.

Aunt Beatrice cleared her throat. "Perdy, I'm sorry for my unkind words."

"As am I, Beatrice," Perdy said.

"I still don't believe going to my brother at this juncture will do any good," Beatrice said.

"Why ever not?" Perdy said. "He's the law. Something must be done."

Beatrice ran her finger around the rim of her mug. "True, but he'll want proof and right now Libby and Ellie's map isn't enough. The salient point at this juncture is that you two are on to something."

Millie leaned close to Libby and whispered. "The what?"

"She means the important thing," Libby said.

"Ahhh." Millie nodded.

"As you said, no one's put all these pieces together before," Beatrice said. "In some respects, it all sounds preposterous, and at the same time quite clever,"

"So, you think these a-a-a …" Eleanor hesitated.

Perdy gave Eleanor one of her do-not-say-that-word-again glances.

"Places Millie's talking about are the ones we are looking for," Eleanor said.

"Perhaps, but I've an idea who we can consult for confirmation," Beatrice said.

"Who?" Libby said.

"Rooksby. He'll be able to confirm the existence of these… places and whether these missing children are being housed there."

"Do you think having this Rooksby fellow's word will be enough for yer brother, Beatrice?" Perdy said.

"We'll just have to wait and see. At least it will be safer than these two wandering around Covent Garden after dark."

"I thought he was a myth," Eleanor said.

Aunt Beatrice wrapped her hands around her mug. "Rooksby's no myth, dear," she said, smiling slyly, "although he does like to think of himself as legendary."

Eleanor leaned across the table and spoke in a conspiratorial voice to Millie and Libby. "They say he knows everything. That he sits at the right hand of the king. My father says he crouches like a wily spider at the center of a vast web that reaches every corner of the empire."

Libby and Millie shuddered.

"He's an old friend of your Uncle Jasper's, Ellie," Aunt Beatrice said.

"Why would the fate of several dozen tradesmen and farmers' daughters interest someone like him?" Libby asked.

Aunt Beatrice rested the heel of her hand on the tabletop and ran her fingertip round and round in a small circle. "We shan't know until I ask."

"Is there anything else you know about these girls, Millie?" Libby asked.

Millie tipped her head and pursed her lips. "They talks funny."

"Funny?" Eleanor said.

"Why, ye canna understand a thing they be sayin'," Millie said. "Me friend, who delivers washin' to that a…"—Millie cleared her throat— "that house was puttin' her clean linens away. One of te girls rushed up to her and grabbed her hand and started jabberin'. There were tears in her eyes. Me friend tried ta understand wha' the poor lamb was sayin'. One of the house tuffs came and hauled her away."

○♂

As soon as Giles and Rodrigo turned onto Frarringdon Street their noses were beset by the pleasant aroma of roasting coffee beans floating above some of London's less pleasant odors—unwashed bodies and moldering refuse.

Giles swung his cane in time to a snippet of dance music that kept
playing in his head from the night before.

A woman walked past. She was about Eleanor's height with chestnut-colored hair. Aside from those two things, she looked nothing like the woman he couldn't keep out of his thoughts. He wished she'd come to the Cunninghams'. He would've liked to inveigle a dance or two out of her.

He laughed at himself and shook his head. "No, that shan't happen anytime soon." Off in the distance he heard the chant of a costermonger selling oranges.

The entrance to Travelers Coffee House lay at hand. The front multi-paned windows revealed the low-beamed emporium chock-full of barristers, ships' captains, merchants, peers, and clerks, all rubbing elbows as they drank the stimulating black brew. An invisible sign hung above the door—*no* females allowed. *What a restful thought.*

Travelers' double doors were propped wide with large lumpy canvas sacks tied off with thick hemp rope expertly woven into sailor knots.

As Giles stood in the entranceway, waiting for his eyes to adjust to the room's dim interior, he heard snatches of conversations mixed with the rustle of news sheets and the *thunks* of many thick-sided coffee mugs being unceremoniously deposited onto scarred wooden tabletops.

"Over here, Giles," Edgerton called. He was standing beside a small table situated beside the farthest window.

As Giles drew closer he noticed the large silver buttons marching down the front of Edgerton's waistcoat and his stick pin that sported a sizeable sapphire lying among the folds of his jabot.

They clasped hands and then dropped into their seats. A scrawny young lad popped up at Edgerton's shoulder. "Oscar, some coffee for me friend here."

"Yes, m'lord. Right away." The boy barely finished his words before he sprinted away.

"Come here often, do you?" Giles pointed to the floor, Rodrigo's cue to lie down, then rested his cane against the windowsill.

The corners of Edgerton's lips curled upward. "Oh, you mean because I know the boy's name? You'll see. It pays to know their names if you want to get anything to drink—at least during this decade."

In the next moment, a steaming mug of coffee landed on the table in front of Giles. "Well now." Startled by the quick service, Giles nodded in appreciation.

Edgerton reached into his waistcoat pocket and extracted a coin and tossed it so it arced high, and Oscar, caught it one-handed.

While at school, Edgerton had never been one to bestow largesse or acknowledge a job well done. There seemed much to admire in this mature Francis Edgerton.

"Thank you kindly, m'lord." The boy had a gap-toothed grin, which he displayed broadly just before he tucked his tray under his arm, pivoted and disappeared into the boisterous throng.

"How long has it been?" Edgerton scrutinized Giles.

The intensity of his gaze made Giles feel a bit like a bug under a glass. He shifted in his seat. "A while."

"Indeed," Edgerton said. "You and Harleigh took off—what was it—nearly three years ago?"

"At least." Giles took a tentative sip. It was still too hot to take a good-sized swallow. He put his mug down, waiting for it to cool. He noted the acidic emphasis Edgerton placed on Harleigh's name. As boys, those two barely tolerated each other; he'd hoped time would smooth things over between the cousins. Apparently, it hadn't. Ah, well … some things change and others don't.

"Harleigh's been back well over a year now, I believe," Edgerton said.

Giles shrugged. "There was too much left to see, and Harleigh was needed back here."

"And you weren't?" Edgerton gave him a shrewd glance.

"Yes, but for me—well, it just wasn't time to come home."

Edgerton leaned forward. "Wanderlust?"

"Have you ever had that feeling that something was calling you?"

"Such as?" Edgerton said.

"As if you had pre-cognition that something was going to happen and *that* knowledge urged you onward."

"Sounds all very mysterious."

"If you mean insubstantial and illogical, it does, does it not?" Giles chuckled. "For certs, my father wanted me home. But I moved around and managed to avoid his letters for quite some time. Tell you, it made me feel damn selfish, but I just couldn't turn back." Giles took another tentative sip of his coffee. It left a pleasantly bitter aftertaste.

"Besides, I knew things were in good hands with my younger brothers, should something happen to our father, God forbid, and I also knew this was my last chance to fly free. So, I ran as fast and as far as I could, knowing once I returned..." Giles let his voice fade into silence.

"You sound like that poor sod, Odysseus." Edgerton sipped his coffee.

"Hah, he angered the gods and had no choice about his extended travels—whereas I was the captain of my own fate. Besides, my man did not turn into a pig."

"Your man Mumby turning into a pig, now that would be something I would pay to see." Edgerton tipped his chair so it rested on its back legs only.

"He has been my valet since I was a boy. Rather think he sees it the
other way around—turning the piglet into a well-groomed man."

Edgerton laughed and sunlight struck the sapphire resting inches below his chin, shooting sparks and reflecting light that bounced into Giles' eyes. The glare blinded him for a moment and summoned a memory of a boat floating on the sparkling Venetian lagoon with the curvaceous Katarina lying in his arms. Giles would swear he felt the shape of her lush breasts pressing into his chest and the musky scent of her skin.

"Helloo-o. Giles. Where are you?"

"Mmmm? What?"

Edgerton leaned forward. "I said *what* was her name?"

Giles looked into Edgerton's eyes, noticing an irritating spark of humor there. "You did not."

"Well?" Edgerton gestured, rolling his hand through the air for Giles to get on with his confession. "Her name was …"

"Katarina. The young widow of a wealthy Venetian merchant. Intelligent, beautiful … lusty." He could see her lying naked, tangled in his sheets.

"And?" Edgerton said.

"And when she was done with me, she told me to go home."

Edgerton cringed "So, that's what kept you in Italy?"

Giles said nothing.

Edgerton laid his open palm over his heart. "A bruised heart is a young man's tragedy. Thank the Lord the affliction is not deadly."

"It's too damn early for all this philosophizing," Giles said and then sipped more coffee. "First, it's my wanderings, now my failed amours."

"We all have failures to live down," Edgerton said. "They're supposed to be character-building,"

"If you're referring to the two of us getting basted regularly by our school bullies …" Edgerton lost his smile so Giles let his comment lay unfinished. He'd often thought Edgerton had provoked those fights to vent his anger on God for turning his life upside down.

After his father's head injury caused Lord Edgerton to forget he even had a son, and Lady Edgerton's sexual exploits had made her a social pariah, their only child had been left to make his way in a very inhospitable world. Damn gossips.

Most people, including Harleigh, only saw or reacted to the wall of bravado Edgerton threw up to keep everyone at arm's length.

Edgerton caught Giles staring at him. "What?"

Giles waved his hand through the air. "This place, the way we're dressed... Damn me, but it is a blaring reminder that I've come home and my wandering days are over." *And where the sex in my marriage bed will be polite, and the future Countess of Margrave's skin will be milk-white, not golden.* "Anyway, when my father's letters finally caught up to me, we struck a compromise."

"I'm all ears," Edgerton said.

Giles shrugged. "The usual."

"Such as?" Edgerton said.

Giles' eyes narrowed. The louse wanted to hear him say the words. He lowered his voice. "I needed to wend my way homeward and when I came back to London I would find myself ..."

"Leg-shackled, tied up like a Christmas goose," Edgerton offered.

Giles bit out each word. "A wife."

"So I've heard." Edgerton sipped more coffee.

Giles frowned.

Edgerton chuckled. "Don't tell me you haven't found at least one who meets your requirements in all the ballrooms you've waltzed through in the last few weeks?"

"Odd you should put it that way," Giles said.

"What way?"

"Harleigh said almost the exact thing to me last night," Giles said.

"Really? How bizarre. Harleigh and I haven't agreed on anything in years."

Silence.

"Speaking of my cousins, have you seen Harleigh's baby sister since your return?"

"Eleanor?" Giles said.

Edgerton nodded. "Christ, remember what a fat, freckled, thoroughly annoying little thing she was?"

As Edgerton spoke, an image of Eleanor came into Giles' mind. But it wasn't a fat little girl he was holding, it was a curvaceous beauty and she was wielding a large hat pin. She was *still* annoying … and obdurate, provoking, dangerous, disquieting, and a whole list of things Giles didn't want to think about.

"Well? Thinking about your Katarina again?"

"No to your last question, and yes to the other two," Giles said.

Edgerton waited.

Giles wanted to steer the conversation quickly into less personally provoking waters. "How's your father doing?"

Like a sudden squall, bleakness settled over Edgerton's features. He became remote and seemed to have wandered off mentally. He twisted his signet ring back and forth, back and forth.

Giles inwardly winced. He'd made a mistake bringing up Edgerton's father as an alternative topic. He wasn't bothered by Edgerton's silence, he was only sorry he'd caused his friend pain.

Edgerton startled out of his daze. "Hmmm, drifted away."

"Nattering on to fill a silence is a waste of breath," Giles said.

Edgerton raised a brow. "You're more a man of action, as I recall."

Those schoolboy fights had been the furnace that had forged their friendship. The two of them against the world, their victories and bloody defeats legion. Why was Edgerton bringing up their juvenile pugilistic history? Did he have a problem now that needed brawn instead of brains to resolve?

Giles expelled a deep breath and rolled his shoulders.

"Tell me more about this compromise you struck with your father?"

"Simple, really. Agreed to keep my ramblings to Britain if he could spare me for a bit longer," Giles said.

Edgerton frowned. "I thought you just got back?"

"To London, yes. Just a few weeks. But months ago, I caught a ship in Rome. Landed in Cardigan a month later, then headed up to the Scottish border. Damnation, sometimes it was hard to believe I'd come home at all."

"Why's that?"

"The difference in the sound of the English language, man. Have you ever traveled north?"

Edgerton was about to take another sip but quickly put his cup down.

"Some time back, why?"

"Wonder I managed to secure a meal, a place to sleep, or a pint, for that matter," Giles said.

"Couldn't have been that bad." Edgerton looked away, searching the crowd.

Something had upset him, but what? Edgerton wouldn't meet Giles' eyes. "Something wrong?"

When Edgerton's gaze finally returned to Giles, the ease between them was gone. "No. What makes you ask?"

Giles persevered, confident he could put the conversation back on comfortable ground. "Oh, it got easier as time went on, otherwise I might have starved—or died of thirst."

Edgerton didn't respond to Giles' jest; instead, he looked over the edge of the table at Rodrigo.

"Where did you pick up your four-legged shadow?" Edgerton asked.

Puzzled by Edgerton's mercurial mood, Giles decided it was easier to travel with the current than against it. "Rodrigo? My boon companion."

Rodrigo raised his head at the mention of his name and gazed adoringly at his master.

"I spent a few weeks laboring for a sheep farmer just across the Scottish border. I slept in his barn."

"You *were* roughing it. A laborer. Let me see your hands."

With mock umbrage, Giles slapped Edgerton's hands away. "Nothing wrong with getting one's hands dirty. Curling up nightly on the fresh hay with a blanket was...well, it was an uncomplicated pleasure. The farmer's collie had dropped her pups a few weeks before I arrived, and when I went to leave, one of the fellows followed me. I brought him back to his mother, but every time I walked away, he followed. The old farmer said he guessed the 'wee laddie' had chosen his master. I gave back my wages and accepted Rodrigo as my pay."

Rodrigo lounged on the floor with his front paws and head draped over the toe of one of Giles' shoes. Halfway through their second mug of coffee, Giles felt Rodrigo lift his head and emit a low-pitched growl.

Giles leaned down and scratched him behind his ear. "What's the matter, boy?"

Rodrigo pushed up on his front paws and drew his ears back. Giles followed the direction of his dog's gaze. He didn't recognize the men who'd caught Rodrigo's attention. One of them gave a slight nod in their direction to his companion and when he caught Giles staring at him he turned away.

"Do you know those fellows? By the door?"

Edgerton gazed in the indicated direction, his mouth turned down. "No. Is that what raised Rodrigo's hackles?"

Was this the reason Edgerton had mentioned their former fights? If so, he and Rodrigo would make sure Edgerton arrived safely at his carriage.

Edgerton, Giles, and Rodrigo exited Travelers. For Giles, standing a head taller than most men was an asset at times like this. He scanned the street. The suspicious men had left Travelers before them and were now nowhere in sight.

Edgerton placed his hat on his head and then leaned down and gave Rodrigo a scratch behind his ear. "My carriage is around the corner. May I drop you two somewhere?"

"We would be delighted." Giles walked beside Edgerton, and Rodrigo trotted along on Giles' left.

The crowd swelled as they drew closer to the corner. Suddenly a wagon raced out of the alley to their left. They were forced to wait for the obstacle to pass. The lead horse reared up and the wagon stalled. The driver stood up, struggling to maintain control of his beasts.

Stomping hooves.

Women shrieking in fright mixed with high-pitched whinnies.

Men's voices barking orders.

Giles felt hands upon his back. Someone roughly shoving.

Edgerton fell against him.

Giles reached out to keep his friend from falling.

Two street urchins threw a sack over Rodrigo's head and pulled him inside the alley.

Another hard push and they were all swallowed by the alley.

That wagon with the balking horses now blocked the exit.

A trap.

The sun had passed its zenith, painting the alley with short dark jagged shadows. A band of muted light bisected the battleground. Two of the three men from Travelers were on Edgerton, an almost toothless jackal holding him from behind and pinning his arms.

Giles' opponent was a bit shorter than himself with a barrel chest and long arms. Giles swung his head out of the way of an oncoming beefy fist. His hat fell to the ground.

Barrel-Chest growled in frustration, revealing a mouth full of broken teeth.

Giles swung his cane up, holding it with both hands parallel to the ground.

Barrel-Chest lunged forward.

Giles pulled the cane back beside his right hip, the metal-crowned end facing Barrel-Chest.

Barrel-Chest raised his arms to grab Giles.

With one quick, forceful thrust Giles drove his cane into his opponent's belly.

Still on his feet, barrel-Chest curled in half and bellowed.

Giles raised his cane parallel to his own chest, placing one hand near each end. He thrust his left arm forward, smashing one end into his adversary's upper left arm.

Another roar of pain from his barrel-chested foe.

Then Giles levered his right arm forward, driving the crowned end into his opponent's right shoulder. He heard the bone break.

Giles spun about. When his back was to Barrel-Chest, he swung his right leg up and brought the heel of his foot into the side of the man's head, knocking him to his knees.

"Ye bloody nob. Where'd ye larn to fight like that?"

"*Marseilles*," Giles said.

Barrel-Chest was on his knees, clutching his upper right arm. Spittle flew from his protuberant lips. "Wha?

"Get up, my friend. I hate to hit a man when he's down."

Barrel-Chest staggered upright. "Ye ain't no friend a mine."

Giles' punch snapped the man's head back.

Barrel-Chest teetered.

Giles swung his right leg up and around, smashing the top of his foot into Barrel-Chest's back, right over his liver. Down he went like a sack full of rocks. This time Barrel-Chest didn't get up.

Rodrigo lay on his belly. A rope around his neck held the rough sack in place. Rodrigo pawed at the bag. The boys were gone.

Giles heard Edgerton's grunt.

The man closest to Giles had red hair. He landed a solid punch into Edgerton's midsection.

Edgerton let out a loud 'oof' and collapsed forward, gasping.

The toothless oaf standing at Edgerton's back yanked him upright, exposing Edgerton's gut to another savage blow.

"Damn them fancy buttons of yers." The redheaded man licked his knuckles.

"We can strips him clean once we're done. Bets we gets a pretty penny for that coat of his and them fancy buttons," Toothless cackled.

Blood trickled down Edgerton's chin and his head lolled to the side.

Giles swung his cane, metal head down, like a cricket bat into Red's ankle.

"Son of a bitch!" Red dropped down on one knee and grabbed his ankle.

Giles planted his left foot. Leaning away, he raised his right leg, bending his right knee back. Cocking it like a loaded gun. He snapped his lower leg forward, driving the top of his foot into the side of Red's head.

Red grabbed his head and fell over.

Edgerton stomped Toothless' instep, then pulled free. He wobbled but stayed upright.

Lying on his belly, Red swiped the sweat from his eyes. He gazed at his barrel-chested comrade. "Ya fancy-pantsed bastard. How d'ye manage to level him?" Red grabbed for Giles.

Giles side-stepped. "I've my ways."

"Well, bully for yous. And I gots mine." Rage propelled Red to his feet. He hunkered down and circled Giles, opening and closing his beefy fists.

"Why not take your friends and leave? If you come closer I'll be forced to give you the same lesson as your friend."

Red spat on the ground. "I ain't goin' nowhere till I finish what I came for." He swung.

Giles danced backward.

His adversary aimed his next punch where Giles' head used to be. "Stand still so I can teach ye to fight like a Englishman."

"Hah! Will you indeed?" Giles said.

With a roar, Red charged Giles.

Giles side-stepped him again.

Red moved past.

Giles pistoned his heel into the back of Red's knee.

Red fell to the ground.

The angle of Red's limb revealed the last blow had broken his leg. Giles felt no remorse.

Toothless saw Red hit the ground. He quit trading blows with Edgerton and ran away.

"Are you all right?" Giles said to Edgerton, breathing heavily.

Winded, Edgerton just nodded.

Giles ran to his dog. "Rodrigo." Giles dropped to one knee near the dog's head. Rodrigo stilled. "Let me—" He held his hand before Rodrigo's covered muzzle. The dog calmed and Giles undid the coarse rope that was binding the sack and pulled it off. Then he ran his hands down the dog's sides and legs.

Rodrigo stood up and started laving Giles' face with his large wet tongue.

"Is he all right?" Edgerton leaned against the wall. His breathing was labored, his right arm wrapping his midsection. He winced.

Giles chuckled. "That'll do, boy." Giles rose and ran his hand over Rodrigo's head. "What about you? Do you need a physician?"

"I'm fine." Edgerton wiped the blood from his mouth with an unsteady hand.

"Well then, let's go find a constable and your coach."

Rodrigo lay on the floor of Edgerton's coach while Giles and Edgerton dealt with the constable. Finally, they climbed in and the coach got underway.

"All right, who the hell were they?" Giles said.

Edgerton's lip had swollen. "How should I know?"

Giles shook his head.

"Oh, you think me their target, do you?" Edgerton pointed to himself.

"Considering you had most of the coverage."

Edgerton adopted a posture of extreme ennui.

Giles crossed his arms over his chest. "Come on, who've you been sleeping with?"

"You think a jealous husband?" Edgerton laughed. "I don't consort with married women, or widows for that matter. I always pay for what I want. And I only buy the best."

"Edgerton?"

"Let me see your cane."

Giles handed it over.

"Christ. Damn thing must weigh half a stone." He tossed the metal-crowned cane back at Giles.

"Not that much. But it's made of good English oak."

"And the headpiece?"

Giles ran his hand over the ornate top. "Brass."

"Where the hell did you learn to fight like that? Not very gentlemanly of you."

Giles flicked a piece of lint from his cuff. "Well, we weren't fighting gentlemen, were we?"

Chapter Six

Eleanor detested the Season and its social swirl. Dressing up and deporting oneself like a sugary, insipid confection in a baker's window was inane and demeaning and she wouldn't miss it one iota.

It was two weeks since their evening adventure in Covent Garden, and Libby was looking very pretty. Not a scrape or a bruise in sight. This was their first night back in a ballroom. Next week, bag and baggage, Eleanor's father was bundling their entire family out of London for the summer, two weeks ahead of schedule.

She and Libby stood on the edge of the dance floor in the Aldridges' crowded, airless ballroom. Her corset restricted her breathing and her lovely Persian rose-colored satin dancing slippers had turned into the bane of her existence.

"I wonder what made your father decide to leave London early?" Libby toyed with a bow edging her sleeve.

Eleanor gave her a baleful glance.

"What?"

"I've a fair notion of what has prompted my father's decision," Eleanor said.

"Well, give over."

Eleanor leaned in and whispered, "A certain interfering nosey-nora by the name of Lord Giles West."

Libby pulled her head back. "You know so? Or ... is that just a guess on your part?"

"In one respect, he's done us a great favor. Once back in the country, we'll resume our daily Sisterhood training schedule. Though there's one unfortunate aspect to our early departure."

"Only one?" Libby teased.

"Aunt Beatrice has heard nothing from the elusive Rooksby," Eleanor said, then pursed her lips.

"I've faith in your aunt. She'll come through for us."

"So do I. So do I." When Eleanor turned her attention from her friend back to the room at large, she spied her eldest brother standing on the opposite side of the room chatting with a group of men. As irritated as she was with Harleigh right now, she admitted to herself he looked dashing in his formal attire.

"Your brother looks quite handsome tonight," Libby said.

Eleanor intentionally looked away from Harleigh. "If you say so."

Libby nudged her in the ribs. "No, not over there. Over by the French doors."

"Quit that."

"What has your brother done now?" Libby said.

"He supported Father's decision to leave early, is what," Eleanor said.

"By the way, you look lovely tonight, although that décolletage is … is a-a…"

Eleanor gazed down at herself. "I swear this corset has me so elevated it feels as though my chin is resting in my cleavage."

"Oh Ellie, you really can be quite inappropriate." Libby bit down on her lip to stifle her laughter.

"I prefer the word candid."

"Of course you do," Libby said, watching longingly as the dancers swirled by. "And I *don't* believe you are as indifferent with Giles West as you want me to believe."

"Pish. That sort of supposition is beneath you, Lib. *His* affairs are no concern of mine," Eleanor said.

"From what I hear Lord West is racing neck or nothing into the parson's mousetrap, which means he's bound to be engaged very soon."

"Which is good news for us. Because with a wife, he'll stay at home and make heirs and mind his family properties and stay out of our way."

"The lady doth protest too much, methinks." Libby's eyes followed the dancers.

One look at her friend's sad face and Eleanor's caustic reply died a sudden death. She gave Libby's arm a squeeze. "It isn't at all pleasant, you know? Most of the men step on your feet."

"They don't," Libby said. "You're bamming me."

"And the old lecherous ones"—Eleanor shuddered—"slide their big hammy paws down your hip and try and pinch your bottom."

"Stop. Stop. Stop." Libby turned away, her shoulders shaking, and spurts of soft laughter erupted from her.

"It's quite true." Eleanor raised her gloved hand as if she were taking a pledge. "I swear.

Oh, and the ones who pull you close with their bellies and body odor..." Eleanor said as she made a face.

More soft giggles from Libby.

Eleanor moved in front of Libby, blocking anyone's view of her while she pulled herself together. One was meant to be seen at one's best, and tearful and pink-nosed from laughter would hardly be considered de *rigueur*. Her nose must have started to run, because Eleanor heard sniffling, so she put her hand behind her back, slipping Libby her handkerchief.

A moment later, Libby appeared beside Eleanor. Her nose was pink and she dabbed her damp cheeks. "I'll return this once it's laundered," she
said, tucking the hankie away. "Eleanor. Eleanor," Libby said as she tugged Eleanor's arm. "Look over there." Libby used her closed fan to point.

Eleanor shoved Libby's fan down. "Quit that. It's undignified."

"Hah. The pot is calling the kettle black?"

"Just tell me where you want me to look," Eleanor said.

ᘓ

Giles stood beneath the arch leading into the ballroom, tugging on his cravat. *Damn, Mumby, you tied this thing deuced tight. I can barely swallow.* Harleigh had told him this was the Barretts' last ball before returning home. Giles had come in hopes of prying a dance out of Eleanor, although he was sure it would be under great protest if he managed it.

The crowd shifted and he spotted Harleigh leaning against a column between the open French doors. He moved quickly to his friend's side.

"Giles, I was afraid we'd miss each other," Harleigh said. "Father's in a flap to get us out of town."

"You mean to get *Eleanor* out of town?" Giles said.

"As a matter of fact. How did you know?" Harleigh's gaze was puzzled.

Giles shrugged.

"Ever since Edgerton informed him she was strolling around Covent Garden. 'Damn it, cannot control me own daughter.' Hah, I love me father but he's delusional if he believes he's ever had control over Ellie's behavior."

Since childhood, Giles had observed how Eleanor managed *all* the men in her family, including her eldest brother. "They were seated, behind easels actually—not strolling," Giles said. "Sketching the place. Drawing quite a crowd, too. No pun intended."

Harleigh's lips twitched. "You saw her?"

"It was me who sent her on her way. Acting in your stead, of course."

"Thank you for that," Harleigh said.

"Hah. Eleanor didn't like it one bit."

"Forget that. You did the right thing. Besides, she never likes anyone telling her what to do, you know that."

"Recognized the coach, thought it was you or your father," Giles said. "I didn't realize who I was arguing with—not until Elizabeth Archer—"

"Ellie dragged Libby down there? Of all the addlepated notions."

Giles scratched his head. "Did not see Edgerton, though. Bet she thinks I let her cat out of the bag."

"No doubt," Harleigh said. "Figures you told me, and I tattled to Father. Well, that certainly explains her coldness of late."

"Forget about it. Our sisters get irked, then they need something and"—Giles snapped his fingers— "phfft, all's forgiven."

"Well, that's rather a bleak assessment of filial devotion, if I ever heard one."

"*Au contraire.* Accurate is what it is. By the way, you said nothing to me about her being back."

"Who?" Harleigh said.

"Your aunt ... No—Eleanor, you great clod," Giles said as he shook his head. Sometimes Harleigh could be as thick as a bowl of cold porridge.

"Does it make a difference?"

"Or that she had..." Giles scrambled to find the polite word to define Eleanor's physical metamorphosis.

Harleigh's stare intensified. "What?"

"Well, what happened to that chubby little girl?"

"She grew up."

Giles coughed to cover his laugh. Eleanor's metamorphosis gave new meaning to the words 'grow up.'

"What?" Harleigh said again.

Giles turned his head away, feigning interest in the other women in the room. "Nothing." To distract Harleigh, Giles tipped his head at the knot of gentlemen standing across from them, at the edge of the dance floor. "What's going on over there?"

"Eleanor and her beaux."

As Giles scrutinized the goings on, he felt a spurt of jealousy. "Do tell."

"Now what's come over you?"

To avoid Harleigh's scrutinizing, Giles tipped his head down and tugged his waistcoat.

He surreptitiously scanned the clutch of animated males.

The room was full of eligible young women. The irony that he didn't care to dance with anyone, save Eleanor, burst whatever was left of his small bubble of affability.

"Now why are you scowling?" Harleigh asked.

"Was I?" *I don't care who she dances with. Liar-liar.* Giles didn't think she would willingly dance with him anyway—not even if it caused him to lose a wager. Hmmm? That gave him a mad idea, one truly fit for the bedeviling Eleanor Barrett.

The question was how to phrase it? He couldn't imagine her passing up a plum of an opportunity to do him a disservice—not after their altercation in Covent Garden.

A moment later, the clutch of gentlemen surrounding Eleanor shifted and Giles got his first good look at her. His jaw dropped. She wore a spectacular dress, which displayed the swells of her plump breasts. Something sparkled just above her cleavage, probably a necklace of some sort, clearly marking the path to heaven. By the angle of their heads, he could tell the men dancing attendance upon her seemed to be talking to her chest.

Those clodpoles probably didn't give a damn that that magnificent body of hers housed an adroit mind that could lay them low with one swipe of her sharp tongue.

A stabbing pain shot up his jaw and Giles realized he was clenching his teeth.

"But she won't seriously encourage any of them—not a one."

"What?" Giles said.

"Mother frets she'll never get Ellie married off. I know for a fact Eleanor would be supremely happy if Mother would let her go live with Aunt Beatrice—you know, our father's sister."

"I've met Lady Whitley. She's … erm … she is a-a …"

Harleigh waved his hand about. "Never mind. I know exactly what my aunt, the very merry widow, is like. Mother's afraid Aunt Beatrice's influence will keep Ellie from marrying."

"That can't be too likely. Look at all those idiots swarming around her."

"Have you paid any attention to what I've been saying?"

"Come along." Giles grabbed Harleigh's elbow and towed him toward Eleanor. Just before they reached her, Giles shoved Harleigh in front of him.

"Sister." Harleigh was a little too loud, a little too bright.

As the last male moved aside, Giles beheld Francis Edgerton standing beside Eleanor.

"Brother." Eleanor arched one brow, lowered her chin and gave him a shrewd look.

Giles stepped out from behind Harleigh.

Edgerton smiled. "You're too late. I've claimed her for the next set."

A soft gasp escaped Libby's lips.

Giles looked from Eleanor to Libby. Eleanor had gone pale and stiff, and Giles felt as though they were all suddenly standing on a sheet of thin ice.

Eleanor allowed herself to be guided onto the dance floor. The music began. The other men departed, seeking dance partners. Giles stood with Elizabeth Archer and Harleigh as they watched the dancers move about the floor.

With each dance of the set, Eleanor moved with less grace and her posture grew
increasingly rigid, and she never smiled.

Libby kept wringing her hands and nibbling on her lower lip. "Lord Barrett, do something."

"There's nothing to be done, Miss Archer, that won't cause talk. This is the last dance
of the set."

"Very well. If that's the best you can do." Libby frowned. As the dance drew to a close, she put her hand on Harleigh's back and shoved him onto the dance floor. "Go get her."

Chapter Seven

Giles watched Edgerton bow to Eleanor. She left him without the semblance of a curtsy. Eleanor's face was a lifeless mask as she walked briskly toward the exit, weaving around the other dancers who were completing their end-of-dance courtesies. Libby Archer dogged Harleigh's heels.

Edgerton appeared at his side. "Well, that was interesting," Edgerton said. "For all Eleanor's improved looks, she's a rather graceless dancer. And *no* conversation at all. Although that might've been a blessing, considering some of her espoused views."

Giles gazed at Edgerton. "What?"

Edgerton looked smug. "My first foray wooing the lovely Eleanor."

"You didn't mention you were in search of a wife."

"Our conversation at Travelers got me thinking. She's just the kind of woman a man can count on to run his home and estate while he's off doing other things. The trick will be teaching her to keep her views to herself. Don't you agree?"

"I suppose." Giles' mind scrambled for purchase. His eyes moved from the doorway through which Eleanor and the rest had departed, back to Edgerton's face. "You sound like you are equating having a wife to training your dog."

Edgerton chuckled. "Precisely so."

"You do know she isn't interested in acquiring a husband?"

"Quite. I've heard her utter that nonsense meself, but that was ages ago. Before she developed those delectable curves, but I must say her taste in friends is rather appalling. Keeping company with that cripple."

"Why are you being an ass about Miss Archer's limp?"

"Didn't know you considered chits who couldn't walk properly desirable prospects."

"Remind me, Francis, exactly why we're friends?" Giles wasn't joking.

Harleigh returned before Edgerton replied.

"Where did you leave them?" Edgerton asked.

Harleigh took up a position beside Giles. "The retiring room."

"They'll be in there forever." Edgerton made a quick survey of the room. "Well, nothing else here interests me. Good night, Cousin. Giles."

ଓ

"Holy hell. Why me?" Eleanor muttered as she burst into the retiring room and flew to the window, threw back the curtains and opened the window wide. She leaned against the window frame, crushing her gown and gulping in air. From behind her a matron's voice squawked about
the night breeze being bad for one's health. Eleanor paid no heed and the matron stomped out.

Libby gently touched her shoulder. "Ellie, you're so pale. Would you like to lie down?"

Eleanor closed her eyes and leaned her head against the cool glass of the windowpane. "I'll be fine. Just need a few minutes."

Libby sat on the settee nearby and waited.

Silence.

"Francis Edgerton always puts me in mind of a pretty snake," Libby said as she shivered. "If there is such a thing."

Eleanor laughed and the feeling like she was about to jump out of her skin eased. She went and sat down next to Libby.

"I always get the distinct impression he doesn't like me," Libby fiddled with the ribbon of her dance card. "Although I can't tell you why, we've scarce said twenty words to one another, *ever.*"

Eleanor removed her gloves and pressed her palms to her cheeks.

"Strange to have such a strong negative reaction to someone and not remember why," Libby said and her brow creased. "When I was little, Mama would give me this red syrupy thing when I had a cough. It smelled like ripe cherries but tasted …" Libby scrunched her face. "Blech, it was awful. It burned going down my throat. To this day, I can't eat cherries."

Eleanor stared down at her lap. "If something did happen, I wish I *could* remember what it was. Sometimes when Edgerton's near I get this whiff of a memory. I turn my mind to examine it and—poof—it moves out of reach."

"Oh, that's so aggravating," Libby said.

"When I was young I never went willingly into a room that he was in, and if it was obligatory, I stayed only long enough to be polite."

"What does Harleigh say?" Libby asked.

"When Harleigh came home from school and in some of his letters he would tell stories about Cousin Francis. All the fights and mean things he did or said to other students. Harleigh's not particularly fond of him either. He thinks I was influenced by his dislike of Cousin Francis."

"Harleigh is your favorite brother," Libby said, then shook her head. "No. You've *never* been one to let anyone's opinion sway you. And I should know. You always make up your own mind."

Eleanor grinned broadly.

"What's so funny?" Libby said.

"Oh, Lib, whatever would I do without you?"

"Well, lucky for you, you'll never have to find out."

"Master Sakegawa used to tell me an African fable about an ant that lived in a kingdom where men weren't permitted to grow beards. One day the ant crawled into the king's walled garden and saw he had a beard. The king had the ant hunted down, killed and his body chopped up and buried in many places so the he could never reveal the king's secret."

"What does that have to do with not remembering?" Libby asked.

"Master said the head of the ant was buried among the roots of a sapling. As the years went by, the sampling grew into a great tree. One day the villagers noticed words had been chewed into the bark of that tree."

"What did it say?"

"The king has a beard," Eleanor answered.

Libby laughed. "And the moral of this tale?"

"There's nothing in darkness that will not come to light."

"A most excellent story. Do you ever wonder where he is?" Libby said.

"Master Sakegawa?"

Libby nodded.

"All the time. I wish he were here now." Eleanor linked arms with Libby. "Are you ready to go back into the ballroom? Who knows, maybe something extremely pleasant will happen to displace the ugly memory of dancing with Francis Edgerton."

cs

Giles noticed Harleigh kept stealing glances toward the hallway leading to the retiring room. "Something wrong?"

Harleigh could not stand still. "Not sure."

The ballroom seemed dimmer when Eleanor wasn't in it. Less lively. Less interesting.

Two attractive young ladies of their acquaintance strolled by. "Good evening, Lord Barrett. Lord West."

Harleigh nodded but his attention returned to the entrance and so the young ladies moved on.

"That was rude, old man," Giles teased.

"What?" Harleigh had a bewildered look on his face.

When Elizabeth and Eleanor rejoined them, Eleanor wouldn't meet anyone's eye and she had all the effervescence of flat champagne. Unfortunately, they soon found themselves in a cluster of her male admirers, again.

Giles raised his voice above the chatter. "Harleigh and I have made a wager."

"And that would interest me, my lord, because…?" Eleanor said.

"Because it is about you." Giles presented his most charming smile.

"Really?" Eleanor scrutinized him through narrowed eyes.

Hah, I've made you angry. Good. Some of the color came back into her cheeks.

"I say, West, that isn't at all the thing, to be wagering on a gently bred
young lady," one of Eleanor's admirers said.

"Sir," Giles addressed the fellow, "it wasn't I who offered up this challenge, but her brother." Giles raised his hand, palm up, and gestured to Harleigh as he sacrificially offered him up for public censure.

Before Eleanor could utter the set-down he knew must be on the tip of her tongue, Giles added, "I told Harleigh that I'm the last man on earth you would dance with. Harleigh said, not so. He thinks you would willingly dance with me."

Eleanor's gaze moved to her brother, then back to Giles.

Harleigh shrugged. "Seemed like an easy win."

"How much will you lose if I dance with you?"

Harleigh spoke first this time. "Fifty pounds to a charity of my choice."

Giles made a choking noise. *Egad, hoist on my own petard.* He couldn't very well deny the amount, now could he?

Giles held out his hand.

Eleanor hesitated, then placed her hand in his.

He guided her from the crowd and onto the dance floor. The next set of country dances was about to begin and he turned to face her. "Lovely evening."

Other couples joined them on the floor.

Eleanor's lovely mouth was pressed into a flat line.

The music began and it was either move or be run over by the other dancers.

"You were actually quite correct, Lord West. I don't care to dance with you."

"But the opportunity to inflict harm on my purse was too great to pass up, is that it?"

"Something along those lines."

"Is this about Covent Garden? I behaved as a brother ought. You didn't belong there, Miss Barrett."

"You, sir, have no idea where I belong,"

An image of her naked in his bed ran through his head and he went hard as a poker.

"But more to the point, I'm not fond of tattle-tales." Eleanor passed in front of him in the pattern of the dance.

Thank the Lord his waistcoat was long. Giles smelled the light floral scent of her skin. It made him want to press his lips to the side of her neck. Giles began to worry she would bolt. He baited her. "Ahhh, so you believe it was I who informed your father?"

"Are you saying it was not?"

"Harleigh told me it was Edgerton."

Eleanor scoffed. "I don't believe you."

No one called him a liar and got away with it. "You are *the* most provoking female of my acquaintance." Now he was the one fighting to control his temper.

Eleanor's voice was full of mockery. "You *aren't* the first man to say so."

"I'm quite sure that's true," Giles said. "Now, my Lady Erroneous, I'm waiting for an apology."

"Then you shall wait until Judgment Day, my lord."

Giles leaned close, towering over her, and whispered, "I can prove my innocence. Now apologize."

Silence was her reply.

He shook his head. "Still don't like to admit when you are wrong, do you?"

"One who has a glass head should beware of stones," Eleanor's said with a satirical smile.

"Quoting Chaucer? Egad, you are well read. Point taken. It's true. I *am* known to favor my own opinions above all others. But I also pride myself on admitting when I'm wrong, unlike others I could mention, and present company is definitely *not* excepted."

"Hah!"

He smiled down at her rather lovely bosom, which was displayed for

his contemplation. Her pique was causing her breathing to accelerate, making her breasts rise and fall rapidly. Maybe he'd been wrong about her bodice. He was quite enjoying the view.

Suddenly, Eleanor's brows drew together as if she were puzzling something out. "I don't know why you wanted to dance with me. Pursuing me is-is illogical. I possess none of the qualities you esteem and require."

"How do you know what I value?"

"My mother has gone on *ad nauseum* about your requirements. I think she wanted me to take note in case I was interested in having you pursue *me*."

"I see," he said.

Eleanor theatrically placed the fingertips of one hand on her chest. "My mother refuses to accept I never intend to voluntarily place myself under any man's paw by committing marriage."

"So, tell me, Miss Barrett, what have you heard are my…"

"Requirements?"

"Well, I wouldn't put it that way," Giles said, and suddenly his cravat felt too tight again.

Eleanor ticked off the words by tapping her thumb against each subsequent finger. "Comely, pleasant, and conventional." Eleanor shuddered at that word. "I believe you've been quoted as saying that your family has a penchant for a long life and you would like to find someone you can tolerate for an extended period."

Egad, I did say something to that effect. Hearing it thrown back at me is most unsettling and I must admit, if only to myself, to sounding like an ass.

"Like every other man in this room you're interested in someone you can control and who won't interfere with your manly pursuits—parliamentary matters, womanizing, high-stakes wagering, and hunting."

The pattern of the dance parted them for several moments, and when they came back together he'd the overwhelming impression Eleanor wanted to bash him over the head. "Perhaps I asked you to dance because I'm being courteous to my best friend's *baby* sister." He saw her wince on the word baby.

She was warring with herself; he could see it in the way she held her jaw. Time passed and he didn't think she'd respond.

"I fail to understand why women don't rise up in revolt," Eleanor said. "Our lot in life is preposterous."

A small spurt of mirth burst from his lips.

Eleanor narrowed her eyes. "You find my statement amusing?"

"You caught me off-guard, is all. That's what made me laugh. I find you challenging. That's the word I would use and I do admire your sharp mind. You're not a bore like so many of your female contemporaries."

"My female contemporaries, as you call them, have poorly trained minds because the men whose children they are haven't deemed it important or necessary to offer the same opportunities to their daughters as they do their sons."

Giles was riveted to the spot.

"It's a poor farmer who blames his crop for failing to thrive when it was the farmer who deprived it of water and sunlight."

He found her argument compelling. What she was suggesting was … revolutionary. He wasn't sure the world was ready for women to be educated.

"And whether my contemporaries are aware of the situation or not, they're frighteningly vulnerable to the whims of the men who control their lives."

"What do you mean?" Giles said.

"Men can beat, rape, or murder their female dependents with impunity. No matter her class, a woman is enslaved by the laws that men write. The fact that you're seeking someone 'compliant' is repugnant and self-serving."

"A man not willing to serve himself by choosing his life's companion with some eye to his comfort is a fool."

"Better he chose the woman to be his partner, rather than his companion. He can purchase a dog to fill the latter role."

Giles blinked. By gad, he did sound like Edgerton—how humbling and humiliating.

Just minutes ago, he'd found Edgerton's similar comments about the wifely role offensive. He wasn't sure he liked this picture of himself.

Eleanor fell silent and her arms dropped to her sides. The intensity of her gaze riveted him to the spot.

The music faded.

Eleanor stepped back. There was a perceptiveness in her gaze. He felt quite naked.

"There was no wager," Eleanor said flatly. No hesitation or question.

He thought about denying her supposition, but he couldn't bring himself to lie to her a second time.

"Not well done, sir. Deliberate deception to achieve one's end," Eleanor said. "How handsomely you prove my point." She walked away.

What an extraordinary creature she'd become. Up until now he hadn't been able to reconcile his boyhood image of Harleigh's freckle-faced, worm-mangling, troublesome little sister with the woman who kept stealing into his dreams. Now he knew that brat had turned herself into a magnificent and formidable woman.

His mind ceased whirring like the insides of a clock, the teeth of one cogwheel engaged with another, dropping into place. It was a very satisfying feeling.

He was done with being confused where Eleanor Barrett was concerned. She might be a handful, but it was a handful he very much wanted to be his. And unbeknownst to her, she had just eclipsed the other contenders for the position of his wife, the future Countess of Margrave.

As she disappeared from view, one man's guffawing pulled him back into the ballroom. He gazed around, looking for the source of that obnoxious sound. Eleanor's words whispered through his mind as he scanned the other males present. She couldn't be speaking of his peers.

He'd seen his share of women sporting bruises and black eyes at some of the taverns he frequented—barmaids and such. But he'd never witnessed anyone striking a woman. He was confident he would have intervened had he been present when the blows were about to be struck, regardless of what class the female in question came from.

A male cleared his throat. Giles startled out of his reverie. Harleigh rocked back on his heels. "Well, that went well."

"Stuff it." Giles walked away.

Chapter Eight

Eleanor and her Aunt Beatrice sat in her aunt's carriage and waited for Rooksby to make his appearance. Six outriders stood guard. The sun had set hours ago. A chill had descended on London along with the fog and the night. One carriage lamp with its flame turned low was a poor substitute for the warmth of a roaring fire. Eleanor leaned over and snugged the carriage blanket around her aunt.

"Thank you, dear."

"He'd better be worth this. My bum is asleep and my toes are nubs of ice," Eleanor said.

Aunt Beatrice chuckled.

Eleanor re-settled herself just as the street-side carriage door popped open and a lithe figure dressed all in black vaulted in and seated himself on the opposite bench, his back to the horses.

Aunt Beatrice addressed the shadowed form. "Good evening, Rooksby."

The long-legged figure tossed his hat onto the seat beside him. "My lady." He took Aunt Beatrice's proffered gloved hand and brushed a kiss across her knuckles.

"Rooksby, allow me to introduce my niece, Miss Eleanor Barrett."

"A pleasure to finally be formally introduced, Miss Barrett. I've been curious to meet the woman with the mind who figured out this delicious puzzle. You possess some..."—he paused— "interesting skills and a piquant sense of justice."

"Indeed." Eleanor held out her gloved hand. She smelled leather and whiskey. "A pleasure to meet the renowned and redoubtable Rooksby."

A sly grin curved his wide mouth as he raised her hand to his lips. "How may I be of service, ladies?"

Chapter Nine

Harleigh and his family had left London over a week ago, and every day since arriving home he'd spent each morning locked in his father's oak-paneled study with his father, his father's steward, Simpson, and an enormous mound of papers. They were currently studying maps, going over ledgers, and making lists. Life in the country could scarcely get more tedious or prosaic.

Of course, it all had to be dealt with, and one day—and Harleigh wished that day a long way off—he would be the one making *his* eldest son sit in this dark study and hash over estate matters, like which cottages needed roofing, tenants' complaints, and the price of oats. He longed to be outside fishing or walking with his dogs, but here he sat.

Unannounced, his mother, Lady Adela Barrett, threw open the doors. His father muttered something about those 'dem'd interferrin' females.' Harleigh coughed to cover his laugh.

Harleigh's father, Emory Barrett, asked with just a bit of asperity tingeing his voice, "What is it, m'dear?"

"There's a large traveling coach coming up the drive." She spun around like a girl of sixteen instead of a matron of forty-plus years, and disappeared, leaving the doors open.

"Suppose she wants us to follow, eh?" Harleigh's father grumbled as he tossed his pen down, removed his spectacles. and got to his feet. "Simpson, we'll resume our work as soon as I see to this business." He motioned after the retreating form of his wife. "Come along, son."

Before the coachman set his brake, Harleigh, his father and mother, his youngest brother, Callum, a few of the household dogs, and several footmen had formed a clutch on the front doorstep.

A footman didn't get to open the carriage door before Giles sprang out like a jack-in-the-box.

Lady Barrett dimpled and clutched her hands to her chest. "How wonderful that you could join us, dear boy."

Harleigh rolled his eyes at his mother's exuberance. He leaned forward and whispered in her ear, "What are you plotting?"

His mother smiled up at him and patted his cheek. "Not a thing, darling, not a thing."

Lord Emory Barrett stuck out his hand. "We just left the boy in London, Adela, what's all this ta-do? Acting like you haven't seen him in an age."

Giles shook hands with and winked at Lord Barrett before he planted a kiss on Lady Barrett's cheek. "Thank you for your kind invitation, Lady Barrett, it's been an age since my last visit to Barrett Hall."

Lady Adela patted Giles' arm. "I'm sorry to have been so neglectful. How long has it been?"

"Just before we went on tour, Mother," Harleigh said.

"My, oh my, *that* has been quite a while, has it not?" Lady Adela took Giles' offered arm and the family processed through the door into the foyer while the footmen began unloading the coach.

"We'll get you settled and then have tea in the family parlor," Lady Adela said.

Lord Barrett put his hand on his youngest son's shoulder. "Callum."

"Sir?" Callum chirped.

"Go find Eleanor. Saw she and Libby heading into the woods."

"They went to the butts in the long meadow for some archery practice," Callum volunteered.

"Oh no, Emory. Send one of the servants, I beg." Lady Barrett wrung her hands.

"Don't fret, m'dear. Taught her meself, Ellie's a crack shot. Callum's safe enough."

Harleigh thought his mother might swoon if his father continued soothing her in this ill-conceived manner. "Never mind, Cal. I've been cooped up in Father's study for hours. I'd welcome a stretch of the legs. Giles?"

Callum dashed out the front door with the dogs in hot pursuit before anyone said another word.

Harleigh and Giles set a brisk pace down the lane.

Giles looked off into the distance. "How far are we going?"

"You heard, they're down at the butts."

"Yes, but I don't remember how far that is from the house anymore."

"I believe your legs were considerably shorter last time you were here. At this pace, we should be there in ten minutes."

Giles put his hands on his hips. "Har-har. Does she know your mother invited me as a houseguest?'

Harleigh couldn't help himself, he loved torturing Giles. His grin broadened. "By *she*, I suppose you mean Ellie?

Giles nodded.

"Worried?" Harleigh said.

"You witnessed her storming away from me on the dance floor."

"Hell, *I* didn't even know you were coming."

Giles grunted.

"Maybe I shouldn't have brought you with me. Who knows, Ellie might take it in her head to use you for target practice."

Giles shoved him hard.

Harleigh stumbled sideways. When he righted himself, Giles was running down the trail into the woods and calling back over his shoulder, "Ten pounds says I beat you to the butts."

Harleigh laughed and started running. "You're on."

⋈

The meadow was surrounded on three sides by trees; a steep grass-covered hill formed the forth side. The flight of the arrows wasn't affected by random gusts of wind in this protected spot. The afternoon sun was at their backs, while the target sat on the northeastern edge of the pasture. Above the tree line, to the east, they could glimpse the rooftops of Barrett Hall. Eleanor stood behind Libby, adjusting her stance and repositioning Libby's hold on the bow.

"I'm going to make this one a bulls-eye," Libby said.

"I always imagine someone I don't like sitting in front of the target," Eleanor said.

Libby nudged her chin in the direction of the butt. "Oh yes, like that nitwit, Lottie Croft."

Eleanor chuckled. "Or her mama. Horrible woman."

Libby dropped her arm that held the bow and sighed. "On second thought, I'd better not imagine Lottie. She is dreadfully dim, but I don't wish her any harm."

"Never mind, then. Just concentrate," Eleanor said.

Libby's arm trembled as she drew the string back toward her chin. Her arrow whistled through the air and skidded into the grass a foot or so before the target.

When Eleanor beheld Libby's infuriated face she burst into peals of laughter.

Libby pointed her bow tip at the target. "You think that's funny?" She swung the bow above her head as if she were going to throw it away. "Damnation!"

Eleanor pressed her hand to her heart and feigned horror. "You cursed."

"You would too if you shot like that," Libby said.

"True," Eleanor said.

There was a moment of taut silence before they both fell to the ground laughing. In the end the two of them lay on their backs gasping for air until their fit of giggles faded away.

Eleanor gazed over at Libby. "Come on." Eleanor stood up. "We'll move a few paces closer."

Libby frowned. "You shot from back here."

"First things first. Right now, let's focus on your accuracy rather than distance." Eleanor nudged Libby's chin with her closed fist. "Hmm?"

"All right."

Eleanor pulled another arrow from the quiver lying on the ground. They moved five paces closer to the target. Libby took the arrow, planted her feet, nocked the arrow, and raised her bow. Eleanor held her breath and said a small prayer.

Libby let go of the string, the arrow flew—grazing the top of the target and sailed into the woods beyond.

Two masculine voices roared, "Hey!"

"Ellie!" One familiar outraged man's voice shouted from within the trees.

Eleanor recognized Harleigh's voice. "What?"

"Was that intentional?" Harleigh asked.

"Using you as a target? Don't tempt me, brother. Anyway, that shot was Libby's."

"We're coming out," Harleigh said.

"You and Cal?" Eleanor wrapped her arm around Libby's shoulder. "Pay him no mind. At least this time your shot did not fall short."

"No, it nearly killed your brother."

"Don't be melodramatic. His fault for not announcing himself."

When the sunlight hit the golden head of her brother's companion, Eleanor muttered, "Damn."

"Now who's cursing," Libby said to.

Lord West was carrying Libby's arrow and rubbing his upper left arm. There was a rent in the fabric of his coat sleeve.

"Thought we were friends, Miss Archer," Giles West said.

"Oh, my word." Libby sighed.

Eleanor bumped Libby with her hip. "Nice shot."

ↃↃ

Eleanor walked beside Libby as they headed back for tea. Lord West and Harleigh brought up the rear.

"Why so glum?" Libby peered up at Eleanor.

"What's *he* doing here?"

Libby dimpled with a mischievous grin.

"What?"

Libby shrugged. "Nothing."

"First, he ejects us from Convent Garden, then he dupes me into a dance, and now he invades my home and interferes with our training regimen."

Libby chuckled. "You make it sound like every time he appears it's because of *you*. I'm sure he's here to keep Harleigh company."

Eleanor said nothing.

"You *do* believe Lord West is here because of you?"

Eleanor gave her one of her stern looks.

"Ha!" Libby tossed her head. "You give yourself far too much credit, my girl. Besides, you're *not* interested, and Lord West doesn't strike me as a man who goes on fool's errands."

On the verge of rebutting Libby's annoyingly insightful comment, Eleanor noticed Libby favoring her weaker leg. "Ow!" Eleanor said, faking a limping step.

"What's wrong?" Libby said.

"A pebble, ooph, in me boot."

"That stump looks perfect," Libby said.

Eleanor turned to Harleigh. "Brother, lend us your coat."

"My coat?"

Eleanor pointed in an imperious fashion. "Just put it over there."

Harleigh huffed.

Giles strolled over, shedding his coat and laying it down over the stump. Then he helped Libby sit. "Does it pain you much?"

Libby blushed. "Sometimes. But then Eleanor contrives some ruse, like this one. She claims to have a pebble in her boot, and so we stop for a rest." She picked up the damaged sleeve of his coat and brushed her fingers over the tear. "I'm so sorry."

"Think nothing of it. It's old and ready for the dustbin. I wear it for traveling because it's comfortable and well-broken in. It drives my man, Mumby, mad when I wear it. On a number of occasions, I've caught him trying to give it away to the rag-picker."

Libby smiled.

Lord West bowed and withdrew to stand with Harleigh.

Startled and touched by his gallantry toward her friend, Eleanor stared in fascination. That coat didn't look ready for the dustbin. Most men treated Libby as if she was wallpaper, if they noticed her at all. And if they attempted to converse with her, Libby grew flustered.

Eleanor sat down beside Libby and focused her attention on her foot as she undid her bootlaces. "I've pushed you."

"You know it's always hard for me at first when we come back to the country. I'm just out of practice, is all. You look worried and I don't think it's about my leg."

"Hush." Eleanor stared at her boot.

"Something wrong?" Harleigh said.

Eleanor waved her hand toward the house. "You and your guest can go along. We'll follow shortly."

"Nothing doing. Father ordered us to bring you home," Harleigh said.

Giles shoved Harleigh in the back and they moved off.

"We'll just move over there to enjoy the shade and the beauty of the day and give you two privacy," Harleigh said.

"Every day we're in the country, more girls go missing." Eleanor leaned in close and kept her voice low.

Libby tapped Eleanor on the nose with her finger. "Worrying about things you can't control is a waste of time. What did Mr. Rooksby say?"

"He's making enquiries," Eleanor said.

Libby motioned with her hand for Eleanor to continue. "And …?"

"Nothing yet," Eleanor said with a sigh.

Libby rested her chin on her fist. "How disappointing. I'd such high hopes based on your aunt's commendation."

Eleanor drummed her fingers against her thigh. "I need to get back to London."

Libby toyed with the leather strap of her quiver. "That's most unlikely, dear."

"True," Eleanor said.

"Have patience."

Eleanor made a scoffing sound.

Libby toed a groove in the dirt of the path. "I wonder what Rooksby will discover?"

"That we're right, of course. But I'll not have him interfering and taking credit for something we began."

"Sometimes your pride speaks louder than your common sense. I don't care who does the rescuing, if those girls get home," Libby said.

Eleanor's thirst for adventure was driving her at the moment. She shrugged in response to Libby's wisdom. "In truth, I don't think he'll do more than get us some information."

"What makes you say that?" Libby said.

"Rooksby swims in a vast political ocean. His concerns involve the stability of the Crown. The missing daughters of merchants and farmers mean nothing to him. He's helping us as a favor to Aunt Beatrice, out of respect for my Uncle Jasper."

"Those girls matter to us and that's sufficient," Libby said.

"Indeed."

"As soon as Rooksby provides the information, we'll meet with your aunt and figure out what our next move should be," Libby said.

"My brilliant strategist," Eleanor said as she thrust her foot into her boot and pulled the laces. "I hate all this waiting."

"I know."

Eleanor pulled a face. "For now, let's return to the house. Hope my mother had Cook prepare more than biscuits for tea—I'm famished."

Giles leaned against a tree several yards away from where Libby and Eleanor sat on their stump, his arms crossed over his chest. The din produced by buzzing insects, foraging creatures and a family of quarrelsome nuthatches nesting overhead kept him from being an effective eavesdropper. "What do you think they're up to?"

Harleigh shuddered. "Something diabolical, no doubt."

"What makes you say that?" Giles asked.

"Those two have always been closer than they are to their own sisters," Harleigh said.

"Was Miss Archer born that way?" Giles asked.

"You mean the limp?" Harleigh said.

Giles nodded.

"A pony stumbled and fell on her when they were girls."

"Was Eleanor responsible?" Giles asked.

"Heavens no. They weren't even together when it happened. But that didn't stop Ellie from high-tailing it over to the Archer's and staying there until she knew Libby wasn't only going to live, but walk again."

Giles gazed over at Eleanor, her head was tipped, and she was totally absorbed in whatever Elizabeth Archer was saying. It was obvious how devoted the two were to one another. Eleanor had all the makings of an excellent mother.

"Good Lord," Harleigh snorted, "Ellie demanded, *not* requested, but *demanded* to stay at the Archer's. It took months before she came home.

As you well-know, where my little sister is concerned the phrase 'lady-like behavior' has no meaning—well, not with any constancy anyway."

Giles chuckled. "Life is never boring when Eleanor's about, is it?"

"Do you think I need reminding?" Harleigh said.

"Now that you mention it ...no."

Harleigh rubbed the back of his thumb across his lips as he stared at his sister, his brows furrowed.

"What?" Giles asked.

"I worry for her. Truth be told, she's my favorite sibling."

"And well she knows it," Giles said.

"She was right to get Father to let her into our school room. What a tragedy it would have been to keep her uneducated. And yet ..."

Giles waited.

Harleigh took a long time before he spoke again. "She thinks too much about matters which are none of her concern, or at least things she has no power or authority to alter. She gets all worked up and thinks she can do something—*must* do something—about these injustices. Here in the country her unorthodox views are tolerated ... well ... more or less." He shrugged. "But in town ... her loyalty, fine mind, and sense of justice are not qualities which our class values in a female. It leaves her reputation and that of our family open to mockery and rampant gossip which at times becomes embarrassing."

"So, you're embarrassed by her," Giles said.

Harleigh cringed and then said. "Sometimes. Father has always had a blindness where Ellie is concerned."

"Unlike her eldest brother."

Harleigh shoved Giles in the shoulder. "As for Mother, she prays daily for Ellie to make a good match and contrives to bring eligible swains into Ellie's orbit whenever possible."

Giles looked away. He wasn't ready to reveal, even to his best friend, that he had the same hopes as Lady Adela. He wasn't sure why he was reluctant, he just was.

"I wish Ellie would restrain herself, at least while we reside in London. That Covent Garden business was making the rounds and definitely prompted Father to take us home early."

Eleanor and Libby rose and started walking, which cut short further discussion on the topic of Eleanor's behavior. When Giles and Harleigh passed the stump, Giles retrieved his coat, shook it out and slung it over his shoulder. They stayed far enough behind to give Libby and Eleanor some privacy.

As they exited the woods, he noticed Harleigh's gaze fastened to Libby Archer's backside. Giles pointed at Libby's derrière. "Rather a pleasant prospect, would you not agree?"

"What?" Harleigh tripped.

"Are you blushing?" Giles chuckled.

Harleigh picked up his pace. "Come along, you great oaf, let's go help them unstring their bows. I'm famished."

"Perhaps they don't want our help."

"I've never let my little sister's wants and desires govern my actions," Harleigh said.

Giles gave him a dubious look.

Harleigh crossed the threshold into the gun room first. Eleanor was hanging her quiver on a hook.

Giles and Harleigh stepped up to Libby and simultaneously said as they placed their hands on her bow, "Allow me."

Libby let go and Harleigh seized the moment to pull the bow free of Giles' grasp. He wore a triumphant smirk. "Go help someone else."

Giles turned and saw Eleanor bracing her bow against the inside of her boot, making ready to release the string. He put his hand over hers. "May I?"

Her eyes flashed him a warning.

"Your stinging wit would be wasted on me, Miss Barrett."

She blinked. "And why is that—are you pretending to be a dullard?"

"Not at all. In fact, just the opposite. I'm perspicacious and well-acquainted with your views on the absurd division of labor between the sexes. I'm choosing to be a gentleman. Now, let go of your bow and accept my offer for what it is."

"And what's that?"

"I'm hungry and ready for my afternoon tea, and I imagine you are as well. This is an interchange between two parties who are both capable of unstringing this bow. Working together shall expedite our arrival at the tea tray. It's as simple as that."

Eleanor let go.

ς

As Eleanor and Libby entered the family parlor, Callum jogged through the open French doors on the opposite side of the room, followed by a pack of five boisterous canines of diverse sizes and ages. Harleigh and Giles moved quickly to corral the dogs and keep them far from the tea tray. Callum, on the other hand, succeeded where his four-legged companions hadn't. He made a beeline for the plates of sandwiches and tea cakes and snatched a butter biscuit.

His father, Lord Emory Barrett, raised his voice above the hubbub. "Sir?"

"Sorry, Father." Callum pulled the biscuit from his mouth and put it back on the tray.

Lady Barrett lifted the offending biscuit from the tray with her thumb and index finger and fed it to her King Charles Spaniel, Sophronia, who lay at her feet.

"I'll go wash my hands first, shall I?" Callum said.

Emory Barrett hid his smile behind his hand. "Where've you been?"

"Here and there." He made a grab for another biscuit and his mother slapped his hand away.

"Callum! Take this rabble back to the kennel." Lady Barrett waved her hand at the dogs. "Then wash."

"I hope you have sandwiches today, Mother, I'm famished," Eleanor said.

Her mother poured a cup of tea. "Eleanor, a lady doesn't say such things."

As Lady Barrett handed her husband his cup of tea, she got her first look at Eleanor and squawked. "Eleanor, you look like a scarecrow."

Harleigh laughed.

Callum winked at Eleanor as he grabbed a fistful of biscuits. "Come on, boys." He summoned his troops and dashed back out the French doors with the dogs in pursuit.

You owe me, little brother. "Not even when the lady is in her home,
Mother?"

Harleigh rolled his eyes. "Ignore her, Mother."

Eleanor leaned down and pecked her mother on the cheek. As she began to stand, her mother grabbed her wrist and tugged her down and proceeded to pluck a few wayward pieces of straw from Eleanor's loose tresses that cascaded over her shoulder.

"Really, darling, were you shooting at those targets or rolling in them?" Adela Barrett let go and Eleanor moved to greet her father.

Eleanor kissed his forehead. "Hello, Papa."

"How did it go, my girl?" Emory Barrett beamed up at her.

"Splendid," Eleanor said. "Libby's getting better all the time."

"Yes, Miss Archer shows quite a talent for the bow, would you not agree?" Giles turned to Harleigh.

Libby turned red. Giles went to her side and took her hand. "I'm so sorry, Miss Archer. I'm an inveterate older brother, you see. Teasing girls is a brother's favorite sport, but I shouldn't inflict my rude habits on you."

Eleanor felt a prickly irritation at the attention Lord West was giving Libby. *I'd better get out of here before I say something untoward.* She heaped sandwiches and biscuits onto a plate, then accepted a cup of tea from her mother.

"Hungry?" Harleigh said.

Eleanor acted as if she hadn't heard him and went out onto the terrace. She set her plate, cup and saucer on the balustrade before she turned and hoisted herself up onto the railing. She crossed her ankles and let her dangling legs swing back and forth as she ate.

She heard Libby chatting with her mother, catching up on all the neighborhood news. Her father, Harleigh, and Giles West were standing before the mantel.

Callum returned with one dog—his favorite yellow Labrador Retriever, Balder, and whispered to her from the shrubbery, "Hist. Ellie. Hows about snatching me another handful of biscuits?"

"Oh no, if I must endure this folderol, then so shall you. And besides, you're getting quite gluttonous in your old age. I don't think I should encourage your consumption of sweets.

"Pshh." Callum dragged his booted feet up the steps. "All right. But why are you avoidin' Lord West?"

"I'm not," Eleanor said.

Callum looked at her suspiciously.

"What makes you say that?"

"I heard you on your walk back," Callum said.

"Perdy was right. Eavesdropping isn't a nice habit."

"When did you see Perdy?" Callum asked.

"A couple of days ago."

"I sure miss her and Mac," Callum said as he snatched a sandwich off her plate. "Wish they lived closer."

"I'll have to add pilfering to your eavesdropping charges."

"I wasn't. Me and the lads were out following some tracks that brought us near the trail you was on."

"Scaring the game away, more like."

"You pick at him, sis."

"Don't," Eleanor said.

Callum snatched a biscuit from her plate. "Doooo." Then he popped the whole thing into his mouth. *Chomp, chomp* and his cheeks filled with partially masticated cookie. "Du."

"Ooo, Cal." Eleanor brushed damp cookie clumps off her lap. "No talking with food in your mouth." Eleanor jumped down from the balustrade. At her feet, Balder began a joyful feeding frenzy of soggy cookie bits.

"You know how every Sunday after church I'm always running after Jenny Crawford?"

"Uh-huh."

"Well, last Sunday I made her cry." Callum grimaced. "Felt awful. Papa pulled me aside. He said I do those things because I really like her."

Eleanor just stared at her baby brother.

"Father says there are better ways to let a girl know I like her."

୯ଷ

After dinner, Giles and Harleigh spent a pleasant evening playing billiards and drinking. When they parted company hours later, Giles leaned against the doorjamb and watched his friend make his way to his own door. They were both a bit foxed.

The click as Giles closed his door roused Mumby from a doze in a chair before the fire. Mumby came forward and helped Giles prepare for bed. As Giles disrobed, his mind wouldn't quiet. When Mumby had him stripped to his shirt, breeches, stockings and shoes, he told his valet to seek his own bed and Giles sat down in Mumby's vacated chair. As he stared into the fire, his whiskey-fogged mind reviewed his activities over the last few weeks. He needed a good smoke to help him cogitate. Lady Barrett detested the smell of cigars in her house, so Giles headed for Lord Barrett's study.

He quickly found the humidor. When he raised the lid the rich perfume of the cured and rolled tobacco filled the air. He inhaled appreciatively, and then selected a cigar. He'd left his penknife in his room. How fortuitous that Lord Barrett kept his near his ink pot. Giles cut away the cap, then tapped the loose bits off.

He picked up the single candle he'd used to illuminate his way to Viscount Barrett's study and retreated onto the terrace. He held the tip of the cigar above the candle flame and toasted the end. Once it glowed evenly he raised the cigar to his mouth and slowly and steadily drew the smoke into his mouth. He let the flavor dance across his tongue and then he parted his lips to let the smoke escape. Nothing like a good cigar to help a man think.

He moved his candle down onto the stone bench, out of the breeze, and hoisted one hip onto the balustrade and leaned back against the fragrant flower-filled planter. He drew another puff of cigar smoke into his mouth. A moment later he exhaled and the breeze lifted the translucent gray trail up and away into the cloudless night sky. His eyes followed it into the heavens. What a breathtaking night, with myriad early summer constellations populating the darkness.

He heard an indistinct sound coming from below him. As his eyes became accustomed to the lack of light, he thought he perceived movement. Something seemed to be spread out over the grass. Curious, he stubbed out his cigar and left it beside his candle, then descended the steps. "What are *you* doing out here … alone? It's well after midnight."

She turned her head, giving him her full attention. "The same as you, my lord—I'm witnessing the magnificence of the heavenly spheres."

"Hmmm?" He couldn't think straight with her lying there like that.

Eleanor lay on her back, her hands cradling her head. "The constellations are so beautiful."

Her position put her well-endowed figure on display and he felt a pulse of appreciation stir his loins. Her physical form was magnificent. An image of her lying naked in his bed, again, his arms wrapped around her and those plump breasts pressed against his bare chest, crossed his mind.

Giles allowed a soft, irritated groan to slip out.

"Did you say something?" Eleanor asked.

As she stared up at him and their gazes locked, Giles took a step back. Putting distance between them.

Eleanor pointed skyward. "Is that Leo?"

Walk away, you idiot. Giles cleared his throat and adjusted his breeches. "I believe it is."

Eleanor stared at him.

"Miss Barrett, even in the country, with few servants about at this late hour, it's imprudent for us to be seen together, partially clothed, after dark."

Silence.

He held his hand down to her, fingers undulating, beckoning her to take it.

She hesitated.

"Come along."

She hesitated, then reached up and placed her hand in his.

The touch of their naked hands sent a sizzling, jangling sensation up his arm. He yanked.

Eleanor flew up.

Giles didn't realize how hard he had pulled.

She fell against him.

His arms wrapped around her.

They wobbled.

Giles tightened his hold, braced his legs to keep them from crashing to the ground.

Eleanor's palms rested on his chest. She sniffed. "You smell like one of my father's cigars."

"You smell ... nice." Good Lord, his mind became a fuddled, inarticulate mess. Because he still held her in his arms, he could feel her body tremble.

She gasped for air. "Haaa-heh."

"You *are* laughing at me."

"Of course, no-ot," she said on a splutter of mirth. "It's been so long since someone paid me such an effusive compliment. He-he-he. Really, my lord, I'm overcome."

"You are ..."—Giles flexed his hands and then he grabbed her by the shoulders and shook her slightly—" aggravating, insulting—" He cut himself off, pressing his lips together to keep from uttering anything he'd regret.

Another small gasp of laughter erupted from Eleanor.

"Well, laugh this off, Miss Eleanor Barrett." His lips crashed down on her taunting mouth.

She stilled.

Giles licked across the seam of her lips and she parted them for him. His tongue swept inside. She tasted spicy-sweet like wine and the sugary drizzle on the cake they'd had at dinner. He drew her closer.

Her arms circled his neck and she pushed up onto her toes. Her tongue darted out, first tentatively, then she began to play with his. She moaned.

Giles never wanted to let her go.

A twig snapped nearby.

They gasped, breaking the kiss.

They turned their heads in the direction of the noise and watched as a hedgehog lumbered out from the undergrowth and waddled across the yard through patches of moonlight.

Eleanor laid her hand over her heart.

"Christ." Giles' word was barely audible. He still held her close.

She dropped her forehead onto his chest.

He expelled a breath and rested his chin on the crown of her head. His hands came up to cradle her head.

She tipped her head back and gazed up at him. She looked soft. He wanted to wrap her in his arms and carry her off to his bed and make love to her all night.

His thumbs massaged her temples.

Eleanor blinked. Her mood changed in a snap, then she stepped back.

Chapter Ten

Eleanor paced her bedroom like a caged animal. After that mad kiss she needed to stay far away from Giles West because, damn him, he made her feel things.

She got ready for bed even though she didn't feel sleepy. Her plan was to rise with the birds and escape the house with little interference. Tomorrow was Saturday. Market day. Going to market gave her a plausible excuse to be absent for most of the day.

She lit a candle and plucked a book from her nightstand. She reread the same blasted page three times but didn't recall a single idea that had been expressed thereupon.

She snapped the volume shut, shoved back her covers and went to her desk. After lighting another candle, she dipped her quill in the inkpot. Her hand hovered over her open journal, but she couldn't think of a single thing to write that didn't have to do with kisses.

Disgusted with herself she tossed down her quill, replaced the lid on the inkpot, and snuffed out both candles and crawled back into bed. Minutes passed.

She kicked off her covers and sat up. Her braid flopped over her shoulder. She toyed with its tail, absently brushing it across her lips, making them tingle and reminding her about Lord West's kiss.

"Ahh!"

She threw herself back into her pillows and squeezed her eyes shut, at which point her imagination began to draw pictures of Giles—naked. Would his torso look like the statuary she'd seen in Florence? Her palms itched, remembering the feel of his warm, well-muscled chest covered only by the fine linen of his shirt.

Lord, when she'd stepped back, that look on his face … Had he been about to apologize? There was nothing to apologize for. Honesty made her admit she'd wanted that kiss.

Eleanor blinked. Well, she'd finally done it—shocked herself. It had been delicious having his arms wrapped around her and he was quite a good kisser, too. He must have had a great deal of practice. She hoped she hadn't come off as a neophyte. Well, she did and she didn't. She didn't want him thinking she kissed every man who made a pass at her, but she also wanted to be someone worth kissing—someone who knew how to get the business done.

Picking up her skirts and running for the house had been an instinct. And a cowardly one at that. And the more she'd thought about it the more she'd regretted it. She should've stayed and brazened it out, like she'd done with so many things in her life.

Eleanor had learned in childhood that prolonged self-condemnation was an exercise in futility. It only made her temper shorter. And eventually, that bottled-up anger would erupt all over some undeserving soul. No, it was best to move forward. Betty's granny used to tell Eleanor: "Be where your feet are, Ellie-girl. The past is over and done with, and tomarra is yet to be."

The sheer drapes fluttered in the night breeze, like siren song. *Go find your breeches.*

Eleanor jumped out of bed and dressed quickly. Everyone must be asleep by now and long ago she'd learned her lesson about visiting the stables alone late at night, so she headed out to the rose garden. Her leather-soled boots squeaked as her strides swept across the dew-covered grass.

Eleanor could have navigated her way to this walled garden with her eyes closed. The night air was fragrant with the scent of hundreds of roses. This garden was one of her favorite spots in the entire world and her friend, Betty, now tended it.

She walked the path twice at a quick clip and thought about running to burn off some of her frantic energy, but she feared tripping in the darkness on the uneven ground. Still restless, she ambled down to the lake and stood under a willow, skipping stones and listening to frog-song.

Resigned, since there was no place left to wander, Eleanor headed back to the house. Walking along the boxwood hedge that bordered the terrace, she heard male voices. *At this late hour?* She inched closer, staying in the shadows. Giles West *and* Harleigh were leaning on the balustrade with a candelabrum between them. Harleigh plucked one of the candles out of its socket and held it to the end of his cigar.

She was about to turn back and find another way into the house.

"What's Eleanor training Elizabeth Archer for? The county militia?" Giles asked.

She froze.

Harleigh laughed. "You believe you're making a jest, but I wouldn't put it past my devious little sister. One never knows what she's up to."

Devious? I'll get even with you for that remark, brother.

Harleigh stared at the end of his glowing cigar. "How did your meeting go with Edgerton?"

"Started off well enough. It's good to see him so plump in the pockets. Remember we wondered if he'd have the funds to finish University?"

Harleigh tipped his head back and blew out a slow trail of aromatic gray smoke. "I remember. What do you mean 'started well'?"

"On the way to his carriage we ended up in an alley."

Harleigh jumped to standing. "Alley?"

"An ambush. Three against the two of us."

"Christ," Harleigh said.

"Afterwards, I asked Edgerton whose wife he was tupping."

"And?" Harleigh asked.

"Claims he's nothing to do with married women. Said the men were after me."

Eleanor held her breath and crept closer. She was below them now.

Harleigh rubbed the back of his neck. A sure sign he was vexed.

"I can tell you want to say something," Giles said.

Harleigh paced. "I've heard things, is all."

Giles prompted with his cigar for Harleigh to continue.

"Would you take my advice?" Harleigh said.

"Depends."

"Spend as little time with my cousin as possible."

"What makes you say that?" Giles said.

Harleigh looked away. "You're putting me in a difficult spot."

"You started this."

Harleigh threw his hands in the air in exasperation. "All right, all right …"

There was a long pregnant silence.

"Just spit it out, man." Giles sounded exasperated.

"Very well," Harleigh said. "I've heard some very nasty rumors of late."

"You've never been one to put stock in gossip, so why now?"

Eleanor leaned so far forward, the twigs of the boxwood stabbed her cheek and she winced in pain.

Giles crossed his arms over his chest.

What have you heard?

"Are you worried he will ask for a loan?" Giles said.

"Nooo."

"Because he already did."

"What?" Harleigh said.

What? Eleanor nearly tumbled from her hiding place.

"Several years ago, …before you and I went traveling. And my man of business tells me Edgerton's quarterly repayments have been complete and on time."

"Why would he need your money?" Harleigh said.

"I didn't ask. I wouldn't ask *you* if you asked me for a loan either."

"I don't think I like being compared with Edgerton," Harleigh said.

CHAPTER ELEVEN

Eleanor overslept. Ominous conundrums were never a passport to a good night's rest.

After returning to her room she'd lain awake for hours trying to figure out what Edgerton had done with Lord West's money. It was another exercise in futility if there ever was one since she didn't have sufficient information to make even a modest supposition.

When she awoke, she dressed quickly, snatched a muffin on her way through the kitchen to break her fast, and set off for the stables. Her sole objective was to leave Barrett Hall without encountering anyone with the last name of Barrett or West.

She leaned against the old oak just outside the stable entrance, eating her muffin and waiting for one of the grooms to ready her mount and one for himself.

"Here we are, Miss Barrett." The groom appeared, leading two horses. He tied his horse to the rail, then led hers to the mounting block.

Eleanor shoved the remainder of her muffin into her mouth, brushed her hands together, and pulled on her gloves as she climbed the steps.

She settled herself into the sidesaddle.

The groom adjusted her stirrup.

Clomp, clomp, clomp. Approaching horses. "Lord West and I shall accompany my sister on her ride," Harleigh addressed the groom.

"Very good, m'lord," the groom said.

The groom gazed up at Eleanor. "Will that do, Miss Eleanor?"

Meaning the stirrup, of course, but Eleanor wanted to scream.

No, damn it, get on your horse. But instead she nodded at the groom and said, "Excellent, thank you." It wasn't his fault her bothersome brother had shown up. She took the reins and tapped her cane against her horse's flank to nudge him into a walk.

As they ambled down the drive, Harleigh rode on one side of her and Giles West on the other.

"You've nothing else to do?" Eleanor kept her eyes forward.

"As a matter of fact, ...not at this moment. Besides, you're heading for Aylesford, are you not?"

She could feel Giles West's eyes on her.

"And since it's market day, the streets will be teeming with all manner of diversions, which is just what Giles and I require at this moment. Is that not so, Giles?"

"If you say so, Harls." The deep pitch of Giles' voice sent a rain of prickling heat down Eleanor's spine. Annoyed with herself for enjoying the effect his nearness had on her body, she nudged her horse into a trot. How could she think when he was near?

As they rode on, Eleanor tried to focus on her surroundings rather than her company. Then a breeze would carry the scent of his cologne or he'd make a comment to Harleigh, and her serenity would shatter.

The traffic increased as they neared town. And since the Barretts were known as a convivial lot, and with their father's standing as the local magistrate, almost everyone they encountered—be they farmer, peddler, or gentry—had something to say.

Eleanor loved the children. A couple of times, with parental permission of course, she would lift a child up before her and canter away. A few minutes later she would return a giggling, pink-cheeked child to their parent, then they would move on.

By the time they arrived at the stable where they usually left their animals, Eleanor was famished. A muffin didn't make for much of a breakfast. She needed something to eat and she knew just what she wanted.

The stable owner greeted them and took hold of her horse's

bridle. She removed her foot from the stirrup and unhooked her leg from the pommel, making ready to slide down.

Large gloved hands wrapped around her waist and lifted her. She could do nothing but put her hands on his strong, wide shoulders to steady herself as Giles West lowered her to the ground. "I have wanted to kiss you since Covent Garden."

Her eyes went wide when he made his revelation and she couldn't tear her gaze away from his mouth. A blush stained her cheeks.

When her booted feet were firmly on the ground, he didn't remove his hands immediately.

Eleanor couldn't move away from him. She was hemmed in between his body and her horse. She cleared her throat and then spoke in a soft voice, "I could've done that myself."

Giles gave her a slow grin, then released her.

Harleigh appeared at her shoulder. "Lift yourself down? Don't be a ninny. Giles just beat me to it."

The horses were led away, allowing her to step back. Eleanor turned away, lifted the edge of her skirt and secured it at her back, under the edge of her jacket's peplum.

Harleigh looked at Giles. "She means she's used to sliding off, losing her balance, and landing on her a-a ... backside."

"Now who is being a ninny? That hasn't happened in an age."

Harleigh rubbed his hands together with glee. "Where to first? I'm famished."

Eleanor's stomach chose that moment to grumble.

Harleigh laughed, while Giles West's lips just twitched.

"What'll it be—Mrs. Lampson's meat pies or fresh gingerbread at the bakers?"

Eleanor rolled her eyes and then took off at a brisk clip with the men in her wake as she sped through the bustling market day's foot traffic.

"Stubborn wench." Harleigh took her elbow to pull her to a stop. "When will you cease to be a pain in my backside, little sister?"

"When she marries me," a now familiar deep male voice whispered in her ear and made Eleanor jump.

"Did you say something, Giles?" Harleigh said.

She hadn't heard or felt Giles come up. He smelled of spice and starch again and ... mint. His breath smelled of mint.

"Only that I don't believe our concern for our siblings ever leaves us."

Harleigh pursed his lips in thought. "Quite so." He turned his gaze back to Eleanor. "There's a tavern just around the next corner."

"I've things to do," Eleanor said.

"Such as?" Harleigh didn't release her arm.

"Errands," Eleanor said.

"Resign yourself, sister. If you think I'm going to allow you to gad about unescorted you have truly lost your senses."

"Good day to you, Lord Barrett." A gentleman walked by and diverted Harleigh's attention.

Giles leaned down. "Please."

She looked over her shoulder at him.

Harleigh offered her his arm. "Where to first?"

"The Brewsters," Eleanor said.

"Ahh, excellent choice," Harleigh said to his sister, then over his shoulder he spoke to Giles. "The Barretts have done business with the Brewsters for generations—the best cheeses, cream, and butter in three counties."

The smell of fresh produce and caged cackling fowl surrounded them. Everything and everybody sat cheek by jowl around the town square. The dairy farmers clustered on the southeast corner.

As they approached the Brewsters' stall, Eleanor noticed the normally jovial Mr. Brewster was frowning and Mrs. Brewster's nose and eyes were red. Eleanor looked about for her favorite Brewster—their eldest daughter, Julia. She squeezed Harleigh's arm to alert him to what she'd noticed.

He frowned. "Something's amiss."

They waited their turn. "Good Morning, Mr. Brewster, Mrs. Brewster."

"Good Morning to you, Lord Barrett. Miss Eleanor." Mr. Brewster's smile was so sad and forced.

Eleanor felt her heart pinch.

"Allow me to introduce you to my oldest and dearest friend," Harleigh said.

Giles stepped forward.

Eleanor looked right and left.

"Giles, Lord West, Mr. and Mrs. Brewster. Mr. and Mrs. Brewster, Giles, Lord West," Harleigh said.

Giles offered his hand to Mr. Brewster and the men shook.

"Where's Julia? Did you leave her at the farm?" Eleanor's gaze returned to Mr. and Mrs. Brewster.

Mrs. Brewster burst into tears, threw her hands over her face and ran behind their stall.

A weighty silence fell and Mr. Brewster wouldn't meet her gaze, instead he darted glances about. Eleanor looked to see what had diverted his attention. Several local gossips had gathered and were whispering and pointing. Poor man. He stood there wringing his hands.

"I'm sorry, sir, that I've distressed your good wife," Eleanor said.

"Tis na yer fault, miss."

"Mr. Brewster, may we speak in private?" Harleigh said.

The poor man, his tears were barely contained. "Aye."

The Brewsters' stall stood before a narrow alley. Eleanor seated herself on a plain wooden bench beside Mrs. Brewster. The three men stood in front of them.

Harleigh broke the strained silence. "It's obvious to my sister and I that something' s amiss."

"Has something happened to Julia?" Eleanor took Mrs. Brewster's hand and gave it a squeeze.

Mrs. Brewster bit her quivering lip and nodded.

Mr. Brewster put his hand on his wife's shoulder. "She be gone. Disappeared."

Eleanor's stomach dropped. Julia was just like those other missing girls. A beauty with apple cheeks and the translucent pink skin of a dairymaid. Everything fit, except the place. Most of the dots on their map came from the west or north. Eleanor felt sick.

"I'm sorry for your trouble, Mr. Brewster," Giles said. "What's been done to locate your daughter?"

"I done looked everywhere I can think of." Mr. Brewster wiped his forearm across his eyes.

"And your neighbors, has anyone seen her?" Harleigh said.

Mr. Brewster dropped his chin to his chest. "Me da was right. In times of trouble ye find out quick enough who yer true friends be."

"They all be sayin' she run off with some boy." Mrs. Brewster's tears ran down her plump cheeks and double chins.

Eleanor pulled a handkerchief from her reticule and closed Mrs. Brewster's fingers around it.

Mr. Brewster raised his hand as if giving an oath. "Our Julia be a good girl."

Harleigh grasped Mr. Brewster's hand and gently pushed it down. "Eleanor and I know Julia would never do anything to shame you or herself."

"Anyone else missing?" Lord West said.

Now that was an astute question.

"None that I know of. Dun know what's to be done now. I canna leave me farm for more than a day." Mr. Brewster rubbed his forehead with a trembling hand.

Chapter Twelve

Eleanor had one thought in her head as they galloped homeward: she had to get to Libby—*now*.

As they neared the fork in the road that led to the Archers', Eleanor shouted above the pounding of the horses' hooves, "I must see Libby." She veered north.

Harleigh caught up with her handily and grabbed her reins and pulled her to a halt.

Giles caught up.

"Let go," Eleanor shouted.

"What are you doing?" Harleigh shouted back.

Eleanor felt frantic. Her horse danced and sidled about. "I must speak with Libby."

"Now? I thought you wanted to talk with Father?" Harleigh said. "About Julia."

"I do, but I need … "She paused. "Harleigh Barrett, let go of my horse." Eleanor yanked on her reins.

Harleigh turned them about as if she were a recalcitrant child.

Eleanor unhooked her leg from the pommel and slid off the animal, landing firmly on her feet. She grabbed her skirts and started marching up
the road toward the Archers.

"Get back here," Harleigh said.

Eleanor kept walking away, stuck her hand in the air and waved him adieu.

"Harleigh, I think we need to trust that your sister knows what she's doing," Giles West said.

Eleanor couldn't believe her ears. She stopped.

"You're bamming me, right?" Harleigh scoffed.

"It's apparent," Giles said, "that she has a need to speak with Miss Archer. I assume it's something urgent having to do with the current crisis over Julia Brewster. I'm willing to give your sister the benefit of the doubt. Besides, I thought the Archers live nearby?"

"Their property borders ours," Harleigh said.

"Well then." Giles West dismounted, handed Harleigh his reins in exchange for Eleanor's and walked Eleanor's horse to her.

She stared at him.

He cupped his hands to give her a leg up. "May I?"

"Very well," Harleigh said and walked his horse toward them. "I tell you, Giles, you'll be sorry you indulged her in this. Come along, Ellie. If it were done when 'tis done, then 'twere well it was done quickly."

Eleanor put her foot in Giles' hands. "We're talking about saving a life,

brother, not taking one." In the next moment, she was seated in her saddle and Giles West had his hand around her ankle, putting her foot into her stirrup. She wasn't sure which was more unsettling—his unexpected support or his touch.

Harleigh held out Giles' reins.

Giles smiled up at her.

Eleanor tapped her cane and got her horse moving before he remounted.

In a brief time, they were in front of the Archers'. A groom came forward.

Giles had already dismounted and was holding his hands up to Eleanor to help her down.

"Will you stop touching me?" Eleanor whispered.

"How else am I to help you dismount?" The devil smiled.

When Eleanor's feet hit the ground, she ran up the front steps. "You two wait here. I must speak with Libby."

The butler opened the door and Eleanor flew through it. Libby was coming down the stairs. Eleanor ran up to her and grabbed her hands. "Can we go back up to your room? I must speak to you in private."

Libby craned her neck to see around Eleanor's shoulder. She was gazing through the open door. "But is that not your brother and Lord West?"

Eleanor began to climb the stairs, pulling Libby with her. "What of it?" Eleanor addressed the Archers' butler, "Excuse me, Perryvale?"

He looked up at Libby and Eleanor. "Yes, Miss Eleanor?"

"Would you put my brother and Lord West in the small parlor and get them some refreshments while Miss Elizabeth and I confer?"

"Yes, miss." Perryvale's lips twitched as he nodded obligingly.

"Lucky for you, Perryvale is used to your autocratic ways," Libby said.

"I'm not autocratic, I'm … "

"Bossy," Harleigh's voice floated up to them.

"Ignore him," Libby said.

Wise, sagacious Libby. This was no time for useless arguments. Her delicate appearance and shy demeanor concealed Libby's sharp analytical mind and keen eye for observation.

"Perryvale, please show the gentleman to the parlor," Libby said.

"Yes, miss."

Eleanor hooked arms with her friend and they continued to climb. Libby had quite a talent for accurately sizing up situations—she seemed to instinctively know when to stand her ground and when not to. Most people, including Libby's family, continually underestimated her, seeming to equate her limp with a deficient mental state. Eleanor slowed her gait.

As soon as they entered Libby's bedroom, Eleanor began to pace.

"What is it?" Libby closed the door.

"The most awful news," Eleanor said as she pulled off her gloves. "Little Julia Brewster's missing,"

"No."

"Yes. And I've this awful feeling in the pit of my stomach that she's gone the way of those other girls."

"Oh, Ellie, are you sure?"

"Not in a factual sort of way, no, but all the pieces fit except for the location—her age, beauty, and she's the daughter of a farmer. And when we were talking to the Brewsters, Lord West asked the most astute question."

"Yes?" Libby said.

"Have any other children gone missing? I think that was what made me think …"

"He's known for his discerning mind, you know," Libby said.

"It was the oddest feeling, like having one's brainbox full of turning gears." Eleanor laid her index finger against her temple and began to draw circles. "When Lord West asked his question, I heard this click in my head, like two gears meshing or a lock popping open."

"Are you thinking it is time to show your father this?" Libby said as she pulled their map out of her desk drawer.

෪

Eleanor bolted out of the Archers' family carriage as soon as the coachman set the brake.

"Wait, Ellie, wait," Harleigh said as he ran up behind her and grabbed the edge of her jacket, pulling her to a halt.

Eleanor batted his hand away. "Wait for what?"

"Elizabeth, for one." Harleigh waved his arm back at the carriage.

Giles West was helping Elizabeth Archer out of the carriage.

Harleigh crossed his arms over his chest. "You had us go out of our way to get her, then the two of you held a secret confabulation, plotting who knows what …"

Libby held Giles West's arm as they joined them on the steps.

"You're being dramatic, my lord," Libby said and moved next to Eleanor and hooked arms with her. "Come along, Eleanor."

A footman held the front door open and Eleanor and Libby progressed through.

"And what, pray tell, is in that folio Miss Archer is clutching so tightly? Secret papers?" Harleigh said from behind them.

They all trooped down the hallway that led to Lord Emory Barrett's study.

Harleigh jumped in front of Eleanor as she reached up to knock on the door. "Ellie, you cannot *demand* Father do something."

"Why not?" Eleanor said. "You saw poor Mr. and Mrs. Brewster."

Harleigh put his hands on his hips.

"Either move out of the way or knock on the door yourself."

Harleigh tapped his finger against her forehead. "This is a time, dear sister, to think with this fine, well-trained mind of yours. Not your tender heart. This is *one* little missing girl. Just because we know her—"

"You see, Lord Barrett," Libby said, "Eleanor and I are of the mind that Julia hasn't gone missing …"

Giles West moved in close. Both men leaned in, hanging on Libby's every word.

"Please continue, Miss Archer." Giles nodded to encourage her to continue.

"Well … we think she's been"—Libby's voice grew very soft as she said the last word— "… abducted."

Harleigh's voice dripped with sarcasm. "*Oh, really.* Now who's being dramatic? What evidence do you two have that supports your sensational pronouncement? Were you two consulting tea leaves when you met privately?"

The door behind Harleigh was wrenched open and his father glared at them. "What's the meaning of this? How's a man to get any work done when his offspring—his grown offspring, I might add—are behaving like squabbling geese?

"Harleigh you promised to keep Ellie out of trouble, not follow her into some scrape." Lord Emory Barrett's eyes went round when he saw Libby standing among those assembled outside his door. "Oh … good day to you, Elizabeth dear."

"Sorry, Father," Harleigh said.

Libby beamed at Eleanor's father and made a shallow curtsy. "Good afternoon, Lord Barrett."

Eleanor scooted around her brother and dashed into her father's study. "Papa, we had terrible news in town. The Brewsters need your help."

Libby and Lord Barrett walked to Eleanor.

Giles and Harleigh were at Lord Barrett's back, motioning Eleanor to calm down.

"What's upset you so, Ellie?" Lord Barrett asked.

"Little Julia is missing, Father," Eleanor said.

"Missing, you say?" Lord Barrett put his arm around Eleanor's shoulders.

"Please, Papa, you could call out the militia and—"

"For one missing child?" Lord Barrett said.

"That's what we told her, Father," Harleigh said.

"Ellie, I know how fond you are of the child …" Lord Barrett squeezed her shoulder.

"Yes, I'm fond of Julia, but what if she's *not* the only child who's gone missing?" Eleanor said.

"Miss Barrett, you were there," Giles West said, "you heard Mr. Brewster say he has heard of no other missing children."

Lord Barrett retreated behind his desk. "I can't do it, Ellie." He waved his hand over the piles of papers on his desk. "Even to please you. Besides, the major and his men aren't even in the area. I sent them off over a week ago, and according to his most recent report they shan't return for at least a fortnight."

"Giles and I'll search for Julia," Harleigh said.

Libby stepped forward and rested her leather folio on the corner of Lord Barrett's desk and untied the strap holding it shut. "Lord Barrett, we've brought several things to show you. We don't think you have all the necessary facts to make an informed decision."

Lord Barrett seated himself. "And you're in possession of the necessary facts?" He clasped his hands and rested them on his desk.

"We think we possess some of them," Libby said.

"Well then, present your case, Elizabeth." Lord Barrett sat at attention.

Eleanor came to stand on the other side of her father as Libby pulled out a large folded piece of parchment.

Eleanor weighted down the corners.

"As you can see, we've a map of England, Wales, and Scotland." Libby cleared her throat.

Lord Barrett pointed at the markings on the map. "What are these clusters of dots here and here?"

"Excellent question, Father," Eleanor said.

"Don't try and butter me up, girl, just proceed with your evidence."

Eleanor rolled her eyes, then said, "For some time we've collected handbills notifying the public that a particular young girl has gone missing."

"You mean like Julia?" Giles West said.

"Exactly like Julia," Libby said. "These dots indicate the towns where the girls we know about have disappeared."

Giles and Harleigh moved closer to examine the map.

"There are a vast number of dots," Giles West said.

"Indeed," Lord Barrett concurred.

"Following your line of thought, Julia's dot would be over here." Harleigh pointed to their county. "There are no other dots in this locale."

"We *know* that," Eleanor said then bit her lip and worked to control her temper.

"Eleanor, continue," Lord Barrett said.

"We're quite aware that Julia doesn't fit the pattern as to location, *but* she does in every other respect," Eleanor said and pointed at Libby's folio. "Did you bring some of the handbills we've collected?"

Libby extracted several worn sheets and handed them to Lord Barrett.

"As you can see," Eleanor said, "all the children reported missing are of Julia's age, all female, known for their fine looks, and are the daughters of merchants or farmers,"

The men looked stunned.

Giles West moved his finger in the air over the map. Under his breath, you could hear him counting. "There are upwards of fifty girls here."

"Fifty children? Over what period?" Lord Barrett asked.

"I noticed the first handbill a little over two years ago," Eleanor said. "At first Libby and I wondered if this was a localized phenomenon. To test our theory, we wrote to our friends who live in other counties and asked them to keep an eye out for this type of handbill."

"As you can see," Eleanor pointed to the map, "only two regions produced any notable results—here in the west and up near the border between Scotland and England."

"Are you telling me that no one else noticed this?" Lord Barrett asked.

"We aren't aware of any organized search for these missing girls, if that's what you mean," Libby said.

"Are you suggesting that all these missing girls have been taken by the same person?" Harleigh said.

"We haven't determined if it is *a* person or a group of people, but yes we think all the missing girls are related," Eleanor said.

"This is monstrous," Lord Barrett said. "What do you think has happened to them?"

"Well, we aren't sure, but recently we came into some additional information," Eleanor said.

"What sort of information?" Lord Barrett pressed.

"We met a young woman … ah, who …a-a-ah … " Eleanor began.

"…Has a friend who is a laundress," Libby added.

How were they going to get to the point without mentioning the word brothel?

"What does *laundry* have to do with these missing children?" The sarcasm was creeping back into Harleigh's voice.

"And what sort of people have you been consorting with, daughter?" Lord Barrett asked.

Eleanor gritted her teeth. She wanted to punch her brother; instead, she gazed heavenward and silently said a one-word prayer: *Help.*

"Well, daughter, what do you have to say?" Lord Barrett said.

Eleanor swallowed. "One of the laundress's customers is the sort of place men like to go. Um …it's the sort of place where they don't take their wives but they engage in some of the activities they do with their wives."

Lord Barrett's eyes grew wide and his face turned crimson. He tossed his glasses down on his desk and roared. "Are you mad? If you're talking about the sort of thing I think you are, I'm going to lock you up, my girl. Who dares discuss such matters with a young girl?"

"Well, actually it was Aunt Beatrice who first explained it to me and …"

"If my sister was here right now I would wring her neck. Of all the addlepated nonsense …"

"What Aunt Beatrice discusses with me isn't the issue at hand. We're talking about what must be done about these missing girls."

Libby moved to perch on the edge of one of the two chairs that fronted Lord Barrett's desk. She was biting her lower lip and wringing her hands.

Harleigh walked up and reached for the map.

Eleanor made a grab for it.

Their father slapped his large hands down on top of the parchment. "E-e-nough! Sit down. Everyone, sit down."

☙

Giles noticed Elizabeth Archer's distress. He went to stand beside her chair.

Eleanor's hands were now on her hips and her expression—mulish.

Elizabeth Archer sighed. Sheepishly, she smiled up at Giles. "This isn't going as we had hoped."

"An astute observation, Miss Archer. What did you expect?"

"That we would be listened to," Libby said.

Giles' brows furrowed.

She tipped her head to the side, studying him. "Julia's life is at stake. Issues of propriety are irrelevant."

"Papa, please let me finish." Eleanor pointed at the map.

Harleigh took Eleanor by the shoulders and gave her a small shake. "Stop it, Ellie. You have outdone yourself."

Eleanor raised her voice. "You and Lord West will be wasting your time and throwing away any chance we have of getting Julia home unharmed if you limit your search to this county."

"Eleanor, be silent," Lord Barrett shouted.

Elizabeth Archer's hands trembled.

Giles leaned down. "Miss Archer, would you care to go for a walk?"

Relief washed over her face, and her shoulders relaxed. Giles offered his arm. As he closed the door behind them, the argument was continuing. He pointed to his left. "Shall we try the gardens?"

"Lord West, I thank you for getting me out of there. You must think me quite the coward for abandoning her. It's only that I've never been very good with shouters. It never seems to bother her. I'll go wait in the parlor."

Giles placed his hand over his heart. "You wound me, that you prefer an empty parlor to my company. As it happens, I think you're exceedingly levelheaded to get out of the line of fire."

Miss Archer chuckled softly. "Very well, the gardens it is."

As they stepped out onto the terrace, Giles recalled Miss Archer's damaged leg, and so guided her to a bench. He stood beside her. She kept shooting worried glances back at the house. "You're worried for her?"

"Julia?" Miss Archer said.

"I was thinking of Miss Barrett," Giles said.

"Both. When Eleanor loses her temper …" Miss Archer's lips pressed into a flat line.

"You're a loyal friend, Miss Archer."

"This has nothing to do with friendship or loyalty."

Giles smiled. He had underestimated Miss Archer—she had pluck. He wouldn't do so again. "A gentleman doesn't disagree with a lady."

"She loves a puzzle, you see, and is quite the deductionist. I know you all see her as meddling and troublesome."

Giles opened his mouth.

Libby held up her hand. "I assure you, m' lord, my loyalty to her doesn't extend to overlooking her character flaws. Ellie sees things—patterns and connections. And right now, I agree with her assessment of this situation."

"Again, I defer to your wisdom."

Miss Archer smiled. "Good man."

Giles' lips quirked.

"She warned me the odds were against us. This is all so infuriating. You men have so many more resources and liberties than we do."

"We mean only to protect and care for ..." Giles began.

Miss Archer gave a soft feminine derisive snort. "Please, my lord, that may be *your* intent, but you can't mean to stand there and claim that protection and care are the intent of every male member of the populace."

A picture of his ne'er-do-well brother-in-law, Lincoln Povey, jumped into his mind. No, not all men were interested in doing well by the women in their care, as Giles' sister Dolly was all too aware.

"I adore Eleanor's father. But right now, I challenge you to see the truth of what's being battled over in that study. It's his perception of his daughter's behavior in the eyes of society, instead of the welfare of those missing girls."

Giles gazed back at the house. Snippets of raised voices could still be heard. Elizabeth Archer was correct. Lord Barrett seemed to be berating Eleanor for her behavior. "I'm not sure how to respond. I would prefer to keep out of the dog's house where you're concerned."

Libby didn't respond.

"I think you and Miss Barrett want to change the world as we know it, and I'm not sure that's possible."

Libby smoothed her skirts. "I'm a patient woman."

"I believe you." Giles smiled, then his gazed shifted back to the house. "I wonder why those girls are the ones chosen?"

Libby perked up. "My, you do ask the right questions. Eleanor believes it's because they are well-fed and well cared for. But their fathers are insignificant and present no viable threat as they possess no political power, no money to pursue a private investigation, or the ability to call out the law."

"Hmmm, that's an interesting notion. Then those families have no recourse."

"I told you Ellie was clever."

"It appears the people in charge of this abduction ring are as well. This is no ordinary skullduggery. It's well thought out and paints a disturbing picture of a human mind that possesses not a shred of decency."

"Indeed." Libby shivered.

"Have you given any thought to the reason for the clustering of the dots?"

"We have, but as yet have discerned no meaning," Libby said.

Bang!

Libby startled.

Eleanor stood on the terrace, staring at the French doors and shaking what looked like their map at the house. "Libby!"

Libby jumped off the bench and moved towards Eleanor.

Eleanor hooked arms with her. "We're leaving."

Ↄ

Eleanor and Libby returned to the Archers'. They quickly secluded themselves in the privacy of Libby's bedroom. This room was pure Libby—the painted pale-yellow walls were inviting and the floor was covered with a thick Persian rug. Such an exotic touch for someone as sensible as her Lib.

This room had always been their sanctuary, the spawning ground for some of their early escapades. At ten they'd written their first Sisterhood manifesto, by twelve they were plotting their early missions—to discover what smoking a cigar tasted like, or to sip whiskey. It was here that Eleanor had first given voice to her dream of starting a secret society to help females less fortunate than themselves.

As soon as the door closed, Libby pounced. "What now?"

"I must send a message to my aunt." Eleanor paced through the middle of the room.

Libby clutched her hands together. "Because?"

Eleanor laced her fingers together behind her back and pulled her shoulders down. The tension in her upper back was excruciating.

Libby unfolded their map, tossed it down on the carpet beside her desk, then lowered herself down and used her hands to press the map flat. "Look here."

Eleanor kicked off her shoes. The woolen carpet felt scratchy beneath her stockinged feet. She knelt beside her friend. "Did I mention your map is exceptional?"

Libby blushed. "Several times, dear." She ran her fingertip over the clusters of dots she'd made on her map.

Eleanor leaned back, propped on her arms and said, "Think there are two gangs of child-stealers?'

"Millie said she knew of two brothels. And who knows, there could be more."

"Mmmmm, I think not," Eleanor said. "Too many similarities. I'm wagering it's one organization. But the thing that keeps deviling me is that bit about not understanding the girls' speech."

Libby cupped her chin and ran her index finger over her lower lip. "Well ... what makes someone *not* understandable?"

"Mumbling," Eleanor said.

"Oh, I hate that. Spit."

"Ewww." Eleanor grimaced.

"Being inebriated or talking too fast," Libby added.

"Accents." Eleanor tapped the fingertips of her hands together. "You know, when a person has a different native tongue."

"You mean like when someone from France tries to speak English?" Libby said. "'Hahow do you do, Meez Baarray?'"

Eleanor snorted and rolled onto her side laughing. "Very good. Once, Father took Mother, Callum, and me down to visit an old friend of his who lives near Penzance." She stabbed the county of Cornwall on the map. "Callum and I tried joining in a game with some of the local children but we couldn't understand them at all."

"Like what?" Libby asked.

"Um, let me see if I can remember any. '*Hanow vy ew* Eleanor. *Dhort Kynt th o'vy devedhys. Pe hanow ow'hwei?*'"

"What on earth did you just say?" Libby asked.

"My name is Eleanor. I come from Kent. What is your name?'" Eleanor drew her finger in lazy circles around and around the cluster of dots that populated the western counties and Wales. Her hand stilled. "Oh. Oh. Oh, my God."

"What?"

"What if the girls taken from Cornwall and Wales,"—she dragged her finger across the map to London— "ended up here?"

Libby thumped her fist down on top of the dots in Cumberland and Northumberland, making the paper crackle. "And these girls ended up in Bath?"

"That must be it," Eleanor said.

"You're brilliant."

"*We* are brilliant. Couldn't have figured it out without you, Meez Arshhrrr. Like always, we're the perfect complement—toast and marmalade."

"But Julia does not fit the pattern. Where do you think they've taken her?"

"Bath, since London is too close," Eleanor said.

"Disgustingly diabolical." Libby scrunched her nose as if she smelled something foul.

"It is, is it not?"

"Julia's speech is perfectly understandable, so why take her?" Libby said.

"She's quite beautiful, perhaps they couldn't resist."

"Ellie, should we go back to your father, now that we've figured this out?"

"We already told them they would be looking for her in the wrong place. All I got out of that interchange is a throbbing head from his scold."

"I seem to recall hearing your voice raised," Libby said.

"Of course, would you expect me to behave otherwise?"

"Ellie …?" Libby's voice held a note of worry.

"By the time they figure out that Julia isn't here, which shall take weeks, it'll be too late," Eleanor said as she rubbed her chin.

"Bath is so far away."

"I don't have all your answers yet,"—Eleanor balled up one hand into a fist and drove it into the flattened palm of her other hand—"but I swore this would *never* happen again."

"You swore? To whom?" Libby rocked forward, and Eleanor helped her to her feet.

"What did you say?" Eleanor had been thinking of Betty and didn't realize she'd spoken aloud.

"You said you swore," Libby repeated.

"It isn't important."

"I don't think you're telling me the truth," Libby said.

Eleanor didn't want to lie, but she'd promised Betty long ago she would never reveal her secret. "Please don't press me on this. It's someone else's secret. Not mine to tell."

"The swearing?" Libby's brows drew together in confusion.

"Not exactly," Eleanor said and she felt a small bubble of hope rising in her chest. She'd failed Betty, even after all these years she and Betty *never* talked about that terrible night. But now Eleanor was getting a chance to redeem herself by saving Julia. "Can you just forget I said anything?"

"For now," Libby said.

Eleanor sighed. She knew Libby wasn't done with this subject. They'd revisit it after Julia came home.

"Wish we knew who was behind this business," Libby said.

"Rooksby may have found out by now," Eleanor said.

"You've a great deal of faith in him." Libby placed her map under a book on her desk.

"The man knows things, Lib, secret things."

Libby shivered. "Ellie?"

Eleanor tapped her fingers against her lips. "Hmmm?"

"What's our next move?"

"To write my aunt," Eleanor said as she moved to Libby's desk, "to tell her to pick me up on her way to visit her bosom beau, Lady Sybil Standish, who just happens to live in Bath."

Libby rolled her eyes.

"You'll remain here and send updates on the search."

"Thought you were certain Julia wasn't here?"

Eleanor opened her mouth.

"I know what you're up to. Keeping me busy and safely out of the harm's way. Where I shan't be a liability, like the night we rescued Millie."

"Information is important too, just ask Rooksby," Eleanor said as she put her arm around Libby's shoulders and gave her a hug.

Libby shrugged. "All right, but on a practical matter, who's going to back you up?"

"We'll enlist Lady Sybil. She's a countess—widowed, poor dear. She used to be on the stage and Aunt Beatrice says she's always up for a lark."

"A lark?" Libby shook her head. "What you're contemplating is *no* lark. And you can't rescue Julia on your own and Lady Sybil is old."

"I shan't be on my own," Eleanor said.

"Who then?" Libby said and crossed her arms over her chest.

Eleanor was reviewing possible candidates.

"No-no-no-no. It's too dangerous."

"I'll ... I, I,"—Eleanor rubbed her forehead—"ask Millie to go. She can be my maid. A couple of weeks with Perdy will've given her sufficient polish."

Libby's brows drew together over her intense blue eyes.

"Don't dismiss her out of hand," Eleanor said.

"I'm not, but we've had no time to train her."

"True," Eleanor said. "But she has courage. And she's clever and not afraid of working hard."

"What's Millie supposed to do if you two get into a-a-a *situation*?"

"I'll figure something out," Eleanor said as she took Libby's hands.

"Time's running out. Waiting means some pox-ridden bastard will force himself on Julia before we can reach her."

"This all feels so tenuous," Libby said. "So many things can go awry."

"You know I can take care of myself."

"What I know is that you *think* you can take care of yourself," Libby said.

Chapter Thirteen

Two days later Eleanor sat beside her aunt, their great traveling coach lumbering westward. Millie sat opposite, looking every inch the lady's maid. She was decked out in a new simple dress of deep blue with a modest neckline, a utilitarian shawl thrown around her shoulders, and a small, no-nonsense straw bonnet perched on her head.

Bored by the endless hours of slow travel and plagued by cramped legs and a bum that had fallen asleep, Eleanor wistfully thought of her horse. "Wish I had my horse."

"Always were a restless child." Aunt Beatrice chuckled.

"Didn't realize I had spoken my thoughts," Eleanor said.

Aunt Beatrice fixed Eleanor with a shrewd gaze. "Im-patience should have been your middle name, not Augusta."

"Hah," Eleanor said.

Millie, who was wiggling and shifting around like someone had dropped a lizard down her back.

Eleanor tapped Millie on the knee. "Stop fidgeting, you look splendid."

"Really?" Millie perked up.

"Quite." Aunt Beatrice gave a nod of approval.

"Only one more night on the road, then we reach Bath." Eleanor pulled a sandwich from the hamper that rested on the floor. "Something to eat? Aunt?"

Lady Beatrice Whitley waved her niece off.

Eleanor pointed to the basket. "Millie?"

Beatrice leaned her elbow on the edge of the open carriage window and propped her chin on her open palm. "Wish Emory and Harleigh had shown a bit more sense."

"What are we supposed to do, linger until they realize the error of their thinking?" Eleanor said. "Your brother, *dear* aunt, called us 'hen-witted' and he turned positively scarlet when I mentioned where we think these girls are ending up."

"Poor Emory." Aunt Beatrice softly chuckled and said, "You're a trial for his poor nerves. Just like I was when he and I were children." She patted Eleanor's hand. "Just remember he provided you with an outstanding education."

"For a woman, you mean," Eleanor said.

"None of us is perfect, Ellie. I'm sure it's at moments like these that my brother questions his sanity."

Eleanor opened her mouth to retort.

"Why do you look at the speck of sawdust in your father's eye, and pay no attention to the plank in your own?" Aunt Beatrice said.

Eleanor looked down at the sandwich she was about to eat. "He's just so—so infuriatingly stubborn."

Her aunt smiled. "You mean like his daughter."

Eleanor laughed. "Point well made, Aunt."

Aunt Beatrice dabbed her handkerchief against her forehead to wipe away the perspiration. "Did Harleigh or Lord West say anything helpful?"

"Harleigh spluttered like a gassy tea kettle on the boil, just like Father," Eleanor said.

"Rooksby's informants say both brothels are owned by the same entity," Aunt Beatrice said.

"I guessed as much," Eleanor said.

"Indeed, the Black Rose Society?" Aunt Beatrice said.

"So, that be how you says it--soe-sy-itty," Millie said.

"Rooksby should have a list of members soon," Aunt Beatrice said. "He'll send his messenger to us in Bath."

"Got any more of them apples?" Millie held out her hand.

Eleanor enunciated each word. "Do you have any more of *those* delicious apples?"

Millie parroted Eleanor's speech.

"Bravo." Eleanor lobbed a shiny red apple at Millie, which she caught one-handed.

"Forcing children into prostitution is an abomination," Aunt Beatrice said. "And putting them where no one can understand their pleas for help… These people are depraved."

"Seems like these fellas have tought of everything." Millie stared at the apple resting in her hand. "But why these girls? There be plenty of chicks runnin' 'round London who've no one who will miss 'em—seems like they would be better pickin's."

"Those poor girls you're speaking of are sickly ragamuffins," Aunt Beatrice said. "These missing girls are well-fed, with sun-kissed cheeks, and shiny hair. The clientele of these establishments are wealthy men who'll pay a lot to bed a bona fide virgin.

"Virgin?" Millie's brows went up in confusion.

"These men,"—Aunt Beatrice's cheeks pinkened—"well, you see, Millie, we suspect that the men who are paying for the privilege of bedding these girls have contracted the French pox."

"You mean these fellas believe that ol' wives tale about virgins curing 'em?"

Aunt Beatrice frowned. "When you're desperate, even decent men will do the unthinkable."

"Don't seem decent to me, ma'am. Poxed or no, to force himself on a
child because he stuck his key in too many of the wrong sorta locks, if you get my meaning, it's—it's—well, it's just wrong is what."

"Well said. So now you see why we're so intent on finding Julia as fast as we can," Aunt Beatrice said.

"Oh, aye," Millie said. "I does. And I be ready to do me part."

Aunt Beatrice took Millie's hand and gave it a squeeze. "I'm grateful that Eleanor has you."

This time Millie's cheeks pinked.

Eleanor swallowed hard. They were risking everything. A ruined reputation was the least of it. She and Millie could be raped, maimed, or killed. She felt for the pistol in the pocket of her skirt. As her fingers wrapped around its wooden grip, she resolved to do whatever it took to bring them *all* home safe.

"You realize, Eleanor, that poor Julia isn't alone," Aunt Beatrice said.

"I hadn't given it any thought. That was certainly very short-sighted of me, was it not?"

"What tosh," Aunt Beatrice said. "I can't imagine the Brewsters not wanting Julia back, so she'll go home. But what's to happen to the other girls?"

Eleanor pondered.

"Having a safe place for those children afterward seems more imperative." Aunt Beatrice gave Eleanor an unwavering stare.

This problem was growing more complicated by the moment. "The school?" Eleanor said. "That was meant for the future, not now. I shan't come into my inheritance for years. How will we pay for a building, let alone a staff to care for the girls?"

"Whatcha talkin' 'bout?" Millie said.

Only Aunt Beatrice, Libby, and her friend Betty knew about Eleanor's dream of providing women and girls with an education and a safe harbor.

"Go on." Aunt Bea nudged Eleanor's arm. "Tell her."

"As it happens, Millie, you're our first ... a-a, hmmm, I'm not sure what to call you."

"How 'bout friend?" Millie smiled.

Eleanor grinned back. "Perdy and Mac were a Godsend to take you in when they did."

"Oh, aye." Millie nodded. "You all ha' changed my life, changed me for the better."

"For some time, we've been thinking about all the girls and women who don't get a chance at something better. We've been thinking of starting a school."

"A school?" Millie said.

"The Sisterhood School would be a haven to get them ready for their future," Aunt Beatrice said.

"Sisterhood?" Millie said.

"That's what we call ourselves," Eleanor said.

"I like the sound of that. I'm an only, never had no sisters." Millie's voice grew wistful. "Someplace safe and warm where they could learn to read and writes, like Perdy be teachin' me."

Aunt Beatrice added, "And numbers, so they could work in a shop."

"Or knows when they be cheated by the baker," Millie said.

"And we would teach each student to defend herself," Eleanor said.

Millie sat up straight. "You mean I could learn to do them things with my hands and feet,"—Millie chopped the air with the side of her hand— "like I seen you do?"

Aunt Beatrice and Eleanor chuckled.

"Would you like that?" Eleanor asked.

"Would I?" Millie cupped her face in her hands. "Good Lord, that would be the best present anybody ever done give me in my entire life." Millie flopped back against the carriage wall. "When does this school business start?"

Chapter Fourteen

Eleanor stepped down from the coach; her joints were stiff and her backside numb.

Visions of falling into a hot lavender-scented bath made her sigh.

"You're here!" A bright contralto trilled from on high.

Eleanor looked up as a lovely, aging beauty with yellow hair streaked with silver and a generous figure wearing a pink morning gown burst out of the townhouse.

"Out ta me way, Honeycutt. Out ta me way." The woman's voice was rich and commanding.

"As you wish, Madame," the man, who must be the aforementioned Honeycutt, said with perfect diction. He rolled his eyes heavenward and followed his exuberant mistress down the steps.

"Beatrice, my love, is that you?" The woman came to an abrupt halt beside the carriage and bounced on the balls of her well-shod feet.

"Good heavens, Sybil. What will your neighbors think?" Aunt Beatrice stepped from the coach, smiling.

"My neighbors be damned." Sybil flapped the air with one hand and then threw open her arms wide. "Give us a hug, Bea, dear. It's been too, too long."

Aunt Beatrice obliged and the two women hugged effusively.

"Good day, Honeycutt," Aunt Beatrice said, addressing the butler.

"Welcome back, Lady Whitley." Honeycutt winked at Aunt Beatrice.

Good heavens, what sort of establishment was this? They seemed to dance to their own tune. Aunt Beatrice was right, this was just the sort of company they needed to keep if they were going to rescue Julia.

"Lady Sybil Standish, allow me to present my niece, Miss Eleanor Barrett, and this young woman is Eleanor's maid, Miss Mildred Nichols."

"How do you do, Lady Standish?" Eleanor smiled and tipped her head.

Millie bobbed a curtsy.

"Oh, they're lovely, Bea. Come along, come along, I'm sure you all could use a freshen-up and a good cup of tea. Hmmm?" Lady Standish lifted her skirts and moved up the steps like a girl of twenty.

As Aunt Beatrice and Lady Standish disappeared into the house, several well-setup footmen appeared from the bowels of the residence. The young males swarmed around the carriage and began unloading. Eleanor spotted Millie giving several of the young men a good looking over.

Eleanor hooked arms with Millie and began towing her up the front steps. "None of that."

"Come now, Miss Eleanor, young single girls like us always have a moment or two to takes—I mean, take a look." Millie chuckled.

When Eleanor, Aunt Beatrice, and Lady Sybil went to the upper parlor following dinner, Honeycutt and Millie soon joined them. They gathered, as Aunt Beatrice pronounced, for a council of war. Not one word was spoken until Millie firmly shut the door behind Honeycutt.

Lady Sybil waved everyone into chairs. "Sit down, Honeycutt, and you too, Miss Nichols."

Millie sat, but Honeycutt stood at attention at Lady Sybil's right shoulder.

"Have we heard anything from Rooksby, Aunt?" Eleanor asked.

"Rooksby?" Lady Sybil said, "my, this must be serious if you're involving that rascal."

"You're acquainted with Mr. Rooksby, Lady Sybil?" Eleanor asked.

"But of course, dear, he was one of my ..."

"Legion of admirers," Honeycutt muttered.

"Yes, well, that was before I met my dear Benjamin." Lady Sybil clasped her hands beneath her chin. "Lord Standish put everyone else in the shade, I'm afraid, even Rooksby."

Honeycutt rolled his eyes and Aunt Beatrice chuckled.

"Rooksby is the best man for the job. As my dear departed Jasper used to advise me, always use the best—lives depend on it." Aunt Beatrice
turned to Eleanor. "There was a messenger waiting when we arrived, dear."

"And?" Eleanor scooted forward.

"We now know the address. The Madame is Dutch. Her name is Dagmar Lutz."

"The owner?" Eleanor asked.

"Rooksby believes she has a secret partner, probably a peer."

"Only one? Then why call it The Black Rose Society?" Eleanor couldn't sit still, so she jumped up and paced.

"Perversity, I suppose. Makes the operation appear larger and therefore more formidable," Aunt Beatrice said.

"Does Rooksby know who?" Eleanor said.

"He thinks he'll have that bit of information in a day or two."

"Not having the name won't prevent Millie and me from taking up our positions within Madame Lutz's establishment. Who knows, we might beat Rooksby to it. But our priority is Julia."

"Agreed," Beatrice said, gazing intently at Eleanor—and there was an entire world of warning in that look. "If Rooksby is correct about the Madame's partner, you realize this makes things more complicated."

"You mean if this were just some avaricious, unscrupulous bastard, we'd just call in the magistrate," Eleanor said. "Instead, we're dealing with an avaricious unscrupulous bastard *with* a title, so justice will *not* be forthcoming."

"Ellie, we'll count our blessings if you, Millie, and Julia come out of this unharmed. You know perfectly well that equality and therefore justice, under the law, has always been an illusion."

"Hear, hear," Lady Sybil said.

Honeycutt's voice was sonorous. "The golden eye of justice sees, and requites, the unjust man."

Lady Beatrice and Lady Sybil snorted.

"I work for that day, Mr. Honeycutt," Eleanor said. "I work very hard."

"Indeed." Honeycutt gave a quick affirmative nod.

Lady Sybil waved them all closer. "Don't worry, dears. Honeycutt and I have it all figured out."

ℭ

The clock in the entryway to the gentlemen's club chimed three o'clock. Sunrise was only a few hours away. Edgerton lounged comfortably in an over-sized oxblood leather chair, when a footman approached with a note. A puff of pungent blue-gray smoke sailed between himself and his companion, Sir Lincoln Povey, the-not-so-esteemed brother-in-law of Giles, Lord West.

Edgerton had few companions and fewer friends. Povey fell into the

first camp. Edgerton gazed at Povey and wondered how long his tolerance for their association would continue. He supposed it depended on how long Povey's company continued to amuse him. Since childhood, loneliness had been Edgerton's *bon ami*, except for the times he spent with Giles. How good it was to have him back in England.

"Business?" Povey pointed with his cigar at the paper in Edgerton's hand.

"Of a sort?"

"Our sort?" Povey leered as he licked his thick lips. His protuberant bloodshot eyes, damp fleshy face, and green-striped waistcoat reminded Edgerton of a lascivious amphibian.

"Most assuredly, dear Lincoln. A new shipment has arrived," Edgerton said as he re-folded the note and tapped his chin with it as he gazed into the fire. "I'm for Bath. Can you come?"

"Not tonight. Have to deal with dear Dolly and the kiddies."

"How is your sweet wife?"

"As much of a pain in my arse as ever." Lincoln Povey's mouth turned down.

"Ah, marital bliss. If not tonight, when?"

Povey shrugged. "A few days."

Edgerton rose and touched the tip of his cigar to the paper in his hand,
when it began to smolder, he dropped it into the fireplace and watched the flames consume it. "Send word and I'll pick you up."

"I can meet you there." Povey sipped his drink.

"It's no bother." Edgerton's smile was slow and tight-lipped.

"You are kindness personified."

"I live to please…" Edgerton bowed his head and laid his hand over his heart in a parody of humility.

Povey let loose a boom of laughter that sounded like a braying ass—not one of his more endearing qualities.

Head still bent, Edgerton rolled his eyes up to look at his companion and completed his declaration, "… to please myself, above all others."

Chapter Fifteen

"It's quiet here tonight." Giles shifted his weight and the leather soles of his shoes squeaked as he planted his feet beside the billiard table in preparation for taking his shot. Leaning forward, he sighted down the slope of the cue. Drawing back the stick, he potted the ball then moved around the corner to take aim on the next.

"You mean *too* damned quiet, now that Eleanor's gone." Harleigh leaned his hip against the table and stared at the tip of the cue in his hand. "Am I going to get a shot, *any* time tonight?"

"You're irked because we've not found the Brewster girl." Giles thought if he ignored the reference to Eleanor, he could keep his attention on his billiard game.

The search for the missing Julia absorbed Giles completely during the day, but the nights… His nights were filled with dreams of Eleanor and plotting how he was going to change her mind about marriage. But first she'd have to come back to Barrett Hall.

That night in the garden, he hadn't wanted to stop kissing her. And he was sure she'd felt the same. He could feel it in the way her body responded to his. Holding Eleanor was like holding fire and passion and joy. He'd thought he'd left that all behind him in Italy, but he'd been wrong. He'd wanted to explore the side of Eleanor's neck with his lips. Feel her shiver with desire. His hands trembled as his body remembered the feel of her skin. He missed his shot.

"Finally, I get a turn," Harleigh said and leaned over the table, taking aim, then he snapped upright. "Yes, damn it. I admit it. I'm— what did you call me? —irked. And troubled. What if my stick-her-nose-in-where-it-does-not-belong little sister is right? What if Julia is *not* here?"

"What do you want to do?"

Harleigh tapped his cue against the table's edge.

The silence stretched.

"Do you think your aunt looked much in need of the salubrious waters of Bath?" Giles asked.

Harleigh came out of his meditation and took aim on a ball. "What? No, not much."

"Want to bet they're up to something?" Giles said.

"Who?" Harleigh said.

"Your sister and Lady Whitely."

"They're women. Women are always up to something, and especially those two." Harleigh pointed his cue at Giles. "In fact, I can say with absolute certainty that there has never been a time when Aunt Beatrice and Eleanor were *not* up to something. I swear sometimes Ellie seems more like Aunt Beatrice's daughter than her niece. Even Father says so."

"I've this gnawing suspicion their rapid departure has more to do with Miss Brewster than your aunt's health," Giles said.

Harleigh interrupted his shot. "Do you?"

"And that map of theirs... I can still see those clustering marks. The ones from the northern counties and the ones in the—."

"West." Harleigh squinted at the table. "Bath is in the west."

Giles tipped his cue downward in a syncopated fashion to emphasize his word. "Precisely."

"Damn it," Harleigh said. "When you put it like that it seems clear as glass. Let's go have another look at that map of theirs."

"I believe they took it with them," Giles said.

"Riiight." Harleigh shook his head.

"There were a lot of dots on that impressive map of theirs, Harls. The plaguy issue of Eleanor and your aunt aside, what if they're correct and Julia isn't here?"

Harleigh looked at him with troubled eyes. He grabbed his glass and took a long swallow of whiskey, grimaced, then wiped his mouth with the back of his hand. "Remember when I said I'd heard rumors?"

"Yes," Giles said, feeling uneasy that this conversation was about to take a turn toward Edgerton.

"Well, some of the talk was about Edgerton, but some of it was of a new brothel. Caters to men who have certain needs."

Giles waited for Harleigh to continue.

"At the club last week, I overheard Lord Taswell—"

"You mean that pox-ridden old fellow?" Giles said. "Thought he'd be dead or in Bedlam by now."

"He was going on about getting his hands"—Harleigh shivered— "on a bona fide virgin."

"You jest?"

"Wish I was," Harleigh said with a look of utter revulsion on his face. "Not the run o' the mill either, he said. Plump, well-fed, clean. That's a quote by the way."

Giles felt like he wanted to cast up his dinner. "Do you think that's what Eleanor and Libby believe is happening to those missing girls?"

Harleigh rubbed his stomach.

"Are you about to be sick?"

"Christ, why did a bunch of girls barely out of the schoolroom see more than we did?"

"Because this is Eleanor we're talking about," Giles said as he put his cue back in the rack. "Mind if we stop playing?"

Harleigh put his cue back in the rack as well. "Not at all. What if Julia's been taken to Bath?"

"As sickly as Taswell is, I'd wager his brothel is in London," Giles said.

"But Eleanor didn't go to London, did she?" Harleigh said.

Chapter Sixteen

Eleanor sat up and rubbed her eyes. The mantel clock said five o'clock. "Hmmph." She flopped back into her pillows and pulled the covers up. Then she heard scratching on her door.

Throwing back the covers, she flew from the bed and cracked the door open.

"Let me in, Miss Eleanor." Eleanor stepped back and Millie slid through the opening.

Millie wore a different dark plain blue dress of modest length. The material of this garment was coarse, and she had a cheap white muslin fichu tucked in around her neck to camouflage her cleavage. Her hair was pulled straight back and pulled up in a no-nonsense arrangement. Her face was scrubbed and she wore a dainty plain cap atop her upswept hair. The whole ensemble was topped off with a small straw hat that tied under the chin with thin strips of faded blue ribbon. The hat looked like a cast-off and so did her gloves, with tiny mending stitches evident between her fingers. She had a rough woolen shawl wrapped around her shoulders.

Eleanor rubbed her eyes. "What's happened to you? And what on earth are you doing up and dressed at this ungodly hour?"

"First off, Lady Sybil and Mr. Honeycutt is what got hold of me. And believe it or not, miss, this is the hour all good servants are up and about."

"Oh." Eleanor felt like a fool. "Well, I guess that's my first lesson."

"So, what do ye' think?" Millie twirled about.

"What happened to your new shoes?" Eleanor stared at Millie's feet.

"Mr. Honeycutt scuffed 'em up. Gotta looks—I mean look—like I'm desperate for a job." Millie winked. "I'm off to apply for a post at Madame Lutz's."

"Well then, I say you look perfect." Eleanor ran to her dresser to get her reticule. "Here, let me give you some money."

"Lady Sybil's done taken care of that." Millie held her gloved hand aloft and a worn reticule hung down from her wrist.

Eleanor heard the jingling of coins. "What about some folding money?"

Millie tapped the top of her left breast. "Tucked nice and safe and outta sight."

Eleanor pursed her lips. "Seems like you three have thought of everything." She pointed to a chair. "Let's review your story once more."

"If we must." Millie sat.

Eleanor paced. "What's your name?"

"Mildred Nichols."

Eleanor gave Millie a hard stare.

"Oh." Millie sat up straighter. "Mildred Nichols, ma'am."

"Right. Don't forget to be extremely proper. Honeycutt says Madame Lutz has a reputation for formality and strict obedience to her rules." Eleanor paused. "You're not from here, Miss Nichols?"

Millie looked startled.

"Well?" Eleanor made her voice sound menacing.

Millie lowered her head.

"Keep your story as close to the truth as possible."

"I am from London, ma'am."

"What brings you to Bath?"

"I wuz promised work by a lady who was comin' here."

"What happened?"

"She sent me on ahead but she never arrived. And I've no money to get back home."

"Why did you come to my house?"

"I heard you might need someone," Millie said.

"From whom did you hear that, Miss Nichols?"

"I ease-dropped on a couple a cooks' helpers down at the market yesterday."

"Did your eavesdropping inform you what goes on here in my house?"

"I need work and I am a hard worker."

"Let me see your hands."

Millie held out her gloved hands.

"Take them off." Eleanor flicked her index finger against the back of Millie's gloved right hand.

Millie took off her gloves and held her hands out.

Eleanor saw Millie's hands tremble. She took Millie's hands firmly in hers and turned them palm up, then rubbed her thumb over Millie's calluses.

"Whatcha lookin' for?"

"Quiet."

Millie shut her mouth tight.

"If you come to work for me, I demand obedience. Do you understand, Nicholz?"

Millie nodded.

"Excellent job. Make sure you get something to eat before you go."

"Oh, no. Mr. Honeycutt says I should go hungry, it will add to my performance as someone desperately needin' a job. 'Tis why he has made me wear a dress that's too big. See?" Millie pinched the fabric at her waist and pulled it out so Eleanor could see the dress was too large. "Said I need to look like I been missing meals. Makes me more needy and more willin' to work for the likes of her."

"He did, did he? He's a crafty one, our Mr. Honeycutt." Eleanor shook her head and smiled. "Remarks like those make me wish I could have seen him and Lady Sybil on the stage."

"Before her Ladyship stole the heart of Lord Standish and married up?"

"Exactly. And who told you she stole his heart?"

"Mr. Honeycutt. Can't figure him out. One minute he is all stuffy, the next he is telling some naughty joke and the next he is treatin' me like a favored child. I tell ye' it sets my head spinnin'."

"Take care of yourself, Millie," Eleanor said.

"I will. Can't wait to see what he does to you." Millie chuckled. "Wonder if I'll even recognize you."

"I'll see you at our lodgings early tomorrow morning."

Millie crossed to the door. "Aye, miss."

"You realize if they're suspicious of you at all you'll be followed home."

Millie nodded. "Bet she trusts no one. I'm countin' on havin' a shadow."

"Just head straight for the boardinghouse. Someone we trust will be watching out for you. And, Millie?" Eleanor hesitated a moment, then threw her arms about Millie and gave her a hug. "Thank you for helping us rescue Julia. I couldn't pull this off without you."

Millie turned pink. "Pish posh."

The door closed behind Millie. Eleanor stared at it as a painful gnawing nibbled at her stomach. Millie was out there alone now.

Chapter Seventeen

The next morning, when the sky was still the color of pitch, Honeycutt escorted Eleanor to the new lodgings she and Millie would share. It was a non-descript boardinghouse overseen by two of Rooksby's people: their landlady, a Mrs. Greystone, and a small boy of indeterminate age who possessed considerable street smarts and answered to the name of Freddy. There were no other boarders.

Eleanor and Honeycutt had arrived just as a town clock had struck half past two. Sequestered behind the false wall in the boardinghouse kitchen's larder, they sat in a secret parlor. This hidden room gave Eleanor the sense that shed stepped out of time. She dozed and awoke, dozed and awoke as she sat in the winged chair. Only the fire in the hearth that had now burned down to ash speckled with a few tenacious glowing embers gave her any sense that hours had passed and dawn must be approaching.

The large, fat candle on the wobbly table beside her was the only source of light. She had tucked her stocking-covered feet up under her and thrown her cloak over her legs.

Her eyes drifted closed.

Something was pushing at her. She cracked her eyes open and beheld
Millie peering down at her. Eleanor swung her legs out from under her bottom and jumped up to greet her friend, but the cramps in her calves and the crick in her neck made her unsteady.

A large warm hand circled her arm.

Eleanor's instincts took over and she jumped out of the hold and whirled around and crouched into a fighting position, ready to strike. In her groggy state, she hadn't heard or sensed anyone else in the room but Millie. Master Sakegawa wouldn't be pleased that she was taken unaware.

"Good morning, miss." A rich baritone voice elocuted beside her.

"Miss, it's just our Mr. Honeycutt," Millie's voice soothed.

Eleanor stood, lowered her hands, and cleared her throat.

"Miss Nichols informed me you were an accomplished fighter."

Eleanor shot Millie a look of displeasure. "Did she?"

Honeycutt stepped closer. "I see she didn't exaggerate. Come along, we've a lot to do to get you ready." He set a rectangular box that smelled peculiar on the table beside the chair Eleanor had vacated.

"What do you want me to do?" Eleanor said.

"Strip." Honeycutt knelt and emptied the contents of his large duffel: one dirty skirt, tattered hose, old boots, garters, petticoats, an apron, an old fashioned misshapen bonnet, and the strangest looking concoction of leather straps and ties.

Millie toed the leather bits. "And what, pray tell, is that?"

Eleanor peered over Millie's shoulder. "Looks to be some sort of harness."

"Excellent guess." Honeycutt handed Eleanor a chemise that had been cut off and looked like it would end somewhere in the region of her hips, and a pair of gray flannel pantaloons.

"Millie, can you help me out of my garments?" Eleanor said.

"Miss Nichols? Have her put these on." Honeycutt handed over garters, holey stockings and a short set of unadorned stays that had some interesting additional pockets sewn into them.

"You keeps your back turned, do you hear me, Mr. Honeycutt?" Millie sniffed. "Even though you been good to me, I'll give you a swift kick if'n I see your face lookin' our way."

"Understood, Miss Nichols."

"And quit calling me Miss Nichols. Call me Millie or do not call me at'll."

"What's the matter, Millie? You're behaving like a wet cat. I thought you were looking forward to seeing what Mr. Honeycutt would do to me?"

Millie sighed. "I'm worried for ye. Ye ha' never been in a place like this."

Eleanor squeezed Millie's hand. "I shan't be alone. I have you." She stripped to her skin and donned Honeycutt's proffered undergarments.

"Now what?" Millie asked.

Honeycutt pointed to the floor directly in front of him. "Miss Eleanor, please present yourself for the next phase of your transformation. Here, put this robe on. We'll do your face, hands, arms, and hair next." He handed Eleanor a pot of dark paste. "Put some of this on your fingertip and rub it all over your teeth and gums. Millie, please light that lamp and bring it over here."

"What is this?" Eleanor asked.

"A concoction of mine. It'll stain your teeth and gums. We'll use it on your hands and nails as well, and when we rub a ring of it on the back of your neck it does an admirable job of making it look as though you haven't bathed in ages."

Eleanor took a whiff and then quickly held the pot at arm's length. "Ooff, smells dreadful."

Honeycutt leaned down and smelled. "Forgot that part, but it'll not harm you aside from the fact that when this escapade is over it'll take many scrubbings to return your skin and teeth to their present pristine state."

Eleanor dipped her pinky into the pot.

Honeycutt pulled several more containers and some brushes out of his box. "You see, we do not dare use paint as I would if you were on the stage. A careless swipe of your hand would divest you of your disguise and that would be disastrous."

"Will this stand up under scrutiny?" Eleanor asked.

"To a point. But I have another stratagem in mind to keep people at a distance."

"And that would be?" Eleanor asked.

"It has two parts." He handed Millie a container. "Miss—I mean Millie, would you be so kind as to go and heat this concoction up just a bit?"

Millie took it and lifted the lid. "P-uuuu, smells like cooked cabbage and onions."

"Righto. Miss Eleanor, you must eat most of it."

"This here's poor folks' food and it's bound to give her, you know ..." Millie waved her hand behind herself as if she were fanning her bum. "Make her windy."

Honeycutt grinned broadly. "Precisely. It'll give her the most stupendously stinky farts."

Eleanor chuckled.

"What's the second part?" Millie said.

He reached into his bag and withdrew a large round object. "Raw onions. I shall be rubbing her skirts with them."

Once Eleanor applied the staining compound and rinsed her mouth several times, Honeycutt applied a fake wart with some noxious smelling glue above her left eyebrow. Millie helped secure Eleanor's hair and then applied a tight cap. Honeycutt set the gray-and-black-streaked wig on Eleanor's head and secured it to the cap with some hateful pins that scraped across Eleanor's scalp. He kept having her shake her head, and every time the wig moved he added another pin.

"And now the *pièce de résistance*." Honeycutt held up the leather strap contraption.

Eleanor and Millie gawked.

"It's my own invention. When I played Richard III, I designed this harness to keep me bent over throughout the performance. It changes your entire attitude when you cannot stand upright. Your whole view of the world and your place in it is altered. This 'contraption,' as you called it, made my performance memorable, I'd even go as far as saying it was the best performance of my career. It also gave me a visceral understanding of the life of a cripple I have never forgotten."

Eleanor clapped her hands together. "You're a genius. We're most fortunate to have you as a member of our troupe."

The first padded leather band circled Eleanor's chest, right beneath her arms, with straps over her shoulders. A second leather band girdled her hips with a strap that passed between her legs.

Eleanor lifted a leather strip that was sewn to the center of the strap circling her chest. "And where does this bit go?"

"It's the tether. As soon as I tie it to the piece circling your hips, you shan't be able to stand erect."

ȡ

When Eleanor, nee Ethel Boggs, left the boarding house over an hour later, she smelled like she hadn't bathed or washed her clothes in a couple of months. Honeycutt had rubbed raw onion over the lower edge of her petticoat, she had small leather pouches in her cheeks that he'd called plumpers, and he'd rubbed a gritty substance over her hands and let it dry, making her skin look and feel rough. She left with her stomach growling.

As Eleanor hobbled down the mews that ran behind the row of houses that included the brothel, she stopped at each carriage house and asked if they knew anyone who could use a good charwoman.

Ethel waited outside the kitchen door of the brothel. When one of the kitchen helpers stepped outside, Ethel was waiting. The girl eyed her up and down and Ethel knew she was about to get the heave-ho so she turned the girl up sweet.

The girl left Ethel waiting on the porch. When the kitchen helper returned, she was accompanied by a large bulky young man with brutish features and whitish-blond hair whom the girl called Mr. Barend.

"You look for work, gran-mudder?" Barend said.

Ethel dipped a wobbly curtsy. "Aye, I be the best charwoman in Trowbridge."

Barend looked enquiringly at the kitchen helper. "Wha' iz dis Trowbridge?"

"Town, next county over, sir."

A tall buxom woman with dark-blond hair piled on her head and wearing a luxurious gown came up behind Barend. "Vhat keeps you?"

"Dis one vants vork." Barend pointed to Ethel.

"Have ve replazed the night charvoman?" Madame asked him.

Barend shook his head.

"Gran-mooder," Madame Lutz said.

Eleanor cocked her thumb and pointed to her chest. "Me?"

"Ja, you gran-mooder, come back tonight at eight o'clock."

"Yes, ma'am." Eleanor bobbed her head. "Thank you, ma'am."

"And, gran-mooder, if you are not here at eight precisely, do not bodder coming at all." Madame Lutz sauntered away.

The sun was full up when Eleanor hobbled back to the boardinghouse.

Honeycutt hadn't lied. Being unable to stand erect gave you a whole new perspective, as well as a sore back. To prevent anyone knowing her destination, Eleanor walked to the next block over and entered the building that backed onto their boardinghouse. She used a subterranean passage running between the two buildings. When Eleanor reached the underground portcullis, designed to prevent unwanted visitors from gaining access, she signaled Freddy, and he'd raise the gate.

Eleanor trudged up to their room. Millie was fast asleep. For a moment, Eleanor thought about slamming the door shut, to rouse Millie, so she could help her out of the harness, but that would be too cruel.

Eleanor toed-off her heavy boots. When the right one hit the floor, her small boot dagger slipped from its sheath. She bent over, picked it up and shoved it back inside her boot top. Retrieving her twig flintlock from the pocket in her underskirt, she placed the gun under what passed for her pillow.

Ready for sleep, Eleanor grabbed the edge of the woolen blanket that covered her cot, turned sideways and collapsed onto the bed, drawing the coarse blanket over her shoulders. She was too tired to think and quickly fell asleep.

It was twilight when Freddy came to wake them; she and Millie ate a Spartan meal and left for work. They planned to make a ta-doo at the brothel tonight that they lived near one another so they'd have an excuse to walk home together.

Eleanor barely saw Millie at the brothel, only if they passed one another in the kitchen. Millie worked as an upstairs maid, changing bed linens, bringing hot water or trays of food to the patrons.

Eleanor scooped up buckets of ash from dead fires, washed floors, dusted, waxed and scuttled around, making herself useful, using every opportunity to discover where the new girls were held.

She could go everywhere except the third floor. Each time she got close to the door leading to the top of the house, Pim, another one of Madame's thugs, or Barend was there turning her away, and not gently either. Pim and Barend reminded Eleanor of each other, big, blond, and dour. She could barely tell them apart.

On her first day, one of them intentionally tripped her. With her harness on she couldn't break her fall. As she lay face down on the second-floor hall runner, the great oaf put his foot on her back and held her down and laughed. Millie arrived and put a stop to his fun.

One afternoon, Ethel plodded through the kitchen door and saw there were fresh green herbs lying on the table waiting for Cook to chop. She found herself longing for just one mint or parsley leaf to chew on to refresh her mouth. She had yet to become inured to the taste of Honeycutt's concoction coating her teeth. Not even bread slathered in butter tasted as it should.

The cook waved her knife at Ethel. "Get yerself back to the scullery where you belong." Life as a servant was eye-opening. When this was over, Eleanor didn't think she would look at an empty chamber pot or a morning fire the same way again.

The end of their work day came just after sunrise. Ethel and Millie would walk out the back door of the brothel together. There was a path that ran beside the house and ended at a gate that led into the mews.

The grooms and footmen liked to stand around that gate, smoking and telling bawdy stories. One morning one of the footmen, who must've been thinking with his nether parts, grabbed Millie's breast as they walked by. Ethel had had enough. She pretended to stumble, knocking Millie aside and falling into the handsy footman.

Ethel ground her boot heel into his toes. He howled in pain and jumped, trying to pull his foot from under Ethel's boot. He was off balance so she brought her head up right under his chin, snapping his head back.

"So sorry, young fella. Did I hurt ye?" Eleanor patted the bastard's cheek like she was his own granny.

Everyone laughed, badgering him for letting an old woman best him.

"Come along, Millie." Eleanor grabbed Millie's arm and they left.

They walked a few blocks in silence. Eleanor strained to hear every sound. It had rained all night. As the day began, the city was still being held hostage beneath a bank of black clouds that seemed chained to Bath's rooftops. The wet pavement with its myriad puddles muffled every sound, making it doubly hard to hear if anyone was following them. Eleanor pulled Millie into a niche between two buildings.

"Wha?" Millie grabbed Eleanor's shoulder. "Yah, hear sumpin?"

"Shhhhh." Eleanor held her finger to her lips.

"Someone's followin' us, ain't they?"

"Just being careful," Eleanor said.

"You got sumpin under them skirts of yers I don't know about? Like mebe a knife?"

Eleanor chuckled softly. "Actually, I have two, *and* a gun."

Millie made a choking sound.

Moments of tense silence, then Eleanor stepped from their hiding place. "Aw, well, must be my nerves and imagination getting the better of me."

"This here business is makin' me as jumpy as a flea on farmer Dubbin's old dog."

"Come along." Eleanor tugged Millie's arm.

"Ye found anything?" Millie asked.

"Not yet. You?" Eleanor glanced up at Millie.

"Alls I can say is they got a lot of secrets in that house." Millie shook her head. "Makes me feel dirty jus to be there."

"Well, they won't let me near that third floor." Eleanor shuffled along beside Millie, her head down against the wind.

"Still?" Millie tucked her shawl tighter and buried her hands in its woolen folds.

"It's been a couple of days—they must at least need the chamber pots emptied." Eleanor sniffled.

"Humph, you would figure, wundcha."

Eleanor thought longingly of a nice clean handkerchief to blow her nose. "Can't imagine Barend or Pim carrying a loaded pot, can you?"

They both snorted with laughter.

"Those two give me the creeping wibbles," Millie said as she tucked a loose lock of hair behind her ear.

Eleanor nodded.

"How're yer hands holding up?" Millie asked.

"I wrapped them in rags, padding them up, see?" She held her hands up.

Millie nudged Eleanor's shoulder playfully. "Yer sumpin' else. Never thought you would make it a single day."

As usual, Eleanor parted company with Millie a block from the boarding house. Millie continued down Saw Close and Eleanor lingered in the shadows long enough to see Millie climb the front steps of their boardinghouse.

At this early hour of the morning, Freddy was still fast asleep so Millie would open the portcullis when Eleanor gave the signal. Once through, it was Eleanor's habit to wait until it dropped closed behind her.

"Ouch." She bumped her elbow on the wall of the passage as she tried to scratch a particularly prickly spot on her lower back. She couldn't smell herself anymore.

Eleanor held her small candle aloft as she made her way through the darkness and tried to keep thoughts of a hot bath and lavender-scented soap out of her mind. She heard a moving, scratching sound coming from the floor and then felt a mouse run over her boot; she told herself it was a mouse, because the possibility that it was the mouse's larger cousin made Eleanor's stomach pitch.

Keep moving.

She reached the portcullis and pulled the cord that would make the peg bauble about up in the hallway, signaling Millie. She pulled twice, but the gate didn't move.

Eleanor's breathing accelerated. Millie must be in trouble.

"Damn it!" Frightening possibilities lashed Eleanor's mind as she backed away. She took a few hurried steps backward and lost her balance when she stepped on something soft that squealed in outrage. She wedged her forearms against the walls to keep from falling. The portcullis began to rise. Eleanor hurried forward. She didn't wait for it to close.

Within minutes, a thin horizontal crack of grayish light appeared ahead of her about ten feet up, indicating she neared the tunnel's end. When she reached the bottom of the ladder, she was panting. She blew out her candle and dropped it. As she cleared the last rung of the ladder, she paused on the ledge and pressed her ear to the door, which was the hidden entrance to the tunnel. Her hand rested on the latch. Suddenly, the door jerked open and Eleanor fell forward. A strong hand grabbed her collar and hauled her through.

Eleanor's nostrils flooded with the aromas of expensive men's cologne, clean skin, and shirt starch. How many? She got a painful, large lump of fear in her throat.

"I'll get the light," a familiar voice said off to her left.

As the single candle on the table flashed to life, Eleanor beheld Millie's fearful face with a large hand covering her mouth.

The harness made it impossible to maneuver into a defensive posture, so Eleanor went by instinct and dropped her weight. Her captor fell to the floor next to her and she broke free and rolled away.

"Christ, what ya' do that for?"

Eleanor got up and backed away until she stood against the wall farthest from Millie in the deepest shadows. What the hell were they doing here? They'd ruin everything.

Harleigh got up off the floor and brushed himself off. "Who the hell are *you*?"

Eleanor made her hands tremble and she wouldn't look Harleigh in the face.

He gentled his voice. "I'm sorry I frightened you. But we're looking for my sister, Miss Eleanor Barrett. Do you know her, old woman?"

He-he-he, you don't recognize me. Eleanor wanted to hop around, shouting 'fooled you.' But *this* was certainly not the time.

She sidled along the wall till she neared Millie. When the light illuminated the face of the man holding Millie, Eleanor squeezed her eyes shut in disbelief. She tugged on Giles' arm to indicate he should let go of Millie. "Gerr off, my friend."

Giles let go of Millie and looked down at Eleanor. "Madame,"— he rubbed the end of his nose, obviously trying not to breathe too deeply— "you smell like the Fleet Ditch."

Eleanor cackled. "And how would ye know, laddie? Spent much time in it, have ye?"

Millie, who now cowered behind Eleanor, let out a small gasp.

"I was using a simile, Madame." Giles scowled down at her.

"Eh? Did no one ever tell ye— 'tisn't nice to talk like that when theres females present."

Harleigh choked on a laugh.

Eleanor turned and grabbed Millie's arm and towed her toward the staircase. Eleanor shoved Millie and she took the hint and raced up the steps.

"Excuse me, Madame, but have you seen my sister here about?"

"I dunno no Miz Brr-ett." With her back to the front door and stooped over, Eleanor began to climb. She made it up to the third step when a soft *woof* came from the darkness behind Giles and Harleigh.

"Let her go, Rodrigo," Giles said.

Eleanor put her hand on the rail and took several steps up the staircase. Hearing claws on the bare wood floor of the entryway reminded her of rats, and she grimaced. The collie trotted out of the shadows. He put his front paws on the first step and he clamped the lower edge of Eleanor's skirt between his teeth.

She grabbed her skirt and tried to take another step. Rodrigo tugged harder. She lost her footing and toppled backward onto Giles West.

He looked disgusted as he pushed her upright. "Terribly sorry, but my dog seems to have taken a dislike to you."

"Huh? Well I ne'er." Eleanor stuck her nose in the air. She looked over her shoulder, up into Giles' face.

He was holding his breath. "Now that is certainly hard to believe," Giles muttered.

"Whatsat you say?" Eleanor gave him the evil eye.

Giles cleared his throat. "Nothing."

Eleanor got up and climbed another step.

Woof. Eleanor felt Rodrigo's paws in the center of her back. She fell forward.

"Down, Rodrigo." Giles rushed forward.

Eleanor lay face down, sprawled up several steps.

Woof. Softer this time and accompanied by a wet, cold nose in her ear.

"All right. All right." Eleanor waved her hand over her head, then she rolled to her side and sat up. Rodrigo licked her face. "Couldn't fool you, could I, Roddy, me boy?"

Rodrigo licked her face again.

Eleanor threw her arm around Rodrigo's neck and gave him a big squeeze and nuzzled him behind his ear. She was rewarded by another sloppy tongue bath.

Harleigh brought the candle closer and leaned down to get a closer look. "Ellie?"

From the top of the stairs, Millie whispered, "You all right, miss?"

"Fine. Go on to bed. I'll be up shortly."

"Oh, no you won't," Harleigh said. "You're coming back to Lady Standish's with us this instant."

Giles West scowled down at her. "His name is Rodrigo."

Harleigh leaned in to grab her arm, then swayed backward like someone had given him a punch. "My word, you smell like a-a—"

"Like the Fleet Ditch?" Giles provided.

Eleanor scowled. It wasn't so much fun now that he knew who he was insulting.

Harleigh shot his cuffs. "I was going to say pungent."

Both Eleanor and Giles stared at him.

Eleanor let go of Rodrigo. "You can't stay, and I can't leave."

"Who says?" Harleigh arms were akimbo.

"I do." Eleanor stood and poked her brother in the chest with her index finger. "What made you change your mind, brother? Didn't find Julia, did you? Decided our map wasn't a lot of nothing after all, hmmm?"

"Stop." Giles thrust his hand out, palm facing them.

Harleigh opened his mouth.

"Both of you. Miss Brewster's life is at stake. This isn't the time for sibling squabbles. Rodrigo, come. Is there someplace we can all discuss this matter, besides this drafty hallway?" Rodrigo trotted back to Giles' side and sat.

Eleanor looked at the floor, breaking eye contact with both Harleigh and Giles West. She rubbed her chin. Maybe they could provide some sort of assistance—if they were managed properly. "Come along. I'll show you three where you can wait while I change."

Eleanor left them in the hidden room and went up to have Millie help her out of her garb. When she finally descended the stairs, she had scrubbed off some of the dirt and had braided her hair into one thick plait that hung down her back. Her teeth and gums were another matter. Honeycutt had warned her it would take days for the stain to wear off once she ceased applying it.

Giles or Harleigh had started a small fire. Rodrigo dozed on the hearth; Eleanor wished she could join the dog. She was exhausted. She plopped down in the only comfortable chair and waited for the inquisition.

Harleigh crouched down in front of her and took one of her hands in his, rubbing his thumb across her knuckles. "Why are you unable to return to Lady Standish's with us, sis?"

Eleanor leaned forward and, with her free hand, brushed his hair back off his forehead with her fingers. "Because we've found Julia."

Giles leaned against the mantel. "You know that for certain, do you?"

"Have you contacted the magistrate?" Harleigh said.

Eleanor looked at Giles. "No." Then at Harleigh. "And no."

"Then what makes you think you've found her?" Harleigh said.

"I'm Madame Lutz's new charwoman."

Harleigh rolled her hand over. "Is that why your skin feels so rough?"

"They let me go everywhere in that awful place except up to the third floor. By process of elimination I'm convinced that's where they're keeping the new girls."

"I see." Giles gazed at her thoughtfully. He came up beside his friend. "What do you want to do?"

Eleanor leaped from her chair, knocking her brother back onto his rump. "Look here, we didn't ask you to come. And how did you find us anyway?"

Giles stared down at Eleanor. "We're here now. And it was your aunt and Lady Standish who directed us here. Said they'd had no news of you in over a day."

Eleanor's voice dripped with sarcasm. "And what may I ask is *your* plan?"

Giles and Harleigh gazed at one another.

"I'm waiting, gentlemen." Eleanor circled the chair and propped her elbows on its back. "I'm breathless with anticipation to hear the superior male logic at work."

"Lord, I hate it when you talk like that," Harleigh said.

"Listen to me, brother, somebody's daughter or daughters are up on that third floor. And they need someone to rescue them. I pray to the Almighty that one of those girls *is* Julia." A long pregnant pause ensued.

Harleigh mumbled as he rolled his hand through the air. "We just got here. Haven't had time…"

"Precisely. Those girls have *no* time. Every moment they're in that house the probability that we'll be too late increases. Millie and I already know our way around. And if I can get you two out of here without being seen, we can move ahead with my plan. In fact, with you two here, we could move sooner."

Chapter Eighteen

Giles and Harleigh stood in the alley behind the boarding house. Giles put his ear to the back door, waiting for the scraping sound of Eleanor barring the door. Before he turned to face Harleigh, he grabbed the handle and tried to open the door. He was unsuccessful. "Good. At least she *can* follow a simple request."

Harleigh opened his mouth.

Giles leaned in close and whispered in Harleigh's ear, "Best wait to talk, until we're back at the stables."

Harleigh nodded.

High above the buildings the sky had turned from deepest black to murky gray. The drizzle felt good on Giles' heated face. Eleanor could make him angrier than anyone else in his life.

As soon as they got Julia back to her family, he was heading home. He needed time away from her to sort things out in his own mind. Did he really want to be wedded to such a vexatious creature?

While the stableman got their mounts ready, Giles paced. Rodrigo sat nearby, his eyes glued to his master.

Harleigh leaned against the open stable door. "What's put that burr under your saddle?"

"What do you mean? You were there and heard her harebrained idea, just as I did."

Harleigh pushed off the wall. "I think her plan is sound. Risky but sound. Millie will make sure the back door is open for us and the guard distracted."

"Do you really expect her to stay out of trouble? Prudence is *not* your sister's middle name."

Harleigh chuckled. "No, it's Augusta."

"What?" Giles said.

"Ellie's middle name. Don't be misled by my calm exterior." Harleigh waved his hand down his front. "I'm frightened." Harleigh rested his hand on Giles' shoulder. "It seems to me I've always got something to worry about when it comes to Ellie. She needs to get married."

"What the hell does that mean?" Giles crouched down to give Rodrigo a good scratch.

"Then she would be someone else's problem, not mine. Besides, having a half-dozen brats to take care of might finally pull some wind out of those trouble-making sails of hers."

An image of Eleanor lying in *his* bed—naked, with a rounded belly and her arms held out to him swam into his mind. "Christ."

"What now?" Harleigh said as his brows knit.

"Nothing. Rodrigo has a large mat in his fur." He hoped that sounded plausible. Giles wasn't sure if he was praying for divine intervention to make him change his mind about marrying Eleanor or help him convince Eleanor to accept his suit.

As they approached Lady Sybil's, the rooftops of Bath had the barest touch of yellow gilding their chimney pots. Giles and Harleigh washed up, changed clothes, ate a hardy breakfast and then went off to find the head of the local militia. Giles and Harleigh were under Lady Sybil's orders *not* to speak with the local magistrate, whose allegiance and sense of jurisprudence came with a negotiable price tag.

○ʒ

That evening, when Eleanor and Millie arrived at Madame's, everything was abuzz. The kitchen staff flew by them. Flour covered every surface. The smells made Eleanor's mouth water. She sidled up to the cook. "Sumpin special? I ken tells." Then she sniffed the air. "Yur a dem fine cook, missus."

The portly woman, who stirred a pot over the fire, turned her heat-reddened face toward Eleanor. "How could you tell what smells good? Good gracious, one would think you never bathe." She shooed Eleanor away.

When the cook opened her mouth, she had the projection of a livestock auctioneer. It was no wonder the kitchen staff all tittered and snickered at Eleanor's expense. She just grinned and bobbed her head. On her way into the scullery to get her bucket and rags, she stopped the youngest kitchen helper. "Sumpin up, dearie?"

The scrawny, pimply-faced girl gawked at her. "Yer lucky ye weren't here earlier. Madame, she came and told us someone important was cumin' t'night. Put the fear of the Almighty into Cook and everyone, she did."

Eleanor patted the girl's shoulder. "Thank ye fer telling old Ethel. I be makin' sure I works extra hard and stays outta ta way."

"Good idea," the girl said as she hurried away with an apron full of potatoes to peel.

Eleanor lingered in the scullery hoping Millie would find some excuse to come there so she could fill her in. She found some rags to tear up and had stuffed her pockets full of them when Millie came rushing in.

"Oh, here ye be, Miss Ethel. Madame says you're to go to her office and make it shine." She said those words loudly. Then she pulled Eleanor back away from the doorway and whispered, "Did you hear?"

"That someone important is due?" Eleanor said.

Millie nodded.

"Yes. Do you know who?" Eleanor whispered back.

"Naw, lots of rumors though," Millie said.

"I just bet there are."

"Someone said it might be the Prince hisself." Millie looked hopeful.

Eleanor snorted. "Our plans haven't changed. Even if it does turn out to be his Royal Highness, you understand?"

Millie nodded.

"Where iz that stupid ol' cow who calls herself the best chrwomon in Trowbridge?"

"I be here." Eleanor grabbed her bucket and hurried into the hall.

⁊

Eleanor spent the next few hours in Madame's office on her hands and knees polishing the floor and the baseboards. Madame came and went. As did Pim and Barend.

Eleanor worked her way around half the room when the door flew open. Madame marched in.

"Ah, gran-mooder." Madame sauntered over to inspect Ethel's work, but due to Eleanor's aroma she quickly backed up. "Goot, I am pleazd." Then she walked behind her desk. "*sluit ogen.*" She waved her hand at Eleanor.

Eleanor sat back on her haunches. "Huh?"

Madame pointed to her own eyes and closed them. "Cloze eyz."

"Oh." Eleanor complied. She heard a soft scraping and then wood squeaking.

"Gran-mooder."

Eleanor cracked one eye open.

Madame was sitting in her great gilded chair behind her desk as she waved Eleanor back to work. From her place on the floor, Eleanor could see Madame was writing.

As Eleanor continued her work, Madame began to hum. What was she doing that was making her so happy? Curious, Eleanor snuck a peek. Madame held a thick stack of scraps of paper in her hand, probably avowals. Eleanor knew Madame had a card room and Millie said that if men needed money to continue playing, Madame would advance them the ready. She was such an obliging proprietor. Lord only knew what that witch charged those fools for the privilege of using her money.

That thought caused Eleanor's mind to whirl. Madame must be working on her ledger of accounts. Now, that would be a delicious plum to fall into their hands. The power attached to a book like that would be enormous. Maybe she could sell it to someone? Or a lot of someones—let the men buy their debts back from someone fronting for the Sisterhood, and that money she could use to fund the school. She wouldn't have to wait for her inheritance.

She needed to talk to Millie. When all hell broke loose in a few hours, one of them might have a chance to come in here and get that book.

Eleanor stumbled to her feet. "I gots to get some clean water." She pointed to her bucket on the floor.

Madame looked up. "Vat? Oh, go. Must be done in here before…" She paused. "*Middernacht*."

Eleanor scratched her head. "Eh?"

"Mmmm, meed-night."

"Oh, you wants me outta here before midnight?"

"*Ja*." Then Madame waved her off.

As Eleanor walked into the kitchen—no Millie. She took her time tossing out her old water and getting new. She sighed in resignation and headed back to Madame's office. As she waddled down the servants' passageway with her heavy bucket, a hand shot out and pulled her into a storage nook.

Chapter Nineteen

"It's me," Millie whispered into Eleanor's ear, then let go of her arm.

Eleanor relaxed. "I'm sick to death of hands popping out of nowhere and pulling me into here and out of there. First Honeycutt, then my brother, now you. I could've broken your arm. If you value your limbs, it's best not to surprise me like that."

Millie giggled.

"Hmph. Glad one of us still has her sense of humor. I've been looking for you." Eleanor threw a rag on the floor to sop up the water that had splashed from her bucket.

"Me too. For you, I mean."

ങ

As the hall clock struck midnight, Eleanor began to fidget. Rooksby had come through; his information about the magistrate's fondness for Madame's house was spot on. The fool was upstairs right now. Thank the Good Lord, Colonel Dutton, the head of the local militia, was someone they could count on.

Tonight, instead of chatting everyone up for tidbits of useful information, Eleanor went to the servants' stairs and plopped herself down
on the bottom step. Her calves were sore so she yanked up her skirts and massaged her lower legs, which were covered in thick black, tattered stockings. When the knots in her muscles began to ease, Eleanor shoved her skirt and petticoat down and leaned forward, elbows resting on her knees.

Dear Honeycutt, had come by early this morning, before sunrise, to check up on them; ostensibly to give her skirts another rub-down with raw onion. It was literally enough to make one weep—the way she smelled. But being repugnant in this situation was truly an asset.

Eleanor's bucket and rags sat on the floor at her feet. She'd gone over their plan a thousand times in her mind. Now each moment tortured her with its slowness. She leaned her head against the wall and closed her eyes, silently beseeching the Almighty to make them successful.

The clack of wooden-soled mules against the uncarpeted back staircase heralded the arrival of a couple of the ladies of the house "Poor old dear, she be sleepin'. Madame works her hard," said the first one.

"Eeewww, she stinks. Think if I shoved her off, we could get by without touchin' her?" said the second.

"Jus lift yer skirts."

Eleanor smelled their perfume—floral for the kind one, something musky and spicy for her companion. She heard their voices fade as they
walked toward the front of the house. Maybe a short light nap wouldn't be a bad idea? Her upper back ached. It felt like someone had tied her muscles in a giant knot. Eleanor shifted to get more comfortable when a great crash startled her. Then she heard the angry roar of men and furniture breaking.

The rapid heavy thud of booted feet moving down the stairs announced the arrival of either Pim or Barend. Eleanor pushed herself up and out of the way before a large blond man careened past. He hurried toward the sound of shattering furniture and jeering male voices.

She left her bucket in a nook at the bottom of the stairs and followed him. With one of Madame's henchmen on the scene, the fracas would soon dissolve, leaving a mess in its wake for her to deal with.

The hall opened into the foyer. A large crystal chandelier—aflame with many candles—and an assortment of wall sconces illuminated the proceedings. Women and the patrons not brawling had formed a ring. Eleanor could hear bets being placed on the outcome. Madame's clientele was an interesting lot, not just men of money, but of influence. She didn't know much about brothels, but many of these men didn't look like they would normally associate with one another. She filed that notion away to mull over another time.

"Twenty on Talbot," bellowed a man with gravel in his voice off to Eleanor's right.

"Are you mad? Look at the size of that fella's fists, would ye'?" responded another man.

"I'll take twenty on the Dutchman." A tall foppish fellow leaning against the wall called out his counter-bid.

"Done," the first man shouted back.

Eleanor saw a ripple in the crowd. A second blond head and broad shoulders moved above the mass of humanity. He was no Moses, but the effect reminded Eleanor of the fable of the parting of the Red Sea. Madame Lutz followed in his wake.

"Vat iz dis?" Madame Lutz held her arms high and waved them about in an all-encompassing manner. Her large jeweled rings glittered in the candlelight. Eleanor lost sight of her, but she could still hear her voice.

"*Maak een eind aan dit.*"

"What she say?" A gentleman nudged his friend who stood in front of Eleanor.

"Think she said the entertainment is over," his friend said.

"Didn't know you spoke the Dutch?"

"Who's sayin' I do?"

They both guffawed.

Eleanor pushed herself away from the wall and went to get her broom, dustpan, and bucket. Even though she hadn't seen the damage, she'd heard it. There must be plenty of broken glass and furniture in the parlor for her to clean away. Botheration, at least cleaning would keep her mind off time passing.

With her pockets over-flowing with rags and dragging her broom behind her, she shuffled into the front room. When most of the spectators drifted away, she got her first good look.

What a mess. It would take hours to put it to rights. Two men lay on the floor, one on his side, the other face down. The man lying face down was sprawled on top of the Aubusson rug in the center of the room. Eleanor noticed portions of a walnut side-chair protruding from under this man. The man on his side was lying in a puddle of liquid. Eleanor crept closer. He groaned and started spasmodically waving his arms about—like an over-turned spittlebug. Eleanor scuttled backward and added an "Ooh, gu-ness," for effect.

For a moment, three tall blonds, Madame, Barend, and Pim glanced her way. They quickly returned to yammering in Dutch.

Barend's chest heaved as he continued to take in great gulps of air. A red trickle ran from one of his nostrils to his mouth. A thick pink tongue darted out. He licked his lips and lapped the blood up like a greedy tomcat finishing a bowl of cream.

Eleanor grimaced.

Several buttons were missing from his waistcoat and the seam at the top of his sleeve was ripped open, exposing a well-muscled shoulder.

Madame motioned with her chin to Barend. "Barend, go. Clean up."

"*Ja, Maitresse.*" Barend nodded, then stiff-backed walked from the room.

A hoarse groan came from the man curled up on the floor. He pushed himself to sitting and swiped his mouth with the back of his hand, then he felt around inside his mouth with his fingers. He moved his jaw about and then spit on the floor.

Eleanor checked her impulse to kick him. Disgusting man.

He grabbed the arms of the chair near him and used them to propel himself to standing. A mistake—he teetered and shook his head. He stumbled, nearly toppling into Madame, but Pim caught him by his collar.

"Werp uit hem." Madame waved in the direction of the door.

Pim dragged Spittlebug outside. Eleanor heard him bouncing down the steps. Then Pim came for the fellow still lying face down and threw him out like the first.

"Grootmoeder?"

Eleanor knew she was being addressed and stopped her sweeping. "Yes, Madame?"

"Maak mijn huis glanzen."

"Eh?"

"Mmmm, make"—she waved her be-jeweled hand about the room— "my house shine. *Snel snel.*"

Eleanor bobbed her head, tossed some rags into the puddle and stepped down to push the rags into what smelled and looked like port.

"Madame." Pim hailed her from the doorway.

Madame turned and two well-dressed men walked in. Footmen came forward, blocking Eleanor's view of the new arrivals.

The delighted expression on her face indicated that Madame recognized them. She glided forward with a smile curving her rouged lips and holding out her right hand in welcome. "You are on time, *mijn vriend.*"

These must be her important visitors.

"Ahh, Dagmar, I couldn't stay away from you a moment longer."

That voice. Eleanor felt chilled.

The familiar masculine voice spoke again. "Madame Dagmar Lutz, may I present my boon companion, Sir Lincoln Povey. Lincoln, Madame Lutz."

"Enchanté, Madame." Must be the aforementioned Lincoln Povey speaking.

Why did his name sound familiar? He made a toadying courtly bow over Madame's hand.

"Lincoln was in a hurry, Dagmar, when he heard about our new shipment."

Madame stepped between the two men and took their offered arms. "Ah, *de heer*, so you are eager to taste some of my new vares? I vill have Pim arrange something special for you, but first you must come to my office. I have some excellent French brandy. We shall drink to *bon chance* that brought you to my door on this auspicious night. *Ja?*"

The three of them walked into the light. Eleanor gasped, then immediately began a sputtering cough to cover her misstep. She dropped to her knees to make herself less conspicuous.

On Madame's left was a vaguely familiar man Eleanor surmised was Povey, and on her right…was her father's cousin, Francis Edgerton.

"What's happened, Dagmar?" Edgerton said and strolled into the room.

Eleanor felt a flutter of panic. She bent her head and gathered more broken glass and other oddments into her bucket.

Edgerton stopped beside the demolished chair. He kicked several of the dismembered chair legs with his well-polished boot. "Replacing all of this will cut into our profits."

Our profits? Eleanor stilled. *Edgerton was a partner?*

She heard him stop behind her. She kept working.

"Not significantly. Come, I vill show you our books. We are doing splendidly, my lord." Madame beckoned Edgerton.

"Good Lord, Dagmar, where did you find this?" He put his boot on Eleanor's backside and shoved, toppling her over. "She stinks."

Eleanor used every ounce of her will to keep from launching herself at Edgerton and beating him to a pulp.

"She eez my best worker. Ordinarily she stay in back but after this disturbance…" Madame cast her arm out in an encompassing sweep.

"If you say so, m'dear." Edgerton took a step away.

"If not for her age, I vould clean her up and let her work upstairs."

"On her back, you mean." Povey chortled. He was the only one laughing.

"Come." Madame beckoned again.

This time Edgerton went to stand beside Madame.

Before they left the foyer, she handed Pim a set of keys. "Go to the third floor. Number four I think vill suit Lord Povey."

Just like that time ran out.

Chapter Twenty

Eleanor hurried into the back hallway. She left her bucket in a nook just outside the kitchen entrance. She pulled a rag from her apron pocket and began sliding it up the rail as if she were dusting as she climbed as fast as she could.

She paused between the first and second floor and listened to hear if anyone else was in the stairwell. Not a peep.

She bent over and retrieved the knife from her boot. Reaching under her skirts and petticoat, feeling for the leather strap that bound the upper part of her harness to the lower, she slipped the knife up and cut through the tether.

Sliding the small blade back into its sheath, she sighed as she unbent. She tapped her fingers against her right hip, feeling the solid shape of her hidden pistol.

She surged up the steps, tossing away the rags she'd stuffed into her apron pockets to camouflage her bola. Finally, her groping fingers closed around the leather thongs of her weapon. As her foot hit the top step, she reached under the neckline of her dress, closing her fist around the velvet pouch with her treasured lucky marble within.

Whatever lay ahead … now she was ready.

Eleanor eased open the servants' door leading into the second-floor carpeted hallway. She paused, listening. Muffled sounds floated up from below. She darted out. Running on the balls of her feet. Dashing the length of the hall. Heading for the door leading to the attic.

She held her breath and turned the handle.

Pulling the door open slowly.

It was dark except for a faint glow moving higher.

Eleanor stepped into the darkness of the narrow-enclosed stairwell, opened her mouth and soundlessly released her held breath.

୭

Invisible chilled fingers brushed the back of Giles' neck, causing him to shiver. His back rested against the stone wall that marked the entry to the mews, leading to the rear entrance of the brothel. He rolled his shoulders. Rodrigo gazed up at him and he ran his fingertips across the top of his dog's head. "I, too, am wondering whether she'll wait for us."

Harleigh stood beside Giles, drumming his fingers against his upper thigh. "I agree. Eleanor isn't the patient sort."

Giles grunted.

Everyone was restless. The militia lieutenant shifted his weight repeatedly. He and his eight men were lined up single-file behind Harleigh, while Colonel Dutton, with the rest of his men, lay in wait out front.

Giles tipped his watch outward, hoping to catch any available light upon its face, but clouds had moved in at sunset, obliterating the moon. Frustrated by his vain attempt to mark the passage of time, he snapped his watchcase shut. That small click sounded huge to his ears. "The colonel must be in position by now."

"Yes, sir." The lieutenant's voice was seasoned and calm.

Giles prayed the young lieutenant proved as efficient as he appeared. They'd need cool heads once they got inside. Eleanor trusted Millie to get rid of the brace barring the kitchen door. He hoped her faith was well-placed.

Harleigh swiped the side of his hand across his upper lip.

"Need a handkerchief?" Giles whispered.

"A little pre-battle humor to ease the tension, eh?"

Giles shrugged.

"Well it failed abysmally. Grabs my guts when I think of what my little sister's been up to and no amount of levity is going to make me forget that. Who the hell does she think she is—the bloody Archangel Michael in a dress?"

"She does have the knack."

"We get her out of this mess, then what?" Harleigh said.

"You might try shackling her to a bedpost."

"Why am I asking you, you great oaf? Your sisters are all married. I'm beginning to wonder if our mother hasn't got the right of it. Who the hell is going to willingly marry Eleanor?"

I would. Giles nudged Harleigh's shoulder. "Come on."

In single-file, they crept through the shadows with Rodrigo in the lead. The smell of horse dung and privies assailed their nostrils as they approached the back door. They climbed the steps and Giles and Harleigh put their ears to the kitchen door's panel.

Rodrigo emitted a low growl.

Giles put his hand over Rodrigo's muzzle. "Quiet, boy. I know you're worried about her too."

"Hear anything?" Harleigh said.

"You?" Giles said.

Harleigh shook his head.

Giles reached up and pressed down on the latch and gently pushed. The thick back door swung open and he let out his breath in a whoosh.

Before he said a word, Rodrigo took off across the kitchen and disappeared through a doorway on the far side. "Come on." Giles ran into the kitchen with Harleigh and the rest close on his heels.

The portly red-faced cook turned and started hollering and waving a big spoon. "Hear now! Get out of me kitchen."

Then they all heard musket butts striking the front door and the colonel's command. "Open in the name of the King!"

The kitchen staff squealed with fright and ran about like chickens—squawking, arms flailing.

Millie hollered, "Quit it, you great bunch of ninnies." She waved her arms at Giles, pointing in the direction Rodrigo had gone. "That way."

Giles charged after his dog. He found himself in the servants' hallway. He strained to listen, trying to decide which way to go.

Millie stuck her head out of the kitchen and pointed upward. "Hurry!"

 C3

The attic stairs were steep. Eleanor stepped on the hem of her skirt. She lost her balance and fell forward, striking her shins on the hard edge of the stairs. Pain shot up the front of her legs. She pressed her lips together to keep from crying out. Her eyes filled with unshed tears. Yanking her skirts up higher, she continued her climb.

The narrow staircase pressed in on her. The hot, fetid air of the attic smelled of over-flowing chamber pots and terror. Eleanor wrapped her arm over her nose and mouth. Her instinct was to draw away from the sickening smell, but she forced herself onward.

She peered over the last step. She was facing Pim's back. He held a candle in one hand and Madame's ring of keys in his other. He was alone, grousing. Through the dim light, she could see a number had been painted on each door.

He put a key in the lock on the door marked "4," but that key wouldn't turn. He put the candle down on a small table a few feet away—the only furniture in this little bit of hell at the top of Madame's house. These rooms had once been the servants' sleeping quarters. He chose another key and inserted it into the lock. It failed as well. He growled and swore. Then he kicked the door with the toe of his boot. A startled girl's cry came from behind the locked door he'd kicked.

"*Zwijg!*"

From behind another door, a girl started to whimper.

"Shut oop, I zed!" Pim went over to that door and struck it once with his fist.

Eleanor nibbled her lip.

Harleigh, where are you?

She listened but heard nothing. She crept over the edge. Pim didn't respond to her presence. She moved as far away from him as possible.

Pim walked back to door four. He grabbed another key and shoved it in its lock.

Eleanor pulled the bola from her pocket and looked at it. Not enough room for a good throw. She bent down, keeping her eyes on Pim, and laid the bola on the floor.

Another key failed and Pim's mutterings grew savage.

Eleanor pulled her pocket flintlock out and unlatched the safety. But she couldn't make herself shoot Pim in the back. "You!"

"Huh?" Pim peered over his shoulder. "No belongin. Go vay."

"*Nr.*" Eleanor raised her arm and cocked the pistol.

Pim turned. "I snap you like tvig, *grootmoeder.*"

Eleanor shook her head.

Pim swung his arm toward the stairs. "Go!"

"Julia Brewster! It's Miss Eleanor!"

"Oh. Please help me," a frightened familiar girl's voice called from behind one of the locked doors.

Other girls started calling out and banging on their locked doors.

The sounds of the chaos from below reached the attic: men shouting, women's screams, and feet running fast.

"*Magistraat,*" Eleanor said.

Pim's eyes darted toward the stairs, then back to her. His nostrils flared as he stepped toward her.

"*You* stop. *Spruit van penis.*" Eleanor pointed her gun at his crotch.

Pim looked shocked. His face flamed.

She'd just threatened to shoot off *his* lock-pick.

He looked again at the stairs, his big hands open and closing.
"*Laat!*" Eleanor shouted above the storm of sounds closing in on
them.

Pim hesitated, then roared and charged. "Bitch!"

Eleanor pulled the trigger.

Heat, a flash, the smell of burning sulfur, and a puff of smoke.
Pim lurched.

For a moment time stopped.

Then he continued his charge.

Powerful thick fingers circled Eleanor's neck and squeezed.

Her head smacked hard against the wall. A shrieking pain
vibrated through her body. She gasped for air. She wrapped her
fingers around his giant wrists and dug her fingernails into his flesh.
Colors danced before her eyes.

Barking.

Claws clicking and scrabbling across bare wood floors.

Growling.

Rodrigo sailing through the air.

Roddy's jaws clamped into Pim's forearm.

Blood spurted up and sprayed her face.

Pim shrieked and his face contorted.

The pressure on her neck eased.

Eleanor's legs gave way. The rough wood of the wall grabbed at
her clothes as she slid downward.

Pim swung his arm, trying to shake off Rodrigo, but the dog held
on.

Teeth gritted, Pim swung again. Rodrigo hit the wall.

A terrible cracking noise.

Rodrigo lay in a heap a few feet away. Pim staggered back,
holding his bleeding arm to his chest.

Eleanor tipped over. Her cheek pressed against the cold floor.
She reached out, trying to touch Rodrigo.

"Up here, they must be up here!" Male voices coming from below.

So far away.

A fast thrumming that made the floor against her cheek vibrate.

Pim lumbered back.

Chapter Twenty-one

Giles flew up the stairs. Before he hit the first landing, he heard the report of a small weapon coming from above. "Hell."

"Oh, God. Eleanor?" Harleigh was on his heels.

Giles' speed accelerated, taking the steps two at a time.

"Where's Rodrigo?" Harleigh panted.

A gaggle of partially clad women clustered on the servants' staircase blocked their way. "Let us by." Giles tried to shove past.

One buxom doxie standing a step above him threw her arms around Giles' neck and yanked his head forward so that his nose was buried deep in her cleavage. "Won't I do, dearie?"

Giles' hands circled the whore's waist and he lifted her up and set her aside, then he and Harleigh surged upward. When they got into the second-floor hallway, chaos reigned. The militia was rounding up the house's occupants.

Giles and Harleigh shoved their way down the hallway, peering through every open doorway.

Nothing but empty beds and the musk of sex.

"Rodrigo!" Giles' heart pounded. They'd run out of rooms. Then he

spotted a slit in the wallpaper at the end of the hallway—the door to the attic. "Eleanor! Rodrigo!"

An eerie, wailing sound coming from the darkness ahead made the hairs on his neck stand on end. The narrow passage upward ended in a small windowless room. One candle sitting on a table was the only source of light.

A large blond head was disappearing into the floor. "Stop!" He ran toward it. By the time he reached the opening, he was staring into a black hole.

"Let us out." A girl's cry from behind one of the doors.

"Help us." Another girl's voice from behind another door.

Harleigh covered his nose and mouth with his hand. "My God, it stinks."

Giles spotted a crumpled form in skirts. "Harleigh, get the light." He dropped to the floor next to the body. "Eleanor." She wasn't moving. He grabbed her by the shoulders and pulled her into his arms.

Harleigh knelt beside them, holding the candle. "What's that on her face?"

Giles' fingers stroked her cheek and the dark wetness smeared. He held his finger up to his nose and smelled the metallic tang. "Blood."

"It's all over her." Harleigh frantically ran his hands across her chest and down her arms. "Do you see a wound? Oh, God, where's all this blood coming from?" Harleigh's hands shook.

"Go get help," Giles said as he grabbed Harleigh's arm. "She needs a surgeon."

"I'll take her," Harleigh countered. "You go."

"We can argue later." Giles put his hand on Harleigh's shoulder and gently pushed him. He wouldn't leave Eleanor now if Harleigh had put a gun to his head.

Harleigh gazed into Giles' face and seemed to come to some kind of decision because he tipped his chin down, leaped to his feet, and ran down the steps. The drumming of his boots against the bare steps faded.

Giles ran his hand up Eleanor's neck and across her chest, looking for a wound Harleigh had missed. She was dying and he couldn't find the damn hole to staunch her bleeding.

Eleanor's head fell back and dangled over his arm, exposing her long neck. The skin at the base of her throat was dotted with purpling blotches. He shifted position and sat on the floor with his back against the wall and pulled her limp body onto his lap. Her head now lay against his left shoulder. He cradled her cheek in his right hand. "Damn you, woman, you can't die. Do you hear me?" He pressed his lips against her forehead.

An animal's whimper.

At the edge of the circle of light spilling from the candle on the floor, Giles could see Rodrigo. In the rush to get to Eleanor, he'd completely forgotten to look for him. One of his front legs lay at an odd angle, probably broken, and his jaw was smeared with blood.

Rodrigo pushed himself up on three legs and hobbled over to Eleanor. He dropped down and licked her hand.

Giles stroked Rodrigo's head.

"Were we too late, boy?"

Rodrigo nudged Giles hand.

A moment later the men arrived and the room filled with light.

Harleigh came first, followed by the lieutenant, and several of his men carrying several large lamps, and an older man brought up the rear.

Girls' frightened voices chorused, "Please help us."

Harleigh picked up the fallen key ring and tossed it to the lieutenant, then he turned to Giles. "This is the company's surgeon."

Rodrigo growled as the large portly surgeon knelt beside Eleanor.

Giles stroked Rodrigo's side. "He's here to help her."

The surgeon put his ear near Eleanor's mouth and then he laid his palm on her upper

chest. "Alive." Then he walked the fingertips of both hands up her neck. "What happened?"

"Found her on the floor." Giles gazed into the surgeon's eyes

"Where's all this blood coming from?" The surgeon kept looking for wounds. "I can find no hole." The surgeon tried to roll her body toward himself, away from Giles. Giles tightened his hold.

"Sir, I need to see her back," the surgeon said.

"Giles." Harleigh's voice seemed to break through his terror of losing Eleanor. He relaxed his grip.

The doctor rolled her limp body over and ran his hands up her back. "No wound. No blood back here, either. I don't think the blood is hers.

"Whose?" Harleigh asked.

Giles spotted Eleanor's gun lying on the floor. "Harleigh, is that Eleanor's? The man who bolted down the trap door…"

Harleigh picked up the gun and ran his fingers down the barrel. "Warm, too. Bet she shot him."

The surgeon rolled her back toward Giles. When he pushed her wig off, the cap came off too. He ran his hands through her hair. "Ah, there's a great lump on the back here. Let's get her out of here."

Harleigh bent down and held his arms out, ready to take Eleanor from Giles.

Giles reluctantly let Harleigh have her. Then he crouched down beside Rodrigo. "I think his leg is broken. Lieutenant, would you send one of your
men for a plank to carry my dog down?"

Harleigh, with Eleanor in his arms, moved to the head of the stairs. The last locked door was opened and a young bedraggled girl with thick black curls flew out like a wild bird being set free. She stared wide-eyed at all the adults who were crowded into that small space. Her gaze caught on Harleigh. "Oh." She dashed to his side and touched his arm. Harleigh gazed down at her. "It's very good to see you, Julia."

"Tis her, I thought I was dreaming when I heard her call me name."

ജ

Edgerton slid into the shadows, across the street from Madame's. The front door stood open. The militia was everywhere. Dagmar waited for him in her coach around the corner. Povey, the damn fool, got himself caught inside the house with the rest of their patrons.

Well, he had no proof, so Edgerton's secret partnership with Madame Lutz was safe.

Several members of the militia held torches aloft. Neighbors were beginning to stir and wander out onto the street. Some instinct made Edgerton linger a moment longer. Giles West appeared. He was moving in tandem with one of the militia men. They each held the end of a plank and something was piled on top. The pile moved. *Rodrigo? What the hell?*

A large portly man exited next, and waved someone to precede him down the steps, a man carrying someone in his arms. One militia man

stood at the base of the steps, holding a torch. Damn. It was his Cousin Harleigh carrying a woman.

As Harleigh drew closer to the coach, the light spilled across the woman's immobile face.

"Is that you, Eleanor?" Edgerton beat his fist against the wall. "Are you dead or merely unconscious?" Another militia man came forward and opened the coach door. "Seems you're up to your old interfering tricks. Are you the author of my troubles here tonight?"

Several curious men walked past.

Edgerton turned and left.

He climbed into the carriage, taking the open seat beside Madame. She wore a heavy wool cloak and the hood was drawn up over her head. Barend sat on the bench opposite with his arm wrapped around his cousin. Pim had a bloody hole in his gut that had been crudely bandaged and another crude bandage about his lower right arm that he was cradling. His eyelids drooped. The cousins kept up a muttered dialogue in Dutch. Pim seemed intent on conveying something. Barend shushed him several times.

"What's he saying?" Edgerton asked Madame.

Madame listened to Pim and Barend. "The one who shot him."

"Who?" Edgerton said.

"He makes no sense," Madame said.

Edgerton leaned forward and shook Pim's shoulder. "Who shot?"

Barend growled and shoved Edgerton's hand away.

"Dagmar?"

"All he says iz te gran-mooder."

೪

Edgerton sat across the table from Madame Lutz. They were sequestered in a private dining room at the Red Gabbler, a posting inn just outside of Bath. The room was toasty and the food good, but the wine was vinegar.

"Will Pim survive, do you think?" Edgerton pushed back in his chair.

"Vill our host ask questions?"

"Nothing that cannot be answered by a few well-placed coins." Edgerton raised his glass, grimaced and lowered it back to the table.

"Even if ve leave him with a body?" Dagmar said.

Edgerton grunted.

"Barend vill not be any good to me until after," Dagmar said. She used her fork to impale the side of the game-bird swimming in brown gravy on her plate; she sliced off a small piece of meat, then raised it to her rouged lips.

"After?"

"After he kills the one vho did this to Pim. They are cousins. Very devoted." She slipped the fork inside her mouth. Her tongue darted out to lick the drip of brown sauce still clinging to the tines of the fork.

"Then the wound is mortal?" Edgerton said.

"If he survives, it vill be a miracle of Biblical proportions," Dagmar said.

Edgerton smiled at his companion. Even though English was her second language, she had a way with words he found amusing. So Barend would want revenge, would he? Edgerton knew just how to use that thirst to his advantage. "A tragedy."

"True." She made a little moue and shrugged. At that moment, she seemed more French than a hardheaded Dutch businesswoman.

"How unfortunate for my dear cousin."

"Cousin?" Dagmar said.

Edgerton nodded. "I recognized her when her brother carried her out of our establishment. She seems to have suffered an injury."

Dagmar's brows rose in confusion. "Are you sure it was she?"

"I warrant the light was poor."

Dagmar's gaze was unwavering.

"It'll be easy enough to discover the truth. I'll make inquiries."

"Vhat vas a voman of your class doing in my house?"

"An interesting question, my dear Dagmar."

"Vhat does she look like?" Dagmar said.

"Tall for a woman. Chestnut-colored hair. Large green eyes."

"Hmmm, I do not recall a woman of that description. Vhat vas she wearing?"

"Rags." Edgerton sniffed. "A dark skirt and an apron—hardly memorable."

She stroked her chin with her index finger. "There vas no one in my house fitting your description and the only one wearing the clothes you describe vas my charvoman."

"Your charwoman? You mean that old smelly hag I saw cleaning up the mess in the front parlor?"

She nodded. "Do you mean…?" Dagmar threw back her head and laughed. "Vhat vas she doing masquerading as my charvoman?"

"Another puzzle I intend to find the answers to before we re-establish our enterprise here in the west."

"Your cousin is very daring. Vas it vhat you English call a lark? Is that vhy she came to my house?"

"A lark, I think not. But curious, is it not, that she arrives on the heels of your new group of girls?" Edgerton rolled the stem of his glass between his fingers. "Something must have impelled Eleanor to take such a risk? That last load of merchandise,"—he put his glass down— "where did it come from?"

"Like usual. Mostly from the north." Madame paused. "There vas one child… Irresistible. Dark thick curls and the deepest blue eyes. She came from the south. Kent or Surrey."

"That was stu—" Edgerton stopped himself.

Dagmar's nostrils flared.

"Unwise," Edgerton finished. "You know the rules. No girls who can be understood. I would wager that 'irresistible' child is what brought my cousin to your door."

"You mean *our* door, *darline*."

Edgerton felt Dagmar's threat in the pit of his stomach. His jaw tightened.

She shrugged. "I plucked the little flower vhile she valked along the road. How vas I to know she had such powerful and resourceful friends?"

"You didn't follow our plan, Dagmar." Edgerton reached across the table and took her chin firmly in his hand. "No more impulsive flower-picking, eh?"

Madame dropped her chin. Her tongue came out and she licked the crotch between his thumb and index finger. He felt himself go hard. "An interesting invitation, Dagmar, but I never mix business and pleasure."

Edgerton let go of her chin. He wouldn't insult her by wiping away her saliva from his hand. Even though he longed to do just that. She was an excellent business partner, but the idea of sexual congress with her would be like shagging a voluptuous asp.

She ran her index finger along his jaw and across his lips. "As you vish, *liefje*."

He forced his lips to curl into a smile. "No one knows of our connection. After a suitable period, I'll purchase another house and we'll start anew, yes?" Edgerton picked up his cutlery and cut into his beefsteak. "By the way, what have you done with our ledgers? I never did get to look at them before we were so rudely interrupted. Are they in your satchel?"

Madame's silverware clattered to the table. "*Goed* God! In the rush to leave … They must still be hidden in my office."

ᴄ઩

When the world came back into focus, Eleanor lay curled up on her side, facing windows draped in a heavy rose fabric. A down pillow cushioned her head and a ruffled linen sheet draped her shoulder. Slices of fuzzy sunlight cut through the dimness where the fabric of the curtains met the molding surrounding the window.

From the angle of the light, Eleanor surmised it must be late morning. Even in the muted light she could see the walls were covered in her least favorite color—pink.

The air smelled of flowers and beeswax. Someone—she could tell it was a woman, for she wore skirts—sat in the chair beside the bed. With the strong light coming from behind her, she was all darkness with no tell-tale features. From the position of her head, she appeared to have fallen asleep.

Eleanor blinked several times and wiggled her toes, then her fingers. She pushed herself up onto her elbow and her head swam and she felt nauseated. "Ergh."

"You're awake!"

It was Libby sitting beside her bed.

"Do not holler. My head." Eleanor eased onto her back. Her forehead itched so she put her hand up to scratch and felt a bandage.

"Leave that alone." Libby jumped from her chair.

"Where am I?"

"Lady Standish's," Libby said.

"How did *you* get here?"

"I talked Lord West and Harleigh into bringing me. Actually…" Libby smiled impishly. "Well, I …"

"You what?"

"I sort of bullied them into bringing me along."

"That, I'd have liked to witness," Eleanor said.

"Bullying isn't the correct word," Libby said. "Coerced is more accurate, I think." She wore a look of triumphant satisfaction. "Yes, I coerced them."

Eleanor chuckled, then winced from the pain the movement caused. She squinted up at her dearest friend. "Did you just call my brother, Harleigh?"

Libby flapped her arms, as she was wont to do when agitated, then moved quickly to the door. "Everyone's been waiting for you to wake up. Must go and inform them."

"Can it not wait?"

Libby's hand rested on the knob. "'Fraid not, dearest."

"Thought you decided it was best to be formal. Him being a man full grown, and my father's heir and all."

Libby stuck her nose in the air, opened the door and rabbited through it.

Eleanor smiled. Libby hadn't called Harleigh by his given name since… Eleanor searched her memory. Well, not since they were all small. After that, it was Lord Barrett, or *your* brother. *Wonder how Harleigh addresses little Miss freckle-faced-shy-as-a-morning-glory? Sweeting?* Eleanor's grin grew wider. *They would be perfect for one another.*

Chapter Twenty-two

Eleanor heard the knock. Before she could answer, the door opened and a troupe consisting of Libby, Aunt Beatrice, Lady Standish, Harleigh, Giles West, Millie, and Julia Brewster came into view.

Julia ran to her bedside and grabbed her hand. "Oh, Miss Eleanor, I'm so happy to see you."

Pain shot up her arm, across her shoulders and up and down her spine, but she hoped it didn't show. "Thank you, Julia. It's a pleasure as always to see you."

Julia blushed. "Miss Ellie, you saved us—me and the others. How shall I ever repay you?"

"Welllll…" With her free hand, Eleanor tapped her chin with her finger. "Next time I come to market you could slip me an entire slice of that excellent cheese your family makes."

Julia wrinkled her nose. "Is that all?"

"I'm so happy you are safe, and soon you'll be home where you belong."

A tear rolled down the girl's cheek.

Eleanor softened her voice and squeezed her hand. "Julia?"

"S-s-so scared. Never thought I'd ever see Mama and Papa again."

"Now you will. But first, I want you to go eat lots and lots—especially the sweets."

Someone had opened the drapes. Julia's face glistened as the sun shone on her tear-streaked cheeks, and her giggle came out on a hiccup. "I like sweets."

"I know you do."

Julia bent down and kissed Eleanor's cheek. "When I'm grown, I want to be as brave and smart as you, Miss Ellie."

Harleigh coughed.

"As a matter of fact, I think you should go get a plateful of sweets, take them out into Lady Standish's garden with a large glass of milk and stay out there until you eat every crumb."

Millie stepped up behind Julia and put her hands on the girl's shoulders. "Come along, lamby." Millie led Julia toward the door.

"May I come to see you later?" Julia turned back and gazed at Eleanor.

"When you come back would you mind bringing me a biscuit or two? I'm rather fond of them myself."

Julia smiled and left with Millie.

"That was kind, sis. According to the staff, none of the girls has slept very well since they were rescued." Harleigh brought a couple of chairs up to the side of the bed.

"Well, gel, you gave us all quite a fright you know," Lady Standish said.

"Yes, niece, how are you?" Aunt Beatrice patted Eleanor's hand before she seated herself beside Lady Standish.

Harleigh, Libby, and Giles West took up positions standing behind Lady Sybil and Lady Beatrice.

"Do you remember any of it?" Harleigh asked.

"When I got to the attic, there was barely any light, except for that candle in Pim's hand. I heard the jangling of Madame's keys."

"Pim?" Aunt Beatrice asked.

"One of Madame's bully-boys." Eleanor shifted, trying to get comfortable.

"You did *not* wait," Giles West said. "You said you would wait."

Everyone turned and looked at him. Lady Standish and Aunt Beatrice nudged each other with their elbows, looking all rather conspiratorial.

"Well?" Giles demanded.

"Shall I tell you what I thought?" Eleanor said.

"By all means," Giles snapped back. "Can't wait to hear this excuse."

She glared at him. "If he got his hands on even one of the girls, he could use her as a hostage for safe passage out of the house. I thought if I could just hold him off long enough…"

"Well, that was a raging success." Giles crossed his arms over his chest, his handsome face marred by a sarcastic twist to his lips.

"Shut up, Giles." Harleigh shoved him.

"Really, my lord." Aunt Beatrice gazed over her shoulder at him. "Your sarcasm adds nothing and delays Eleanor's recounting." She swung back to face Eleanor and her voice lost its caustic edge. "Do continue, dear."

"I never would have thought someone so large could move so fast."

"What about your gun?" Libby said.

"I shot. I swear it. I must have missed." Eleanor cocked her head, seeing it all replay in her mind. "He grabbed me around the throat with both his hands, shoving me back against the wall." Eleanor touched her neck and stared into the sunlight. When she swallowed, it felt like he still had his hands around her neck.

"He pinned me with one hand, and drew back his other, getting ready to throttle me."

Giles muttered. "I know that feeling."

"Rodrigo flew through the air," Eleanor said. "He sank his teeth into Pim's arm. Pim roared and let go of me. Rodrigo saved me. Is he alive?"

"One of his front legs is broken," Harleigh said.

"I want to see him," Eleanor said.

Harleigh turned to Giles.

"Now," Eleanor added.

"Go on, lad," Lady Standish said as she waved her beringed hand at him.

Giles left and when he returned, two footmen carried Rodrigo on a board. A splint and a large white bandage covered one of his front legs.

Eleanor lay in the middle of the bed.

"Put him here." Eleanor pointed to the area on the bed beside her, on the mattress.

"Are you mad?" Giles put his hands on his hips.

"*Here*," Eleanor said.

"Do as she wishes." Lady Standish rose and moved out of the way.

"Libby, help me. I need to move over." Eleanor pointed to the opposite side of the bed.

The footmen moved in and placed Rodrigo, board and dog, onto the bed.

C3

Giles never thought he would envy a dog. How lowering. Eleanor Barrett fell asleep while snuggled up next to Rodrigo. As far as Giles was concerned, this entire situation gave new meaning to the words 'lucky dog.' Sometimes, life made no sense at all.

Her thick chestnut braid hung down over her shoulder, he could still see the tell-tale purple necklace of finger marks circling her throat—they'd almost been too late. A chilling thought. The ladies preceded him and Harleigh from the room. The footmen brought up the rear.

Aunt Beatrice put her hand on Harleigh's arm. "What they both need is lots of rest. Why, in no time she'll be back to her old self. You just wait and see."

"Heavens forfend." Harleigh looked heavenward.

His aunt swatted Harleigh's arm. "Petulant boy."

He instructed one of the footmen. "Best leave the door ajar." He turned to Giles. "I'll ask Honeycutt to station a man at her door."

"Oh, you mean if my dog's needs…"

Harleigh shook his head and waited for Elizabeth Archer, Lady Sybil, and his aunt to move out of earshot. "I'm uneasy. Can't put my finger on it. Julia is going home, but this whole business doesn't feel finished."

Chapter Twenty-three

Two days later, Giles tapped on Eleanor's door and waited.

"Come." Eleanor was partially tucked up under the covers. Her eyelids drooped. She appeared to be trying to keep herself awake. Her lids fluttered closed and then she would open them wide. The surgeon had mentioned the blow on her head could leave her lethargic.

What he could see of her, above the waist, was modestly covered in a heavy robe made of moss-green fabric. She lay curled up on her side, her arm slung across Rodrigo's shoulder. He walked across the room and stood beside the bed, deliberately putting himself in her line of vision. He scratched Rodrigo behind the ear.

Eleanor obviously wasn't attempting to be provocative or seductive, yet he found himself overwhelmed by the urge to lift those bed sheets and climb in behind her and wrap her in his arms and nuzzle her neck.

She had a fresh bandage about her head, making her look rather piratical, which in his mind fit her to a T. The air smelled of herbs. Millie must have recently reapplied the doctor's poultice to the swelling on the back of Eleanor's head.

Eleanor's eyes opened wide when she caught sight of him. "Have they left?"

"Not yet."

"I must speak with Harleigh before he goes," she said.

"There's no need for concern. He and Miss Archer will take excellent care of Miss Brewster."

"What? Oh, it's not that," Eleanor said as she wadded the corner of the sheet in her fist. "Millie, would you go find my brother? Tell him I must speak with him before he leaves."

"Yes, miss," Millie said and made sure to leave the door wide open.

"May I sit?" Giles indicated the chair beside the bed.

"If you desire."

Giles saw a book on the bedside table. "Shall I read?" He took the small book into his hands and opened it. *Robinson Crusoe*. His shoulders relaxed. Thank the Almighty—no Aphra Behn.

Eleanor's lips quivered with suppressed laughter. He could tell because the laughter that wasn't coming out of her mouth was dancing in her eyes.

"Perhaps Lady Standish has a newssheet somewhere in the house."

Giles cleared his throat. "I was afraid it'd be *Oroonoko* or some such."

Eleanor chuckled. "I surmised by the look of relief that washed over your countenance."

"Am I so easy to read, then?" Giles said.

Eleanor's grin was sly. "As a book."

A seductive silence fell upon the room. Giles leaned down, wanting to steal a kiss from her laughing mouth.

Harleigh strolled into the room, startling them both. "Have I interrupted?" Harleigh said. He had on traveling clothes. "I'd have come before I left."

Eleanor cleared her throat and rolled slowly to face her brother. "I need to speak with *you*."

Giles put the book back on the table. "Shall I return later?"

"Yes," Eleanor said.

As Giles walked from the room, he heard Harleigh and Eleanor's voices. "What has your feathers ruffled?"

"Close the door, will you?" Eleanor said.

Giles stood in the hall, watching the door close. He didn't realize he was still staring at her door until he saw the quizzical look on the footman's face. Embarrassed to be caught woolgathering, Giles shoved his hands in his pockets, pivoted, and ambled away.

As he trod the thick, well-carpeted steps downward, the silence of his footsteps made him imagine how easy it'd be for someone to steal up to Eleanor's room unnoticed in the dark. Perhaps they should move her to another room. Bah, all Harleigh's talk of keeping her safe was making him twitchy.

He stopped his descent and pondered. Sunlight poured through the beveled glass above the front door and glinted off a massive crystal vase sitting on a round table in the middle of the foyer. A lush bouquet of blossoms filled the air with a heady perfume. The floral scent and the fractured light sent his thoughts spiraling back to Venetian lagoons and a passionate woman in his arms, but this time, it wasn't the Italian widow he held, this time it was the passionate woman lying upstairs. He turned his head and gazed up the stairs and whispered, "*Siete il tesoro del mio cuore*—you are the treasure of my heart, you just do not know it yet."

He smiled as he imagined what kind of bedmate Eleanor would make—eager, unpredictable, adventurous, loving. He wanted to teach her things. He wanted to show her pleasure. Those thoughts careened through his mind, tightened his bollocks, and scared the hell out of him. How was he to woo her? He needed a plan.

CB

As the door closed, Eleanor pointed to the chair beside the bed that Giles had just vacated. "Sit." She waited, giving Giles time to walk down the hall, away from her door.

Harleigh tossed himself into the chair. "Well?"

Eleanor couldn't figure out how to begin.

"This has to do with the bordello, does it not?" Harleigh said.

Silence.

"Ellie, give over."

"Cousin Francis…"

That brought Harleigh to attention. "You saw him?"

Eleanor nodded.

"Do you think he recognized you?"

Eleanor laughed. "*You* didn't."

Harleigh sulked. "Hrumph. Don't remind me."

"I think he's part owner of that dreadful place," Eleanor said.

"What makes you say that?"

"Some furniture and other things got broken before you arrived. He said replacing the broken bits would decrease *their* profits."

Harleigh rubbed the back of his neck. "Christ."

Eleanor sat up straighter. "You're not surprised." She squinted at Harleigh.

He wiggled in his chair.

Eleanor stabbed her finger at him. "You knew."

Harleigh grimaced. "Not really. I'd heard rumors. But nothing about the child-stealing."

"I never imagined Edgerton was involved," Eleanor said. "Even Rooksby—"

"Uncle Jasper's man?" Harleigh said.

Eleanor bobbed her head. "The same."

"Good Lord, you've been rubbing elbows in some lofty circles. Or should I say, some low circles."

"Ha-ha. Most amusing. We needed sound information. And he knows everything."

"Did you meet the …?" Harleigh asked.

"Abbess? Dagmar Lutz?" Eleanor nodded.

"Such language. Mother would faint if she heard you."

"You know," Eleanor said as she rolled her eyes, "it wouldn't surprise me in the least to find out Rooksby was already cognizant of our cousin's involvement."

Harleigh stood. "Why would that old spymaster care a fig about that brothel?"

"I've nothing solid to go on, mind you—more a feeling, but things there just didn't add up," Eleanor said. "Some of Madame's guests were odd, not the sort to have the chinks to spend on an expensive…"

"Don't say it. It's bad enough I agreed with your plan and allowed you into that place."

Eleanor snorted.

"And just how would *you* know what a-a …" Harleigh rolled his hand through the air as he struggled to find an appropriate word— "those *things* cost?"

Eleanor flopped back into her pillows. "Stop being obtuse. Of course, I don't know exact numbers, but the furnishings and wine were first stair, so I merely extrapolated."

"What made these men odd?" Harleigh asked.

"Well, they looked and sounded more like government clerks."

"Clerks?"

"Uh-huh. Their coats were unadorned, and their shoes not well-maintained, like they didn't have a valet to look after things."

"What makes you think they were government men, and not your run-of-the-mill business clerk or merchant?"

"When they were foxed, they said things that sounded like they should never be spoken about in public."

"What sort of things?" Harleigh said.

"Troop movements. Supply chains. Things of that nature."

"That's strange and imprudent to be sure," Harleigh said. "But, Ellie, are you sure we're not looking for trouble where there is none? This may just be a group of debauched gentlemen with a predilection for pubescent bed-partners. Disgusting, I grant you, but nothing more."

"No, there's something we aren't seeing," Eleanor said and yanked
her covers higher. "I feel it."

Harleigh paced. "You're impossible." The clock in the foyer chimed. "I have to get on the road."

"You can't leave until you speak to Lord West about Edgerton," Eleanor said.

Harleigh's eyebrows shot up toward his hairline. "Nooo." He stuck his index finger in the air and wagged it rapidly. "I can't. No. No. Very much no. Out of the question. No."

"Why not?" Eleanor said.

"My feet are practically out the door. I can't just say 'oh and by the way, Giles, Edgerton is involved in the kidnapping of Julia Brewster. See you in a fortnight.'"

Eleanor took a breath to launch into her argument.

Harleigh sat on her bed. "This isn't going to go down well, you know that, Ellie."

"He has a right to know that a man he trusts is involved in this mess, and you are Giles' best friend," Eleanor said.

"Have faith in my judgment on this matter. Giles is a lot like you about his friends, deeply, blindly loyal."

"Some friend," Eleanor said.

"That's my point, *he* considers Edgerton his friend."

"Only in Lord West's mind," Eleanor said as she leaned back into the pillows and fussed with the turn-down of her covers.

"Ellie?"

"Hmm?"

"What is it with the two of you?"

Eleanor tensed. Was her brother talking about her and Edgerton or her and Giles? Eleanor held her breath, waiting for Harleigh to elucidate.

"You have never gotten on with Edgerton. And now when you believe you have the goods on him, you seek to cut him off from the one friend in this world he does have. It seems vengeful."

Whew, not Giles. That was a matter for another time—not now.

"Stop trying to divert me," Eleanor said. "We're *not* talking about my opinion of our cousin. The matter under discussion is you informing your best friend about a man he holds close before you leave this house."

Harleigh took her hand and squeezed. "Believe me, I wish they weren't so close. Giles and I've nearly come to blows over his defense of Edgerton on more than one occasion, but there's nothing more I can do right now. I must get going if we're to make the first posting inn before nightfall."

Eleanor turned her head away.

"When Giles learns about all of this, he'll confront Edgerton and I need to be here when that happens."

Eleanor was getting ready for another assault on Harleigh's argument.

"This isn't going to go down any easier for our father than it will for Giles when he learns Francis is mixed up in this heinous business," Harleigh said and hung his head. "You know how protective he is of Edgerton's mother. Good Lord, this is a nightmare."

"I hadn't thought of that." Eleanor sighed. "Poor Papa."

"Show a little pity for the messenger, will you?" Harleigh said. "I'm the one who must deliver the news."

Eleanor laid her hand on her brother's arm. "Edgerton must be dealt with; there's no getting around it. Who knows how many other Julia's there are?"

The clock in the foyer chimed, again, announcing another fifteen minutes had passed.

Harleigh jumped up. "I *must* go."

"But ..."

"What a mess." He leaned down so they were eyelevel. "Promise me not to say a word."

Eleanor turned away.

Harleigh took her chin and lifted it so they were eye to eye.

"Very well," Eleanor said. "Though I think you're making a great mistake."

"Are you positive Edgerton didn't recognize you?"

"Don't fret on that account."

Harleigh sighed. "Maybe I should ask Giles to take Julia home instead."

Eleanor didn't want anything to interfere with Libby spending more time with Harleigh. Who knew what could happen. "Rodrigo can't travel yet. And you must deal with Father."

"Very well." Harleigh flinched. "I'll return quickly."

"I still think you should tell Lord West—"

A knock came on the door.

"Quit nagging. That subject is closed."

Giles strolled in with a tea tray in his hands. "Told Millie I would bring this up." Giles had his back to them as he placed the tray on the table.

Eleanor kept moving her mouth, silently speaking the words, "tell him, tell him, tell him."

Harleigh sliced his hand through the air in front of his mouth.

She squinted at him and pursed her lips.

"Brother, *this* isn't going to turn out well, and time isn't going to make the news go down any easier either," Eleanor said.

"What news?" Giles asked.

"It should take less than a fortnight to get Julia home and return," Harleigh said.

"What's bothering you, Harls?" Giles said as his brows knitted. "You're not one to state the obvious."

"I…" Harleigh cleared his throat. "I'm worried about Eleanor. After all, we don't know who's behind this ugly business."

"Certainly, we do, that Madame Lutz." Giles poured out the tea.

One tick, then another of pregnant silence.

"You think she has partners?" Giles held out a cup of tea to Harleigh.

Harleigh waved him off. "It's a likely supposition."

Giles shrugged. "I suppose." He pursed his lips. "Any notion who?"

Harleigh cleared his throat. "Not yet."

Eleanor made a disgusted sound. Both men turned to look at her.

"The important thing is that *no* one knows Eleanor is here. And it *must* remain that way," Harleigh said.

Chapter Twenty-four

Giles sat in his usual spot beside Eleanor's bed, watching her sleep and waiting for her to awaken. Since Harleigh's departure, his entertainments had been reduced to reading, playing whist with Lady Beatrice and Lady Sybil, who had to be the worst card sharks in the Northern Hemisphere, solitary walks about town, and dodging the deluge of invitations from mothers with unattached daughters of marriageable age.

The room was *pink,* his least favorite color, and full of frills and lace. His big hands rested on the arms of the chair that was covered in some blushing floral pattern, and his long legs disappeared under the bed-skirt. He felt like he was sitting in a lady's hatbox.

He must have made a sound because Millie, who was seated on the opposite side of the bed, scowled and put her finger to her lips. The heavy rose drapes were closed, but the intensity of the late morning sun made everything quite distinct, the paintings, the furniture, and the lovely woman lying on her side, facing him.

Eleanor's fist was tucked under her chin, creating a deceptively winsome effect. The copperish rope of her braid fell over her shoulder, and Giles' fingers itched to slide across her cheek.

Millie returned her attention to the mending in her lap. Time for the slumbering beauty to awaken. To expedite matters, Giles surreptitiously knocked the book off the bedside table. It missed the carpet and slapped the floor.

Rodrigo growled.

Giles leaned forward to pick up the book and looked his dog in the eye. "Traitor."

Eleanor smothered a yawn. "What's the time?"

Giles looked at the mantel clock. "Eleven."

Eleanor buried her nose behind Rodrigo's ear and nuzzled, which put she and Giles eye to eye. Suddenly he had Eleanor's undivided attention. "What concerns you, my lord?"

"Hmm?"

"Your brows are a veritable pucker," Eleanor said.

I'm wondering how to circumvent your trajectory toward spinsterhood—that's what, Miss 'I'm-never-getting-married' Barrett.

"What do you think, Roddy? What has your master so bedeviled?"

Rodrigo turned his head and gave Eleanor's cheek a lick. Her sleep-roughed chuckle was maddeningly erotic.

Giles felt his groin pulse. "His name is Rodrigo." Giles pushed himself out of the chair.

Woof.

Damn. Giles strolled to the window and drew back the curtain, hoping something in the outside world would distract him and he could will his rod to quit dancing in his breeches. This whole scenario was the stuff of Shakespearian comedies. Eleanor Barrett wasn't even trying to be provocative and he was hard from her nuzzling his dog—longing for her to be nuzzling him, and not behind the ear either.

"I *said*, what's bothering you? Too many mama's trying to get their hooks into you?"

"What?" Giles let the curtain fall and he turned toward the bed. Eleanor had pushed herself up onto her elbow. This caused her robe to gape open, revealing the swell of her breast covered by an enticing bit of lace-edged fabric.

"What's going on that has you so bumble-brained?" Eleanor said.

Rodrigo began to whine.

"Sorry, boy, guess you need a trip out to her ladyship's garden," Eleanor said. "Millie?"

Millie walked out of the room, and when she returned she had two able-bodied footmen, one carrying a plank. Giles helped load Rodrigo onto the board for his trip down the stairs.

Giles noticed the way the second footman and Millie eyed each other. *Ah, flirtation.*

"Go along, Millie," Eleanor said and made a shooing motion. "I'll be fine until you return."

"Yes, miss." Millie's steps were quick as she left the room. She didn't look back. In fact, in her haste, she closed the door behind her.

Giles stared at the closed door.

"Humph, guh. Bother." Eleanor struggled to rearrange her pillows at her back.

"May I provide some assistance?" Giles ambled toward the bed.

Eleanor yanked one of the pillows free from behind her back, when something small shot out. When the projectile landed on the carpet, it made a muffled *plunk,* but that was not the end of its journey as the plunk was shortly followed by a *wrr-wrr-wrr* as the object rolled across the bare wood floor beneath her bed.

She stared over the edge of the bed, then lifted the covers. Her bare toes appeared as she swung her legs out.

"Stop," Giles said as he rushed forward. "What do you think you're doing? I'll get whatever fell. Stay put. It's only been a few days since you got throttled."

"I was *not* throttled."

He knelt on one knee, reaching under the bed and running his hand over the floor. He located something small and hard and closed his fingers around it.

Eleanor sat back, pulling the covers up and squeezing her eyes shut. She looked distressed.

He pulled the object out. For a moment, it crossed his mind to hand it back to her without looking, but his curiosity got the better of him. He opened his hand to see what had caused Eleanor such consternation.

He gazed at the small, blue, misshapen roundish object lying in his palm. It resembled a marble except one part had been flattened. What was all her fuss about a child's toy, for heaven's sake?

Something niggled at the back of his mind. This blue lump felt familiar. As if he were used to holding it. Giles ran his fingers over it, rolled it across his palm. Then it struck him. This was *his* lucky shooter.

He remembered the moment he'd given it to her. That morning after her eighth birthday, when she'd been hurt. He'd told her it had always brought him luck and she looked like she could use some. Giles cleared his throat. "You kept it?"

With that flattened side, it wouldn't even roll anymore. It wasn't broken off either. It looked like someone had held it and repeatedly run her fingers across its surface. He just stared at the misshapen object resting in his palm.

Still kneeling beside the bed, he watched her staring down at her hands. "Eleanor?"

She didn't answer.

"Sweetheart," Giles whispered.

When she did look up, her eyes were filled with such unconcealed vulnerability.

He leaned forward and kissed the corner of her mouth. Eleanor trembled and turned her head and pressed her lips softly to his. He was lost in the feel of her mouth, lips so soft. This kiss wasn't that mad, frenzied embrace in her parents' garden; this was slow and sweet like honey.

When it ended they stared at one another He planted his hands on either side of her hips and kissed her again. He drew back just enough so he could gaze into her eyes, so he could be sure she wanted him as much as he wanted her. She tunneled her fingers through his hair and pulled his lips back to hers.

Giles tasted strawberries and the tang of tea. He came down on the bed beside her and rolled to the center of the mattress, his arms around her. She lay across his chest and he felt her hands under his coat, sliding up his back.

Eleanor winced.

"We should stop." Giles tried to sit up. Eleanor gripped his shoulders and pulled herself up his chest. Then she dropped her weight and he flopped back and an *oof* escaped his lips.

Eleanor smiled, then she nipped his bottom lip.

Giles took control and brought up his hands to hold her head still. His tongue brushed across her sealed lips and her mouth opened and she eagerly participated. For a flash, he wondered who had taught her to kiss that way, and then all thought fled. His mouth left her lips and traveled across her jaw to her ear. She let out a throaty sound. She turned her head so he could nuzzle behind her ear. Open-mouthed, he slid down her neck.

Her skin felt warm against his lips and tasted salty against his tongue. Eleanor shifted, and Giles felt her slide her bare toes up his legs. She dropped her knees down upon the mattress so that they bracketed his hips, straddling him.

Giles' hands left her head to cradle her knees and his fingers slipped beneath the edge of her night-rail as she gripped his hips with her warm thighs. She had the legs of a horsewoman, strong and firm. She rubbed and rocked against his throbbing cock. Even through the fabric of his breeches he could feel her heat and need. She dropped her head forward. Her braid came undone and her loosened hair fell over her face. He heard her quick gasps of pleasure coming faster and faster.

Giles got his hands under Eleanor's arms and lifted her up.

Eleanor raised her head, grabbing his lapels, trying to stop him from moving her.

Her lovely eyes were nearly black with passion. "Shhh." He pulled her forward, dragging her right across his swollen cock. He groaned. He lifted her farther above him and her robe gaped open. Her breasts, barely contained behind the lace-edged fabric came into view, round and firm with the dark rosy tips of her nipples begging for his attention. He had to put his mouth *there*.

Eleanor gasped as he bit down on her nipple. He began to suck her through the thin linen of her gown. He sucked harder and her hips rocked against him in a frenzy and her breathing grew faster and more frantic.

Suddenly she threw her head back and her whole body arched. Giles felt the vibration of her release. He pulled her against his chest and felt the damp heat of her skin. With her head tucked under his chin, he wrapped his arms around her.

They held each other until her breathing calmed.

"My goodness. That was even better than anything that I have given—"

"What?" Giles pushed Eleanor away far enough so he could look up into her eyes.

Eleanor cleared her throat and her eyes darted away. "I mean—"

"Are you telling me that—" Giles huffed, unable to bring himself to finish his sentence. "Your Aunt Beatrice again, no doubt."

Eleanor dipped her chin and looked at him from the corner of her eye while a very satisfied grin spread across her lips. "But of course. That was lovely. As for Aunt Beatrice, she simply made sure that I knew my own body and how it worked. What's more, she says men take care of their own needs as well. I mean …"

Giles stared at the ceiling. "I can't believe we're speaking of such things." He felt Eleanor's lips on his neck. "You're incorrigible," he said.

She chuckled and the vibration of her laugh against his skin tickled. He cupped her jaw. Her skin was damp and soft.

A door shut somewhere, rousing him from his reverie and reminding him where he was and what they were doing. Giles slipped out from under Eleanor. "I must go."

She ended up face down in the rumpled sheets, her brows knit and mouth turned down. He chuckled and took a step away and lost his balance as he rocked backward. He recovered and leaned down and picked up his marble from the rug. He put his large hand about her wrist and pulled her hand forward, turning her palm upward. He placed a kiss in the center of her palm and then placed the marble where his lips had been, closing her fingers around it, as he'd done so long ago—without the kiss, of course.

Giles put his ear against the door. No voices or footfalls. He opened the door then disappeared.

Chapter Twenty-five

After a few days at the Red Gabbler, Pim was no longer among the living. After burying his cousin, Madame Lutz prevailed upon Barend to remove with her to a small property in Clevedon, to lay low and wait for Edgerton to locate their prey. Edgerton saw them off, then returned to Bath.

Barend would make the perfect executioner. Edgerton couldn't wait to locate the bothersome baggage and set his plan in motion.

The Bath gossip mill revealed his cousin, Lady Beatrice Whitley, was visiting an old chum, Lady Standish. If Eleanor was in town, she would be with Lady Beatrice. He sent a note, asking permission to make a call.

The town clock chimed two as he stood waiting for the front door of Lady Standish's impressive townhouse to open. He held two nosegays. A rather odd butler, who looked more like the comic lead in one of Goldsmith's plays than her ladyship's major domo, informed Edgerton that Lady Standish and Lady Whitley would receive him in the parlor. When he entered the room, the two women were standing before the fireplace.

Edgerton bowed and walked toward them. "How pleasant to see you again, my lady," Edgerton addressed Lady Beatrice as he took her hand and brushed a respectful kiss above her knuckles. He presented her a nosegay.

"Thank you, Edgerton." Lady Beatrice raised the posies to her nose, sniffed and smiled benignly. "I wasn't aware you were acquainted with my old friend, Lady Standish." Lady Whitley gazed at him with utter inscrutability.

"Alas, I'm not." He smiled with as much boyish earnestness as he could muster at Lady Sybil Standish. "Lady Beatrice, I heard you were in residence and chose this opportunity to beg an introduction."

By gad, I'd hate to play cards with this old virago—she gives nothing away.

Beatrice Whitely paused, then turned to her companion. "Lady Standish, may I present my second cousin, Sir Francis Edgerton."

Edgerton handed her the other nosegay. "Charmed."

"So, thoughtful. Thank you, my lord." Lady Standish gazed at the flowers. "My late husband was quite fond of giving me nosegays," —she paused— "especially when he'd done something … he knew would upset me."

A fine riposte. You're smarter than you look, Lady Sybil.

Lady Standish motioned him to the settee. "Will you join us for tea, my lord?"

"Delighted." Edgerton accepted his cup.

Secret non-verbal communication buzzed through the air between the ladies. The by-play was all vastly amusing. These two were truly worthy adversaries, up to a point; no one of his acquaintance was truly his match. More the pity, for he liked a good challenge and hadn't had one in a very long time.

⁓

Giles closed the book he'd been reading to Eleanor and Rodrigo. The rise and fall of her chest denoted deep sleep. Standing, he walked to the side of the bed. Rodrigo stirred and looked up at him.

"Shhh. Don't wake her." Giles leaned down and lightly kissed Eleanor on the forehead. Her skin was warm and soft under his lips and her hair smelled of lavender. "Dream of me."

Giles stoked Rodrigo across his silken head and gave him a good scratch behind his ear. "Watch over her, boy." Giles' stomach growled. Rodrigo eyed his midsection. "Hmmm, seems I'm in need of some sustenance."

Giles trotted down the stairs, hoping to find tea and a pile of sandwiches waiting for him in the parlor. When the footman opened the door, Giles was surprised and happy to see his old friend sitting with ladies. But as he stepped across the threshold, Harleigh's warning rumbled through his mind. *Don't let anyone know she's here.*

He felt as though he was having a premonition, like in those fables he used to read as a boy. But that was nonsense; this was Francis. Bah, Harleigh and his fanciful imagination seeing danger behind every turn.

"Giles." Edgerton put his cup and saucer on the table and rose to clasp hands.

Giles smiled and shook hands, then accepted a cup of tea.

"I understood that my Cousin Harleigh Barrett is also visiting you, Lady Standish, as well as his sister, Miss Eleanor."

Giles stared at Edgerton. Odd, Edgerton hadn't been surprised to see him, and how the devil did he know about Harleigh, let alone Eleanor? Giles felt the skin across his forehead tighten, while a prickle skittered across his shoulders. He shrugged to ease the tension. It didn't relieve his apprehension.

No one except Lady Standish's staff knew Eleanor was in town. Giles lost his interest in food; he placed his cup on the mantel.

Lady Beatrice nibbled on a biscuit. "I'm sorry to inform you, but Harleigh's visit was cut short. A need arose for him to travel back to Kent."

"And Eleanor? Is she unwell? Is that why she's failed to present herself?" Edgerton looked about the room, as if he expected her to suddenly appear.

Lady Whitely lowered her cup. "Eleanor caught a bit of a cold. Her throat." Lady Beatrice touched her neck. "So, I ordered her to bed. A few days' rest will prevent it from turning putrid."

"Wouldn't want that, would we? What brings you to Bath, West?"

"Accompanied Harleigh," Giles replied.

"Family business drew him home, I suppose." Edgerton sipped his tea.

"Something like that." Giles grew more uneasy.

"Is he expected to return?" Edgerton asked.

"In a few weeks, I suppose," Giles said.

"Well, when he does we can make a night of it. Although, I'm sorry to say, Bath has nothing to compare with the delights of London."

Giles nodded.

The mantel clock chimed the half hour.

Edgerton rose. "Should be off. Ladies, West." He bowed to all.

"I'll see you out." Giles walked Edgerton to the door.

A brawny footman came forward with Edgerton's hat, gloves and cane. The footman held them out to him. Edgerton didn't notice his garments being offered, as his attention was elsewhere. He was staring up the stairs.

Giles felt a discomfort he'd never experienced in his old friend's company. He cleared his throat loudly enough to snag Edgerton's attention. "Your things?"

"Ah, yes," Edgerton said.

As Giles watched the front door close, denial warred inside him with fond childhood memories. He'd an overwhelming sense of loss, as if something precious had just been knocked off a shelf and shattered beyond repair.

A well-enunciated baritone spoke from behind him. "The ladies are awaiting your return, my lord."

Giles startled. He hadn't heard Honeycutt approach.

He returned to Lady Beatrice and Lady Sybil. Honeycutt followed a few minutes later accompanied by a maid carrying a fresh pot of tea and several large plates piled high with sandwiches and cakes.

Lady Sybil poured Giles a fresh hot cup of tea and Lady Beatrice lifted an empty plate. "My lord, may I fill a plate for you?"

Giles looked at the tempting food and realized his hunger had flown. "No, thank you, Lady Beatrice. Tea is all I require." Lady Sybil handed him his cup.

His stomach rumbled. Lady Beatrice gave him a questioning look. He sat down and drank his tea, hoping it would soothe his now sour and agitated stomach.

Honeycutt waved his hand in the direction of the nosegays that rested on the table. "Shall I remove *those*?"

"Rumpled your feathers, has he, Honeycutt?" Lady Standish chuckled. "Do as you like."

Honeycutt plucked the nosegays from the table and tossed them unceremoniously onto the now empty tray as the maid was departing.

Giles stared down into his cup. "Odd. He didn't seem surprised to see me, did he?"

"That's true, dear boy." Beatrice Whitley sipped her tea.

Lady Sybil's brows drew together. "Bea dear, was Lord Edgerton the one to bring up Harleigh?"

Beatrice Whitely drummed her long fingers on the arm of the settee. "And Eleanor. How did he know they were in Bath? I feel like we're missing something. I believe we need to consult my niece." Lady Bea put down her cup and saucer.

"You read my mind, Lady Beatrice," Giles said.

Millie opened Eleanor's door and Giles followed the ladies across the threshold, while Honeycutt brought up the rear.

"Whatcha all about?" Millie said. "She needs her sleep."

"She needs to wake up and tell us what she didn't tell us about the brothel," Giles said as he pointed at Eleanor.

"We done told it all." Millie put her hands on her hips.

Giles adopted his lordliest posture, looking down his nose. "Have you, indeed. Tell us, Millie, did *you* recognize any of the patrons?"

"Whatcha talkin' 'bout, yer lordship?" Millie shifted from one foot to the other.

Lady Beatrice went to the side of the bed and leaned down and stroked Eleanor's cheek. "Ellie-sweet, wake up, we need to talk to you." Then she patted Rodrigo on the head.

"This is most intriguing, is it not?" Lady Standish said and beamed at Giles as she seated herself. "I simply adore a good puzzle."

Giles wondered when he had taken up living inside Astley's? His life seemed to be turning into a circus. He paced as Millie stuffed several pillows behind Eleanor's back and threw a floral shawl around shoulders.

"Seal the portal, Honeycutt," Lady Sybil said and waved her hand at the door with her usual touch of the dramatic. "We've news, dear. Lord Edgerton just paid us a visit."

Eleanor wrinkled her nose.

"Yes, well, we know you're not fond of the boy, but the point is he presented us with a conundrum," Lady Beatrice said.

"Really?" Eleanor gazed about the room.

Giles stood at the foot of her bed. "Miss Barrett, how does he know you are *here*?"

Eleanor fiddled with the fringe on her shawl but said nothing.

"How does Cousin Francis know you are in Bath?" Aunt Beatrice cocked her head.

"And Harleigh, too," Giles said as he moved to the head of the bed and loomed over Eleanor. "Harleigh made it very clear to me before leaving that I was to let *no* one know you were here."

"I've no idea," Eleanor said.

"Now, unannounced and without any preamble, Edgerton shows up and says he wants to see,"—Giles thrust his finger at Eleanor — "*you.*"

Eleanor flushed and then batted his hand away. "Not nice to point."

Giles put his hands on his hips. "Does he inquire if you're in residence? No … he does not. He states it as fact that you *are* here. It's the understanding of everyone in this room that no one knows you are in Bath, so how can this be?"

Eleanor crossed her arms over her chest. "I don't believe it."

"Calling me a liar, are you?" Giles said.

"Edgerton stood right beside me," Eleanor said, "and didn't recognize me, I swear it. Just like you and—" She slammed her mouth shut.

"What?" everyone said at once. All eyes trained on her.

"This is no time for secrets," Aunt Beatrice said.

"I told Harleigh that. But he made me promise to keep quiet," Eleanor said. "He decided it was best to wait until he returned to speak about this."

"I see." Aunt Beatrice folded her hands in her lap.

"Are you confirming Lord Edgerton was at that house?" Honeycutt asked.

Eleanor hesitated, then nodded.

Giles wandered to the window. The burning in his stomach intensified. He pushed the sheer drapes aside, hoping something in the outside world would distract him.

"Nothing unusual about a young buck visiting a high-class brothel, missy," Lady Sybil said.

Just like in a fight when you know the next blow is coming, Giles felt the punch moving at him and there was nowhere to go. He had to stand there and take the hit. "Let's have it all."

Eleanor sighed. "Edgerton didn't arrive alone. The fellow's name sounded familiar, but I couldn't place it."

"What name?" Aunt Beatrice said.

"Povey."

"Lincoln Povey?" Giles said.

"Yes," Eleanor said.

Giles made a disgusted sound. "My sister Dolly's husband. I curse the day my sister ever met that poor excuse for a man."

Aunt Beatrice cleared her throat.

"Anything else?" Honeycutt probed.

Eleanor cleared her throat. "I don't believe Edgerton, ah-h, came to patronize the establishment."

Giles let his hand drop to his side and the sheer curtain closed. He turned toward Eleanor.

Eleanor cleared her throat. "I believe he's one of the owners."

"Really?" Lady Sybil said. "Goodness, now that's a bit of interesting news, is it not?"

Aunt Beatrice moved to the edge of her chair. "Remember what Rooksby told us? The rumors of someone of consequence being involved?"

Eleanor nodded. "Lady Sybil, this can't get about."

"I understand, dear. Honeycutt and I..." She pantomimed trapping her lips between her index finger and thumb. "Mum's the word, eh, Honeycutt?"

"Indeed, my lady," Honeycutt said.

"None of this explains how he knows you're here, dear," Lady Beatrice said.

"I can't explain it," Eleanor said.

Giles' world tilted. Every sound became muffled, like when he was under water. He looked up and Eleanor's sympathetic gaze made him wince. He didn't know who this Rooksby was and right now he didn't give a damn. He had to get out of this room, find Edgerton, and prove he had nothing to do with the missing girls.

Without another word, Giles strolled out of the room and flew down the stairs. He was standing in the foyer with the footman handing him his hat and gloves when Honeycutt's voice pierced his red haze.

"My lord?"

"Yes, Honeycutt," Giles said.

"Might I inquire?"

"Where the hell do you think?" Giles said. "To find Lord Edgerton, of course."

"Do you know where he's staying?" Honeycutt's voice was smooth and controlled. The rich timbre of it felt like a balm against Giles' frayed temper.

Giles hesitated. "What? No, I have no idea." He looked at Honeycutt out of the corner of his eye as he pulled on his gloves.

"Very good, sir. Might I venture an alternative?" Honeycutt said.

Was there no end to this man's gall? Giles shook his head and turned. "And that would be what precisely?"

"Let me make some inquiries regarding Lord Edgerton," Honeycutt said.

"And what would you suggest I do in the meantime?"

"I'd have Robert here," Honeycutt said, and waved the robust young footman forward, "escort you to *Señor Saviolo's* fencing salon."

"Master *Vincentio Saviolo*?"

Honeycutt nodded. "You could post an open challenge. Take on all comers, as it were." Palm up, Honeycutt moved his hand before him like he was casting bread upon the waters.

"And burn my unbridled anger to a crisp, thus leaving me to deal with Lord Edgerton with a clear head and a sober temperament; is that the general idea, Honeycutt?"

"Precisely, my lord."

"You are a wise man." Giles looked up the stairs. He felt like he was abandoning his post. "Miss Barrett?"

Honeycutt stood straighter. "Her ladyship has many able-bodied men in her employ, my lord. We shall keep her safe."

"Adieu, Mr. Honeycutt."

Chapter Twenty-six

Edgerton raised a sour pint of ale to his lips, knowing no amount of spirits, good or bad, could wipe away the memory of that bleak look in Giles' eyes back at Lady Standish's. The brothel and the girls were easily replaced, but not his one faithful friend. *Eleanor, you interfering bitch. This is all your fault.*

The air in the main room of the tavern was thick with smoke, smelling of cheap pipe tobacco and charred wood. His eyes burned and as he rubbed them he glimpsed a pair of small dirty feet in his peripheral vision, standing beside the back legs of his chair.

The boy cleared his throat to announce himself. The arrival of the lookout bearing news banished Edgerton's maudlin musings for the moment. He needed to focus on pressing matters, like how he was going to get to Eleanor. He'd bet a monkey she was upstairs at Lady Standish's right now plotting his demise. He laughed to himself. *Not if I get you first, cuz.*

"Podge?" Edgerton sat low in his chair before the inn's fire, his long legs stretched out before him.

"Sir?"

"Have you ever been too clever?" Edgerton said.

"Huh?" Podge scratched his dirty hair. "Oh, yeah, all the times. Me mum says I asks too many questions. Is that whatcha means?"

"In a way," Edgerton said.

"Whas got you in the mopes, m'lord?"

"Someone is spoiling my fun."

Podge made a derisive sound.

"Should have snapped her neck when I had the chance. Back when she was eight. Now *that* would have been a fitting birthday present." Edgerton chuckled as he laid his thumb across his index finger and pressed down to crack his knuckle.

Podge bobbed his head, eager in his agreement.

"What do you have to tell me?" Edgerton said.

Podge craned his neck, left and right.

"Don't worry. I pay them plenty *not* to listen." Edgerton's throat felt dry. He raised his mug, then thought better than to take another swallow of this piss, and put the mug down.

Podge eyed the pint on the table and licked his lips.

Edgerton huffed out a laugh and pushed his mug to the boy.

"Thank you, sir." Podge took it and gulped down the contents, then wiped his mouth with his torn coat sleeve.

"Well?"

Podge threw his hand over his mouth to muffle his burp, "Beggin yer pardon."

Edgerton nodded.

"I done followed that footman, the one they calls Robert, and that tall blond fella you sets me to watch. To a building on Priory Street."

"What building?"

"It had a sign hangin' 'buv the door." Podge raised his hand over his head.

"What was on the sign?"

"A big hairy beast. With huge head and teeth." Podge opened his mouth wide and bared his teeth.

"Was it red?"

"It twer."

"A red lion perhaps?" Edgerton said.

"Is that what you calls it, a lion?"

Edgerton knew that building well. "Interesting choice." He lobbed a coin in the air and Podge caught it.

"Anyfing else, sir?"

"Return to the house. I'll send a few others to join you. Mind, stay well hidden. Wouldn't want you taken up by the constable."

Podge shook his head several times. "No, yer lordship, don't want to get nibbed fer nuffin'."

"Off with you."

The boy darted away like a minnow.

Edgerton climbed the back stairs of the tavern. At the end of the hall, he knocked once. Daylight had given way to dusk and the only illumination came from the meager fire. Barend sat on the hearth, a great lump of woebegone man staring into the dying embers. Edgerton endured his proximity to this saturnine creature because when the time came he would kill Eleanor without hesitation.

Edgerton laid his hat and cane on the table. "Would you care for something to eat or drink?"

"Vhat newz?" Barend said.

"Lord West has gone out, to practice his fencing."

Barend turned his head and gave Edgerton a quizzical look. He put his hand on the hilt of his own sword.

"It vill do him no goot."

"If you would be so kind, try not to damage Lord West. He is my only friend. Miss Barrett is your target."

Barend grunted.

"By morning we should have sufficient information from my little web of spies to make our plan."

Chapter Twenty-seven

The moon had traversed more than half its arc by the time Giles and Robert returned to Lady Standish's. Several of her ladyship's robust retainers stood guard inside and outside the front door. Giles wondered about the rest of the property—was it as well-guarded? He didn't think someone bent on hurting Eleanor would use the front door.

The house was deadly quiet except for the sound of his and the other men's heels striking the marble floor, which reverberated in the cavernous foyer.

"How are things?" Giles asked the footman who took his gloves, cane, and hat.

"All quiet, m'lord."

"And the perimeter?"

"There, too. Our Mr. Honeycutt's thurrah. No one'll get past us, m'lord."

"Excellent. Goodnight, gentlemen." Giles walked to the foot of the staircase and stared upward. His bed seemed miles away at that moment. Fatigue washed over him. His thighs, shoulders and arm muscles burned from the abuse he'd given them at Master Saviolo's fencing studio.

He placed his bare hand on the banister and began to climb. The wood was warm against his palm. An image of Master Saviolo came into his mind. When they'd been introduced, the old master clasped Giles' hand with both of his, and looked him directly in the eye. Giles had the impression he was being measured by that keen, perceptive gaze.

"Ah, I see," Master Saviolo said as he pursed his lips and nodded his head. "Betrayal is a difficult emotion. One tends to blame the self, instead of the one who deceived. Come back to me when you are *not* fighting with yourself, eh? I can teach you something then." He released Giles' hand and glided away to watch and instruct the other men.

It had been unnerving to be stripped of one's social mask so quickly. But Giles sensed no judgment or malice in the old master, he was just an astute observer of humanity. The fencing matches had indeed helped Giles vent his anger. But now, in the quiet house, the faces of the rescued girls flooded his mind, and Eleanor. *Damn you, Edgerton! And damn me for a fool!*

By the time Giles reached the second-floor landing, he'd shed his heavy blue coat and slung it over his shoulder, unbuttoned his waistcoat, stuffed his cravat into a coat pocket, and opened his collar.

He toed off his shoes to silence his footfalls before he continued down the hallway. When he bent down to pick them up, he noticed Rodrigo's hair clinging to his hose. Giles hesitated, but decided to check on his dog before retiring.

He hoped Rodrigo and Eleanor would be fit to travel soon. His shoulders sagged as he acknowledged that leaving Bath wouldn't mean leaving his troubles behind.

He left his discarded clothing on a bench in the corridor, and walked down to Eleanor's door. He didn't knock. It was late. Eleanor and Rodrigo must be asleep. Once inside, he closed the door and leaned back against it, waiting for his eyes to adjust to the darkness. The air smelled like her, a lemony woodsy fragrance.

Images of what had happened the last time they'd been alone in this room leaped to mind. *Damn, maybe this isn't such a clever idea.* His hand was on the door latch. Ready to make his retreat. But Rodrigo hadn't uttered even one soft *woof* of greeting.

Giles tensed. Had an intruder evaded Honeycutt and his watch? He slid his feet across the thick carpet as if skating and headed towards what, he assumed, were the drapes. Groping around in the dark was a disorienting business. At last he felt the heavy brocaded fabric against his open palm. He pushed the curtain aside. A slice of the blue-white moonlight cut into the darkness. He turned.

Eleanor was sitting up in bed with a gun in her hand, pointing straight at him.

"Good God, woman! What in the blazes are you doing?"

"I'm *not* the one creeping around in the dark, my lord."

Giles came to stand beside the bed and stared down at the place his dog usually occupied. "Where's Rodrigo?"

Her legs were under the covers and drawn up toward her bottom, tenting the covers and obscuring his view of her breasts. She sighed and replaced the pin that served as her pistol's safety and laid it onto the bedside table. She then wrapped her arms around her legs, and rested her chin in the notch between her knees. Her night-rail was sleeveless, held together at the shoulders with some bits of ribbon, tied into floppy bows.

"I should go," Giles whispered as he stood still, staring down at the bed.

"What?" Eleanor cocked her head to the side like a voluptuous, quizzical bird.

Giles didn't realize he'd spoken the words aloud until he heard her question.

She peered over the side of the bed. "Pray tell, what does the whereabouts of your dog have to do with you standing, in your stocking feet, in my room after midnight?"

"After three, actually. Just got back."

Eleanor sniffed, then waved her hand before her face. "You stink of cheap tobacco."

Giles huffed and pointed his finger emphatically down at the bed.

"Oh, Roddy and the cook's son have become fast friends. They're spending the night together down in the cook's quarters."

"His name is Rodrigo."

Eleanor shrugged, nonplused. "Where have you been? We've been worried about you."

"Have *you*?" Giles said.

"Have I what?"

Giles put his hand on the headboard and leaned down. "Worried about me?" She looked other-worldly with her features rimmed in moonlight. It gave these moments a dreamlike quality.

"Are you drunk, my lord?"

On you. "No, just incredibly sore and tired." *Damn, I'm fashed.*

"I distinctly heard myself use the inclusive pronoun 'we', which should indicate to anyone of average intelligence that I was including myself among those who were worried."

Giles closed his eyes to block out the sight of Eleanor, and gave his head a slight shake. Lord, what an infuriating creature.

Time passed. Neither spoke.

"Well?" Eleanor said.

Giles opened his eyes. Had he fallen asleep on his feet?

One of Eleanor's ribbony straps had drifted down her arm. She had lovely shoulders, creamy white. He wanted to press his lips right there, where the ribbon stopped, and kiss his way back to that delicate notch at the base of her throat and then he wanted to go on an exploratory journey south, into the valley between her luscious firm breasts.

Eleanor poked him hard with her finger in his upper arm.

"Ow. Quit that, you murderous wench. First a gun, now you are attempting to stab me to death." Giles let go of the headboard and rubbed the sore spot on his arm where she'd poked him. "What do you want?"

He knew what *he* wanted … Eleanor naked and under him, for starters, but only after she agreed to marry him. He needed to get out of there before they were caught. He would *not* compromise her to force her hand.

"My, my, you must be tired," Eleanor said. "You're being positively surly."

Giles ran his hands through his hair, dislodging the black ribbon at his nape. His hair fell to his shoulders. This situation was absurd. He walked to the door.

"Wait. You didn't answer my question. Where were you?"

Giles had his hand on the door latch. "*Señor Saviolo's.*"

"The fencing master?"

Giles nodded.

Eleanor said as she leaped from her bed, "Oooo, he's a genius." She grabbed her wrap and shoved her arms down the sleeves. "Will you take me next time you go? Do you think he might be persuaded to take me on as a student?"

He made his voice stern. "Eleanor."

She took a step in his direction as she tied her wrapper closed. "What's this?" She bent down and picked something off the floor and held it up.

It was his hair ribbon.

He held out his hand. Good grief, nothing of his should ever be found in her room. *Never. Ever.* "Give me *that*." When she didn't, he closed his eyes against the vision of her. "Damn you, Harleigh."

"Oh, yes indeed." Eleanor made a tisking sound and shook her head. "Harleigh's going to be positively furious with me."

With you? Giles opened his eyes. Eleanor was absentmindedly weaving his hair ribbon through her fingers. Being angry with her was nothing compared to what her brother was going to do to him if he learned Giles had been in his sister's room without a chaperone.

"He made me promise not to say a word, you see," Eleanor said as she walked closer.

Giles leaned his back against the door and held out his hand. "Eleanor give. Me. My. Ribbon. So I can get out of here."

"Everything got so muddled. If only Harleigh had confided in me about his suspicions."

"I need to *go*." But Giles needed his damn ribbon first.

"I'm sorry. We know how much you care for our cousin. You're such a loyal man and ..."

Giles pressed his fingers gently against her lips to silence her. With the moonlight behind her, he could not see her features, but her voice was full of tender feeling. He couldn't seem to breathe deeply. And then she pressed her lips against his fingers. There was a roaring in his ears and his fingers tingled where her lips touched his skin.

Giles moved his hand away and leaned forward, hovering, waiting for her to turn her head away.

Instead, Eleanor tucked a loosened lock of his hair behind his right ear, then rubbed the ends between her fingers. "It's so soft." She kissed him high on his cheek.

"You missed the mark." Giles tapped his finger against his lips.

"Did I?" She kissed the end of his nose this time.

He chuckled. "Come here, you minx." He tunneled his fingers through
her hair. He held her still while he brushed his lips lightly against hers.

When she didn't protest his first kiss, he filled the second with ardor and lingered. When he pulled back, she made a sound of protest.

He wrapped his arms around her and pulled her in. She snuggled and laid her head on his shoulder. Her hand rested on his chest. He picked it up and wove his fingers through hers. "Eleanor?"

"Hmm?" She sounded sleepy.

"Eleanor Barrett, I'm in love with you. Please do me the honor of becoming my wife."

She stared at him, at their joined hands.

Dear Lord, please make her say yes.

Finally, she took a breath and looked up at him. "I believe if I was ever going to say yes to anyone, it would be you."

"Gaaaauullll." Giles stared at the ceiling. "Lord, why is *she* the one?" He paused, hoping for an answer, but when none came he returned his gaze to Eleanor's. "It is beyond my *average* intelligence..." He paused and cocked one brow at her.

Eleanor snorted.

"...to comprehend the meaning of this improbable situation. I've met others during the Season who would say yes without hesitation. But no, I have to be drawn to you, only you." He jabbed his finger in her direction.

"Well then, by all means go ask one of those females." Eleanor tossed her hands in the air and stepped away. "You know I don't want to be anyone's ..."

"Egads, you were a child when you made your declaration never to marry."

"You believe my decision never to be subject to a man's dominion childish?"

There was no right answer to *that* question. Best keep his mouth shut.

Eleanor's spine stiffened.

"I know you love me," he said. "I know it like I know my own name." Giles cocked his thumb and pointed to himself. "The way you look at me, touch me, kiss me. You know we belong together."

She opened her mouth.

He sliced his hand through the air, cutting off her rebuttal. "You're *not* a liar. Don't even try denying it."

"Very well." Eleanor crossed her arms over her chest. "Let's hypothesize for a moment, shall we? If we did marry, and the need arose—like it did with Julia Brewster—for me to go and help another woman, would you support my efforts?"

"Of course not, you nearly died," Giles said.

"You prove my point nicely. And that's why my feelings for you are irrelevant. I could *never* sit by and do nothing."

"Irrelevant? Your feelings for me are *not* irrelevant. Not to me. This is preposterous. You are willing to throw away the life we would have together because I'll not aid you in your reckless behavior?"

"Just because you have a bishop in your breeches, sirrah, doesn't give you the right to judge my behavior as reckless. I did what was right. If we'd followed the course of action you, Harleigh, and my father had set out, Julia would've been raped by now."

She was right, damn her. She'd saved that poor child. But that didn't stop him from wanting to grab her and shake her. Good Lord, she seemed to care nothing for her own life. By losing his temper he'd lost control of this situation. Arguing with her now wasn't going to aid his cause. His fear and lust were clouding his reason.

Eleanor pointed at the door. "I think you should leave."

"What a *brilliant* idea."

Chapter Twenty-eight

Giles strode with ferocious intent down the hallway away from Eleanor's door. *That blasted woman—so stubborn.*

He was a few paces from Eleanor's room when the sole of his unshod foot landed on something sharp buried in the pile of the carpet runner. That pain put an end to his rant. "My damn shoes?" Then he recalled where he'd left them and the rest of his garments.

"Blast." Giles quickly retraced his steps and grabbed his belongings off the bench. As he turned, he heard the soft click of a door's latch closing nearby. *Damn it to hell and back.*

Inside his room, his man Mumby had left a candle burning on the dresser and a window open just a crack. Giles tossed his things down and threw the window wide. The rush of the cool air racing over his hot skin didn't do much for his erection. He leaned his forehead against the cool glass of the window. What a maddening creature. He'd never felt such an intense need to be with anyone—ever.

Something darted through the hedge below his window, followed by the screech of a bird of prey. Out in the dark, dinner was being served. Food? Hmmmm, he could almost feel cold milk running down his throat and the taste and feel of flakey butter biscuits against his tongue. He smacked his lips. Perhaps a trip to the kitchen was in order? Something sweet to counter his mood.

No. Stay put. No more wandering around the house tonight.

He disrobed and got into bed and closed his eyes and tried to empty his mind. But the incessant chirps of the insects inhabiting the shrubbery caught his ear and summoned images of his parents' house and the omnipresent female chatter that filled it. His mother and sisters were forever nattering on about this or that. Last time he was home he stumbled into a heated discourse on the enhancing effect of peach-colored cloth over some other color. And an entire dinner's conversation had been dominated by commentary and unsolicited suggestions on the correct way to discipline one of his nephews. He'd been bored witless. He snorted. He couldn't even imagine Eleanor bothering with either topic. She'd tell her modiste what she wanted and if a child of theirs misbehaved she would sit him or her down for a chat.

The workings of his dearest female relatives' minds sounded trivial compared to Eleanor's. This need of hers for self-governance presented a significant barrier to his plans to marry her. He'd blundered badly when he'd dismissed it as childish. Until their recent run-ins he'd been ignorant and quite content with the status quo, and from what he could tell so were his mother and sisters, but then he'd never asked them, had he?

He was his father's heir, born to privilege and the rank his family's title bestowed. He'd never once considered he was also born to the privilege of being a man. What must it be like to never have a say in your own life?

He put his hands behind his head. As a boy, he was forced to submit to his father. But as a man he ruled his world. But a girl never matured in the eyes of the law. He shook his head. How the hell had checking on his injured dog led him to question the foundations of his existence?

It was all Eleanor's fault. She kept raising questions and prodding him to examine things. Why couldn't she accept the way things were and get on with her life? He sighed.

All he wanted was to love her and awaken beside her every day for the rest of his life. Was that too much to ask? Now he had to figure out how to present his proposition in a way that would be palatable and amenable to someone who saw no gain in marriage, only servitude and the loss of herself and the ability to shape her destiny. He needed sleep. He needed his brain to work so he could sort through this tangle.

Much later … the sound of a clock somewhere in the house indicated another hour of sleeplessness had past. Giles rolled over and stared into the darkness. He tried boring himself into unconsciousness by conjugating irregular Latin verbs: *sum, es, est, sumus, estis, sunt.*

He soon depleted what he could recall of his schoolboy vocabulary. When the clock struck the next hour, Giles gave up, rolled off the bed, found his robe, pulled a comfortable winged chair in front of the open window, and propped his bare feet on the window's ledge. Watching daylight creep over the sill was about all he could manage, too exhausted to figure anything out or make a decent plan.

At half six, he splashed cold water on his face, did a pitiable job scraping the whiskers from his cheeks, dressed quickly—without Mumby's aid, and dashed down the stairs, certain he had managed to beat the rest of the inhabitants to the breakfast parlor. He'd fill his stomach and drink great quantities of coffee before he summoned Honeycutt to enquire if he'd discovered Edgerton's direction.

When the footman opened the door to the breakfast parlor, his hope for a solitary meal vanished like the steam rising off a cup of hot tea. There at the head of the table sat Eleanor's inscrutable aunt, Lady Beatrice Whitely.

Oh hell.

Being associated with Harleigh's family for nearly two decades made Giles well acquainted with this woman's fierce intellect, unerring moral compass, and iron will. Lord, it must be a female Barrett family trait.

She was immaculately groomed, which made him wonder how long she'd been awake. As Harleigh's long-time close friend, he'd spent many hours in her company and had always felt comfortable. But not at this moment. At this moment, he felt off-balance. Maybe it was his lack of sleep or, better still, his conscience. He stumbled over his own feet as he walked into the room.

"Not sleep well, my lord?" Lady Beatrice asked.

"Not really." Giles wondered if Lady Beatrice was aware of his interest in her niece. And if she was, did she approve? Eleanor's resistance was bad enough, but if her aunt was against the match too, he was doomed. What he needed was an ally not another opponent.

He expelled a long breath and made eye contact with her. "Good morning, Lady Beatrice." He went directly to the sideboard and started filling a plate.

"And to you, my lord. I'm so pleased someone else is an early riser. Sybil still keeps her theatrical hours and never rises before noon. Even though it has been thirty years or more since she set foot on any stage." She waved her hand to motion him to the seat beside hers.

He sat where she wanted him. "I'd no idea you favored this time of morning."

She dabbed her serviette at the corner of her mouth and then returned it to her lap. "Disappointed not to be left alone with your food and the newssheet, sirrah?"

"Not in the least." Giles caught the look in her eye; she didn't believe him.

"When you get to be my age, you tend to savor every moment of every hour."

"My lady, I know the age of Harleigh's father, your elder brother, and you're several years his junior, so I can't take you seriously when you paint yourself in your dotage."

She chuckled and set her elbow on the table, rested her chin in her hand and gave him a bittersweet smile. "It's not always the passage of time that can make one old; sometimes it's the events of life that make one act beyond their years."

"Such as?"

She released her chin and sat back in her chair. "Such as the early death of a beloved spouse who had much to live for and many years ahead of him."

"I never met Lord Whitely, but I did hear of his riding accident."

"Pish-posh, my husband was murdered."

Giles opened his mouth, but nothing came out. She had outdone herself in startling her audience into silence.

Lady Beatrice waved him off. "Yes, I know what was put about. My husband was murdered while in service to his King."

"And you know who?"

"Oh yes, indeed. Although he's someone beyond my reach to bring to justice, I strive daily to make his work as tedious and fruitless as possible." She sighed and stared at something on her plate. She held her knife in one hand and her fork in the other.

Giles studied her. "Since his death was dressed up, I'll assume, unless you contradict me, that your husband served His Majesty in secret matters of state."

She nodded. "That's how I came to be acquainted with Mr. Rooksby, you see. He's an old and trusted associate of Lord Whitley's."

"Ah, the gentleman you and El—your niece—made mention of yesterday."

"Indeed. But there's nothing gentlemanly in the least about Rooksby—except his exterior. He'll do whatever he thinks necessary. But enough about my lost love and his odd associates. Why are you up so early?" She cocked her head to the side and studied him. "You've the look of a man with a troubled mind—not just a sleepless head."

Giles didn't want to talk about what had caused his lack of sleep, and it appeared Lady Beatrice had no further wish to discuss the death of her husband, so another topic was in order. "Yesterday you mentioned this Rooksby aided your efforts to locate Miss Brewster."

"Aid is too mild a word. Truly a *sine qua non* of the first order, really. A momentous combining of Eleanor and Libby's acumen with Rooksby's web of informants."

Giles gave her his undivided attention. "Indeed. If by acumen you're referring to their map, I must concur. A brilliant and painstaking piece of reasoning."

Lady Beatrice nodded. "As I understand it, when Eleanor noticed the handbills she made a point of reading each one, in case she spotted one of them."

"Did she?" Giles said.

"Never. But over time she noted patterns."

"And your Mr. Rooksby helped you—how?" Giles said.

"Mmmm, yes." Lady Beatrice's brows knit together and she fell into a thoughtful silence.

He was grateful; it gave him a moment to digest what she'd revealed. My God, Eleanor was swimming in some very deep waters—with men involved in secret government affairs. Giles lost the battle with his patience as he waited for Lady Beatrice to continue. The words burst from his lips. "Exactly what service did this Rooksby perform for you and Miss Barrett?"

Lady Beatrice put her cup down. "When we approached him, he already knew about an establishment here in Bath that catered to men with a particularly disgusting taste in bedmates, but he was unaware of how and who they were procuring. It was Eleanor and Libby who provided that information."

"You're bamming me?" Giles said.

"You know me better than that, my lord."

"How could you condone, let alone encourage, Eleanor in this matter?"

She gave him a reproving look.

"My apologies, Lady Beatrice."

She regally waved him off. "Your outburst only strengthens my opinion that you care deeply for my niece."

Giles stilled. *Damn.*

A footman approached with the chocolate pot in one hand and the coffee pot in the other.

"No more for me." She placed her serviette beside her plate, in preparation for rising from her seat.

Giles stood.

"I'll be in the library, my lord. When you finish your meal, would you join me?"

So much for making my escape.

Giles took his time and ate his fill. The confrontation awaiting him in the library slowed the pace of his eating. When he finally joined her, Lady Beatrice was alone, standing before a crowded bookcase on the far side of the room. Several tall windows, with their drapes drawn back, bathed the room in soft early morning light.

Most of the available wall space was covered with white bookcases. The hearth was surrounded by a pinkish marble mantel. Large theatrical masks were carved into the stone. All the chairs were plump and covered in one of Lady Sybil's ubiquitous floral patterns.

A large portrait hung over the fireplace. The composition was of two handsome young people standing back to back, a boy and a girl. They looked as though they were related. Their clothing was a tad flamboyant and they both had a wicked gleam in their eyes, leaving the viewer with an impression they shared a secret.

Lady Beatrice cleared her throat. "Do you like the painting?"

"It seems familiar to me, though I'm sure I've never laid eyes upon it."

She chuckled. "That's because you've met the original."

"Mmmm?"

"You're her guest. That's a painting of Lady Sybil playing Viola in *Twelfth Night*. Lord Standish loved her in that role. Poor man, he attended performances for weeks to work up the nerve to visit the green room and
make her acquaintance. The painting is a jest. Standy said it was a reminder of the suffering he endured in his pursuit of loving Sybil."

"And the boy?"

"Standy had the artist paint it as if Sybil had played both parts."

Giles hadn't moved from his position by the closed door. Right now, he felt a kindred spirit with Lords Standish and Orsino; love wasn't bringing him joy at the moment either. "Is there something I can do for you, Lady Beatrice?" His deliberate brusque transition back to present dissolved the intimacy that was floating around them, threatening to put him at ease. He didn't want to feel comfortable in her presence. He needed his wits about him.

She didn't respond to his rudeness, and pointed to a book several rows above her head, obviously beyond her reach. "There's a volume on that shelf; would you be so kind to get it for me?"

He walked over and pulled the requested volume down. He glanced at the spine before placing the book in her hand. It was a stud book, a breed registry. "You've an interest in animal husbandry, my lady?"

Lady Beatrice gave him a wry look. "Only as it pertains to certain species, Lord West."

He thought about asking which species, but even sleep-deprived he possessed enough good sense and civility left to let *that* sleeping dog lie. Besides, he already knew which species interested her—the two-legged kind, Homo sapiens to be exact.

Time to go.

"If that's all you require, Lady Beatrice." Giles strolled to the door, he tasted freedom.

"As a matter of fact…" She paused until he turned to face her. "There is something else." She tapped the unopened volume against her palm.

A long pause ensued.

"If you're not ready to discuss whatever matter is pressing on your mind, perhaps it can wait until I return from my walk." Giles reached for the door's handle. *Last night, that door click—had that been her?*

She walked closer. When she was within a few feet of him, she stopped. "I offer you my aid and support, my lord, in your wooing of my niece. Have a pleasant walk."

Giles turned and opened the door, then he shut it. "I have a question."

"Only one?" Lady Beatrice sat on the settee.

Giles lowered his chin but remained silent.

"Very well, ask away. Though you understand, I won't break any confidences," Lady Beatrice said.

"Agreed. Why does your niece fear marriage?"

"Fear?"

"Yes, fear. What other explanation can there be?"

"She and I are both uncomfortable that marriage creates an unequal alliance between a man and a woman, but that isn't fear, just fact."

"That's the law, madam, both for church and state."

Lady Beatrice snorted and waved off his response. "If that's the depth of your thinking on this matter then I've misjudged your mental capacity and you'll not succeed where Eleanor is concerned, even though she seems attracted to you."

Giles felt as though he'd been slapped. He recovered when Lady Beatrice's words sank in. "Are you saying Eleanor is interested in me?"

"I've never known her to desire any man's company before. Although she's much sought after for her looks and fortune, once she opens her mouth most men look elsewhere. I've noted, on more than one occasion, that her intellect doesn't dissuade *or* offend you."

Giles smiled. "On the contrary, Lord help me."

Lady Beatrice's smile was a wry quirk of her lips.

"I'm an arrogant man, but I despise people who toady to me. I prefer to surround myself with smart people, not just the quick-witted, but real thinkers."

"Even as a wife?" Her gaze intensified.

"When I started this marriage business, I'm chagrinned to admit that intelligence wasn't a trait I sought in a spouse."

"And now?" Lady Beatrice said.

"I find I can't live without it."

Lady Beatrice nodded. "You *are* indeed a smart man."

"Because I've come around to your way of thinking?"

"Not entirely, you've many traits I admire; chief among them is your flexible mind. Most women of my acquaintance are content to follow in their mother's footsteps. For them marriage is a state devoutly to be wished for, and they haven't the good sense to notice the powerlessness and loss of self that state bestows. The moment they say 'I do' they cease to exist."

"You're *not* describing your niece," Giles said.

"Precisely."

"You and Eleanor consistently make me turn over rocks I'd rather let lie, or for that matter not even notice."

She threw back her head and laughed. "Glad to hear it, my boy, glad to hear it. You've promise. Must be what Eleanor sees in you."

Giles' head felt stuffed with information but still nothing seemed clear. The marriages of Eleanor's parents and her aunt and uncle were as different as night from day and yet they were both happy unions. Why was Eleanor so adamant in her refusal to participate in one herself?

Lady Beatrice slowly drummed her fingers on the arm of the settee "Eleanor speaks of never marrying; I've counseled her on more than one occasion not to refuse to consider the possibility with the *right* man. Her father and I argue about many things, but in this we're in accord: marriage would be a good thing for Eleanor. Except my brother's idea of the right man for Ellie would be one who would rein her in."

"And you, Lady Beatrice, whom do *you* think the right man for Eleanor would be?"

"Someone who loves her passionately, who isn't intimidated by her intellect, and who won't permit her to run roughshod over him."

Giles sat in the chair opposite Lady Beatrice. "You forgot to mention patient. For Eleanor would try even the patience of Job."

Lady Beatrice laughed. "She *is* a lodestone for unconventional trouble, and her thoughts and pursuits will always be driven by what she believes is right. So yes, patience would be an asset in any man who wished to wed Eleanor."

"Do you believe these aforementioned 'pursuits' will continue to include the raiding of brothels?"

"Good Lord, I hope not. One was quite sufficient."

"Sometimes she seems more your daughter than Lady Barrett's," Giles said.

"What an astute observation, my lord. Whitely and I were blessed with only sons. If I'd had a daughter I'd want her to be just like Eleanor."

"For the moment, let us put aside the issue of inequality that marriage creates," Giles said.

"As you wish."

Giles stood and began to pace. "My instincts tell me there's something beneath her intellectual pursuit of equality. Something driving her to risk her life as she did to save little Julia."

Lady Beatrice pursed her lips. "Again, you amaze me, sir. Over the years, on countless occasions, I've sensed in Eleanor a refusal to draw back even when she knew she was putting herself in harm's way. She behaves like she has no choice."

"And you have no idea what's motivating her?"

"Whitely and I were out of the country for a few years, on government business." She gave him a significant look, which he interpreted as secret business for the King. "Eleanor was not yet seven when we left and a charming scamp. She was nearly ten when we returned and she was changed. When I asked my brother, he told me there'd been an incident on her eighth birthday."

"You're referring to the stable?" Giles asked.

"You know of it?"

"I was at Barrett Hall for her birthday celebration."

She moved to the edge of her seat so Giles felt compelled to continue. "The morning following the celebration, Eleanor was found in the stable."

"Yes, yes, I know all that."

"And the fact that she wouldn't talk?" Giles said.

"Yes, that too."

Giles rubbed his forehead. "Then I'm not sure what I can add."

Lady Beatrice pulled a handkerchief from her pocket and twisted it about.

"So, she's never confided what happened, even to you?" Giles said.

"Not a peep. In fact, her refusal to speak to anyone regarding the event convinces me it's the wellspring of her drive to protect and care for women and girls who can't care for themselves. I believe it also holds the key to her reluctance to marry."

Giles nodded his agreement. "How the hell ..." Giles coughed after his verbal stumble. "Excuse me, Lady Beatrice, but how can we address something she has kept locked inside herself for ten years?"

Chapter Twenty-nine

Eleanor was fed up with her life as an invalid. Her back and hips still ached from being thrown against the wall, but it was time to venture outside this room. Giles was out of the house, a prerequisite for her making her painful and slow journey down the stairs. She'd have to be in his company eventually, just not yet. Her feelings were all raw and jumbled. He made her think about things that were better off never crossing her mind.

Honeycutt appeared as Eleanor descended the last step. "My aunt?"

"The library, miss. And might I say, it's a pleasure to see you up and about."

"Thank you, Mr. Honeycutt."

Eleanor walked with measured steps into the room. "What has you so thoroughly engrossed, Aunt?"

Aunt Beatrice lowered the pamphlet and smiled. "Bravo, my girl. You braved the steps at last. And where's your four-legged shadow?"

"I believe he's out enjoying the sunshine and watering Lady Sybil's flowerbeds."

Eleanor pointed at the papers in her aunt's hand.

"An essay from Lady Montagu."

"Something new?" Eleanor asked.

"I hadn't read it until now, 'On the Mischief of Giving Fortunes with Women in Marriage'."

"That woman has almost as much gall as you, Aunt."

Beatrice Whitley snorted. "In that aspect, I believe Lady Mary and I are equals. However, I think I made the happier marriage."

"Uncle Jasper." Eleanor sighed as she settled herself back into the soft cushions of the chair nearest her aunt.

"I miss him too. I just don't let myself mope over-long about things I can do nothing to change. Speaking of marriage…"

"Were we?" Eleanor said.

"Listen, my dear girl, I know you're charting a course of heroic spinsterhood, but Sybil and I've been noticing."

"Nothing heroic about it, it's practical," Eleanor said.

"You can't rule a heart the way you can a head," Aunt Beatrice said.

A noise from outside the door saved Eleanor from enduring any more of these ominous pronouncements. "Sounds like a visitor."

The door swung open and in bounded Harleigh, fresh from the road. He hadn't bothered to remove his topcoat, and a footman followed in his wake to collect assorted items as her brother discarded them—his hat and gloves, and finally his coat along with a plume of road dust, and a pungent whiff of *eau* de lathered horse.

Eleanor pushed herself to her feet, but before she took a step, Harleigh grabbed her up and held her high off the floor. "Sister!"

Eleanor laughed and beat her fists on his shoulders. "Happy to see you too, brother!"

"How are you?" Harleigh smiled up at her.

"Exceptional, until you man-handled me."

"Harleigh, put her down and come over here and give me a kiss." Aunt Beatrice raised her cheek for him to peck.

Harleigh repositioned Eleanor in his arms and carried her to the settee. He deposited her beside their aunt, then took Aunt Beatrice's face in his hands and planted a smacker on her lips.

He stood back, grinning like a fool. "Will that do?"

"Impertinent boy." But Aunt Beatrice couldn't hide her smile.

"Where is West? How could he bear to be parted from such loveliness?"

C3

Everything Giles put in his mouth that night was tasteless. There were no provoking comments spicing up their evening meal since Eleanor chose to take a tray in her room, leaving him in the company of Harleigh and the Ladies Beatrice and Sybil.

How could they resolve their impasse if she continued avoiding him? Well, in her mind, he supposed, the matter was resolved. But he wasn't finished, not by miles.

It was their last evening in Bath. Giles and Harleigh stood before the decanters on the sideboard in the parlor after dinner.

"What's got you sighing like a maid?" Harleigh nudged his arm. Eleanor. "Woolgathering."

"Changing your mind about accompanying us back to Barrett Hall, are you?"

"No, just stewing in my troubled thoughts."

Harleigh held a glass aloft. "What's your pleasure?" *Eleanor.* "Whiskey."

Harleigh filled their glasses and motioned to the French doors. "I need some air."

A fat quarter moon sat high in the heavens while thick bands of clouds raced across the darkening horizon, showing intermittent clusters of stars. Constellations. That night he'd almost tripped over Eleanor. Was that only a few weeks ago?

Harleigh sipped his drink. "The ladies seem to think you spend your days being pursued by hordes of unmarried females. Honeycutt said I wasn't to disabuse them of that notion. Why's that?"

"It's complicated." Giles wanted to laugh at the absurdity of his remark.

Harleigh huffed. "Are you being sarcastic?"

Giles placed his hand on his friend's shoulder. "Not in the least."

"Damn it. Ellie promised she wouldn't say a thing ... I didn't have time to speak with you myself 'bout Edgerton before I left to take Julia home."

"She got boxed in after Edgerton made his unexpected visit. We put two and two together and confronted her. You should be grateful, she saved you the unpleasantness."

Harleigh snorted. "That's the sort of sideways logic she likes to use on me."

"No one has seen Edgerton since that day he came here asking after you and Eleanor."

"And you know that because?" Harleigh asked.

"I've been looking for him. Honeycutt, too. But there's no trace of him."

"Giles."

"Don't give me that." Giles leaned in close and poked Harleigh in the chest. "Edgerton has a debt to pay. I can't close my eyes without seeing the faces of those little girls we rescued."

"What do you plan to do?" Harleigh asked.

"Hunt him down."

"Then what?" Harleigh said.

Call him out and kill him. Eleanor's life was at stake and he would do anything to keep her safe. "I'm not sure." Giles stared into the distance. His blindness to Edgerton's machinations and his new understanding of Eleanor had transformed his internal landscape. "What did your father say?"

"Shocked him. He turned purple with rage. At one point, he grabbed my lapels and shook me, yelling 'are you mad' over and over. 'My Ellie in a place like that. Pray your mother never hears of it'."

Giles muttered. "As if she gave us a choice."

"And Edgerton asking for Ellie … do you think he knows she was the charwoman?"

"I would bet on it," Giles said. "Otherwise, his visit makes no sense."

"When I told my father, Edgerton was part of the ring kidnapping young girls, including Julia Brewster, he went stone-cold quiet. He wants irrefutable proof. Then he'll issue the warrant."

"As far as I know there are no documents proving Edgerton's involvement. And no one to attest to his complicity in the kidnappings."

Harleigh grunted. "We're playing a dangerous game of cat and mouse."

"Agreed. Having played innumerable games of chess with Edgerton, I can tell you he's the patient-planner-type-cat who'll wait by the hole, knowing the mouse will eventually make an appearance."

Chapter Thirty

Eleanor knelt on the rug, before the fire, eyes closed, slowly breathing in and out.

"What ya want me to do with these?" Millie said as she came back into the room. "Oh, I'm sorry, Miss Eleanor." She was carrying a book and a handful of papers.

Eleanor sighed, and rolled to her feet. "It's all right. My mind won't quiet itself tonight," she said as she stood up. "What are those?"

"Stuff from Madame's hidey-hole. Ye know, the papers ye asked me to snatch the night of the raid."

"Really? Anything good?" Eleanor said

"How should I know? Perdy's just beginning ta teach me me letters and such." Millie laid the book and papers on the desk.

"You made quite a haul," Eleanor said.

"Well, I grabbed everything tha was under that floor board."

"Excellent work," Eleanor said as she opened the book. "Just as I thought."

Millie looked over Eleanor's shoulder. "What?"

"It's a ledger."

"What's that?" Millie said.

"A record of who owes Madame and how much."

"You gotta be dumber than a tin pail fulla holes ta be in tha woman's debt."

Eleanor laughed. "Agreed. But you and I both know that when men start thinking with that thing dangling between their legs instead of what's on their shoulders, they tend to make some very stupid decisions."

Millie chuckled, then sobered. "Sometimes you talks too old, ye know tha?"

Eleanor looked up from the ledger. "What does that mean?"

"Well, yer only just eighteen, right?"

Eleanor nodded.

"If'n you'd been raised like me, well, I would 'pect you ta talks like ye does. Makes me wonder if you seen things a girl like you shouldna ever see."

Eleanor turned her face away to hide her shock at Millie's insight. "It doesn't matter."

Millie squeezed Eleanor's shoulder. "Ahh, but it does. I can see you don'ts wanta talk about it, if'n you ever does ..."

A companionable silence settled between them.

Eleanor gathered up all the papers and handed them back to Millie.

"Wrap all these together in some paper and string, then put the package in a good spot in my trunk."

"All right."

Eleanor opened the ledger flat and drew the candelabra close. She ran her index finger down the column of numbers, adding and subtracting the sums in her head as she went.

Millie pressed against Eleanor's back as she leaned forward to get a better look at the ledger. "Is all tha writin' there English?"

"Hmm, no," Eleanor said. "The parts we can't read I would guess are written in Dutch. Rooksby's bound to know people who can read and write Dutch. More important, I need Libby and my father to look at this. I can do calculations, but a ledger's a different matter. It can tell a story."

"What kind a story?"

"Besides the basics of who owes and how much, it can also tell us when they paid and what was used to pay the debt."

"Money, of course," Millie said.

"Not always. Sometimes a gentleman doesn't have the ready, so he might hand over an avowal or sign over something of equal or greater value than the money he owes, like a horse, or a piece of property, or information."

"Information?" Millie said.

"Oh yes, indeed. Sometimes what a person knows can be worth a king's ransom."

"You pullin' me leg?" Millie said.

"No," Eleanor said as she laughed. "Let's say you went to be a maid to a young woman who was about to be married. Someone who knew nothing about the things that go on between a man and woman."

Millie laughed. "I could tell her a thing or two, I could."

"Exactly," Eleanor said. "And suppose you were the kind of woman to take advantage of the young woman's ignorance."

"I'd ne'er do no such a thing," Millie said, a touch of indignation tingeing her voice.

"I know that." Eleanor deepened the pitch of her voice. "Dear Miss So-and-so, if you pay me ten pounds I'll tell you the things your husband expects from you on your wedding night."

Millie started to laugh. "I see whats ye mean. Bet little miss-so-and-so would pay much more than ten pounds ifn I tell her the really good stuff she could do to her husband."

Eleanor joined in the laughter. "Now you are getting the idea."

"What kind of information do you think Madame wanted?" Millie said.

Eleanor tapped her chin with her index finger. "That's an excellent question—something she could sell. Those loose papers may provide a clue to what the men used." Eleanor banged her fist down onto the open ledger. "Rooksby."

"What 'bout him?"

"My Uncle Jasper used to say Rooksby was a great admirer of Walsingham's."

"Who?" Millie said. "I swear, Ellie, sometimes yer mind jumps faster than a flea on a hot griddle. First yer talkin' 'bout that Rooksby fella and now Ham-something."

"Sir Francis Walsingham. Queen Elizabeth's spymaster," Eleanor said.

"Queen Elizabeth…aint she dead?" Millie said.

"Quite."

"Then why are we talkin' 'bout her now?"

"The point is … our dear departed Queen Bess had a very clever man who worked for her by the name of Walsingham. He was a brilliant boss of spies and he liked to use people he referred to as invisible to do his spying. You know, the kind of people a gentleman or a lady considers beneath their notice, like a tailor, a shipping clerk, or a—"

"A smelly ol' charwoman," Millie said and her grin was effusive. "He-hee."

"Yer thinkin' Madame be a spy? And them fellas that might be clerks paid her with information?" Millie said.

"Maybe. Suppose they were clerks who worked in government offices? What if they knew where and how many troops were being sent somewhere? Or when those troops would be getting food and ammunition?"

The following morning Eleanor gathered in the back servants' hallway with Lady Sybil, her aunt, Harleigh, and Mr. Honeycutt. She and her aunt wore heavy traveling cloaks. The carriage carrying Lady Beatrice's maid, Millie, Mumby, and Harleigh's man waited out in front of Lady Sybil's house.

"Really, is all this necessary?" Eleanor directed her comment to Harleigh.

"No more arguing. Just do as I say." Harleigh pushed Eleanor toward Lady Sybil. "Go make your good-byes, sis."

Lady Sybil hugged Aunt Beatrice and then it was Eleanor's turn. "You're a wonder, my dear. So brave. Now, be a sensible lass and listen to your big brother. He'll get you home safe."

Eleanor kissed Lady Sybil's cheek. "I'll miss you. Thank you for opening your home to our motley band."

Lady Sybil sniffed and wiped her eyes.

Eleanor moved to stand before Mr. Honeycutt. They gazed at one another and then Eleanor rose on her toes, threw her arms around his neck and gave him a hug. "You're the best of men, Mr. Honeycutt. I'll never forget you." Then she kissed his cheek.

Honeycutt took her hand before she turned away and raised it to his lips. *"Farewell! Thou art too dear for my possessing."*

Lady Sybil tapped him on the arm. "Shakespeare, Honeycutt? You must be truly melancholy at our guests' departure."

Honeycutt still held Eleanor's hand and gazed into her eyes. A sweet smile curved his lips. "I wish you all happiness in your future endeavors, dear Miss Barrett."

Eleanor returned his smile and pulled the hood up over her head.

Harleigh took his aunt's arm. "No more dawdling. Good-bye, Lady Sybil, Mr. Honeycutt."

As she walked to the coach, she saw Rodrigo lying on a cushioned board nearby. She stooped to stroke his head. "Hello, boy." Eleanor felt Giles eyes upon her.

"Is that hairy beast to ride with Eleanor and me?" Aunt Beatrice stood on the coach's step.

"I didn't think you would mind, considering his hero status," Harleigh said.

Lady Beatrice shook her head. "Oh, very well." She ducked her head under the doorframe and sat down.

"You next, Eleanor." Harleigh held out his hand.

Eleanor put her foot on the step, grabbed the sides of the open door and propelled herself inside the coach.

Harleigh shook his head. "Ellie, your ordeal has done nothing to improve your maidenly behavior."

"Wishful thinking, brother?" Eleanor said.

They reached Salisbury late in the afternoon and the women

chose to dine together in their rooms, leaving Giles and Harleigh to share a meal in the inn's private parlor. Both men paid more attention to their own thoughts then conversing with one another. day gone and he hadn't gotten Eleanor alone. Giles needed help.

After the dishes were cleared, Harleigh cleared his throat several times. "Is something going on between you and my sister?"

Had Harleigh taken up mind-reading? "What?" Giles said.

"I know I may sound like a nutter, but I'd swear she's avoiding you and when I catch you looking at her ... Well?" Harleigh said.

Giles leaned forward, elbows on the table, fingers interlaced. "When we found her in that attic—my God, I thought she was dead. I cursed myself for a fool, wasting time with milksops who can't hold a candle to her."

Harleigh opened and closed his mouth, but not a word came out.

"Have I shocked you into silence?" Giles said.

"Christ, man, Ellie meets few of your espoused criteria."

"For a wife, you mean? Am as puzzled as you. Well, maybe not completely baffled. And yet I'm quite sure she is the one."

Harleigh scratched his jaw and stared at his friend. "You're bamming me, right?"

Giles chuckled. "Are you asking me why I would want to take to wife someone who would never be compliant?"

"Who'll always challenge you if she thought you were being a pompous ass."

"She would, would she not?" Giles smiled.

"For certs," Harleigh said.

"You know, most of us—me included—turn away when life is grim. Make choices based on what is convenient. Eleanor walks right up and faces the ugliness down. There's no tossing a few coins in the poor box for her, brushing her gloved hands off and walking away as if she's done with the matter."

"Egad! You can't mean it. You know she's stubborn, willful, and intermittently the biggest pain-in-the-backside you'll ever encounter."

Giles chuckled. "You're too late."

"Am I?" Harleigh took a deep swallow of his wine. "And this you find attractive?"

"You above all others know how much I value my own opinions."

Harleigh smirked. "I did mention the words 'pompous and ass'."

"Arrogant nodcock."

"Lackwit," Harleigh said.

"Pompous ass," Giles said.

"'fraid not," Harleigh said, "that's your nom de guerre, remember?"

Giles snorted. "Having Eleanor as my wife will be …"

"Humiliating?" Harleigh provided.

"Humbling. Also, lively, passionate, provoking and infuriating. At the start of my bride-hunt, someone convivial and easy-going seemed the best fit. Good Lord, imagining myself chained to one of those docile creatures, who never steps out of line or voices her unsolicited opinion, makes me question my sanity. Can you imagine how utterly boring that would be?" Giles shuddered.

Harleigh chuckled.

"Eleanor's easily all those things you enumerated and one more."

"What's that?" Harleigh asked.

"The woman I love."

Harleigh grunted. He leaned forward and rested his arms on the table. "I tease and torment her mercilessly about not being marriage material. The truth is, my little sister is a gem and not many men of my acquaintance are worthy of her. And I must admit having a sister like Eleanor and an aunt like Beatrice has given me a taste for a woman with a bit of extra starch in her petticoat myself."

An image of that limping ball of fire Elizabeth Archer popped into Giles' mind. "I've noticed," Giles said.

Harleigh's glass stalled on the way to his lips. "Ahem."

Giles grinned.

Harleigh raised his glass. "Here's to you getting Ellie to say yes."

Giles raised his glass to acknowledge the toast. "I need your help."

"Want me to put in a good word for you?"

"Nothing so bromidic," Giles said.

○3

The next day, they processed to Winchester where they lunched and changed horses. Out of Winchester they swung north and headed for Guilford. The road was long and dusty and gave Giles plenty of time for contemplation.

Tired of being avoided by Eleanor, he decided to take Harleigh and Lady Beatrice's advice and do something unexpected. Throw Eleanor
off her stride.

Giles rode out in front of the carriages, mentally running over his options. They'd just passed the sign for Sevenoak, their last night on the road before reaching Barrett Hall.

Harleigh came up beside Giles and said, "Wish Libby were here to advise?"

Calling her Libby now, are you? Well, well, she'll make you a good wife, old friend. "More so than you and Lady B?"

Harleigh shrugged. "I'm no good at this cupid business. This is our last night on the road. Once we get to our parents, Ellie will have all matter of excuses to keep out of your company."

Giles rolled his shoulders, trying to relieve the tension. "I've come to the same conclusion."

"You must waylay her before she gets into her room, or you'll not see her again until tomorrow morning."

Giles nodded. "Have you ever wondered what happened in the barn that night of Eleanor's eighth birthday?"

Harleigh's brow furrowed. "We were speaking of wooing my sister. What made you think about that ghastly night, after all these years?"

"I was talking to your aunt."

"Now, there is a dangerous occupation for a man, if I ever heard one. Beware, or she'll try and convert you."

"To what?' Giles asked.

"Women's rights."

Giles shrugged. "I'm beginning to think their argument has some merit."

Harleigh groaned. "Look, if all women were as smart and capable as those two, I'd have no problem at all with these radical changes they'd like to see instituted. But women weren't created equal. I shudder when I think of my own mother and other sisters governing their affairs.

"Eleanor thinks it's a matter of education, not intelligence or gender."

"Did she mention she thinks women and girls need to go to school?" Harleigh said.

"No, but if she's correct in her assumption that it's a lack of training and knowledge, then a school seems a practical solution."

Harleigh threw his hands in the air. "Gaah." His horse shied. "Easy, boy. Of all the misguided, unsubstantiated nonsense."

"We've strayed from the point; Lady B and I are of a like mind," Giles said.

"About women's rights?"

Giles shook his head. "Your aunt and I believe Eleanor's declaration never to wed should be viewed as a personal rebellion against the act of marriage, and is a response to what she endured in the stable on her birthday."

"Because?" Harleigh said.

"Because it forwards no identified cause. She isn't petitioning anyone in government to change the law or even soliciting support by encouraging her friends to remain unmarried." Giles shook his head. "No. This is a personal act."

Harleigh's eyes grew round. He looked shocked. "Good Lord, I wonder why I never figured that out."

"It occurred to me only after my conversation with your aunt," Giles said.

"Your notion has merit."

"Has Eleanor ever confided to you what happened?

"Never. Aunt B?" Harleigh said.

Giles shook his head.

"My God, that's a long time to keep a childhood secret."

"Indeed."

Harleigh stared into the distance. "So many things about Ellie changed after that night. When she came home from London she talked little and attacked everything with an iron determination, her studies especially. She made us boys look like idiots on many an occasion. Before that night, she would laugh easily and often. Afterwards, she quickly lost patience with us. She stopped arguing and engaging. No chess, no hide-and-seek, no challenges of any kind."

"Your aunt said the same."

"Ellie's smiles became as rare as fossils."

They rode on in silence.

"What about Miss Archer?" Giles asked.

"If Libby knows anything, she wouldn't betray Ellie's confidence," Harleigh said.

Chapter Thirty-one

The smell of his unwashed male companion and the lack of fresh air inside the unmarked coach made Francis Edgerton's stomach roil.

His companion's large, thick hand pushed aside the leather flap covering the coach's window. "Vhat iz dis place?"

Edgerton used the tip of his cane to push the window covering back down. "A safe harbor, Barend."

Barend glared. "Vhy do I need such a place?"

"Because you're the most conspicuous person I've ever met, aside from your late lamented cousin Pim, of course." Edgerton meant to be witty but that sort of humor was lost on the dour Dutchman who sat across from him. "Only for a short time."

"She comes?"

Edgerton nodded. He was disappointed about the outriders, of course. Their presence caused his hope of arranging Eleanor's demise on her trip homeward to evaporate like morning dew in his father's rose garden.

But with the Edgertons' estate being a short distance east of Viscount Barrett's, the adjustment as to the location of her death was a small matter. Plus, moving onto his home turf made keeping tabs on Eleanor's movements child's play.

Edgerton struck the head of his cane on the trap door in the roof of the carriage. The hatch opened. "Drive around to the back."

"Vho lives here?" Barend said.

"No one you need concern yourself with."

Barend glowered.

"You will stay in the gamekeeper's cottage. In the woods. I will arrange for food to be brought. No one must see you."

Barend grunted. "How long?"

"Patience. The longer we wait, the more they will relax. And the more they relax, the easier it will be to get to her."

"I vant to do it now," Barend said.

"I know you do. Have you never heard the saying that revenge is a dish best served cold?"

One side of Barend's mouth curled upward.

Edgerton nodded. "They are keeping a tight rein on her. Her restlessness will drive her into doing something foolish and when she does, we will be there to put an end to her once and for all."

When the carriage halted, Edgerton put his hand on the door handle. "Stay here."

"Drink."

"I will send something." When Edgerton stepped down, he closed the door to the coach immediately.

His father's head groom greeted him. "My lord, will you be staying?"

"No. There is a passenger within. Bring him a drink of cold water," Edgerton said.

Edgerton entered his family's home through a side entrance. He headed directly for the steward's office to get the key to the cottage. On his way down the rear passage, he came face to face with his father's butler and longtime retainer, Gormley. "My lord, when did you arrive?"

The old gent seemed genuinely happy to see him. Edgerton couldn't remember the last time his presence had elicited that sort of happy response. Then his mind flashed to his meeting with Giles at Traveler's Coffee House—that had been a sweet moment.

Edgerton smiled. Gormley was a very kind and loyal man, who—like the rest of the staff—took great care of Edgerton's father. "Just arrived. I'm looking for the steward."

"He's in his office, m'lord." Gormley pointed behind him. "Shall I summon him for you?"

"I'll go to his office. Have Cook prepare several baskets of food.

Tell her she'll be feeding a very large, very hungry man for several days."

Gormley gave an emphatic nod and departed.

In short order, Edgerton provisioned and deposited Barend in the gamekeeper's cottage, then paid off the hired coach and returned to the main house.

He found his father in the lower level of his beloved gardens with the head gardener and a young boy. As Edgerton came off the terrace and headed across the lawn, his father caught sight of him and waved his welcoming greeting with unbridled enthusiasm.

"Ah, my young friend. So good of you to come for a visit." Edgerton clasped his father's large outstretched hand and smiled.

"Have you met my head gardener, Mr. Fielding? Mr. Fielding, allow me to introduce my young friend here, Mr. Francis. And Mr. Francis, this is my son, Daniel. Daniel, shake hands with Mr. Francis."

Edgerton was thunderstruck. He had a half-brother. A bastard off one of the housemaids, no doubt. He'd never even considered such a thing. He looked down at the boy who was gazing up at him with his—no, their father's—blue-gray eyes. The same eyes that stared back at him each time he peered into a mirror.

Daniel offered his small hand. Edgerton had left his hat and gloves in the front hall and when his bare hand touched his brother's, the first wave that struck him was tenderness, but the one that followed was sizzling anger, which he quickly hid.

"A pleasure to make your acquaintance, Mr. Francis," Daniel said. The "s" at the end of his name became a sibilant sound as the boy was missing a front tooth.

Edgerton couldn't speak without revealing his feelings, so he nodded and released the boy's hand.

Mr. Fielding stepped forward and took Edgerton's hand, as if they hadn't known one another for years. As their hands joined, the elder gardener leaned in and whispered. "It's very good to see you, young master." Edgerton began to smile at the old man's greeting, but the look of pity in the gardener's eyes made Edgerton press his lips together in bitterness. He let go of the old man's hand and turned his head away. "God is my judge."

"Sir?" the gardener asked.

Edgerton cleared his throat. "The meaning of the boy's name."

The old man beamed at Edgerton. "Quite so. You was always such a bright lad and a good student as I remembers. Always knew them Latin names of things here in the garden."

Edgerton did smile this time at the memory of wandering the grounds with Mr. Fielding. "How old?"

"The boy?" Fielding said.

Edgerton nodded.

Daniel crouched low beside their father. He was lifting leaves and looking beneath.

"Spot any of 'em nasty rose-eating bugs, Danny-boy?" Edgerton the elder said.

"No, Papa."

"Daniel just passed his fifth birthday. He's a grand lad and, next to these roses, the light of your father's life.

Edgerton stiffened. "I see."

"Forgive my impertinence, young master, but I don't think ya do. You and yer mother, well, yer city dwellers. When tha' fall from tha' horse of his erased yer father's memory like chalk on a blackboard, your mama put you in school and left. Never comin' back."

Edgerton saw himself dressed in his dark suit, sitting beside the family solicitor, rolling away from his home—from this place. No one on the step waved him off, not even his mother. His jaw clenched. Such raw feelings for something that happened long ago.

"And, well, you had no way did ye to get back here when you was a little 'un, like Daniel, so we ne'er saw ye. But when you was growed up, well, now I think I can count on both my hands the times you been to see us—him, I mean. I don't even know where you lives?" The old man stuck his hand under his cap and scratched his balding head.

Fielding put his hand on Edgerton's shoulder. "It must hurt like the dickens that he don't know who you are. But Daniel there, he can't take nothin' from you, not really."

Ah, but you're wrong, Fielding. Without intent, the boy has taken everything that matters.

"Yer still your father's heir, whether your papa knows your name or not, and that's a fact."

Edgerton thought he'd become inured of longing to hear his father utter the words 'this is my son' but *that* folly seemed to be long-lived. He swallowed hard. "As usual, Fielding, your assessment is both accurate and fair. I've been neglectful and shouldn't judge my father or hold a grudge on the boy. It's good they are happy." He only wished he could say the same of himself.

"Our lives can take unexpected turns, do ye not think, young master?"

"They can indeed." Edgerton gazed at the tableau before him, at the second chance that life had offered his father with his new son. When he
gazed into his own future, he saw Barend with his hands around Eleanor's throat, and nothing more.

"It's what we do with what's given us that's the measure of our days," Fielding said. "Yer future lies before you, young master. Go out and do something with yer life to be proud of."

⳹

Giles entered the Tabard Inn's coaching yard in Sevenoaks ahead of the rest of their party. As he dismounted, a young stable boy ran up and grabbed his horse's reins. "Thank you, lad." Giles pressed a coin into the child's hand. "Give him a good rubdown, plenty of water and oats, and there'll be another coin in it for you."

"Aye, sir. I'll make him shine, I will, sir." The stable boy gave Giles a broad, gap-toothed grin as he led his horse away.

Harleigh arrived next, followed by the carriages. When Harleigh's feet met the ground, Giles came to stand beside him.

Harleigh muttered out of the side of his mouth. "Well?"

"I'm going to ask her to take a walk with me."

Harleigh grunted affirmatively.

The footmen came forward and removed Rodrigo from the floor of Eleanor and Lady Beatrice's coach.

Lady Beatrice appeared in the doorway. "Nephew, your hand, if you please." Once on the ground, she said with a sniff, "I refuse to reenter this benighted contraption again today."

"Agreed, Aunt. We stop here for the night," Harleigh said.

Giles stepped forward with a smile on his face and waited. Eleanor looked away and ignored his presence. He continued to wait even though his nerves were frayed with anticipation. He wanted to reach through the opening and yank her out.

The coach shifted and bounced on its springs as the men unloaded the boot and climbed on top to release the straps holding the luggage. She must have a strong stomach if the coach's movements weren't making her nauseated. Excellent, she'd be a good traveler.

"I don't need any assistance to disembark," Eleanor said.

Giles raised his arm in an overblown theatrical fashion and addressed his comment to a groom who was passing. "Behold! She speaks." The young man he'd addressed ducked his head and hurried on. Giles turned to Eleanor and spoke through clenched teeth. "You may not want it, but you will accept it. Now come over here so I can help you down."

Eleanor took her time pulling on her gloves and sliding across the bench. She finally extended her hand, but instead of taking it, Giles encircled her waist with his hands and lifted her out. They were eye to eye and he felt her body go rigid. "Déjà vu, is it not? Me and you and a carriage. Only, last time I was helping you in, was I not?"

Eleanor demanded in a raspy whisper, "Put me down."

"Or what?"

Eleanor's eyes narrowed. She moved her arms, her fists clenched.

Giles thought she was about to throw a punch. He pulled his chin in to make it less of a target.

She smirked.

He gave her a hard shake, then lowered her to the ground. "You've been seated for hours. Walk with me."

She turned her face away.

He'd have sworn he could hear the war of emotions raging inside her.

The air was hazy with heat and dust. A voice inside him cautioned him to wait. A light breeze pulled at tendrils of auburn hair that framed Eleanor's face, the humidity causing the loosened hair to spin into curls.

Giles cupped her cheek and gently turned her head so he could see her eyes. She didn't resist. "Even covered in road dust, you smell like a garden after it rains."

"You should see a doctor; your nose has ceased to function properly."

"Should I?" He smiled.

There was a twinkle in her eyes and the barest hint of a smile on her lips.

He was still caressing her cheek, and she tipped her head just a bit, pressing her cheek deeper into his palm. Her lids lowered for a fleeting moment. Then her mood changed, her eyes opened and she stepped back. "What do we have to say to one another that we've not said before?"

Giles lowered his hand to his side. "You won't find out unless you walk with me."

"Then I choose ignorance." She pivoted toward the inn.

"Coward."

Her body stiffened.

A hit.

"Ellie." He offered his arm.

Eleanor leaned in the door of the coach, retrieving her bergère broad-brimmed straw hat. She clutched the hat's ribbons tightly but made no move to place it on her head. She stared at his offered arm.

He bounced it upward in an encouraging fashion. "It will not bite."

Eleanor rolled her eyes, then placed only her gloved fingertips on Giles' arm.

A tall wooden whitewashed gate stood open and provided the main access into and out of the yard. To the side of this portal, still within the confines of the coaching yard, stood a massive oak with a bench nestled between two protruding roots. He guided Eleanor to this shady patch.

At the last minute, he wanted more privacy, so he walked her around behind the tree. As he stepped from bright sunlight into the seclusion formed by the over-arching tree limbs, thick foliage, and massive tree trunk, Giles' eyes perceived nothing but blackness.

Eleanor fell against him. "Botheration."

Giles' hands shot out to keep her from falling.

"Let go." Eleanor pushed his hands away.

Giles released her. His eyes began to adjust to the change in light and he watched Eleanor's arms flail, then she pitched backward. He pulled her against him. "What's the matter?"

"My foot," Eleanor snapped out.

"Hold still."

She twisted about and pushed her skirts aside.

Giles waited as she ignored his council.

"These stupid traveling garments are supposed to make one's movements easier." She grunted and twisted about. "I can't see a thing." She lost her balance again and her arms flew out.

He grabbed ahold of her. "Are you done flailing around like a mackerel wiggling on a hook?"

Once she regained her balance, she went stiff as a board.

He released his hold.

Eleanor huffed and tossed her hat to the ground. "None of this would've happened if I had not gone on this walk with you."

"Is that the way you intend to play it? You make a misstep and foist the blame to me?"

She grabbed his jabot and yanked, nearly strangling him in the process, but now their faces were on the same level. He knew he deserved her ire for his remark. "My foot is caught under something, probably a root. I'll push my skirts to the side, then you'll kneel and unbuckle my shoe. I'll then slip my foot out."

"No," Giles said.

Clearly shocked, Eleanor let go of his neck cloth. "What?"

Giles leaned against the tree's massive trunk and crossed his arms over his chest. "Say please."

Eleanor bit her lip.

Giles pushed away from the tree. "On second thought, I want you to say, 'Giles, please help me."

"This was all your idea."

Giles gave her a look of utter incredulity. "Your foot getting stuck? I don't think so, but it does add a nice touch though." He placed his thumb against his forehead and scratched as he thought. "You know, in all the years we've known one another, I don't think I've ever heard you ask for help."

Eleanor gave up talking. She bent over in a most provocative way, folding herself in half with her backside in the air and her face hidden in the folds of her skirt, trying to reach her shoe's buckle. The ground was uneven with protruding roots, which made finding a flat place to plant her free foot difficult. Her bottom swayed, and Giles went stiff with desire. To distract himself, he began to whistle a tune.

Eleanor growled.

He let out a bark of laughter. "Come on, Ellie, just say:"—as he repeated each word of the short phrase, he popped up another finger— "Giles,"—his pinky came up— "please"—his ring finger— "help"—up came his middle finger— "me"—finally his index finger joined the other three. "Four little words and I'll free your foot."

Eleanor threw herself harder at the task. It became obvious that she'd rather do herself an injury, maybe even break her ankle, than ask for help. And based on his recent conversations with Harleigh and Lady B, he didn't think her reluctance to ask for help was exclusive to him; it applied to everyone. My God, who'd failed her so?

"Stop. Stop. Stop." Giles fell to his knees before her and grabbed her shoulders. "Stop, Ellie. You'll hurt yourself."

More of her hair had fallen out of its pins in her frenzied attempt to free her foot. Her face glistened with perspiration. Wet curls were stuck to her cheeks, forehead and neck. Her fichu had disappeared, her chest was flushed and damp from her inverted exertion and her breasts were nearly falling out of their confines.

"Hold your skirt out of the way, will you?"

She complied without another word.

"You were correct, it's a root," he said as he tugged off his gloves and tossed them on the ground. When he slid his hand over her trim silk-stocking-covered ankle and then down to the shoe's buckle, he heard her soft gasp. Giles liked where his hand was, he liked it a lot, and decided to reward himself by letting it rest on her leather-covered instep for a moment or two.

Eleanor softly cleared her throat. "Lord West, I perceive that you've located the buckle of my shoe."

"Indeed. I was just thinking—"

"What a novel experience for you. Now, if you would just—" Eleanor began.

He didn't let her provoke him. "Your personality is so large and yet your ankle is so small—dainty, even."

"I'm not fragile. Furthermore, I don't believe a female's physical attributes are a subject a gentleman should discuss with a lady."

"Especially when he has his hands under her skirt, you mean? And I didn't say 'fragile'. I said 'dainty'."

Eleanor's face flamed.

Giles unbuckled the strap. "Pull your foot out."

When Eleanor's foot was free, she cocked her knee, holding her shoeless foot above the ground and hopped on her shod foot to the tree trunk.

He freed her shoe, rubbed the scuffed toe of it against his buckskin-covered thigh and turned the shoe over and shook out debris. When Giles turned about to face the tree, his mouth went dry. Eleanor lounged back against the trunk. She'd tipped her head up and her eyes were closed. Her clothing was rumpled from her fight to free her foot and thick curling ropes of her hair hung down her back. Dappled sunlight pouring in from above added to the ethereal picture before him. Hah! If ever there was a misnomer that was it; there was not a single thing angelic about this woman. She was trouble from stem to stern, and she was his.

Giles dropped to one knee, like a knight before his lady, and held up her shoe. *"Mademoiselle, votre pantoufle de verre."*

She opened her eyes, scoffed, and reached for her shoe.

Giles pulled it away.

"Give me my shoe. Glass slipper, indeed."

Doggedly, Giles kept a smile on his face. *"Aahhh,* no. *Votre pied, s'il vous plait."*

Eleanor rolled her eyes, then raised the hem of her skirt and presented her shoeless foot, arched like a ballerina's, toes pointed downward.

Giles cupped the heel of her foot in his hand, then leaned down and kissed her instep.

Their eyes locked. She didn't yank her foot away but cocked her head to the side and gave him the most perplexed look. "Why did you do that?"

He eased her shoe on, placed her foot on his thigh and closed the buckle. She dropped her skirt. The hem fell against the back of his hand. He ran his fingers over the buckle and continued upward. Eleanor's breath sped up and a flush rose up her neck and darkened her cheeks.

He caressed her calf, his hand continuing until his fingertips touched her ribbon garter wrapped about her thigh. When she made no protest, his fingers went higher. Just above the garter he found bare skin and laid his hand against the firm smooth flesh at the back of her thigh. With his thumb, he began to massage. He felt the tremor in her leg muscles. Suddenly she collapsed. His hand was under her skirts and once again they were eye to eye.

Eleanor blinked. "Ahh, h-have you changed your mind? Are we going to engage in relations outside of marriage?"

"We most certainly are not."

"Is this your idea of a walk, then?" Eleanor said.

"This is as far as we're going."

"That's a shame." She gave him a sly grin. "That was very…"

Giles let go of Eleanor's leg and pulled his hand out from under her skirts, as much as he would rather not. "Stop it. I never should've done that. And it shan't happen again. Well, not until you marry me." Damn me for a fool. I shouldn't have said that. "I'm supposed to be protecting you." He jumped to his feet because he was rock hard and he was damned uncomfortable crouched on the ground and he had to put some distance between them.

"Protecting me? From whom?" Eleanor asked.

"Harleigh's worried about those people from the brothel and so am I."

Eleanor still sat on the ground. "You mean Madame Lutz, the man I shot, or maybe you're worried about … Edgerton?"

Giles flinched. Well, that's getting straight to the point. "Since you insist on being blunt, allow me to follow suit. Yes, to all three. We may not know the how of it, but Harleigh and I believe that Edgerton has deduced you are the cause of the raid upon his business, otherwise his visit to Lady Sybil's and his declaration that you were in Bath makes no sense at all."

"I see." Eleanor's hand trembled as she laid her palm against the tree's trunk, got her feet under her and pushed upward.

Chapter Thirty-two

Eleanor was numb. Giles' logic was irrefutable. Her arrogant and imagined advantage over Edgerton had just dissolved. She felt rather exposed and weaponless. Maybe Madame's ledger and papers would provide a clue or some leverage with which to thwart him. With Giles' words, she understood with unambiguous clarity she'd never be free of his malice. Having Edgerton as her eternal enemy was an extremely unpleasant prospect. She shivered. The sooner they got home, the better, then Libby and her father could get to work.

Eleanor took a misstep as she crossed from the packed dirt of the coaching yard into the inn's entryway. Giles was there to steady her. He walked her up the stairs. When they reached the top, Aunt Beatrice appeared. "Ah, there you are."

"I need to find Harleigh." Giles jogged back down the stairs.

Eleanor walked through the open door to their left. "Is this bedchamber yours or mine, Aunt?"

"Yours, dear."

Eleanor went to the open window and stared out. She couldn't pull her thoughts into any coherent form.

Then the curtain beside Eleanor was shoved aside by a well-manicured hand. "What's so fascinating out there?"

Eleanor shrugged.

Aunt Beatrice wrapped her hand around Eleanor's arm and turned her so they faced one another. Her aunt's eyes narrowed as she surveyed Eleanor. "Come sit with me."

The bed made a few companionable squeaks as the two women descended onto the mattress.

"You look different," Aunt Beatrice said.

Eleanor attempted nonchalance. "Oh, really?"

Her aunt leaned closer as if inspecting her for ticks. She pointed her index finger at Eleanor's face and wagged it back and forth. "For one, you have a lovely pink color in your cheeks."

"The sun." *Or maybe abject fear.*

"La girl, you must think me born yesterday. That boy puts me in mind of your Uncle Jasper. He could put that sort of pink in my cheeks," her aunt said and waggled her brows at Eleanor.

Eleanor choked on a laugh.

Beatrice slapped Eleanor on the back to assist her breathing.

When Eleanor caught her breath, she spoke with finality, "It was the *sun.*"

Beatrice Whitely chuckled. "Well, if you ask me, dear, you could use with a little more of that sort of *sun* in your life."

Eleanor's mouth fell open.

"When you behave like this, Ellie, you put me in mind of your mother. And I'm not paying you a compliment."

Eleanor shook her head. "Are you sure I'm not your child?"

"Funny, he said almost the same thing."

"He who?" Eleanor asked.

"Lord West. He said sometimes you seem more a child of mine."

"Is that so?"

"When I see you two together you put me in mind of Jasper and me."

"He looks nothing like Uncle Jasper."

"Don't be obtuse, Eleanor."

Eleanor laid her head on her aunt's shoulder and wrapped her arm around her waist. "I miss him too. But you and Uncle Jasper are one thing, Lord West is something else."

"Is *that* so?"

Before Eleanor could respond, her aunt continued. "That lad is special. Known it since I first laid eyes on him when he was a boy."

Eleanor made a scoffing sound.

"I remember once, Giles and Harleigh were on the lawn playing. I was with your father in his study. You'd gotten away from the nursemaids, as usual, and you kept trying to join in. Harleigh, the rascal, called you a nuisance and told you *loudly* and repeatedly to go away. Your father opened the window and was about to intervene when Giles West tossed you the ball, then scooped you up and took off around the house, leaving Harleigh behind. Oh, that look on your brother's face. And I can still hear your peals of laughter as you disappeared around the corner. Your father and I laughed so hard. Poor Harleigh."

Eleanor jumped off the bed.

"You're in love with that boy and he's in love with you."

Eleanor leaned down so she was nose-to-nose with her aunt. "I'm in lust."

"Luuve," Aunt Beatrice said.

Eleanor threw her hands in the air and spun away.

"Of course, lust in a marriage bed is quite delightful," her aunt said.

"Marriage bed? No, no, no, no. I can't marry, and he's made it quite clear that he would not pursue anything with me without the bonds of marriage. And you know as well as I, that I must remain independent. The Sisterhood—"

Aunt Beatrice slowly got to her feet. Her shoulders were back, spine erect.

Eleanor knew that look. She was in trouble.

"The Sisterhood needs *all* of us, not just *you*," Aunt Beatrice said. "If you choose to turn your back on what I believe your heart is telling you to do, then so be it. But do *not* use the Sisterhood as an excuse. I'll not listen to you say anymore that the Sisterhood requires that kind of sacrifice from you. It's the most egregious lie and you demean the commitment of the rest of us when you talk like that. You're not any more valuable to this organization than any other member."

"I never meant …" Eleanor realized just what a pompous ass she was being. Had been. Aunt Beatrice was correct in her assessment; she did act like she was more important than the others.

"Then why do you keep saying it, dear? It's quite unfair, you know."

Gazing into her aunt's eyes, Eleanor saw how her promise to Betty, and her own desire for vengeance, had acted as an arbiter for her life. That night in the barn had set her life on a course she'd held to for ten years. Everything she did or learned was in preparation to find and punish the man who'd raped her friend.

It never counted for much with Eleanor that she had only been eight. Not as the days turned into years and her sunny, happy friend transformed into a lonely, frightened young woman who never mentioned or alluded to that night, even to Eleanor.

Her aunt took Eleanor's chin. "A life is made up of many things, child. Family, friends, pursuits, triumphs, failures, love, grief and so on. You understand?"

Eleanor nodded.

"A life well-lived is a symphony. You have it within you to create the most extraordinary symphony."

A symphony?

Eleanor's eyes drifted away from her aunt's face as she let herself contemplate holding a child of her own and being Giles' wife. What if she never figured out who had attacked Betty? What then? Her hatred of that one man had burned inside her for so long, an everlasting flame lighting her way into the future. But should she allow her life to continue down this narrow channel? "I need to speak with Betty."

"Betty?" Aunt Beatrice sounded shocked.

Eleanor's focus came back to Aunt Beatrice's face. "What? Yes. My friend Betty Longley. And you're right. I'm no worthier than any other member. I'm sorry I've behaved so badly."

"All I'm asking you to do is think about your future without these strictures you've imposed on yourself since childhood. Look at your life with the eyes of the compassionate adult you've become. Extend to yourself the same kindness you offer your sisters."

Chapter Thirty-three

Since returning to Barrett Hall, Eleanor's father had restricted her to the house and grounds—and only those grounds that lay close to the house.

Giles lingered. His excuse: Rodrigo needed a respite before they traveled on to his parents. But when he didn't make one single attempt to be alone with her, she wondered if he'd changed his mind about her.

Then Mother Nature made things worse with an oppressive change in the weather. Thick banks of clouds blocked the sun, as a wave of moist summer heat settled over the valley, making it feel as if they were living under a soggy woolen blanket. With hardly a breath of wind to ease the stifling effects of the heat, everyone's temper sported a shortened fuse.

"Enough!" Eleanor jumped from her bed. She went to the wash basin and splashed her face, neck and chest with cool water, then leaned out of the open window. This morning the eastern sky was streaked in pinks and lavenders.

She spun on her heel and pulled her night-rail over her head and used it to wipe the water from her face before tossing it into a nearby chair. Naked, she threw open the doors to her armoire and pushed aside her fashionable gowns. When she found what she sought, she tossed it onto the floor behind her, then knelt to rummage through the drawers in the base of the cabinet for the few undergarments she was willing to don during this ghastly weather.

Dressed, she pulled on her most decrepit short boots, braided her unruly hair without even attempting to get a brush through it, and raced out of the house. As she marched down the hill, a cool breeze bussed her cheeks and lifted her sprits.

The walled rose garden came into view, and over the wall Eleanor spotted Betty Longley moving about, getting her tools out of the shed. Eleanor smiled as she recalled the war of wills Betty and her grandfather waged over that one small shed. When Betty finally acquiesced, and let them build it, she'd insisted it be made of the same stone as the wall, thereby making it invisible.

The enclosing wall was eight feet high with a lovely decorative motif of cabbage roses and leaves cut into the coping stones that topped the entire wall. Eleanor headed for the formal ornamented iron gate that was embedded in the center of the northern wall. The gardeners used a wide, utilitarian, wooden gate that was in the southern wall, and hidden from view by a large tree. That tree was the bane of Betty's existence, but it had invaded the garden over seventy years ago and she didn't have the heart to cut it down. It wasn't in Betty's nature to harm any living thing. But it didn't stop her from wishing for a lightning bolt to strike that tree and burn it to the ground.

Since the incident, Betty preferred to work alone, and didn't like anyone coming upon her unannounced. Eleanor stood outside the northern gate and hailed her friend. "Betty!"

A smiling face crowned with a braided coronet of honey-brown hair popped up above a hedge of light red apothecary roses. "Here comes trouble."

Eleanor opened the gate and smiled broadly. "Hah, look who's talking."

"Took you long enough to get yerself down here. Ye've been home fer days."

"Sorry, Father's being a worry-wart." Eleanor secured the gate behind her.

"Yer leather gloves and apron are where you left them," Betty called after her as Eleanor headed for the shed.

Eleanor disappeared inside the door-less hut, which smelled of sunshine and bundles of drying rose hips Betty had hanging from the rafters. Eleanor donned her apron, hat, and work gloves and then hurried back outside. "What do you want me to do first?"

Betty motioned with her cutters to several rows of *Quatre Saisons* roses. "I need to finish some pruning. You can start on the weeding over there."

Eleanor could've found those roses with her eyes closed—their smell was heavenly and unique. She plucked a weeder out of Betty's box of tools and went to her assigned spot and dropped to her knees. It was good to work hard. To forget about everything and everyone accept what was right in front of you. She finished one row and stood, stretching to ease her back muscles, and moved to the next row.

Time flowed on. Every low-hanging bloom beckoned Eleanor to lean forward and hover just above its center and inhale. Bees swooped in. Some landed. Fascinated, Eleanor watched one crawl over the center of the several blooms, its segmented limbs ceaselessly pumping up and down. It had sacks of yellow attached to its hind legs.

The bladed end of a hoe chopped into the earth only a few inches from Eleanor's fingertips. "Whoa." Eleanor reared back and gazed up into Betty's frowning face. "What?"

"I've been calling you *and* calling you," Betty said.

"Have you?"

Betty reached down and grabbed Eleanor's arm and yanked her to standing. "Time for a break and some talk. My grandmother sent enough food for ten men."

When the two had devoured honey cakes and drunk lemonade, Betty leaned back on her hands and gave Eleanor her undivided attention. "Out with it. What has you so fuddle-headed?"

"Am not."

"You let me come upon you unawares. Yer the one who taught *me* to always be vigilant."

Eleanor twisted her mouth up tight. "You know how much I hate having my words thrown back at me?"

Betty scratched her cheek. "Not much, I'd warrant."

Eleanor snorted.

Betty stayed quiet.

"Well," Eleanor sighed. "I've several things on my mind."

Betty was the most patient person Eleanor knew.

Eleanor fidgeted. "Well, by now I'm sure you have heard most of the tale of little Julia."

Betty gave one quick, forceful nod.

"Did you hear where we found her?"

"Ye know how close my grandparents are with the Brewsters. Is that what's bothering you?"

"You know I was working there?"

"Aye." Betty chuckled. "Woulda like to ha' seen you tricked out like an old woman."

"Well, my father and brother think someone may be looking for me because of us rescuing Julia and the other girls."

"I heard Mr. Harleigh and Mr. Giles telling Grandda to keep a look-out for anyone new coming round askin' fer work. Ellie, they're not just lookin' fer ye, they want to hurt you for interferin' in their business."

Just hearing Giles' name made Eleanor squirm. "I'm sure they're worrying for nothing."

"I know too well na ta swallow whole what comes outta yer mouth, Ellie Barrett."

Eleanor pulled a face.

Betty touched Eleanor's arm. "Are you worrit?"

"Not like you mean. Besides, I can take care of myself."

"If that isn't what's worryin' ye, then what is?" Betty asked.

"What do you think of Lord West?"

"Hard to think of him as a lord, seein' how he and Mr. Harleigh ran riot here as boys." Betty tucked her hand under her chin. "Do you like him, Ellie?"

"What made you ask that?"

"Well, ye never asked my opinion about a fella before."

"Really?" Eleanor said.

"No, never. Are ye maybe thinkin' of lettin' him court you?"

"You know I plan never to marry."

"You made that vow a long time ago. You can't let what happened to me make you mad and suspicious of every man ye meet."

"Is that how you feel?" Eleanor asked.

"We was talkin' about *you*."

So, *that* subject wasn't open for discussion. A companionable silence fell between them.

"You asked me what I thought of Lord West. Well, Granddad thinks he's a good man. And the way he looks at you ..." Betty whistled.

Eleanor ducked her head.

Betty chuckled and then playfully shoved Eleanor in the shoulder. "Are ye gone on him?"

"Maybe. He asked, but I said no."

"Why?" Betty sat up straighter.

"I don't care what you say, I'm going to finish what I started."

"I didn't ask you to do that," Betty said.

"It was a promise as much to myself as to you. He needs to pay for what he did."

Betty threw her hands in the air. "You're a stubborn one. Anything else on yer mind?"

"At the brothel, I saw someone. From *our* family."

"Not one of yer brothers, was it?" Betty asked.

Eleanor shook her head. "A cousin. And I think he may be an owner."

"Are ye believin' this cousin is responsible for what happened to Julia? That's evil, that is. Which cousin?"

Eleanor fiddled with her bootlace. "The son of my father's favorite cousin."

Betty went pale. She'd picked up her trowel, clenching it in her fist, like a dagger.

"What's the matter?"

Betty's voice shook. "A-are you talkin' 'bout Francis Edgerton?" Betty stabbed the trowel into the ground.

Eleanor nodded slowly, her eyes never leaving her friend. The rage rolled off Betty. Eleanor watched and waited, looking for any sign of her tender-hearted friend instead of the vengeful warrior who sat beside her.

"Damn his black heart." Stab. "May he burn in Hell." Stab. Stab. Stab. Betty finally seemed to become aware of Eleanor again and she rolled away and stood up.

Eleanor stood up, not wanting Betty towering over her in her strange mood. "I didn't realize you had such a powerful grievance against Edgerton."

Betty grabbed Eleanor by the shoulders. "Are you mad?" Betty shook Eleanor hard. "*You* just said you were gonna punish him for what he done to me?"

Eleanor felt as though someone had stuffed her head with cotton batting.

Betty brought her face close. "Ellie, he's *the* one."

"The one?" Eleanor felt ripped open. "Oh, my God, how could I've not remembered?"

Betty gasped and let go of her. "What?"

Eleanor staggered back but then grabbed onto Betty's sleeve. "In my dreams, I couldn't see his face. The one who did it. All these years, it's been a shadow and a mocking voice. I would wake up screaming from the dreams of that night."

"Is that why they took you away?" Betty asked.

"I never told anyone what happened."

"Aye, I know that." Betty squeezed Eleanor's hand. "Grandfather said when you woke up you wouldna talk at all Not even to Mister Harleigh."

"I remember a voice telling me he'd come back and kill my pony if I told anyone anything. I was so scared, so I said nothing."

"Why didn't ye jus ask me?" Betty said.

"You never wanted to speak about it," Eleanor shrugged. "I figured one day all the pieces would fall into place and I would remember. Papa took me to these doctors in London. They looked down my throat and pulled my tongue." Eleanor grimaced. "Then one day I was sitting in the coach, waiting for Papa. I saw three men picking on this strange little man. I snuck out of the coach to help him, but he fought the bullies off by himself."

"Was that little man tha' Sekegawa fella?"

Eleanor nodded. "When he taught me to defend myself, I didn't feel afraid all the time. Sensei Sakegawa said in time I would remember. I've waited and practiced. I taught you and Libby what he taught me so you would trust yourselves, and feel capable and strong, too. Since that awful night, every man I met I would close my eyes and listen to his voice and ask myself, 'Is it him?'"

Chapter Thirty-four

Eleanor sat alone in her room, like a lump of iron slag. She'd been in this same spot for hours—ever since leaving Betty. Millie came and retrieved Madame's papers, saying something about giving them over to Libby and Lord Barrett.

Eleanor didn't care. She felt sick and ashamed. *How could I've forgotten it was him? How?* It was as though part of her mind had deliberately wiped away the man's identity. *I must make this right.*

"Ellie, can I come in?" Libby said from the hallway, from behind the closed door. She didn't wait for a response. The door cracked open and Libby's smiling, inquisitive face appeared. "Millie said you wanted to be left alone, but this is *really* important."

Eleanor turned her face away.

"What's wrong? You look awful." Libby came and put her palm on Eleanor's forehead.

Eleanor pulled away from Libby's touch.

"Did I do something?" Libby said.

Eleanor pushed herself out of the chair and moved away from Libby. "You never do anything wrong."

Libby's brow furrowed. "What's that mean?"

"Did you and Father find something?"

Libby blinked several times in rapid succession. A sure sign she was fighting tears. She got control of herself and walked back to the door, back stiff as a poker, her voice devoid of any brightness or warmth. "You need to come and see for yourself. Those papers and *that* ledger... well, if what your father and I suspect is true, you've stumbled on a very dangerous woman, Ellie. Your father sent for Mr. Rooksby."

"What?" Eleanor turned about.

Libby was gone.

Forgive me, Lib.

೮

When Libby reached the stairs, she heard a roar of female frustration followed by a crash from inside Eleanor's room. "Oh dear." She used the heel of her hand to wipe away her tears and hurried down the steps.

As she re-entered the library, Lord Barrett looked up. "Is she coming?"

"Mmmm, I don't know. Ellie's upset about something."

Lord Barrett slipped his thumb and index finger beneath his glasses and massaged the bridge of his nose. "Ah well, some of what we have to tell her shan't improve her mood certainly, but some will lift her spirits. Think we should batten down the hatches and prepare for unpredictable weather, Captain?"

Libby went to his desk. "You're the captain. I'm just a tag-along."

Lord Barrett put his arm about her shoulders. "Tag-along? What tosh. You saw things in these papers I missed."

Libby gazed up into his kind eyes. "Wonder what happened to upset her? She looked dreadful."

The door to the library was thrown open and crashed back against the wall. "Father."

Libby jumped.

Eleanor stomped in.

Lord Barrett tossed his spectacles onto his desk and moved to greet his truculent daughter. Eleanor stood, hands on hips, in the center of his library. He took her by the shoulders and turned her a bit to the right and then to the left. "You've been down with Miss Longley, I see,"—he sniffed— "and smell."

[298]

"You're most observant today, Papa."

Lord Barrett put his hands behind his back and strolled around Eleanor like a general reviewing his troops. "Are you accusing me of ignoring you, daughter?"

"Not any less than I want to be ignored. I know how to get your attention if I want it."

Lord Barrett laughed. "That you do, m'girl, that you do." He reached up and ran a thumb over Ellie's cheek and then presented his dirt-smeared thumb for her inspection. When she leaned in for a look, he swiped the dirt onto the tip of her nose.

"Really, Papa." Eleanor wiped away the smudge with the back of her hand. "Libby said you have something important ..."

Lord Barrett's voice was gruff but not demanding. "We'll get to that in a moment. What's put you in this mood?"

Eleanor rolled her eyes. "Old news."

Her father's brow lowered. "Old news indeed. It must be positively rancid to produce this kind of response. And you're not willing to air this bit of news with Elizabeth and myself?"

"I'm not at liberty to discuss it."

"Intriguing." Lord Barrett went back to his desk.

Libby laid her hands atop the ledger. "Perhaps we should wait to discuss the contents of Madame's papers until—"

The door opened again, this time by a footman, and in strolled Harleigh and Lord West.

"Waiting for us, were you?" Harleigh asked.

"Not really," Libby said.

"Have you finished?" Harleigh asked.

"In a manner of speaking." Libby wished he'd take the hint and leave. Eleanor was right; men didn't understand subtlety.

Harleigh looked at his sister and then pointed to himself and Lord West. "Well, this way's better; you kill three birds with one stone, eh?"

"That's an ill way of putting it," Libby said.

Harleigh came and stood beside Libby. "Ill? Is it not a better measure of time to do something once, rather than for the lack of a bit of planning, be doomed to repeat yourself?"

Libby shuddered hearing the word doom.

Lord Barrett came to stand on Libby's other side. "It'll be all right, Elizabeth."

Libby crooked her finger and motioned Lord Barrett to lower his head. "I beg you, sir, please put this off. I don't think this a good idea at all considering Eleanor's present state of mind …"

Harleigh and Giles rested their elbows on the high back of one of the vacant chairs before Lord Barrett's desk.

Eleanor's voice trumpeted. "Father?"

Libby startled.

Eleanor walked to the door. "If you two aren't ready, I've things to do."

"Wait." Lord Barrett held up his hand, then motioned Eleanor to a chair.

Eleanor paced the perimeter of the room instead. Neither her perpetual motion nor flaring temper had wiped the pastiness from her skin.

Lord Barrett laid his hand down on the ledger and nodded at Libby. "Let's start with this."

Libby sighed, then cleared her throat. "This a-a establishment is—I mean, was—quite profitable."

Harleigh rolled his hand forward in the air in an encouraging fashion. "And…"

"They'd several ways of generating revenue," Libby continued.

"My, how industrious," Giles said.

Giles and Harleigh elbowed each other like schoolboys who shared a joke.

Lord Barrett shook his head in disapproval. "Boys, I assure you what we're about to reveal is hardly cause for levity." He cleared his throat. "The usual way, of course—and then it seems the madam made loans to some patrons."

"Loans?" Eleanor said.

"With excessively high rates of interest, too," Libby said. "If the numbers in this ledger are to be believed," she added.

Harleigh turned his head to Eleanor. "Covering gambling debts, No doubt. Colonel Dutton said his men broke up a card game during the raid. Pots of money on the table."

Eleanor pointed to the papers on her father's desk. "And those papers there, are they avowals?"

"Some, yes, but only gentlemen use avowals, dear," Lord Barrett said.

Eleanor snorted.

Libby shifted her weight. "Ellie, we believe you had the right of it all along."

"The right of it?" Harleigh said.

"When Eleanor told us some of Madam Lutz's customers didn't look like they belonged. She said they looked more like clerks than gentlemen."

Harleigh's brows furrowed. "Madame extended credit to clerks? Where's the profit to be had in that?"

"Be patient, son. All that we know at this point shall be revealed," Lord Barrett said.

"Some, um, debts were paid off with coin, while others were expunged by other means," Libby said.

"What does that mean?" Eleanor said.

Libby's voice quavered. "Well, it's a kind of puzzle. The way someone keeps their books reveals a great deal about their thought processes as well as their character."

"Now there's a scary thought," Harleigh said.

"Shhh." Giles nudged him.

Libby laid her hand upon the open ledger. "Some entries are straight forward, with the left-most column containing names of gentleman, some of whom Lord Barrett recognizes. Then there are other notations in the left column, which are initials only, or what he and I think might be pseudonyms. And there are some strange notations we've yet to decipher besides those initials and pseudonyms."

Lord Barrett twirled a quill. "All the handwriting is of the same florid style, which tells us only one person kept these books. Probably Madame Lutz."

"Then perhaps the strange notations are Dutch," Harleigh said.

Lord Barrett pursed his lips and nodded. "That's only one of the reasons I sent for Rooksby."

"Rooksby? What's he got to do with this?" Giles said.

"Whose names did you recognize?" Harleigh said.

Lord Barrett gestured to Harleigh, Giles, and himself. "There are some men the three of us would know on sight and some only by reputation. Of those names I do recognize, they share a common trait … they all hold government posts or are all well connected to men who do. The other men's names that are written out are ships' captains and a few wealthy
merchants I know only by reputation."

"Are you suspecting blackmail, Lord Barrett?" Giles asked.

"Of a sort. And the fact that these men would have access to secret government affairs, matters of state, troubles me greatly."

"And so, you've summoned Rooksby?" Giles said.

Lord Barrett nodded.

"Honeycutt said Dagmar Lutz has a predatory reputation. I'd not want to be one of those men who became indebted to her without the means to repay," Harleigh said.

"Yes, but what if she deliberately arranged for them to be in that vulnerable position?" Giles said.

"You're ahead of me, Giles." Lord Barrette nodded. "In our circle a man might put up any number of things to cover his debt, but why court persons without the means to pay … unless that was your intent all along. In the right hands, what those clerks and ships' captains possess is something worth far more than a horse, and could change the fate of a nation."

Viscount Barrett's frown deepened. "The picture forming here is quite disturbing. One of the clerks listed in this book works for Lord North. I've seen the fellow for years in my comings and goings."

"The Chancellor? You're joking." Harleigh said.

Lord Barrett looked his son in the eye. "Now do you understand why I sent for Rooksby?"

Harleigh lost his smile. He jumped out of his seat and marched over to his sister. "Good Lord, Ellie, what've you gotten yourself into now?"

Eleanor spoke through gritted teeth. "There's nothing either good or bad, but thinking makes it so."

Harleigh waved his hand around in a mocking and theatrical fashion. "I'll think what I damn well please, you brat, and as it turned out, that Hamlet fellow got himself into quite a fix, did he not?"

Lord Barrett raised his voice. "Children!"

The rising tension made Libby's neck and shoulders ache.

The library fell into a charged silence.

Libby repositioned herself in Lord Barrett's chair and the squeaking broke the quiet.

Giles stepped to the desk. "Besides what you've already told us, do any of these documents provide the proof Lord Barrett requires to issue a warrant for Lord Edgerton?"

Libby shook her head. "His name hasn't appeared on anything thus far."

Giles rubbed his jaw. "I suppose that would be too convenient."

Harleigh's laugh was bitter. "Sly is what I would call it. Probably has someone fronting for him."

"If the proof isn't here—well, then we'll look elsewhere. I shan't give up." Eleanor said.

"No more brothels, daughter, do we understand each other?"

"Yes, Papa."

Harleigh came closer to the desk. "Anything else useful in these piles of paper?"

Libby folded her hands on the open ledger. "Well … there are several regular expenses, which include the wine merchant, her modiste, the butcher, and the like. Then there's one regular dispersal, and it dates back several years."

"Why did this expense catch your attention?" Giles asked.

"Uhmmm …" Lilly hesitated.

"This recurring amount—for how many years?" Harleigh said.

"Is there a name beside that amount?" Giles asked.

Libby felt like crying. "No, no, just initials."

"The amount she's referring to appears every three months, like clockwork," Lord Barrett said.

"The same amount each time?" Giles asked.

Libby nibbled her nail and nodded.

"Sounds like a loan she's paying off," Harleigh said.

Giles crossed his arms over his chest. "What kind of man loans money to a brothel?"

"A bad man," Eleanor said.

Harleigh rounded the desk like an eager young hound. "Perhaps she has a partner. If we figure out who—that should move us closer to that warrant for Edgerton. May I see?"

"Well…" Libby threw her hands, palms down, on top of the open ledger. Her temples throbbing.

"Elizabeth …" Lord Barrett's voice was calm and authoritative.

She gazed up, silently beseeching him to stop this.

"Let Harleigh have a look." Lord Barrett sat heavily in one of the chairs before his desk. Harleigh lifted the book from the desk. "Yes, a fresh pair of eyes and all that."

His eyes followed his finger as it ran down one page and then on to the next. "I see what you mean. At least four times a year. The same amount."

"How much?" Giles asked.

"Twenty pounds." Harleigh looked up.

"That comes out to eighty pounds per anum. For how many years?" Giles asked.

"Give me a moment. Haven't finished tallying yet." Harleigh continued turning pages.

Giles looked stunned. He rose slowly from his chair.

"What initials?" Eleanor said.

"Good Lord, you were right, her handwriting is execrable … The first letter seems to be … I would guess a G, and I think this other one might be a W. Yes, it's a W." Harleigh paused, his eyes growing round. He swallowed as he raised his eyes from the page to his friend. "You told me you'd made Edgerton a loan."

Giles placed his hand on the back of the chair. "That's correct. Before we left on tour."

"What was the money for?" Harleigh asked.

Giles stood stock-still. "I told you, I didn't ask. I'd the funds and I gave it gladly. My man of business reports Edgerton has been diligent and timely with his repayment."

"You didn't ask?" Eleanor said.

Harleigh and Giles had moved to face one another. Harleigh still held the ledger. Eleanor was circling the two men and with each pass she moved in closer.

"If *you* needed money—" Giles said.

Harleigh drove his finger into the open ledger like he was hammering a nail home. "After what we've found out—you're equating me with *him*?"

"I figured he was bettering himself. Investing in shipping, or purchasing a horse for stud."

"Or a building, my lord?" Libby said.

Giles tossed his hand in the air. "See, Miss Archer understands."

The knots in Libby's stomach twisted tighter.

Giles raised his voice and sounded proud. "Edgerton could've purchased a building with my money."

Libby picked up a folded document.

Lord Barrett took it from her. "No, Elizabeth," Lord Barrett said and turned to Giles. "This is a deed."

"You see?" Giles said.

"And carries *your* signature—not that of Francis Edgerton," Lord Barrett said.

"What property?" Eleanor asked.

Libby felt as though she were standing inside a storm cloud just before a thunder clap.

Giles took the deed and flipped through the pages. "This isn't *my* signature."

"Let me see." Eleanor took the document from Giles and scanned the pages. "This is a deed to the building used for the brothel in Bath." She waved the papers under his nose.

The volume of Giles' voice notched louder. "I swear I don't own that building."

Eleanor shouted back as she stabbed him in the chest with the deed. "You swear? You swear? Because that isn't what this says."

Red-faced, Giles shouted back. "It's a forgery. Ellie, I had nothing to do with it."

Eleanor hollered, "You had everything to do with it! You gave him the money, damn you. That makes you responsible. He's paying you back with a portion of his profits from girls like little Julia."

"I-I…" Giles said.

Eleanor rolled up the deed and drove the end into Giles' chest. "You what? We told you over and over and over. Don't trust him."

Giles grabbed Eleanor by the upper arms. "Are you thinking if I'd not given him the funds then there would be no brothel? Julia wouldn't have been kidnapped? Is that it? Ellie, you aren't *that* simple-minded. Think." He gave her a shake.

Eleanor's right arm shot forward. She twisted it just before she drove her knuckles into Giles' shoulder.

He stumbled back. Eleanor got her foot behind his ankle and yanked his feet out from under him. He hit the floor.

Eleanor tossed the deed onto the floor. "I'm done with you." She angrily swiped at the tears running down her cheeks as she ran from the room.

Chapter Thirty-five

He'd made Eleanor cry. Giles felt sick. "What a hash I've made." Giles threw himself into one of the two chairs before Lord Barrett's desk.

Harleigh put his hand on Giles' shoulder. "Why, because Ellie *is* crying? Listen, you great simpleton, if she cared nothing for you at all she wouldn't have shed a single tear."

"She blames me." Giles dropped his head into his hands.

"It was a shock for all of us, seeing your name on that deed," Harleigh said.

"Harleigh's correct," Lord Barrett said. "Eleanor isn't known for tears. I believe you've cause for hope. That's if you're still interested. I mean, it isn't every man who can say his wife knocked him down, is it?"

Giles' smile was melancholy.

Lord Barrett scratched his head. "Gad, can't remember the last time Ellie shed a tear."

"Exactly," Harleigh said.

"Are you two accusing Eleanor of being heartless?" Libby said.

Lord Barrett shook his head. "Heavens no …" He stared off into space. "Well, frankly, I can't remember the last time I saw a tear on her cheeks."

Harleigh leaned forward against the arm of his chair and pointed at his father. "When her cat died? No, that isn't it. She was a bit older. Around eight, I think."

"Eight?" Giles said.

Lord Barrett's face darkened. "Your mother told me Ellie didn't make a sound when the doctor examined that terrible bruise on her abdomen. Said Ellie just lay there like a broken doll. I thought your mother was being fanciful, but I'll never forget looking down on Eleanor lying motionless and silent in that bed."

Harleigh sat back. "Hard to believe after all these years we're no closer to solving the enigma of the night."

⋄

Eleanor felt like a damn fool. She rolled over. Tears were spilling from the
corners of her eyes, running down her temples and dripping into her ears. Giles had made her cry. Damn him.

Why? Why? Why did she listen to her heart and body where Giles was concerned? Both were extremely unreliable sources.

She tilted her head toward the open window, hoping for relief and a bit of distraction for her troubled mind. But there were no soft afternoon breezes to cool her hot cheeks, burning eyes, and frayed spirit.

Someone rapped on her door.

Eleanor startled. She sat up. The sky was no longer pale yellow but a deep dusk.

How long have I slept?

She didn't answer the knock.

The tapping began again and then a soft pleading voice. "Ellie, please let me in."

Eleanor stayed where she was.

"If you don't let me in, I'll take up residence on the floor outside your door until you do open up."

"Bah." Eleanor propelled herself off her bed. She'd never let Libby sit on the drafty hallway floor, and Libby knew that. She unlocked her door. "Drat you. Playing on my sympathies."

As Eleanor walked to the basin, Libby came in. Eleanor poured some water onto a towel and wiped her crusty eyes and tear-stained cheeks. Then she plopped down in her favorite reading chair, the one she kept before the window. She gazed into the dark and listened to the branches brushing against the house.

Libby sat quietly on the bed. Eleanor knew she'd just sit there as she always did and wait until Eleanor wanted to speak. The first stars appeared before Eleanor pulled her thoughts together and opened her mouth. "I don't believe he knew what Cousin Francis did with his money."

Libby rested back against a pile of pillows against the headboard. "That's a good start."

"Brat." Eleanor pulled a cushion from behind her and hurled at Libby.

"And the deed?" Libby said.

Eleanor shifted and stretched her legs out in front of her. "Remember, Mr. Rooksby told us people in high places were involved. Giles' family reputation is impeccable. Many would look the other way if it ever came to light that a West owned a brothel."

"Maybe they have already," Libby said.

Eleanor made a disgusted face.

"Extraordinarily mean, betraying his friend like that." Libby toyed with a fringed pillow. "Poor Lord West, I don't know what hit him harder: his gullibility or your accusation."

"Well, he did provide funds."

"Ellie."

"I know. I know. I shouldn't have said he was at fault."

"Someone once told me if you're patient in one moment of anger, you'll escape a hundred days of sorrow," Libby said.

Eleanor stared fixedly at the print of her dress material as if it held the wisdom of the ages. "Not fair, using Master Sakegawa's words against me."

"Do you not think you should go down and—"

"Tomorrow," Eleanor said as she pulled the pins from her hair. What if Aunt Beatrice was correct? That marriage to *the* right man would be sublime. Was she throwing the right one away? The whole notion of throwing Giles reminded her anew what she'd done to him. "Was he hurt?"

"Besides his pride, you mean?" Libby's smile was impish.

Eleanor snorted.

"No. But now your brother wants to know who taught you."

"I can deal with Harleigh," Eleanor said as her fingers plucked at the fabric covering her legs. "Aunt Beatrice thinks I've held myself more important than the rest of you in the Sisterhood."

"She's right."

"You too? That was never my intention," Eleanor said.

"I know that."

Eleanor flopped onto her bed, belly first. "How will I be able to circumvent the law to impose *feme covert* if I marry?"

Libby tossed a pillow to Eleanor. "I think you're selling Lord West short. Seems to me a male partner who shares your views would be an asset, not a liability. We'll not see *feme covert* change in our lifetime, Ellie, but that shall not keep us from getting around it and doing what's right and good."

Eleanor stuffed the pillow under her chin. "Well, that's the rub, isn't it? What a man professes before his marriage vows are spoken, is like believing morning mist will linger in bright sunshine. To trust my future and dreams to any man's promise, I think may be more than I am capable of."

ങ

Giles watched Harleigh and Lord Barrett gather up Madame's papers and lock them away. "Do you think there is more they can tell us?"

"Not today," Lord Barrett said. "I feel like I need a long hot bath and a good scrubbing after looking into that woman's business affairs."

"Sir, would you mind if I asked you a few questions about the aftermath of Eleanor's eighth birthday celebration?"

"Not at all. But you were here, as I remember it," Lord Barrett said as he seated himself at his desk.

"I was, but childhood has a way of coloring the past, and limiting one's point of view," Giles said.

"Fire away, lad."

"I've always been curious why you didn't have her pony put down."

"Put down? Why ever would I do that?" Lord Barrett said.

"You mentioned the bruise on her stomach. I recall Harleigh telling me her new horse had kicked her."

Harleigh scratched his head. "Did I? I think I overheard the doctor say something to our parents about Ellie being kicked."

"There was no cause to put the horse down." Lord Barrett took off his spectacles and wiped them off with his large handkerchief.

"But if he kicked Eleanor?" Harleigh prompted.

"You're only half right, son. She was kicked." Lord Barrett shifted in his chair. "But the mark on her abdomen was from a boot not a hoof."

A boot! "Who kicked her?" Giles said. The thought of anyone hurting her made him crazy. No wonder she didn't trust men.

"I've no idea," Lord Barrett said. "She was listless and that no-talking business, that's why I took her to London."

The image of that small, wounded eight-year-old Eleanor huddled in the corner of her father's traveling coach came into Giles' mind. He hadn't given it a second thought when he reached into his pocket and pulled out his lucky marble. She still had it.

A footman knocked on the door. They all startled.

"Enter," Lord Barrett said.

"Message for Lord West." The footman handed Giles a sealed missive. "The rider's waiting for your answer, m'lord."

Giles broke the wax and read. "Tell the rider I'll be ready shortly."

The footman withdrew.

"What's happened?" Harleigh asked.

"My sister Dolly. My father has asked me to come home immediately."

CB

Less than twenty-four hours after riding away from Barrett Hall, Giles and Harleigh strode into Giles' family's home. Even road weary and covered in dust, Giles needed to see Dolly.

As they handed off their hats, gloves and coats, both men were descended upon by a gaggle of shouting children of various ages— mostly boys.

"Uncle Giles!" seemed to be the most popular salutation.

His parents appeared, and Lady West took the children off.

"Harleigh?" Giles' father, the Earl of Margrave sounded surprised to see him.

"Sir. When I heard Dolly was in trouble I couldn't let Giles come alone."

The earl nodded with approval and motioned for them to follow him. "My son has chosen his friends wisely. Come into my study."

"Sorry, Father, I must go see Dolly." Giles' raced up the stairs and all way to her old bedroom door. He knocked. No reply. "Dolly, may I come in?"

A long, pregnant silence. Finally, she answered, "Come."

The heavy drapes were drawn. As a boy, Giles accompanied the gamekeeper when he tracked a wounded fox to put it out of its misery. Dolly's room smelled of fear and pain, just like the cave where they'd found the dying fox.

"Dolly?"

"Over here." She was sitting in a winged chair before a dead fire.

"Would you like me to stir the ashes?" Giles said.

"No, thank you. I'm quite comfortable." Dolly's speech sounded odd.

Giles knelt beside her chair and took her hand.

"I asked Papa not to bother you," Dolly said.

Giles felt like he was walking through a forest with traps hidden beneath the undergrowth. One wrong question and…snap. He waited. Dolly shifted and withdrew her hand from his.

"Sweetheart, why are you sitting here in the dark?"

"I've a headache."

Giles felt a sharp pain in his chest. "Where's Povey?"

Dolly sucked in her breath. Giles needed to see her eyes, headache or no. He rose and threw one side of the drapes back. Dolly gasped and threw her hands over her face.

Giles knelt again beside her chair. "Please, look at me."

He waited.

Dolly lowered her trembling hands.

Giles breath caught. Her upper and lower lips were split and swollen, and a large bruise purpled her soft cheek.

Eleanor's words, from that night at the ball, came flooding back. Calling him naïve about the brutality visited upon women of their class.

"I noticed Con wasn't with the other children."

"Abed. Next door. H-h-his arm's broken."

"How?" Giles hoped a fall from a tree had caused the break. He'd a sickening feeling that wasn't the case.

"He stepped between his father and me." Dolly started to sob. "He was protecting me."

First Edgerton and now Povey. *Lord, please, I don't need any more proof of my utter stupidity. No more.* What would he have done without Eleanor in his life to wake him up? "Dolly-love, how long?"

His answer was more tears. A whole host of them. He handed her his handkerchief. Hers ceased to be of use, it being sopping wet. He put his hand on her arm. "Just nod, all right?"

She did.

"Was this the only time?"

She shook her head.

"A year?"

She shook her head, and Giles felt a flutter of relief that his sweet Dolly hadn't endured beatings for years. But nothing would absolve him of this new black mark against him as a neglectful brother.

"More," Dolly whispered.

"What?!"

She drew back.

Damn it! I've frightened her. "May I hold you?" Giles asked.

She looked so unsure it broke his heart. When Dolly gave a slight nod, he gently pulled her from her chair and slowly enfolded her in his embrace. "I swear to you, sweeting, this will never happen to you or Con again—not to any of your children."

CB

Giles found his father and Harleigh in his father's study. Lord West paced before the large windows, his brows knit. Harleigh wore a perplexed look.

His father came to a halt. "Well?"

Giles had never felt this sort of ungovernable rage. "Do you know where he is?"

"I've not made enquiries. As soon as he left home and the doctor took care of Con's arm, Dolly came here. Then we sent for you."

"Who?" Harleigh came up beside Giles.

Giles said through his clenched teeth, "Povey."

"Your brother-in-law?" Harleigh said.

"He struck Dolly and broke Con's arm."

Harleigh's mouth was agape. "Was he drunk?"

"Does it matter?" Giles asked.

"Of course not.

"Eleanor once accused me of being blind to this sort of 'affection' a husband shows his wife. And all under the impunity of the law."

"I didn't realize you two talked of such things," Harleigh said. "She usually restricts that kind of discourse to our family and women friends."

Giles laughed with bitterness. "We didn't *discuss*. I was lectured."

"Now that *does* sound like my little sister," Harleigh said.

"Don't make light of this, Harleigh. I think she believes that, given the opportunity, all men will turn into Poveys."

"Son, I beg you, don't go looking for Povey. Not when you're in this frame of mind. Dolly and the children need you."

"What do you want me to do, Father?"

Harleigh put his hand on Giles' shoulder. "I think Dolly should spend some time with Eleanor."

"What can she do?" Giles' father asked.

"Here's what's true: one, when Povey sobers up he'll come home;" Harleigh said. "Two, when he doesn't find Dolly and *his* children there, he'll come here; three, Eleanor is correct—under the law, you and your father have *no* say, she's *his* property. And he can do what he likes to her—even lock her up in Bedlam. She must do what he says. *But* … if he can't find her…" Harleigh's voice trailed off.

Giles' father shook his head. "I don't know, Harleigh. Dolly and Eleanor are like—well, Dolly possesses a conventional nature and your sister is rather…rather a-ah uncommon."

"Eleanor's not speaking to me right now, as you may recall?"

"Eleanor's just what Dolly needs," Harleigh said. "Trust me. With an added bonus, she and the children will be safe at my parents' home. I know my sister. She'll not hold it against Dolly that she's related to *you*."

Giles snorted. It was the first time in more than a day that he'd found anything remotely amusing.

"Moving Dolly and her children to my parents' will give you time to cool your head and choose an appropriate course of action, one suitable for making sure your brother-in-law gets his just desserts and leaves you legally and morally blameless."

Chapter Thirty-six

Three days later, Giles and Harleigh rode beside two coaches laden with children, nursemaids, and Lady Dolly Povey. Harleigh sent word to his parents so rooms could be readied for their guests.

Giles was happy to see Eleanor emerge from the house with her mother as the coaches drew near the front door. As soon as the doors opened, the children sprang forth whooping and hollering. Rodrigo trotted around the side of the house. Giles wasn't sure which happened first, the children spotting his dog or Rodrigo spotting the children, but suddenly the air was filled with joyful barking and laughter as the dog and children collided.

Harleigh helped Con and Dolly from the carriage. Through the black veil Dolly wore over her hat, Giles saw her smile at the sight of her children and Rodrigo playing. Lady Barrett ushered Dolly into the house. He walked up the steps and Eleanor walked down.

"Miss Barrett, I know how you feel about me. I've been a stubborn fool, but my sister—"

Eleanor lowered her chin. "I didn't know you read minds, my lord?" With her a step above him, they were almost eyelevel. "Harleigh said Dolly needs my help."

Giles nodded.

"Then she has it." Eleanor bussed Harleigh's cheek. "Greetings, brother."

Harleigh tapped Giles on the shoulder. "Come along. I've ordered fresh horses. Let's get changed and have something to eat." Harleigh gave Eleanor a squeeze. "Thank you, Ellie."

"Leaving?" Eleanor looked back and forth from her brother to Giles.

"I must deal with my brother-in-law. And then there's the matter of Francis Edgerton. They're known to keep company."

"I see. What exactly do you have in mind for Lord Edgerton?"

"I haven't decided." Giles tugged his ear. What was he going to do? Beating him to a bloody pulp had its merits. Master Saviolo was right; Giles did blame himself for being duped, rather than placing the blame where it belonged—on Edgerton for betraying their friendship. A bitter taste lingered on his tongue.

"And Lord Povey?" Eleanor said.

Giles ground his teeth. "Something extremely unpleasant."

Eleanor spoke in a flat matter-of-fact tone. "No."

"It's not up to you." Giles' anger flashed and his hands curled into fists.

"If you want me to help Dolly, you *will* listen to what I have to say."

Giles stepped up to stand beside her. Doing so had him towering above her. She didn't flinch or draw back.

Eleanor raised her hand, her index finger pointing heavenward. "First, he's your brother-in-law and therefore the father to your niece and nephews, so if you kill him that'll always hang between you and those children. Two…"—another of Eleanor's fingers went up — "he's vermin and not worth hanging for,"—she raised her ring finger— "three, in the likelihood that he hurts or kills you, that would be a tragedy of another sort—your family needs you and not just because you're the heir,"—finger four went up— "and four, there's a more judicious way to handle Lord Povey."

Giles took her hand and pulled her thumb away from her palm and caressed it, running his fingers across the pad of her finger and down to its base. He saw her shiver. "And five?"

Eleanor cleared her throat.

Giles laid her hand over his heart. "You were saying?"

"What?" Eleanor said.

"The more judicious…?"

Eleanor shook herself. "He's fathered four sons. Speaking practically, he's no longer necessary for the continuation of his line."

Harleigh's brows shot together. "I thought you were advocating *not* ending his life?"

"Shhh, let her finish," Giles said.

"Lord West murdering his brother-in-law would be imprudent. On the other hand, I see nothing ill-considered about lending fate a hand. Let us say that Lord Povey was prevailed upon to leave England, and not for the continent, either."

Giles warmed to the idea. "You were thinking perhaps of India?"

"Or the Colonies, or the East Indies, or Timbuktu as long as he *never* comes back. I've a feeling that the inhospitable weather and native conditions would prevail and in the natural course of things Sir Povey would cease to exist. But not by *your* hand."

"And exactly how are we to bring this about?" Harleigh voice dripped sarcasm.

"I believe Uncle Jasper's old acquaintance Mr. Rooksby can be of assistance in that quarter. He's returned to London. I'm sure Aunt Beatrice can be prevailed upon to make the introductions."

Harleigh took her by the shoulders and turned her to face him. "All right, I admit that's a brilliant plan, but I want your promise *not* to wander from the house while we're gone. Until we deal with Edgerton, you aren't safe."

Chapter Thirty-seven

Edgerton rapped once on the gamekeeper's cottage, then let himself in.

"Tired of vating." Barend sat at the table, hunched over a plate of food.

"As am I. My source tells me that Giles West and Harleigh Barrett left days ago, and today they returned and then departed almost immediately." Edgerton walked into the room and circled the table so he faced his machina de mort.

"Vhat goot iz diz newz?"

"Well, for one thing—I believe they've gone off to London to search for Lord Povey."

"Who?"

"Never mind, an acquaintance of mine. Once Giles gets a hold of him, I'm afraid poor Lincoln shan't be long for this world."

Barend lowered his chin and gave Edgerton a look of 'why-are-you-boring-me-with-all-of-this?'

"Then, of course, he hopes to find me in London, but alas he shan't. And last but certainly not least, Eleanor hasn't left the property in over a week."

Barend grunted and continued to shovel food into his mouth.

"I think it's time to make a little mischief."

Barend's head came up and his gaze was sharp and attentive.

"Ah, I see that idea interests you. Good. I've arranged for some trouble to visit a laundry woman in the town."

Barend shrugged.

"Eleanor knows this woman. When she hears of the laundress's plight, she'll come to put things right."

"She vill come?"

"I'm counting on it. Eleanor can be impulsive, and right now I'd guess very restless, which will drive her right into our hands."

"How vill ve know vhen?"

"My watcher will tell us. Tomorrow we move closer."

Barend nodded.

"I'll come for you at dawn." Edgerton crossed his arms over his chest. He let thoughts of watching Eleanor die play across his mind. It gave him great comfort to know that soon he would be rid of her.

○ঃ

Eleanor sat on the edge of her bed and pulled on her boot. "Libby, I'm only going to look."

Libby snorted. "What a great heap of farradiddle." She paced back and forth, back and forth. "Ellie, we've not done any reconnaissance. You're not prepared, it's dark, and you'll be alone. At least take Millie."

"She's abed."

"As we all should be." Libby jabbed her finger in Eleanor's direction.

Eleanor looked at Libby askance.

"I'll get to bed once I know you're staying *here*," Libby said.

"This'll not take long. It's probably some merchant's son who's had too much to drink and who doesn't like hearing the word no. Hmmm?" Eleanor pulled on her other boot and then stood and stomped to settle her feet into her boots. "I'll show him the pointy end of my sword and he'll no doubt run off into the night, never to cross the laundress's path again."

"I think you're tired of being penned up and your common sense has gone on holiday."

Eleanor picked up Harleigh's old coat and her sword in its scabbard. She rolled the coat around the sword and put both into a large canvas bag. She stuffed a battered tricorn in last and pulled the draw cord. "You may be right. Either way, I shan't be long. If you want, stay here in my room. When I come home I'll fill you in."

Eleanor opened her window wide, leaned out, and dropped the canvas bag to the ground. Next, she slung one leg over the sill.

Libby rushed over and grabbed Eleanor's arm. "Ellie, not the tree?"

"From its base, it's a straight shot to the stables."

Libby tugged.

"What? You want me to parade out the front door? I bet Harleigh and Lord West are downstairs right now playing billiards or some other manly pursuit. I've no intention of letting them know I'm out of the house." Eleanor eyed Libby. "Promise me not to say a word."

Libby wouldn't meet her eyes so Eleanor squeezed Libby's hand. "Lib?"

Libby kept her head down but gave a quick nod.

"Wish me luck." Eleanor turned about and grabbed onto the thick branch just above her window.

॰ॐ

"I'm not surprised." Giles dismounted and tethered his horse next to Harleigh's under a large fan-shaped elm that shadowed the village schoolhouse.

"We've only been back from dealing with your brother-in-law a few hours," Harleigh said. "Honestly, what was I thinking? I should've tied her up."

"Well, in her defense, you only made her promise to stay put while we were away."

"Don't start." Harleigh shoved Giles in the shoulder.

Giles exaggerated his stumble as he fell sideways. "You didn't know she'd go out the window?" Giles walked quickly to catch up with Harleigh.

"Like hell. She's been using that tree as an escape hatch since she could walk. Father and I've threatened, on more than one occasion, to cut it down."

"Where are we going?"

"Shhhh. Libby said Eleanor was here to help the laundress. Her cottage is just down that lane there. She makes the last of her deliveries at the inn and must pass this tavern on her way home."

"How do you know so much about her?" Giles nudged Harleigh.

"She's the daughter of one our father's oldest tenants. Her husband died a year or so ago. Her father wants her and her children to move back with him, but she wanted to stay here in town, be an independent woman."

"Another of Eleanor's protégés?" Giles asked.

Harleigh's chuckle was soft and nearly drowned out by the sounds of the night. "That obvious, is it?"

Giles and Harleigh hunkered down in the shadows.

Harleigh leaned out around the corner.

Giles heard a noise and yanked Harleigh back into the shadows.

"What did you do that for?" Harleigh said.

"Heard something."

"What?" Harleigh said.

They both strained to listen.

Giles' eyes were becoming accustomed to seeing by moonlight. "Guess it was nothing."

"Well, I hope my sister hurries up and says yes to marrying you, then *you* can be the only one gallivanting after her in the dark of night."

"I've other plans for Eleanor and me to pursue during the dark of night—or the light of day for that matter."

Harleigh cleared his throat. "'Fraid that's a bit too much information concerning your future activities with my baby sister." Harleigh pulled his collar up. "Smells like rain."

Giles made a soft chuckle. He was amenable to changing the subject since thinking about doing those things with Eleanor would only make his rod spring to painful attention and there was nothing he could do about it at present.

They settled into watchful silence.

The tavern door swung open. The screech of a bow drawn across unturned fiddle strings, smoke, and lantern light spilled into the street, along with three men.

"I recognize two of them," Harleigh said. "That one's the miller's eldest son, and the other one there, I've seen about the village. But the third one, I've never seen."

"Strange companions," Giles whispered back. "The one you don't know is better dressed than the other two—sort of fancy to their plain workman's garb. And the two you know are a bit foxed." They were leaning into one another for support as they walked. The fancy-man kept darting furtive glances about, which put Giles on the alert.

"I'm for home," the miller's son announced.

"I'm witcha," said the second man.

"What's yer hurry, gents? Come back inside and I'll buy you another."

"Aww, thas grand of you, but me father'll skin me alive see if'n I'm late ta work tamarrah."

Fancy-man snapped to attention. A couple was heading their way. The laundress with her basket on her hip, accompanied by a slim man in a coat and tricorn—Eleanor.

Giles elbowed Harleigh.

"What've we got here?" Fancy-man dragged his two intoxicated comrades toward the couple.

Giles felt a prickle of warning. He pulled Harleigh out of their hiding place. "This feels like a trap." Giles thought about drawing his sword, but there were too many people, and in the moonlight, it'd be hard to distinguish friend from foe.

The three men surrounded the laundress and Eleanor.

Fancy-man drew his sword.

Eleanor pushed the laundress into a nearby doorway.

Jumped in front of her.

Sword drawn.

The two drunks stumbled about. Giles used a few well-placed kicks and rendered them unconscious.

Harleigh and Eleanor were fighting the fancy man.

Giles came up behind Eleanor. Grabbed her about the waist and tossed her off into the doorway with the laundress.

"I can take care of myself." Eleanor was angry.

Too bad. She would just have to get used to him taking care of her. "Stay put." Giles turned. Drew his sword. Fancy-man was damn good with his blade.

Harleigh slipped.

Fancy-man lunged.

Giles jumped between them. "Take care of the women," Giles said to Harleigh.

Harleigh scrambled to the doorway.

"We' re fine. Help him." Eleanor tried to shove past her brother.

Harleigh held on tight to Eleanor.

Bang.

Harleigh fell into Eleanor, knocking her to the ground.

"Harleigh Barrett, get off me," Eleanor said as she pushed at her brother. "You great lump."

Harleigh groaned.

Eleanor smelled the metallic tang of blood. "Harleigh? Oh, no! Giles, help us!"

Giles was yards away, running after Fancy-man. Then in a flash, he was crouching beside her. Giles rolled Harleigh off Eleanor.

She sat up. Held her hand up to Giles. "Someone shot him."

℞

Eleanor waited with Giles, Libby, and her father in the upstairs parlor. Her mother was with the doctor in Harleigh's room. Eleanor sat alone in the window seat, staring down at Harleigh's blood on her boots.

Libby drew near. "Ellie, dear."

"Libby, what have I done? You were right. If I'd not gone out, then Harleigh ... What if he ...?

Libby wrapped her arm around Eleanor's shoulder. "Shhhh. I *absolutely* refuse to entertain that sort of notion."

"I'm scared," Eleanor said.

The doctor appeared and Lord Barrett went to him.

"The shot went through his lower arm," the doctor said. "He's lost a great deal of blood."

Her father nodded. "What now?"

"We must wait to see if he can use his arm. Many have lived full lives without the use of two arms, but if the wound turns putrid ... well, that's my biggest concern. Your wife and housekeeper are with him. I left instructions."

"Very good," Lord Barrett said.

"I'll take my leave and return tomorrow." Their butler showed the doctor out.

"I'm so, so sorry." Libby's head was bowed and Eleanor could barely hear her.

"What?"

"I was afraid for you out there alone. I told them where you were going."

Eleanor stared. "A-are you saying … "—she leaped off the window seat— "Harleigh would've never been there if you'd not broken your promise?"

Libby backed away.

"Stop it, Eleanor." Giles came to stand beside Libby. "She saved your life."

"What she did was get Harleigh shot."

Libby's lip quivered. "I didn't think—"

"You certainly did *not*," Eleanor bit out. "You gave me your word. If I can't trust your word, how can I trust *you*?"

Giles drew Libby into his arms as she burst into tears.

ɣ

Eleanor couldn't stand being inside another moment. She ran out of the house. She cut across the lawns, keeping her head down to avoid eye contact with any of the gardeners. If only she hadn't left the house last night.

Her spirits were lower than the soles of her boots swishing across the dew-soaked grass. The cost of her avenging had never been so high. Now Harleigh might lose his arm, or his life, and she'd blamed Libby instead of herself.

When the path forked, Eleanor veered right. Straight toward the walled rose garden. She found Betty kneeling on the ground, tending a spectacular golden rose near the southern edge of the garden. A large straw bonnet lay discarded on the bench beneath that misbegotten eyesore of a hornbeam tree near the gardener's gate.

Eleanor went and plopped down on the bench. When Betty was ready she would come and sit with her.

The beauty and calmness of the garden eased Eleanor's troubled spirit. A thick layer of hornbeam seeds lay on the ground under her boots. She picked up a stick and dragged it through the seeds, writing the letters L-I-B.

"Whatcha doin' there with the bane of my existence?" Betty stood before her, wearing solid work boots. A heavy canvas apron covered her dress, and she wore thick workman's gloves. She kicked a spray of seeds with the toe of her boot into the air, then looked at what Eleanor had written. "Uh-oh, whatcha done now?"

"Hah, how well you know me. I made Libby cry, is what."

Betty shook her head. "You and your temper." She scooped up her hat, tossed it on the ground, and settled herself down beside Eleanor. "Why did ye make Miss Libby cry?"

"Have you been practicing those new fighting moves I taught you?"

Betty made a scoffing noise. "You didn't come down here to check on my practice. She put her arm around Eleanor's shoulders. "Come on, out with it."

○ℨ

Giles decided to stop by Harleigh's room to check on him before going down for lunch. The door was open so he walked right in. Harleigh was sitting up. Miss Archer sat beside the bed, reading to him.

She lowered the book and smiled at him. "Shall I leave you to your manly matters?"

Giles stood at the foot of the bed. "We can discuss manly matters later. For now, I just wanted to see how Harleigh is getting on."

Harleigh's lower right arm was bandaged and rested on a pillow in his lap. This scene was all too reminiscent of him and Eleanor in Bath. Giles felt an overwhelming need to go find her.

"Have you seen Eleanor?" Harleigh asked.

Giles shook his head.

"Libby stopped by her room but she wasn't there." Harleigh smiled at Libby.

My God, is that the way I look at Eleanor?

"She's avoiding me," Harleigh said.

"Give her time," Giles said.

"Trust me on this," Harleigh said. "I need to see her."

"And you want me to find her, is that it?" Giles said.

Harleigh nodded.

"I've not the faintest idea where to begin such a search."

"Oh, I know exactly where she is." Harleigh leaned back in his pillows, closed his eyes and grimaced. "The same place she always goes when she's troubled."

Libby frowned when she saw Harleigh's pained expression. "She goes to the rose garden, my lord. If you exit through the French doors on the terrace, any of the gardeners can show you the way."

"All right. But what if she's not there? Where do—"

"Oh, she'll be there," Libby stated with utter certainty. "That's the garden her friend Betty tends."

Harleigh opened his eyes. "Betty Longley. They've been thick since childhood. Her grandfather was the head gardener when we were boys. Now Betty is the wizard of the rose garden."

And that is exactly where Giles found her. Sitting with a tall, pretty woman who was wearing a heavy apron and thick boots under the only tree in the rose garden, so engrossed in their conversation they didn't hear him approach. "Helllooo," Giles waved from outside the gate.

Both their heads came up. Eleanor scowled. Her companion scurried away, heading for a small, unobtrusive shed several yards away, and disappeared inside.

Giles said in a bright voice, "May I come in?"

"Suit yourself." Eleanor rose. "I'm leaving."

"I've come looking for you. Actually, I was sent on a mission to find you."

Eleanor said nothing.

"By Harleigh."

Silence.

"He thinks you're avoiding him."

Eleanor looked away.

Giles wanted to shake some sense into her and kiss her senseless at the same time. Last night had been a brutal reminder of what he'd almost lost, *again*. "Apparently that incident in Bath failed to teach you a damn thing."

She looked at him and then quickly turned away. The pain in her eyes shocked him. "Eleanor." He reached for her. She backed away. Why did she always muddle his thinking? She'd hurt Libby and nearly gotten them all killed.

Eleanor pivoted.

"You thoughtless, selfish, immature brat. Harleigh was out there because of you. And you blamed your dearest friend for it. Not well done, not well done at all." Giles grabbed her arm. "Come along. Harleigh's waiting, and you owe Elizabeth Archer an apology."

Eleanor spun and drove the toe of her boot into the back of his knee. Giles staggered and crumbled to the ground. Eleanor raised her arm, preparing to deliver another blow. She stopped. Dropped her arm.

Looking up at her with sunlight striking her eyes, he saw her unshed tears. "Eleanor." He reached for her.

She stepped back. "Get out. You delivered the message." Eleanor sped toward the shed.

Betty came to her. Put her arm around Eleanor's shoulders. They walked away from him.

Jealous and dejected, he left. As Giles pulled the rose garden gate closed behind him, he gazed back at the two young women. *Where the hell did Eleanor learn to fight like that?*

ଔ

Eleanor scrubbed her eyes. "Gah! No more tears."

Betty waved her hand at the iron gate. "He cares for you."

"Are my gloves in the shed?"

"Aye." Betty gave her a hard look. "Mayhap workin' with me roses might be just the thing. Give ye time to think. I'll get 'em for ye."

Eleanor knelt and stuck her nose into a large open rose. *Heavenly*. A bee landed nearby. The sunlight struck its wing segments, flashing iridescent sparks.

"Well, well, well, what do we have here?" a familiar voice drawled.

Eleanor's head shot up. She hadn't heard him approach. She clutched the hidden pocket in her skirt. Empty.

Eleanor stood slowly and pivoted. "How did you get here?"

Edgerton strolled out from behind the hornbeam tree. He held a cocked pistol. "I've my ways."

Another man appeared behind Edgerton's right shoulder, lean and dressed as a gardener. As he came closer, Eleanor studied his face. Something was familiar about his wide, mean mouth, thin lips and his long nose. *Tis Fancy-man, from last night.* "What happened to your clothes?"

"My finery? Fancy-man shrugged. "Today it doesna serve me purpose."

"You've been spying for *him*." Eleanor's gaze moved to Edgerton. "What do you want?"

Edgerton didn't answer for a long time. "You."

"I don't think so," Eleanor said.

"Once again you underestimate my desires, cousin. Bring her."

Edgerton pointed his pistol at the shed. A big blond man, Pim or Barend, came around the corner with Betty slung over his shoulder. *Oh, God.*

Her legs were bound. Her arms, too, behind her back. There was a gag in her mouth. And she was whimpering.

Calm, Little Eleanor, be calm, Sakegawa's voice cautioned.

"Barend, put her there." Edgerton pointed to the ground.

As Barend moved forward he limped and there was a bruise forming on his cheek. Ah, Betty had not surrendered without a fight.

Betty whimpered again and Barend bounced her on his shoulder and slapped her hard on her rear. "Silenz."

Betty quieted.

Barend knelt and as he pulled Betty from his shoulder, Eleanor saw the terror in her friend's eyes. He drew a large knife from a sheath on his belt. He grabbed Betty's braid to hold her head steady and then placed his blade against Betty's throat.

"Do as I say and we shan't hurt her."

Eleanor sucked in a breath.

Edgerton stepped close. "Only you can save her."

Eleanor gazed into Edgerton's cold eyes. "Why not kill me now?"

"Oh, I intend to be the means to your end, just not here."

A vision assailed her. Time slowed. Sakegawa had called this state of mind *mushin*. Like when Eleanor sat before a chess table, watching her opponent make *the* mistake that would cost him the game. Edgerton was blundering. His mistake: giving her time to find a way out of his trap. For now, Eleanor bowed her head and surrendered.

"Put your hands behind your back." Edgerton's look of smug satisfaction nearly drove Eleanor over the edge. "If you do anything, she dies."

Fancy-man stepped behind Eleanor and tied her hands tightly with a coarse rope. When he was done, Edgerton came and tugged on the bond. "Excellent." Edgerton shoved Eleanor down onto the ground. "Now, bind her ankles and knees."

Fancy-man knelt and when he wrapped the rope around her ankles, he ran his hand up her leg. Eleanor kicked out and caught him in the chest and knocked him onto his arse.

Edgerton laughed. "Told you to be careful, did I not?"

Fancy-man jumped to his feet. "Bitch." He raised his booted foot to kick her.

Eleanor rolled away from his kick.

When his leg passed over her, she rolled and swept his other leg out from under him. Fancy-man came down hard.

Edgerton laughed again.

Furious, Fancy-man roared to his feet.

Barend stepped in front of Eleanor. "Mine."

Red-faced, Fancy-man backed off.

"Barend." Edgerton nodded at Betty.

Edgerton gazed down at Eleanor. "Do anything else, cousin, and she pays."

Eleanor sat still. Fancy-man finished trussing her up.

"Go back to your work in Lord Barrett's gardens. Wouldn't want anyone to get suspicious, now would we?"

Fancy-man stood up, looming over Eleanor. "Shame. I would ha' liked te be there to hear you beg for mercy, sweeting."

Chapter Thirty-eight

Even with the sack over her head, Eleanor could tell they were moving in a southerly direction. The smell of the sea grew stronger with each rotation of the cart's wheels. Hours away from home now. There would be no one riding to her rescue.

As always, I have only myself to rely on, and only myself to blame.

The cart jerked to a halt. Eleanor rolled across the cart's floor. Her elbow collided with something hard. Excruciating pain radiated down to her wrist. A rush of cold terror stole her breath away. Like a scavenger's beak stabbing at unprotected flesh, fear tore at her confidence. She hadn't felt fear of this magnitude since the night in the barn with Betty.

Master Sakegawa whispered inside her head, *Little Eleanor, focus your mind.* His imaginary presence strengthened her.

Master, I am so scared.

The rope about her ankles was grabbed. Eleanor's clothing snagged on the rough wooden surface as she was dragged across the bed of the cart. Her feet hit the ground. She wobbled, then fell.

"Pick her up." Edgerton's voice came from above.

"Now—ve do eet now," Barend insisted.

"No."

"Vhat you mean?"

"Your grievance with her is new," Edgerton said. "Mine is old. I want to savor this moment."

An angry huff. Then a heavy silence. "No like." Barend kicked her in the rump.

Eleanor cried out.

"I said she would die and she shall." Edgerton dragged the last words out. "Very slowly."

Eleanor squeezed her eyes shut. Tears she didn't want to shed ran down her cheeks as images of Harleigh, Giles, and Libby entered her mind. *I'm so sorry.*

"Pick her up. It's a long way down."

Eleanor was lifted and thrown over Barend's shoulder. He had a long gait. She rolled and bounced against his back as he moved. She swallowed hard to drive down the bile that rose and burned her throat.

Barend stopped.

Jangling keys. The scraping of a lock.

When they moved again she no longer felt the sun's warmth. It smelled musty. The rasp of a flint and the smell of tallow. Then they began a descent. Goose bumps and a stinging sensation crawled across her skin from the chill. Down, down, down. What was this place?

They stopped again. An oily smell. A lantern being lit. *Count the steps.* From that point on, as they continued their descent, Eleanor counted. It became harder to breathe, and not just for her, Barend also labored with each inhalation.

He stumbled and fell against the wall, bumping Eleanor's head against stone.

"Much farder?"

"'fraid so. We're not even halfway down."

Eventually they came to a sloping passage. It wasn't as narrow. Her feet and head didn't brush the walls as Barend maneuvered through. Eleanor felt a growing pressure in her ears. A soft roar began that kept getting louder as they moved on.

A cold breeze smelling of the sea raced over her. Edgerton's footfalls sounded different.

"Ahh, here we are," Edgerton sang out in a parody of good cheer.

Metal sliding against metal. Then clinking metal. The turning of a well-oiled lock and the sound of a heavy chain sliding. A gate or door swung on oiled hinges and the echo of water slapping a hard surface.

"Over there. Put her down," Edgerton said.

Barend dragged her off his shoulder and dropped her on the stone floor.

Eleanor let out an 'oof'. She landed on her side. She drew her legs up and shifted her weight to bring herself to sitting.

"Oh, my, he doesn't seem to like you, m'dear," Edgerton said. "Take off the hood."

The binding around her neck fell away. The cloth lifted off. Edgerton leaned close, smiling. "Perhaps it's because you killed his cousin. Hmmmm? You remember Pim?"

Eleanor's eyes shot to Barend's. She swallowed. She'd had no choice. "*Droevig.*" She was sorry she'd killed his cousin.

Barend stared at her, his brow furrowed.

Edgerton back-handed Eleanor across the mouth. It split her lip. "He hates you almost as much as I do."

Eleanor touched the tip of her tongue to her bloody lip.

"Wait outside." Edgerton waved Barend away.

The big Dutchman hesitated.

"Go." Edgerton was emphatic.

Barend left.

Eleanor was sitting on the upper-most shelf in a cave. The lower portion was submerged. Daylight bounced off the water and illuminated the bleak gray walls. Refuse belched from the ocean floor—sand, driftwood, and hanks of seaweed—lay about her.

"That gate,"—Edgerton pointed to the sea gate— "and the one we used over there are the only ways in or out of here. In a moment, I'm going to untie your hands. But before you've a chance to untie your legs, I'll be locking you in here. In a few hours when floodtide is complete, this cavern will be inundated…completely.

"While you are here, trapped, and gasping your last, I'll be above, enjoying a picnic I brought along to celebrate the occasion." He waved a hand in the air. "And when it's all over … I'll come down here, open the sea gate, and let you float away on the tide." He pointed at the open water. "Who knows, someone may even find enough of you to bury in the family crypt."

⚜

Frustrated, Giles stomped around the grounds with Rodrigo until his temper cooled. He knew he needed to go back and make things right, speak with Eleanor. When he got back to the rose garden gate, though, something felt wrong. "Hello?"

No answer.

Rodrigo frantically pawed at the gate.

Giles' unease grew. He and Rodrigo entered the garden.

Rodrigo ran to the shed.

Giles followed.

Betty, bound and gagged, lay on the floor, facing the wall.

Rodrigo pawed Betty, trying to roll her over.

Startled, she made a muffled cry.

"Sit, Rodrigo," Giles commanded.

Rodrigo complied.

Giles knelt and rolled Betty over. The look of stark terror in her eyes took him aback, for it mirrored his own agitated state. *Go slow. Be gentle. God, where is Eleanor?*

"Betty, I'm Lord West. Harleigh and Eleanor's friend. May I?" He motioned to her gag.

She nodded.

"Now, your bonds." First, he undid the rope circling her legs. He felt her trembling. He helped her stand. He then moved behind her and undid her wrists. "Where's Eleanor?"

Betty took him by the arm and pulled him outside the shed into the light. Her brows drew together. "You're the one who loves her?"

"Yes."

Rodrigo was circling them, snuffling, with his head down.

Betty gazed around the garden. "Gone. H-h-he took her."

"Someone took Eleanor away?"

Betty choked on a sob and nodded.

Giles gave her his handkerchief.

"She saved me."

"Do you know who took her?" Giles asked.

"Her cousin."

"Lord Edgerton?"

Betty nodded.

Giles cursed himself for a prideful fool. If he hadn't lost his temper, Eleanor would still be here, safe.

"Betty, do you know where …?"

Betty began to run toward the iron gate. "He knows."

Rodrigo ran in front of her.

"Who?" Giles kept pace with Betty.

"Come." She opened the gate. "The gardener."

Once beyond the wall of the rose garden, Rodrigo took off. Giles and Betty ran to keep up. They broke through the shrubbery and out onto the lawn. Gardeners were everywhere: in the flowerbeds, pruning trees, cutting grass.

Betty twirled about, searching. "That one." She pointed to a gardener off by himself.

So, Edgerton had a spy on the property after all. He was a damn clever gamester.

"Rodrigo." The dog gazed intently at his master. "Find the man who hurt Eleanor." Rodrigo took off, barking, heading straight for the gardener Betty had singled out. As the dog drew near, the man's head shot up. He threw his rake down and bolted.

Rodrigo gave chase and knocked him flat.

The man rolled over and tried to scramble to his feet.

Growling, Rodrigo sank his teeth into the man's pants leg and pulled him down.

When the man was on his back, Rodrigo lunged, planting his front paws on the man's chest, his teeth bared and hovering over the man's throat.

"Ger off! Gettim' offa me!" the man shrieked.

The head gardener ran up. "My lord, what's happening?"

"Miss Eleanor's been kidnapped," Giles said. "This man's responsible."

Everyone, including Betty, circled around. "Quiet, Rodrigo." The dog ceased barking but didn't move off the man's chest. Giles squatted down beside the spy. "Ah, the fancy-man with the sword. One of your friends shot Harleigh Barrett."

The crowd gasped.

"Twernt me. I ain't done nothing. Get him off."

"Liar. You've one chance. Tell us where they've taken Miss Barrett. Keep silent and I'll let Rodrigo have you."

Chapter Thirty-nine

Giles left Rodrigo in Betty's care and grabbed the fastest horse in Lord Barrett's stables.

When he arrived on the bluff, a large workhorse, released from its trace, stood hobbled near an abandoned cart.

Edgerton leaned against a boulder on the cliff's edge fifty yards along. He didn't turn around as Giles approached. "I was resting here, hoping against hope you would *not* come," Edgerton said. "You've made a bad choice, my friend."

"Are we friends?" Giles said.

Edgerton looked over his shoulder. "Do friends hold guns on one another?"

Giles looked at his pistol, then lowered it. "As my friend, tell me where she is."

A long, pregnant pause.

"Francis." When Edgerton didn't answer, Giles stepped closer. "Don't do something you'll regret."

"Ah, but you see, I shan't regret it. Not in the least."

Giles heard Harleigh and Eleanor's warning: '*You really don't know him.*'

"I'd forgotten all about that escapade in her father's stable all those years ago, until she reminded me. Should've taken care of her that night when she found me with that servant's daughter. But I was too soft, you see. Shan't make the same mistake again."

"Her eighth birthday?"

"As a matter of fact, it was her birthday."

"*Where. Is. She?*" That was the last thing Giles uttered before daylight shattered into pain and blackness.

Eleanor stood thigh-deep in the frigid water. Her petticoats, stockings and boots lay discarded on the highest ledge. She'd gathered her skirts above her knees.

She'd wrapped strips of linen torn from her petticoats around each hand, to pad her grip as she yanked, rattled, and pulled on the sea gate to no avail. It sported a pair of new brass hinges and a chain with links that were forged from metal as thick as her thumb, and one of the new-styled padlocks.

Frustrated, she leaned against the gate. Her eyes wandered upward. The ceiling was blotched with patches of barnacles and other sea creatures. So, Cousin Francis had told the truth—this entire place would inundate during floodtide.

She leaned her forehead against the cold damp iron and stared out at the blue sky, open water, and soaring birds. Sadness lapped at her like the water swirling around her legs. She let out a deep choking sob.

"Poor little Eleanor."

She hadn't heard Edgerton enter. She spun to face to him. She slipped on something slimy, but managed to keep herself from falling underwater by clutching the gate. She imbued her voice with as much sangfroid as she could muster. "Thought you had a picnic to attend?"

"My, my, even facing death your tongue is barbed. You really are incorrigible." Edgerton raised a gun and pointed it at her. Was he bored of waiting? "Stay where you are. Bring him in."

Barend lumbered forward, carrying a man over his shoulder.

"Put him there." Edgerton waved his pistol at the pile of Eleanor's discarded clothing. As Barend moved closer, Eleanor recognized who he was carrying.

"Why?!" Eleanor charged through the water and scrambled onto the upper ledge. By then Barend had returned to Edgerton's side.

Eleanor rolled Giles over and ran her hands over his torso, looking for wounds.

"I'm afraid Barend was rather heavy-handed when he struck him."

She found a lump at the back of Giles' head. "Why?"

"Because he loves *you*," Edgerton sneered.

"He's your friend." Eleanor reached out her hand in supplication. "Please, you can sell him to a ship's captain bound for India or China. He's strong. You would get a good price."

Edgerton paused, then shook his head. "It'd never work. Giles would hunt me down."

She was shocked that even Edgerton knew the depth of Giles' feeling for her. He'd risked everything to save her. She hung her head and tears broke free, spilling down her cheeks and dripping from her chin.

Exhausted, Eleanor laid her head down on Giles' chest and closed her eyes.

"Eleanor?" Giles voice was raspy.

Her head popped up.

Giles' eyes were barely open and he was smiling at her.

"Oh." She looked around. Edgerton was gone. She leaned forward and kissed him gently on the lips.

"Is that all the thanks I get? Come here, woman." Giles wrapped his arms around Eleanor and pulled her on top of him and kissed her thoroughly. When the kiss ended, he stroked his thumbs across her cheeks, wiping the wetness away. "Tears, my brave virago?"

Eleanor tried to move off him. "I've turned into a useless watering pot."

Giles held her fast against him. "Water makes things grow and you are *never* useless."

Eleanor tugged to move away from him.

He tightened his hold. "I know why you thought you had to do everything on your own."

Eleanor gasped. "You do?"

"Before Edgerton tossed me in here, he blathered on about something that happened ..."

Eleanor planted her hands on his shoulders and pushed.

Giles held her tighter.

"I wanted to see my new pony," Eleanor said.

"I remember Sir Gawain." Giles stroked her back.

Eleanor sniffled. "Afterwards, I changed his name to Bumble."

"Because he didn't defend the maidens, you mean?"

Eleanor choked on a sob. "So, foolish. And now you." Her lip quivered.

Giles scoffed. "You were a little girl. Now, an apology to Libby I'd agree is in order. When we were boys, especially after Edgerton's father's accident, I felt sorry for him. I had two loving parents and a gaggle of siblings. He had no one. He was so miserable. Then our schoolmates began a relentless and cruel campaign against him. I couldn't let him deal with it by himself. That forged a bond between us that blinded me. But none of it excuses what he did to Betty."

"It doesn't matter anymore."

"Help me up. My head's spinning. Perhaps if I sit here a moment..." He looked around. "What is this place?"

"A very old smugglers warren, I think." Eleanor shifted to sit beside Giles. He pulled her close. She rested her head on his shoulder.

Giles nudged his chin in the direction of the sea gate. "Sturdy?"

"Very. I tried my knife in the lock but the blade ... well, I couldn't get the purchase I needed to trip the mechanism."

"I shan't ask how you know how to do such things as picking locks."

Eleanor chuckled. "It's a very useful skill."

"Help me off with my boots. I want to have a look."

Eleanor huffed. "You doubt my ability to assess our situation?"

"Don't waste time. We must work together." He held up his booted foot.

Eleanor tipped her chin down.

"You're putting me in mind of a young ram. Are you going to butt me or help me off with my boots?" Giles wiggled his foot at her.

She grabbed hold and tugged.

The water had risen to her waist by the time Giles and Eleanor returned to the ledge. "I was so sure I would find a way."

Eleanor planted her hands on the ledge and pushed up. Giles stepped behind her, wrapped his hands about her waist and lifted her onto the ledge.

"I could've done that myself."

"You could just say 'thank you'," Giles said.

"I don't like others doing for me what I can do for myself."

"I think you don't trust anybody to be there for you, that's what I think."

"Who asked you?" Eleanor said.

"You've made yourself independent as a defense against being hurt. Not because it is your natural inclination, or even to prove you are a man's equal. Those have been corollaries."

He saw her so clearly. damn him. Why now when the end was upon her did she finally find a man she could rely on?

When he joined her on the ledge, he wore nothing more than his shirt and breeches and he'd lost his ribbon holding back his thick golden locks so they hung in disarray around his handsome face. Gone was the impeccably dressed stuffed shirt who'd accosted her a few months before on the streets in Covent Garden. This man was better.

"What an utterly predictable and supremely masculine response to our dilemma. You thought your mind would find a way out of this trap that mine didn't?"

"I was hoping it would be a matter of brawn over brains, actually."

Eleanor snorted.

Giles cupped her face in his hands as the cold water washed over their bare feet. "Looks like we'll need a miracle to get out of here."

Eleanor pressed her cheek into his palm, enjoying his touch. "I'm sorry I said no."

"Are you?"

"I was so sure, given the opportunity and the impunity the law provides, you would all turn into Edgertons."

"And now?" Giles said.

"I was wrong."

Giles took Eleanor's hand.

"I asked him to send you away," Eleanor said.

Giles pulled her close. "Did you? Well then, I'm indebted to Edgerton for saying no. I wouldn't want to go on without you, Ellie."

Eleanor rested her head on his chest. "Please don't say that."

"You mean the world to me. I'm proud of you and all you've accomplished. You'd make a splendid, if reluctant, countess, you know."

Eleanor snorted. "Hah, I'd give your father palpitations, is what I'd do."

"He wants me happy. You're what makes me happy."

She gazed at the rising water, then back at him. "I'm sorry it's taken so long for me to tell you... I love you, Giles."

He smiled down her. "And I love you, Eleanor Augusta Barrett."

Eleanor put her hand over his heart. "We can't stop the tide, but we can choose how we use the time that is left. Make love to me."

Giles grabbed Eleanor by the shoulders and held her at arm's length. "On one condition."

"You want to negotiate at a time like this?"

He gave her a light shake. "You agree we're man and wife."

"What does it matter?"

"It matters to *me*." Giles seemed to be holding his breath. Silence.

"All right."

"No, I want to hear you say the words, Eleanor."

She bit her lip. She took a deep breath, let it out and looked him in the eye. "I…accept."

He pulled her over to their discarded clothing. "Take these." He shoved Eleanor's discarded petticoats at her. He picked up her stockings. "Those shan't help at all." He tossed them back down.

"Help?"

Giles scooped up the discarded clothing. "Don't dawdle, wife." He marched over to a spot beside the wall on the highest ground and dumped the clothes on the floor and arranged them into a nest. "I'm now ready to play lady's maid."

Eleanor turned her back to him. She felt Giles' unsteady fingers undo her laces. As her dress slipped down her shoulders, he brushed her hair aside and ran a string of warm kisses across her shoulder.

"I love the feel of your skin against my lips," Giles said.

"Giles?" Eleanor spun to face him, holding her dress against her breasts.

He pulled her close and kissed her thoroughly. She melted into him. When the kiss ended, her dress was puddled around her ankles. "Step out of it, sweeting." He laid her dress with the rest of the pile.

"Your turn." Eleanor pointed to Giles' chest.

He reached over his back. In a wink his shirt fluttered down onto their make-shift bed.

He ran his index finger just inside the embroidered edge of her stays and whispered, "Lovely." She quivered as his fingernail lightly abraded her nipple. The heat from his touch shot straight to the juncture of her thighs, making her ache.

Eleanor pressed her lips to his chest. His skin tasted salty and smelled of sandalwood and…Giles. He wrapped his arms about her and she felt his fingers plucking at the strings of her stays. He held her so tightly against him that through the fragile cotton of her chemise she felt the press of his cock, still held captive inside his breeches.

When her stays hit the floor, he sank down on their bridal bed. "This'll do nicely." Giles pulled her forward. "Put a foot on either side of my hips." The dark curls at the juncture of her thighs were right in front of his nose. Her musky scent filled his nostrils. He leaned forward and pressed his lips into the dark, shadowy juncture.

"Giles?" Eleanor squeaked as she wobbled.

"Shhh," he purred as his hands slid up her firm thighs, pushing the fabric of her chemise higher. "Lift this leg, darling." His right hand slid down to her calf. He wrapped his hand around her ankle. "Put this knee on my shoulder."

This time Eleanor did lose her balance. Giles grabbed her thighs to steady her. She planted her hands on the wall above his head. "What?"

"Trust me." Giles nuzzled the juncture of her legs through her chemise. "Mmm, I wonder if you taste as good as you smell?"

Eleanor slapped him on the head. "Stop that."

"Come on, wife. You've come this far, don't lose your nerve." Giles nudged her right leg. He felt her unlock her knee and she raised it and placed her shin on his shoulder, granting him access.

Eleanor felt his large, warm hands roam up the back of her thighs. He ran his fingertips up the cleft in her bum.

Giles loved the feel of her nice firm behind in his hands.

She trembled. "What *are* you doing?"

He didn't answer; instead, Giles kissed his way up the smooth, soft skin of her inner thigh.

Eleanor made a strangled incoherent sound.

Time was moving away from them. Giles wanted to make their first and last time together go on forever. He rested his head against Eleanor's thigh. Her skin was soft. He looked up to fill his senses with only her.

He ran his tongue up her thigh. With his hands on her bum, he held her steady as be began probing her center with his tongue. When he found her nubbin, he circled it with his tongue and then sucked it into his mouth. She was wet with her desire and her whole body vibrated with her impending climax.

He sucked harder.

Eleanor heard herself scream his name as she shattered. From her center to her scalp, every nerve hummed and sparked.

Her standing leg gave way. She slid down onto his lap. His hands sliding up her sides guided her down. Her head pillowed on his shoulder.

Her thighs hugged his hips and her shins rested on the cold stone floor. "Now what?"

"You are going to ride me."

Her brow furrowed.

"There are many ways to make love. Up on your knees, my treasure."

A cool breeze brushed her nether curls and she shivered. The cry of a seabird nearby made Eleanor look back at the water. "How long do you think we have?"

Giles put his hand on her cheek and turned her face back to him. "Long enough." Then his mouth came down on hers in a fiery kiss. Eleanor wrapped her arms around his neck. His tongue entered her mouth and circled her tongue.

She used her tongue on him as he was doing to her. She heard a deep rumbling groan and knew he liked what she was doing.

She felt his hand on her breast rubbing her nipple through the thin fabric. Hot spirals of pleasure coursed downward and she rocked her core against the hard ridge of his shaft. She couldn't get close enough.

"This is getting in the way." He grabbed her chemise and pulled it over
her head. As the chilly air hit her passion-heated skin, her nipples puckered into hard points. Giles stared at her chest.

Eleanor's hands flew up to cover herself.

His gaze returned to her eyes "You're so beautiful."

She lowered her hands. "What are you waiting for?"

"You." He placed his palms on the cave floor next to his hips, leaning slightly back to give her better access. "Go on."

Eleanor narrowed her eyes.

He waggled his brows at her and an impish grin curved his lips.

This time with him was precious beyond measure. He was daring her. Hah! She'd show him. She felt powerful in a way that was different from donning her mannish attire, rescuing, or fighting. This new feeling called to her, pulled her.

She ran her fingers up the front of his pants. His eyes drifted shut. His head fell back against the cave wall. When she finished undoing his buttons, the fabric fell away and she slipped her hand through the slit of his smalls. The hair of his groin was coarse. In the soft light of the cave, she could see it was fair. She found his erection and wrapped her fingers around it. It pulsed. She liked the feel of it in her hand. Who would have thought such a thing?

"I said I want to be inside of you. Up on your knees, wife."

Eleanor pushed up.

"Come closer."

She walked forward on her knees until her most tender flesh hovered above his erect rod. He moved his hand between them and when she looked down he held his cock in his fist. "Now lower yourself."

She did as he asked until she felt a searing pain. She closed her eyes and grimaced.

Giles caressed her shoulder. "Shall I help?"

Eleanor's eyes flew open. "Aunt told me it only hurts the first time and won't last."

Giles shook his head and laughed. "Is that a yes ... or a no?"

Eleanor bit her lip, put her hands on his shoulders rose enough so the pain eased. Then cupped his dear face in her hands and kissed him with all her heart. When he responded, she dropped her weight and impaled herself completely on him.

"Ahh," Eleanor tore her mouth from his as she cried out, then closed her eyes, rested her forehead on his shoulder, and breathed into the pain.

Giles stroked her back. "I promise it will get better."

"It better."

Giles let loose a boom of laughter. "Such a demanding bed partner."

"This is no bed," Eleanor said.

"But you *are* my partner, now and always, Lady West."

The smile he gave her pierced her heart.

He moved his hands to cover her breasts and played with her nipples. Her body responded to his touch, as the muscles of her passage gripped him.

Eleanor put her hands on his shoulders and hugged his hips with her thighs, she rose a little, then lowered herself. "Like so?"

He gritted his teeth. "God, yes. Do it again, Ellie."

Something urgent thrummed through her. She never wanted to stop. The pleasure was raw and wild. At first her ups and downs were slow and steady, then she felt compelled to move faster.

His head rocked from side to side as he groaned. He shifted. Eleanor felt his shaft rub against her womb's wall. A spike of heat and pleasure shot through her. Giles wrapped his hands about her waist and pushed her down onto him as his hips thrust upward. Her back arched. Gasping—they were both gasping.

As their passion climbed and coiled tight, it came. Her womb convulsed around his rod and a roaring in her ears like a great wind and the pounding of her own heart came with an explosion of such ecstatic joy it hurled her out of the cave. She broke apart. Giles cried out and she felt his release.

She slumped forward against his damp chest. She felt his pounding heart. He enfolded her in his strong arms. She closed her eyes, savoring the feel of him inside and surrounding her. So much love. She dreamed of little boys who looked like Giles racing across a green lawn and leaping over girls sitting in the grass making chains of clover and wildflowers. Eleanor whispered against his chest, "Maybe a child."

"What?"

Her eyes opened. "Just dreaming. It doesn't matter."

"You were hoping we made a child?"

Eleanor nodded.

"What did you see?" Giles' chin rested on her head.

"A great many children, actually."

"Truly? We haven't talked of such matters, but I would like many children. I hope you do not mind." He held her close and kissed the top of her head.

She thought he was being preposterous. But she wouldn't ruin this moment for him—for them.

Still holding Eleanor close, Giles gazed from the sea gate to the internal hillside gate. "I wonder…"

"Hmmm?" Eleanor mumbled.

"I tell you, wife, I'm *not* willing for that bastard to beat me—beat us."

Giles rolled to his side, taking Eleanor with him. He gently disengaged himself and stood. As he re-buttoned his falls, he gazed down at his wife sitting naked among their discarded clothes. He sighed and tore his eyes away from her and surveyed their prison. "There must be a way out of here."

"We've tried—"

"You're not going to turn fatalistic on me now, are you, Ellie?"

"Ha."

Giles ran to the gate that led back to the hillside. He put his arms through the bars and pressed close, groping with his hands.

"What are you doing?" Eleanor pulled his coat from the pile she sat on and wrapped it about her.

He felt for the hinges. He turned toward the seaside gate. "I bet I'm right." He ran back, pulled her to standing, then searched the pile of clothes. He scooped up her chemise and his shirt. He took his coat from about her shoulders and dropped first her chemise and then his shirt over her head. "Where's your knife?"

Eleanor pointed. "The sheath is inside my right boot."

Giles found what he was looking for. They had less than an hour of light left, and even less time before that damn gate became submerged.

Giles jumped into the frigid water and waded to the sea gate. The Water level was up to his shoulders now. The topmost hinge was partially submerged and he ran his fingers over it, discerning its configuration and construction mostly by feel. Then he ducked under the water to feel if the two hinges were the same.

When he reappeared, he shoved his wet hair back from his eyes. "These hinges are identical." He held his fingers under his nose. "And well-greased."

Eleanor leaped into the water and swam to his side. "What of it?"

Giles pointed to the cliff-side gate. "That gate was set to keep intruders from getting into the passages so its hinges are on the cliff side, and there's a bar which is secured with a lock, but this one"— Giles smacked the sea gate with his palm— "was meant to keep invaders from entering the cave from the sea so their hinges face into the cave."

"Then we can reach the hinge pins!"

"Exactly, and they should move easily if we can pry them up high enough for me to grab a hold."

"That blade is thin but very strong." Eleanor pointed to her boot knife that he held in his fist. Giles slipped the blade under the upper hinge's pin head.

Eleanor grabbed his arm. "No-no, do the bottom one first, but only pull it part of the way out. Wait here." She swam away. When she returned, she had two large pieces of her petticoat in her fist. She shoved one at him. "Wedge this cloth under the pin head to keep it from reseating."

"Excellent. Stay put," Giles said.

She snorted, rolled her eyes and then dived down.

Giles shook his head and followed her under water. Beneath the cold waves, their movements were slow and clumsy. Their hands slid over the rails of the submerged portion of the gate until they found the bottom hinge, returning several times to the surface for air before succeeding in wedging her petticoat under the pin head.

The upper hinge was easier to deal with since the pin head was still above the waterline.

They could no longer stand, so both were treading water. "We must pull the pins out at the same time."

"Agreed," Eleanor said.

"I'll take the bottom one, and when I'm ready to pull my pin I'll touch your leg. Count to three, then pull your pin free. Are you ready, Lady West?"

Eleanor's lips were tinged blue from the cold but she gave him a wobbly smile.

He kissed her quickly, took a deep breath, then went under the water. A few moments later she felt him touch her leg and she pulled the top hinge pin out.

Giles broke the surface, laughing. "It's done!"

"We've done it!" Eleanor shouted.

Giles chuckled. "Together we're unstoppable." He braced his feet on the wall of the cave and pulled. At first the gate didn't budge. He gave another mighty tug and the hinges parted and the gate swung drunkenly open, tossed about by the current, dangling on its chain. He heard Eleanor swimming away. "Where're you going?"

"I need something." She swam in the direction of the ledges, which lay deep in shadow.

"What could be so important?"

"Don't nag," Eleanor said.

He heard a splash. It seemed an eternity before she was back at his side. "What was so important?"

"I had to get my lucky marble."

He roared with laughter. "Dear Lady West, have I told you how positively mad I am for you?"

The waves of the incoming tide scraped them against the rocky outcropping that camouflaged the cave's mouth from the outside world. Once free of that obstruction, Eleanor laughed.

Treading water, Giles put his hand over her mouth. "Shhh, sweetheart. We don't know where Edgerton and his man are."

೦೩

Up on the cliff, a chilly wind blew down from the north as Edgerton leaned against a boulder while smoking an excellent celebratory cigar. He turned up the collar of his greatcoat and gazed down at Barend, who lay on his side a few feet away in a bloody pool of fecal matter that had seeped from his breeches.

"Thank goodness the wind is behind us, eh?" Edgerton waved his hand before his face. "Afraid your aroma is rather dreadful."

In death, Barend's cup had slipped from his fingers. His lips were now drawn back in a pain-filled rictus, which Edgerton found unpleasant to behold. He pulled his lace-trimmed silk handkerchief from his pocket, held his breath, leaned down and tossed it over the man's face to block it from his view. "Much better."

Edgerton addressed the corpse. "I'd lay a hefty wager that dear Dagmar never envisioned me using the Jericho rose elixir on you when she gave it to me, eh."

Edgerton startled. *Laughter? Can't be.* He pulled a spyglass from his pocket, walked as close to the brittle edge of the cliff as advisable. He put the glass to his eye and gazed out to sea.

The horizon was now a burning orange line, and the sky above faded from golden-blue to hazy purple. He stared down at the water. Something white moved on the surface, away from him. The longer he watched, it seemed to him the white object was moving with a purpose.

He tossed his cigar away. "Impossible! They can't beat me." Edgerton gazed at the immobile Barend. "Perhaps I acted in haste, my brutish companion."

Edgerton kicked Barend's empty cup. "Damn it!" He gathered his horse's reins and mounted. "I shan't be gainsaid. You two shall never leave this place."

ℭ

The sun was down. Giles held Eleanor by the elbow as they stumbled through the surf. She was shaking. "Just a bit farther."

"Th-hat's what-t-t you said an hour ago."

"Shh, darling." As they stood on a sliver of beach, Giles pulled Eleanor close, wrapping his arms about her to infuse her with some of his heat.

"Now, w-w-hat?"

"There." Giles pointed to a narrow winding path rising from the beach up the cliff face.

Eleanor walked out of his embrace. "The sooner we start, the sooner I'll don something dry."

Giles snorted.

They trudged upward in silence, with him in the lead. A few feet from the top, Giles reached back and took her hand because he had to touch her. She was as necessary as air to him now. Nothing would stop him from making her his wife. "I want to begin calling the bands this Sunday." Giles pulled her over the edge.

"Bands? Is someone getting married? No, I rather think a funeral is what's in store for you two." Edgerton cocked his guns.

He was standing a few feet away. The wind set Edgerton's great coat flapping about him like a large raven's wings.

Giles moved in front of Eleanor. His muscles screamed with exhaustion. Could he move fast enough?

"How gallant." Edgerton's voice dripped with insincerity. "How the hell did you get out?"

"Where's your partner?" Giles said.

"Indisposed," Edgerton said.

Giles stepped toward Edgerton. Eleanor sank her fingers into his forearm. "Talking with him is a waste. He's not sorry for anything."

"*Sorry?*" Edgerton parodied the word. "Apologies are for fools and simpletons. I'm neither, little cousin."

"If you leave now, you could disappear," Giles said.

"I've no intention of leaving." Edgerton raised his gun and aimed for Giles' heart.

"Nooooooooo!" A woman's enraged scream startled them all.

Edgerton turned.

The thunder of hooves as a horse and rider bore down on them.

Edgerton raised his arm to shoot.

Giles cocked his leg and kicked Edgerton hard in his mid-back, right over his kidneys.

Edgerton hit the ground hard. His guns flew out of his hands.

One gun discharged but missed the oncoming rider.

The rider pulled the horse to an abrupt stop and slid from the saddle.

Edgerton rolled onto all fours and was halfway to standing.

The rider kicked him in the side, in his liver.

Edgerton crumpled as his attacker danced back out of range. As he struggled to regain his feet, the figure moved in quickly and delivered a blow to his groin.

Howling, Edgerton fell to his knees.

"Get up, you bloody bastard. Get up!" came the woman's angry invective.

Now Giles knew who it was.

Edgerton lay on the ground, wheezing. "Who the hell are you?"

A long pause.

"Betty Longley."

Edgerton sneered. "Is that supposed to mean something to me?"

"I forgot. You never did ask my name the day you promised to teach me to kiss like a lady."

Edgerton rolled onto his knees. "You stupid bitch. Lay a hand on me again and I'll have you transported."

Giles put his arm around Eleanor to keep her from interfering with Betty's punishment of Edgerton. He deserved anything Betty doled out. When she was done, he'd tie Edgerton up and turn him over to the magistrate.

Edgerton lunged.

Betty parried his attack.

Giles had seen Eleanor block a blow just like that.

Edgerton made another grab. He'd been weakened by both Giles' and Betty's kicks. He stumbled.

Betty pivoted, raised her right foot, and drove it into the back of his knee.

He hit the ground. Cursing, he rose slowly.

When Betty turned to face Edgerton, she was inches from the cliff's unstable edge.

He charged. Hands out like grappling hooks.

At the last moment, Betty stepped aside.

Edgerton swung about, eyes wide with horror. He teetered.

Betty's leg shot out, connecting with his midsection and sending him over the precipice.

Epilogue

Giles, Eleanor, and Rodrigo stood on the terrace at Barrett Hall. The bride and groom stood sandwiched between Eleanor's parents and his. Rodrigo sat between them, on guard duty. They were receiving everyone's good wishes for a happy marriage and a long life.

Giles leaned down, buried his nose in Eleanor's hair, just behind her ear. "I can't wait to get you alone, Lady West. Will you taste as sweet in a real bed as you did in that cave?"

Eleanor had been chatting with Julia Brewster's mother. She choked. And even in profile he could see the effect his bawdy words had on his wife's skin.

He chuckled.

Mrs. Brewster leaned forward and patted her hand. "There, there, Miss Ellie. Marriage is a trial, to be sure." She winked at Giles, then moved on to greet his parents.

Betty came through the line next with her grandparents. Eleanor gave her a fierce hug and Betty returned the embrace in full measure.

Harleigh walked up and handed them each a cup of punch.

"Where is your betrothed?" Giles smiled.

"You finally asked Libby" Eleanor said.

When Harleigh nodded, Eleanor bussed his cheek.

Giles laughed. "I'm confused. Are you not the fellow who swore he wasn't getting leg-shackled for at least a year or two?"

Harleigh shrugged. "Things change."

Giles smiled down at Eleanor. "They do, indeed."

"Where's Libby now?" Eleanor said. "I must congratulate her.

And as for you brother, never thought you had the good sense to ask her." Eleanor beamed at her brother.

"Speaking with Mr. Rooksby. Cannot believe Aunt Beatrice asked him to be her escort," Harleigh said.

"What's Libby got to say to him?" Giles asked.

"No idea. But they are deep in conversation," Harleigh said.

Wedding guests peppered the lawn and gardens. Giles and Eleanor strolled arm-in-arm through a wooded portion of the grounds that bordered the lawn. Rodrigo was by their side.

"You look thoughtful ... should I be worried?" Giles said.

Eleanor gave him a cheeky grin. "Perhaps."

Giles pulled her to a stop. "What troubles you?"

"Reflecting how my life has changed."

"Seems an appropriate observation for your wedding day." Giles brushed a curl behind her ear.

"When you stormed back into my life and challenged my ideals, my work, my purpose—I thought you were a pretentious windbag."

Giles choked on his laugh. "Well, in all fairness, wife, I've been accused of liking my opinions *too* much."

"Do tell."

This time Giles let lose a boom of laughter.

"Then Aunt Beatrice delivered the same challenge." Eleanor's brow furrowed.

"Always thought your aunt a remarkably astute woman."

Eleanor snorted. "Oh, really? Just wait until you find yourself in opposing camps."

"I'll look forward to it, for you've given me a taste"—he waggled his brows at her— "for curvaceous, strong-minded females."

Eleanor cheeks flamed and she slapped his arm.

Rodrigo jumped to attention.

Giles held up his hand. "Easy, boy." He turned back to Eleanor. "Sweetheart."

"You're the most provoking man."

"Yes, but now I'm *your* provoking man." He smiled.

"Yes, I suppose that's true."

"Tell me your thoughts."

"I was mulling over how a single event can frame and focus one's life."

Giles knew she was speaking of her childhood encounter with Edgerton. "It's all right, dear. You don't have to avoid speaking his name."

Eleanor squeezed his arm.

"I think you needed to feel safe," Giles said.

"I was frightened ... all the time. And I hated myself for it. Master Sakegawa changed that. But there's no getting around it. I made a mistake holding on to my childhood beliefs. They constrained my thoughts, my vision."

Giles cupped her cheek.

"You proved to me not every man would turn into a ... a Francis Edgerton."

They walked on.

"I'm grateful for your perseverance," Eleanor said.

"Good. I'm sure in the years to come I'll have numerous opportunities to remind you that you said that," Giles smiled.

Eleanor laughed. "And I'm doubly grateful Libby was her usual magnanimous self and accepted my apology."

"Indeed," Giles said.

"We should get back to our guests," she gazed about.

"Not yet. I wanted to give you your wedding gifts."

"I left yours up in my room."

He gave her a wicked grin.

"Did anyone ever tell you that you've a vulgar mind, my lord?"

Giles pulled her close. "Only where you're concerned." He kissed her quickly. "And since we're married, it can hardly be considered vulgar, now can it?" Giles handed her a pouch.

She opened it and out spilled a leash. "What?"

"I'm giving you Rodrigo. That's his leash. I trust him to keep you safe when I'm not around."

"Oh."

"And then there's this." Giles pulled an officious-looking document out of his inside coat pocket.

Eleanor opened it and read. Her eyes grew wide.

"The property is a couple of hours from here. It'll make an admirable home for your Sisterhood School. As you see, the deed's in your name."

"Yes." She swallowed hard.

"Since, from all appearances, I owned that blighted property in Bath, I took possession and sold it for quite a pretty sum. Then I turned around and used the money to purchase Hartwell for you."

Eleanor chuckled.

"I see the irony isn't lost on you," Giles said.

"Using *his* money to do good for women and girls is elegantly ironic." She tapped the deed against her chin. "Hartwell?"

"If you don't like it, you and the others can rename it."

"I love it." Eleanor took his arm and the three walked on. "Thank you. Do you know what I think, husband?"

"I don't know if I'll ever figure out the workings of that mind of yours. But, I intend to spend the rest of my life pursuing just that course."

She chuckled. "I'm thinking it's time we expand the Sisterhood. And in alignment with my new perspective ..."

"Yes?"

"I want you to be its first male member."

-The End-

Acknowledgments

There have been many people over the years who have believed in my talent and ability to tell an entertaining story—their numbers are legion, as I have been at this pursuit for quite some time. They know who they are, and I hope I had the humility and grace to acknowledge their contributions to my work, even when I didn't agree with them.

I shall take only a moment longer to say there are four people I would like to call out for special recognition: my husband and our children. I wouldn't have made it this far without your love and support.

My last acknowledgment goes to you, Reader. Thank you for taking a chance on me, and sharing in my adventure. If you enjoyed "The Reluctant Countess", would you take a moment and pop over to my product page on Amazon and leave a review. It can be as long or as short as you'd like. What you say has a tremendous impact.

You can also check out my author Facebook page at: Annieparnellauthor and I have set up a separate Facebook page for the Sisterhood at: @yoursisterhood. Please think about joining the Sisterhood Community. My work is about more than my books and entertaining my readers, it's about the chain we form when we work together for good.

All the best,

Annie P.

Novels by Annie Parnell
The Reluctant Heart Part One
(released exclusively on Amazon.com, Fall 2017)
The Reluctant Heart Part Two
(released exclusively on Amazon.com, winter 2018)

Novellas by Annie Parnell
The Griffin and the Rat-catcher
(e-book only, available exclusively on Amazon.com)

Made in the USA
San Bernardino, CA
12 December 2017